THE
COWBOY'S
MAIL ORDER BRIDE

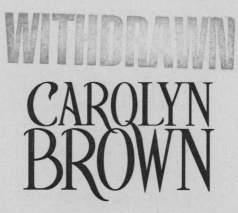

CAROLYN
BROWN

sourcebooks
casablanca

Published by Sourcebooks Casablanca, an imprint of Sourcebooks, Inc.
P. O. Box 4410, Naperville, Illinois 60567-4410
(630) 961-3900
Fax: (630) 961-2168
www.sourcebooks.com

Printed and bound in Canada.
MBP 10 9 8 7 6 5 4 3 2 1

Praise for
Just a Cowboy and His Baby

"I love my cowboys and there are none better than Carolyn Brown's."

—Fresh Fiction

"Brown provides an up close and personal look at the rodeo arena, with exciting action scenes written in her vivid, you-feel-like-you're-right-there style."

—USA Today Happy Ever After

"Another great read by Carolyn Brown... these two are steaming hot whether they are fighting or giving in."

—Night Owl Reviews Reviewer Top Pick, 4.5 Stars

"Brown's writing holds you spellbound as you slip into the world of tantalizing cowboys and love of family, with a lot of fun added in for good measure."

—Thoughts in Progress

"I know when I read a book by Carolyn Brown, I'm in for a treat."

—Long and Short Reviews

"I can't turn down Carolyn Brown's cowboys. They're as addictive as Janet Evanovich's Ranger."

—Drey's Library

"A witty, adrenaline-packed contemporary romance that I read in one sitting, unable to put it down."

—Romance Junkies

Also by Carolyn Brown

Lucky in Love

One Lucky Cowboy

Getting Lucky

I Love This Bar

Hell, Yeah

My Give a Damn's Busted

Honky Tonk Christmas

Love Drunk Cowboy

Red's Hot Cowboy

Darn Good Cowboy Christmas

One Hot Cowboy Wedding

Mistletoe Cowboy

Just a Cowboy and His Baby

Billion Dollar Cowboy

Cowboy Seeks Bride

The Cowboy's Christmas Baby

Women's Fiction

The Blue-Ribbon Jalapeño Society Jubilee

*This book is dedicated to Karen Garrison Sanders...
time and distance might separate us,
but we will always be friends.*

Chapter 1

EMILY TOOK A DEEP BREATH AND RANG THE DOORBELL.

The cold February wind swept across the wide porch of the ranch house and cut right through her lightweight denim jacket. Her heavy coat was in the pickup, but this job wouldn't take long. Hand the box of letters over to Clarice Barton and she'd be back in her truck and on her way. Then her grandfather's spirit would rest in peace. He'd said that it wouldn't until the box was put in Clarice's hands.

She heard footsteps on hardwood floors, and then something brushed against her leg. She looked down just as a big yellow cat laid a dead mouse on her boots. There were two things that Emily hated and mice were both of them. Live ones topped out the list above dead ones, but only slightly.

She kicked her foot just as the door opened and the mouse flew up like a baseball. The woman who slung open the screen door caught the animal midair, realized what she had in her hand, and threw it back toward Emily. She sidestepped the thing and the cat jumped up, snagged it with a paw, quickly flipped it into its mouth, and ran off the porch.

"Dammit!" The lady wiped her hand on the side of her jeans. "God almighty, I hate them things, and that damned cat keeps bringing them up to the porch like she's haulin' gold into the house."

The woman's black hair was sprinkled with white. Bright red lipstick had run into the wrinkles around her mouth and disappeared from the middle. When she smiled, her brown eyes twinkled brightly. Sure enough, the hardwood floor to the big two-story house was so shiny that Emily could see the reflection of the woman's worn athletic shoes in it.

"I'm sorry," Emily gasped. "It was a reflex action."

The woman giggled. "Well, now that we've both decided that we hate mice, what can I do for you, honey? You lost or something?" she asked.

"Is this Lightning Ridge Ranch? Are you Clarice Barton?" Emily shivered against the cold and the idea of a mouse touching her favorite boots.

"Yes, it's Lightning Ridge, but I'm not Clarice. She's making a run out to the henhouse. We're making a chocolate cake later on and I used up all the eggs makin' hot rolls. It's cold. You better come on inside and wait for her. I'm Dotty, Clarice's best friend and helper around here. I'm going to have to wash my hands a dozen times to get the feel of dead mouse off." The lady stepped aside. "What do you need Clarice for?"

"I'm here to deliver this box."

"Your nose is red and you look chilled. Come on in the living room. We got a little blaze going in the fireplace. It'll warm you right up. This weather is plumb crazy these days. February ain't supposed to be this damned cold. Spring ain't that far away. Winter needs to step aside. What'd you say your name was?" Dotty motioned her into the living room with a flick of her wrist.

"I'm Emily, and thank you. The warmth feels good," she said.

"Well, you just wait right here. She won't be long. Go on and sit down, honey. Take that rockin' chair and pull it up next to the fireplace. Can I get you a cup of coffee or hot chocolate?"

"No, ma'am. I'm fine," Emily answered. She would have loved a cup of anything hot just to wrap her chilled fingers around, but she didn't want to stick around long enough to drink a whole cup.

"Well, I'm in the middle of stirrin' up some hot rolls. Just make yourself at home until Clarice gets here."

Dotty disappeared, leaving Emily alone in the living room. She held the ancient boot box in her lap. Her grandfather had worn out the boots that came in the box and now it held letters from a woman who was not her grandmother. His passing and her two promises to him in his final days seemed surreal, especially sitting in the house of the woman who'd written the letters more than sixty years before.

Warmth radiated out from the fireplace as she took stock of her surroundings. The room was a perfect square with furniture arranged facing the fireplace to give it a cozy feel. A framed picture of a cowboy took center stage on the mantel. She set the box on the coffee table and stepped in closer to look at the photograph. He had dark brown hair and green eyes behind wire-rimmed glasses. It had been taken in the summer because there were wildflowers in the background. One shiny black boot was propped on a rail fence, and he held a Stetson in his right hand. His left thumb was tucked into the pocket of his tight jeans, leaving the rest of his hand to draw attention to the zipper. And right there in the corner of the frame was a yellow sticky note with the words, "Miss you, Nana!" stuck to it.

The crimson flushing her cheeks had nothing to do with the heat rising from the fireplace and everything to do with the way she'd mentally undressed this man she'd never even seen in real life. *Get a grip, Em*, she thought to herself. She backed away quickly and stood by the door, but when she looked over her shoulder, the cowboy was staring at her. She moved to the other side of the room and shivers shot down her spine when she realized he was still looking at her. She tried another corner and behold, those green eyes had followed her.

She was tired. It had been a long, emotional week and this was the final thing she had to do before she could really mourn for her grandfather. She'd driven since daybreak that morning, and her eyes were playing tricks on her. That must be it. Her dark brows knit together as she glanced at the picture from across the room. Did he have a wedding ring on that left hand? Determined not to let a picture intimidate her, she circled the room so she could see the photograph better, and his hand was ring-free.

How old was he, and when was the picture taken? Not one thing gave away a year or a time other than it was spring or summer. He might be a fifty-year-old man with gray hair nowadays and bowed legs from riding too many horses through the years. Or he could be a lot younger than he looked in the photograph and still be in college, just coming home to work on the ranch in the summertime like she had when she was getting her degree.

Unless he came looking for a warm spot to take the chill off, she'd never meet him anyway. Her mission was to deliver letters, and studying the picture was just a diversion while she waited on Clarice.

"My grandson, Greg Adams," a woman said from the doorway.

"Fine-lookin' cowboy, isn't he? His daddy and momma wanted him to be a businessman in a big old office in Houston, but he's got his grandpa's ranchin' savvy. He's down in southern Texas at a cattle sale. Cute little sticker he left there, isn't it?"

Emily swallowed hard at the mention of a grandpa. She fought even harder to keep from blushing again. "Yes, ma'am, he is surely handsome. I'm Emily Cooper, and you are Clarice Barton?" She quickly crossed the room and held out her right hand.

Clarice's handshake was firm and her smile sincere. "Do I know you? Dotty said you had a box or something to give to me."

Her thick gray hair was cut short to frame her round face. She wore jeans and a Western-cut shirt, boots, and no makeup, and she had the same green eyes as the cowboy in the picture.

"No, ma'am, you do not know me. You *are* Clarice Barton, aren't you?"

"No, honey, I'm Clarice Adams. I haven't been Clarice Barton in more than sixty years, but I was before I got married. Let's sit down while we talk. Dotty is bringing us some hot coffee in a few minutes."

Just out of curiosity, Emily glanced at the picture and sure enough, the cowboy followed her as she crossed the room and sat down.

She picked up the box from the coffee table and held it out to Clarice. "Marvin Cooper was my grandfather.

He made me promise I'd bring these to you. They are the letters that you wrote to him when he was in Korea during the war."

Clarice laid a hand over her heart, and the color left her cheeks.

"Marvin," she whispered.

"Marvin Cooper?" Dotty set a tray holding three cups of coffee on the coffee table. "I'll be damned. Did you tell her that you were playing kickball with a damned old dead mouse?"

"No, ma'am." Emily's nostrils curled just thinking about it. She looked down at her boots. Should she simply leave them in her hotel room or try to wash the mouse from them? She could visualize the thing right there on the instep.

"Well, it took half a bar of soap to get it off my hand." Dotty went on to tell Clarice the story. "She don't like mice either, so I've decided that she's my new friend."

Clarice giggled. "I wish I'd been here to see that sight. Dotty hates mice and I hate spiders." She ran a hand down the side of the box, but she didn't take it. "I can't believe he kept them all these years or that you've brought them to me."

Emily pointed to the one that had been slipped beneath the faded red ribbon tied around the box. "This one is from him to you. It got stuck in a mailbag and then the bag got shoved back into an old desk drawer down at the post office. They didn't discover it until last week. According to the postmark, it should've been mailed sixty years ago, but it never left Happy. You might want to start with it. They brought it out to the ranch and apologized for losing it all those years ago.

Gramps told me to put it with the others, and he didn't even open it. He said he remembered right well what it said."

Clarice's hands trembled. "Gramps? That would make you his granddaughter, then? He got married and had children?"

"Yes, he did and he is—was—my grandfather. He's only been gone four days and I'm still not used to the idea of saying 'was.' It sounds so final."

"I understand. When my husband died, it took me a long time to use the past tense too. So Marvin had a granddaughter and I have a grandson," Clarice whispered.

Dotty shook her head slowly. "Marvin Cooper! When I first met Clarice she told me all about Marvin, but we never thought we'd hear that name again. And you drove all the way across the state to bring those letters? You are talking about Happy, Texas, right?"

"Yes, ma'am."

"You aren't plannin' on drivin' all the way back tonight, are you?" Clarice asked.

"I'm staying at a hotel in Sherman," Emily said.

"Please stay with us for supper. I've got to hear all about Marvin and how his life went." Clarice's eyes misted over and Emily couldn't have refused her request if it had meant standing in front of a firing squad.

Besides, it was just supper and a couple of hours' worth of talking about her grandfather. It would make Clarice feel good, and Gramps would like that. Maybe it would even give Emily the closure she needed so badly.

"And if that damned old mama cat brings up another rat, we might have to stick together to get rid of it," Dotty said.

"Thank you. I'd like to stay for supper, but Miz Dotty, if that cat brings up another one of those vicious rats, you're on your own," Emily said.

"Rat, my hind end. It was probably just a baby mouse. Every time that Dotty tells the story it'll get bigger and bigger," Clarice said.

"You didn't see it. It was only slightly smaller than a damned old possum," Dotty argued.

Emily giggled and wished that she could take Dotty to Florida with her. That old girl would be a real hoot to have around all the time.

Clarice's phone rang and she fished it out of her shirt pocket. "Greg, darlin', the most amazing thing has happened." She gave him the one-minute shortened form of Emily bringing the box of letters and told him that she'd tell him the rest of the story when he got home.

Emily looked at the blaze in the fireplace, at the ceiling, and finally settled back on the picture of Clarice's grandson. She locked gazes with him, wondering what he would be like in the flesh. Was he really that handsome or just very, very photogenic?

"That's her grandson, Greg," Dotty whispered.

"She told me." Emily nodded.

"He's gone right now, but he'll be home tomorrow night. We miss him," Dotty said.

"I bet he misses being home," Emily said.

"Emily," Clarice said.

She whipped around when she heard her name, and an instant flash lit up her face.

Clarice giggled like a little girl. "I'm so sorry. He asked me what your name was again and I told her. It's a good picture of you. You have your grandpa's eyes.

This is a new phone and I keep taking pictures of things rather than hanging up. I miss the old corded phones that we used to have and cameras that used a flashbulb. This new technology is enough to drive a person crazy."

Dotty picked up her cup of coffee and sipped at it. "Ain't that the truth. Us old dogs havin' to learn all these new tricks is frustratin' as hell, and that damned computer shit is the worst thing of all. Y'all best drink that coffee before it gets cold. Want some cookies to go with it? It's a while 'til supper."

"No, this is fine." Emily covered a yawn with her hand. "I'm sorry. I drove all day, stopped at the hotel, and then got lost twice trying to find this place."

"How did you find me?" Clarice asked.

"I stopped at the post office and the lady there said that there wasn't a Clarice Barton around. The only Clarice she knew was Clarice Adams and I might check to see if that was you."

"She's new in town. Ain't been here but ten years or she would have known the Bartons helped to build Ravenna." Dotty pointed to the door. "I know Clarice is just dyin' to dig into those letters. And I've got things to do in the kitchen. Would you like to take a nap until suppertime? You can rest in the first room on the left upstairs."

"I wouldn't want to be a bother," Emily said.

"No bother at all. You go on up there and rest. If you aren't awake by supper, I'll holler for you," Dotty said.

Clarice reached across the space separating them and patted her arm. "And thank you so much for bringing these letters."

"I promised Gramps I would do it. Is it all right if I

take this upstairs with me?" Emily picked up her cup
of coffee.

"Of course it is," Clarice said.

Dotty stood up at the same time Emily did. "Clarice
was right about Marvin. She said that she thought he
was about to ask her to marry him. She's the only one
of us four that isn't a mail-order bride. That's the way I
come to live in these parts. I was from Kentucky and he
lived here. I thought any place was better than Harlan
County, Kentucky, so I climbed on a bus and come out
here. Married Johnny and loved him to his dying day,
but the best thing that come out of me bein' a mail-order
bride is that I met Clarice and we become best friends."

"Four of you?"

"Yep." Dotty nodded. "Me and Rose and Madge all
come to Texas right after the war was over more than
sixty years ago. I got here first in January and the other
two came on later that spring. It's a long story how it
all happened. Rose and Madge are cousins. Madge was
writing to a soldier that she met through the church pen
pal group. So she came out here to meet him, and then
Rose came to visit and wound up married to a local guy
too. Our husbands are all gone now and we are widows."

"You were all kind of like mail-order brides?"

"Mainly me and Madge were, and Rose kind of got
in on the deal like shirttail kin. Clarice is the only one
of us that was raised right here in Ravenna," Dotty said.
"Now get on up there and get some rest."

"Supper is at six?" Emily checked the clock and
glanced at that picture one more time.

"Yes, it is." Dotty smiled.

A two-hour nap, supper, some talk about her

grandfather, and then back to the hotel. Tomorrow she would be on her way to Florida for a whole month on the beach.

"Oh, my!" Emily gasped when she opened the door into the bedroom.

Back when she was in high school she would have hocked her tomcat, Spurs, to have her own room like the one before her. A queen-sized four-poster bed covered with a pretty quilt and lacy bed ruffle sat on one side of the room. A big, deep recliner and a vanity with a three-way mirror were located over beside the door into the bathroom, which sported a deep claw-footed tub. She'd always shared the one bathroom in the small three-bedroom ranch house with two men who did not understand why one girl needed so much hair spray, lotion, bath oil, and her own pink razors to shave her legs.

She washed her hands, dried them, and then rubbed lotion into them—sweet-smelling lavender lotion that reminded her of Great-Aunt Molly, grandmother to her favorite cousin, Taylor.

Her grandfather's words the day that he and Molly went to the courthouse together came back to her as she looked in the bathroom mirror. Molly had deeded her ranch to Taylor, and Marvin had given what was left of his adjoining ranch to Emily. On the way home he had said, "I'm not real sure your future is on Shine Canyon Ranch, Em."

When she'd asked him why he'd say a thing like that, he'd just smiled and tapped his heart. "Ranchin' is in your heart and you'll always love it, but something in my soul tells me your future is not on Shine Canyon. When I'm gone, I want you to take a month and think things through before you commit to this land for the rest of your life. You'll have a hard row to hoe even with family to help with just a hundred acres. I'm not sure in today's economy that you'll ever make it without taking a job in town, and that means ranchin' at night after you work your ass off all day at your job."

She blinked away the tears and turned away from the mirror. "A hundred acres might not be much, but it's mine, Gramps. And I love the land as much as you did. I'm not afraid of hard work, and piece by piece I'll buy our land back from Taylor. He promised he'd sell it to me when I could buy it, remember. That was the rule when you sold it to him."

Lacy curtains covered the narrow window overlooking the backyard. She drew a corner back and peeked out. She dropped the curtain and took a step back, stumbled over a small footstool, and went down on one knee.

She wanted to cry, to curl up in a ball and weep, but she couldn't. She limped over to the recliner, flipped the handle on the side, and leaned back as far as it would let her, looked up, and right there on top of the chest of drawers was another picture of Greg. A bust shot of him in his high school graduation robe and mortarboard hat with a tassel hanging to the side. The gold charm told her that he'd graduated two years before she did and that his school colors were orange and black. A sticky note attached to the side of the frame held the message, "I'll bring home the best bull. Miss you!"

He was younger, but the eyes were the same and they still looked right into her soul like the picture down in the living room. She threw her arm over her face and forced herself to think about the beach, to hear the seagulls and the slapping of the waves against the sandbar. The soft smell of the lotion on her hands sparked a deep memory of her mother in her dreams. They were playing in the wildflowers like the ones in the picture of Greg Adams. She was a little girl with dark braids and a cotton dress. The grass was soft on her bare feet but cool, so it had to be spring. They'd sung the "Ring around the Rosy" song, then fallen back in the flowers. Her mother touched her cheek and said, "Don't ever give up your wings. Always know that you can fly, my child."

Then out of nowhere there was a door right in the middle of the pasture of wild, colorful flowers, and there was a yellow cat peeking around the corner. A mouse darted through the cat's front legs and was coming right at her when she sat straight up in bed and her eyes popped wide open.

"Damn it! I don't get to dream about Mama very often. Why'd you bring that thing into my dreams?" she asked.

Someone rapped gently on the door, but she thought it was part of the dream until it happened again. She cocked her head to one side and said, "Come in."

Clarice pushed inside and sat down on the vanity bench. "Thank you. It's been more than an hour and I was hoping you were awake. Would you please tell me more about Marvin? I read the letter and it said what I thought it would. Strange, that something sixty years old can still be so bittersweet."

"Is it all right if I sit on the bed?" Emily asked. "This chair would be a lot more comfortable for you than that bench."

"Honey, this is your room right now. Make yourself at home."

"Is that your grandson in that picture too?" Emily asked.

Clarice nodded. "When he graduated from high school. He leaves me little notes when he has to be gone. It's to convince me that he's coming back. I have a fear that he'll change his mind about ranchin'. Now please tell me about Marvin."

Emily kicked off her boots and crawled up in the middle of the bed. She crossed her legs Indian-style, kept her gaze on Clarice and off the picture on the chest, and said, "He fought cancer for five years and last week the battle ended. It won. I thought he'd kick it for sure right up until that last week. He was diagnosed the week I graduated from college five years ago. I had planned on coming back to the ranch anyway, so it didn't change my life drastically. I took care of him. He was always too stubborn to hire a foreman, so I took care of that too. As the ranch dwindled to pay for his bills, there was less ranchin' and more caretakin'."

"How many children did he have?" Clarice asked.

Emily held up one finger. "Just one son, my father. But Nana's family lived on the next farm over. She came from a family that had five girls, so I had lots of family around me and lots of cousins to play with when I was growing up. My father died nine years ago in a horse accident. I was a senior in high school and the shock was horrible. Even worse than when Mama died, but I was just barely four that year and too little to really understand what an aneurism was. He was fine that morning at breakfast, and that evening he was gone. I thought it was the worst thing I'd ever endure, but watching

Gramps go by degrees was even tougher. How many children did you have, Miz Clarice?"

"Just one son, Bart. He and his wife, Nancy, only had one child—Greg. He's thirty now. And you?"

"Twenty-eight," Emily answered.

"Did Marvin ever mention me?" Clarice asked softly.

"He talked about you that last week and to you the last hours of his life. I really thought that you were probably dead and had come to help him cross over into eternity. He made me promise that I'd find out if you were alive and see to it that you got those letters and understood that he hadn't been a jackass. It all started when the mailman drove out to the ranch with that letter they found at the post office," Emily said.

"Thank you for keeping that promise. You'll never know what this means to me. Did Marvin, was he, did he suffer?" Clarice dabbed at her eye.

Emily shook her head. "He was sick for a very long time, but for a while he was still able to be up and around. It wasn't until that last round of chemo that he wasn't able to at least sit on the porch swing with me every evening. At the end I prayed that God would take him on to a place where he wouldn't hurt anymore. That sounds ugly, doesn't it?"

Clarice shook her head. "No, it's the way life is. Why didn't he come to Ravenna all those years ago? He knew where I was."

Emily shrugged. "I asked him that, but he just smiled and said that God must've had other plans for both of you or that letter wouldn't have gotten lost."

Clarice nodded. "Can't undo history. I was happy with Lester Adams. We had a good life, raised a good son, and he married well. Now I have Greg to help me run the ranch. I'm glad you brought the letters home to me, Emily, and I'm glad you agreed to stay for supper."

"Thank you," Emily said.

"Want to come with me to the kitchen and help Dotty get things on the table?" Clarice asked.

"I'd love to." Emily bounded off the bed, stomped her feet back into her boots, and followed Clarice on down the stairs.

———∿∿———

Greg checked out every square inch of the big black bruiser of an Angus bull. He was one of the finest specimens he'd ever laid eyes on, and Lightning Ridge would be lucky to have him.

He took his phone out of his shirt pocket to call his grandmother to tell her that he'd discovered the perfect new bloodline for the ranch, and found that Clarice had sent a picture. She hadn't learned the art of texting with the new phone he'd gotten her, but apparently she had figured out how to take and send pictures.

He adjusted his glasses and stepped away from the bull pen to the shady side of the sale barn so he could see the picture. So that was Emily that Nana had called three times about in the past two hours. She'd been adamant that he stop what he was doing and look at the picture the last time she called.

According to Nana, Emily was an inch or two shorter than she was and had come to the house in jeans, boots, and a lightweight denim jacket. She didn't have tattoos, and the only thing Nana could see that was pierced was her ears. He'd told his grandmother that there might be a whole raft of surprises under those jeans and jacket, but she was so excited about some old boyfriend she'd had back when she was a teenager that she didn't hear a word Greg had to say. He held the phone up to get better light and had to admit that Emily was striking with all that dark hair and those crystal, clear blue eyes.

"So is your body covered with tats? Do you have a belly ring and a tongue stud?" he asked. "Are you a ranchin' woman, or do you just like jeans and boots? Nana is quite taken with you, but I'll never meet you in real person, so it doesn't really matter, does it?"

His phone rang, surprising him so much that he almost dropped it. "Yes, Nana. I just saw the picture. You did a good job. What's her name again—Emma? And Dotty called to tell me about the mouse. That would have been a sight to see, the way that Dotty hates those things," he teased.

"It's Emily," Clarice said. "I told you already that her name is Emily. What do you think of her? Did you find all my notes? I only found two that you left me."

"She is a very pretty lady. And yes, I found your notes and I left more than two, so you'd best start lookin' around. It's past time to clean off the fridge if you can't even find a new note on it." He chuckled.

"I have offered her that job we've been talkin' about," Clarice said bluntly.

"Nana! I called an ad in the newspaper to be published next week that we would take resumes for that job. And I had in mind that we'd hire a man for the job, not a woman that we don't even know. Hell, we could have hired Prissy," Greg said.

"Emily has got a degree in agriculture business and

has been working on her grandfather's ranch for five years. I don't think any man could beat her credentials. And it's just for a month. She's got a hundred acres out in west Texas that she wants to get back to by the first of March. That way I get to see if I really want someone in the house to help me or not, and I get to know her better. So call the newspaper and take the ad out, and believe me, Prissy has a job and she won't ever live on a ranch," Clarice told him.

"Did Emily take the job?" Greg asked.

"She's stayin' at a hotel in Sherman until tomorrow. She's going to think about it. Marvin died after a long battle with cancer and she took care of him. He made her promise to do two things: bring my letters home to me and take a month off. Her cousin is running things while she's gone, but she will be going back. I swear she talks about that ranch like it's a real person," Clarice said.

"I still think a man would be better," Greg said. "But if it's just for a month, then whatever you think is fine, Nana. And Nana, you talk about Lightning Ridge the same way."

Clarice laughed out loud. "I'm the over-romantic one, and you are like your grandpa, ever the businessman. That's what makes us such good ranchin' partners, Greg."

"You are right about that. It takes both of us to run Lightning Ridge, doesn't it?" Greg said.

He adored his grandmother even if she was more sentimental about everything since his grandfather passed five years before. A month with someone to help her in the office with the new computerized bookkeeping and to drive her and her friends around would show her just how valuable an assistant could be. And then they'd hire a man to do the job. It was a win-win situation.

But right now, he had a bull to buy. He said a few more words to his grandmother and hung up. On his way back into the sale barn he brought up Emily's picture one more time. There was something about her eyes that was downright mesmerizing.

But still, a ranch was a business, and running one was hard work. Maybe Emily would work out just fine for a month, but Greg had a feeling that the whole reason his grandmother wanted her around was to drag up the past. She and Dotty seemed obsessed with it lately, constantly arguing about what had happened when they were younger or when someone had died or given birth. Maybe it was the fact that they were both eighty years old, or maybe all elderly folks relived their glory days as they got older. He got a kick out of their close friendship and a bigger one out of all four of the old gals—Clarice, Dotty, Rose, and Madge—that made up their circle.

He'd only been gone three days, but his heart was back at Lightning Ridge. He wanted his own bed and Dotty's chocolate cake. He didn't give a rat's ass if his grandmother hired a dozen women. If that made her happy, then he'd write the paychecks out of his personal account, but when the permanent hire was put on the ranch payroll, he wanted someone who could protect those four elderly women. He'd rest easy if he hired someone who could pick one of them up and carry them to the hospital if they fell and broke a hip while walking into the ice cream store.

He sat down in the bleachers with his bidding card and took his phone out of his pocket. "Nana, how old was you when you wrote all those letters to that soldier?" he asked when she answered his call.

"I was a senior in high school and I read the letter that got stuck in the mailbox. In it he says that he's got something important to ask me when I get out there to his ranch. We'd talked about me riding the bus out there when he got out of the service and I got out of school that summer. I really thought I was in love with him and he was about to ask me to marry him," she said.

"And you never met him?" Greg asked.

"I have a picture of him in my box of letters up in the attic," she said. "But I never did actually meet him or even hear his voice. We didn't make phone calls in those days like we do now."

"You kept letters from another man after you married Grandpa?" he gasped.

Clarice laughed. "Yes, I did. That part of my life had been over for two years, but I couldn't throw those letters away. I took them to the burning barrel just before I married your grandpa, but something wouldn't let me throw them in the fire. So I tied them up with some bailing twine and put them in the attic. I'd forgotten about them until today. Emily has her grandfather's eyes."

"How do you know that, Nana? Is the picture you have in color?"

"No, but I can tell they are blue and he told me they were," Clarice said.

"This is just for a month, right?" Greg asked.

"Yes, it is. Did you buy that bull?"

"It's the next one up on the block. How high should I go?" he answered.

"The sky is the limit. I trust your judgment," she said.

That was Nana's way of saying that he should trust her as well. If she and Dotty wanted to go on a month-long cruise around the world, he would have booked it without so much as blinking. So if she wanted to hire Emily to drive her around and help out on the ranch for a month, then he wouldn't fight her.

"Okay, then. And Nana, make Emily an offer she can't refuse. It would be nice for you to have someone to take you and the ladies to all your beauty shop appointments and auxiliary meetings. Time to start bidding. I'll see you late tomorrow night."

"I love you, Greg. Drive careful now, and when you get home, don't turn that bull loose in the pasture until I get a good look at him," Clarice said.

Chapter 2

EMILY SAT CROSS-LEGGED IN THE MIDDLE OF A KING-sized bed in her hotel room and opened up her laptop. She typed Lightning Ridge Ranch into the search engine and immediately a link came up for the ranch website. There was a picture of Greg with a foot propped on a rail fence, one of Clarice sitting on the porch swing, but she wore a pretty flowing skirt and sweater instead of jeans and boots, and one of a whole pasture of Black Angus cattle. It had a page that told all about the cattle sale in the fall; how many cow and calf combinations, bulls and steers they'd sold. Yes, sir, it was a big operation; ten times the size of her ranch when it was at its prime. It would swallow up the little hundred acres that she had these days.

She flipped back to Greg's picture. She stared at him so long without blinking that the image became fuzzy. What was it about him that made her heart flutter around in her chest? Was it the eyes?

She pushed the laptop to one side, picked up the remote, and hit the power button. The CMT channel popped up with a video of "I Feel a Sin Comin' On" by the Pistol Annies. The volume was so loud that at first she didn't hear her phone ring. It was the flickering light on the nightstand that caught her attention. She rolled to one side and grabbed it, answering without even check-ing the caller ID.

"Do I hear Miranda Lambert?" Taylor asked.

"Yes, you do." Emily pressed the mute button on the remote.

"Did you find the lady that the letters belonged to? I bet you are in Louisiana tonight, aren't you?" Taylor asked.

Emily sighed. "I did find Clarice and she's offered me a job for a month. Her grandson has been after her to hire an assistant. Someone to help with the computerized ranch stuff, payroll, taxes, and then help drive her and her friends around when they need to go places. I think she just wants to hear more about Gramps, but I'm thinking about stayin' on. You'll never believe what happened right smack off the bat when I rang the doorbell."

"You are shittin' me," Taylor stammered. "If you want to ranch, come on home."

"I promised Gramps I'd take a whole month. And after all the times you've teased me with dead mice, I figured you'd get a kick out of that story."

"You also promised him that you'd sell me the final hundred acres if you found something else you wanted to do. I don't see that happenin', the way you've hung on to this last parcel like a bulldog with an old ham bone. And darlin', I hate cats, but I could kiss that old yellow critter for that trick. And since they've got mice on that ranch, don't you think you better get on back here to God's country, where you belong?" Taylor asked.

"To begin with, all ranches have mice. And I'd kiss a mouse on the nose before you'd kiss a cat. And about sellin' the ranch, it ain't never goin' to happen, Taylor. I'm not selling the last of Shine Canyon to you. And those promises go two ways, remember. You have to sell my land back to me a hundred acres at a time as I get the money saved up. My roots are firmly planted in that dirt out there. I'll be home in a month." She could visualize his dark brows knitting together in a fine line over his light blue eyes. "Are you lighting up a cigarette? I swear, they're going to give you cancer just like they did Gramps."

"He was eighty years old," Taylor said.

Emily heard the click of a cigarette lighter and then the whoosh as Taylor blew out a stream.

"If I come home will you quit smoking?" she asked.

"If you'll come on back to Happy, I'll think about it," he answered.

"Gramps said I was supposed to take a month and figure out what I really wanted before I make a decision. I reckon I can do that working for Clarice as well as I can sitting on a sandbar. Besides, I heard it rains a lot during this time of year in Florida. You won't quit until you are ready anyway, so don't be usin' your smokin' as blackmail," she said.

"I knew you couldn't survive a whole month away from the smell of hay and cattle any more than I can survive a whole day without a cigarette," he said between puffs.

"I don't want to watch you die like Gramps did," Emily begged.

Another click of a lighter and Taylor said, "I know, darlin'. And I promise I'll quit on my thirtieth birthday. You know I keep my promises always, and I'll be thirty next fall, so how's that?"

"If that's what I can have, then I'll take it. Taylor, I

have to do this. Please understand, but also know that I meant it when I said my roots are in the land out there. I could never leave it completely or I'd wither up and die. I just need this month to regroup," she said.

"I know, and it's okay. This dirt, it ain't goin' nowhere. It'll be right here when you come home, and you'll have family around you to help you settle those roots even deeper."

Emily swallowed hard to get the baseball-sized lump out of her throat, but she kept the tears at bay. "I'll call every couple of days. Things all right out there?"

"It's fine, Em. I'll look for you to be home by calving season, or else sell this place to me. I brought Old Bill and the other dogs over here to our place so I don't have to go over there and feed them every day," he said.

"Thank you, Taylor," she said.

"Night, honey," he said.

Emily pushed the button to hang up and laid the phone beside her on the bed. She could always depend on Taylor and Dusty to help her, and she could take a job in Amarillo for a steady income to supplement growing a few calves and as many acres of alfalfa as she could plant. There was comfort in knowing that.

By mid-morning Greg and his big black bull were just inside the Conroe city limits sign. He fished his phone from his shirt pocket and punched in Jeremiah's business number.

"Conroe Investigative Services, may I help you?" a feminine voice asked.

"Could I speak with Jeremiah please? This is Greg Adams."

"I'll patch you right through to him. He's been expecting your call."

In seconds Jeremiah's big booming voice came through the phone. "Hey, what's happenin'? Mama said you might call today because you'd be comin' through town. Got time for coffee? I'll meet you out at the coffee shop on the highway."

His size, looks, and voice didn't match. He was short, bald-headed, and slightly overweight, but his voice made him ten feet tall, bulletproof, and movie-star handsome. In a crowd there wasn't one thing that made him stand out from anyone else. Maybe that's what made him such a damn fine private investigator.

"I know just the one you're talkin' about. I'll be there in ten minutes," Greg said.

Greg parked behind the coffee shop where they'd made room for a couple of semitrucks, and Jeremiah pulled his dark SUV in beside him. Greg shook the legs of his jeans down over his boots. Jeremiah adjusted the collar of his black knit shirt and pulled on a black leather jacket.

"You still don't look mean even in black leather." Greg laughed.

"Well, you just barely look like a cowboy even in boots and a Stetson. It's good to see you. Been a while."

They didn't shake hands but did a man-hug in the middle of the parking lot.

"Dotty fusses that you don't come home often enough," Greg said as they headed inside the shop.

"I hear it on a regular basis. Don't tell Mama, but I've

got a girlfriend. She'd have me married with three kids and the president of the PTA within twenty-four hours." Jeremiah laughed.

Greg stepped up to the counter and ordered two black coffees. "You still drink it the right way? You haven't gone all double latte with skim milk, have you?"

"Still drink it black." Jeremiah nodded. "I talked to Mama last night. She told me a story about your nana and an old boyfriend's letters. Clarice has offered the girl who brought her the letters a job at the ranch."

They found a table in the corner and sat down across from each other.

"Nana needs someone to help her. She's eighty and we don't let her drive anymore. It was tough on her to let her license expire, but she'd had three fender benders and I was afraid the next one wouldn't just be a fender bender. It's only for a month, and then she'll see how nice it was and let me hire some real help," Greg explained.

"Givin' up her driver's license was the toughest thing Mama did. I think it was even worse than giving up the bourbon." Jeremiah chuckled. "I'll be home for the church bazaar, and I'm bringing Stacy to meet Mama. I want to surprise her."

"And you don't want to listen to all that sentimental shit between now and then, right?" Greg laughed with him.

"Women! And the older they get the worse it is. Everything has to do with the heart and little with the head," Jeremiah said.

"Says the man who is bringing home a woman to meet Mama."

"Man, you know what I'm talkin' about. You're the one who's going to be living with three women in the house now."

"Three?"

"Clarice offered room and board with the job. I haven't talked to Mama this morning, so I don't know if she took the job or not. She's a looker, though. Mama sent a picture of her. Pretty blue eyes," Jeremiah said.

"And your new woman? She got blue eyes?"

"Sometimes. Sometimes they're green. Naturally they are gorgeous brown."

Greg cocked his head to one side.

"Contacts. She matches them to her mood. I don't mess with her when she has green eyes. I just find something to do outside the office and leave it with her." Jeremiah smiled again.

"So she's your new secretary?"

Jeremiah nodded. "Six months now."

"Is that a record?"

Jeremiah's head bobbed again. "Oh, yeah, by a whole week. I think I'm in love."

"You better know you're in love before you bring her home, because you will be afterward."

"Crazy ain't it, the way we love those two old gals? Love 'em like they are our real mamas."

Greg held out his cup and Jeremiah tapped his to it. "I was always more at home on the ranch than in Houston."

"And I was a sinkin' ship when Mama jerked me up by the collar and took me in after my real mama died," Jeremiah said.

—⁓—

Nothing was as beautiful as a sunset in Ravenna, Texas. Bright yellow laced with orange, sprinkled with a bit of hot pink and some baby blue. No artist's palette could ever string the colors together the way that nature did when the sun set out over the bare mesquite trees and scrub oaks.

Greg parked his truck out by the barn and jogged all the way to the house. He took the stairs two at a time. Cooking smells filling the house promised that Dotty had kept her word and made his favorite meal, which included hot yeast rolls and Southern fried chicken. But he flat-out had to hit the bathroom.

No one waited in the foyer when he started back down, so evidently he'd managed to sneak in without anyone knowing. He tiptoed across the foyer, leaned on the doorjamb leading into the dining room, and waited in the shadows.

Nana and Dotty's voices drifted from the kitchen where they argued about whether it was time to pour the gravy in the bowl. Dotty said cold gravy was terrible and she hadn't cooked all damn day for supper to be spoiled by putting it on the table too soon.

Nana said that he should be driving up any second. And then Emily carried a bowl of salad to the dining room table and Greg's chest tightened. The picture did not do her a bit of justice. She was shorter than he'd imagined. Her waist nipped in above rounded hips, and her hair was so black that the light from the dining room chandelier gave it a deep blue cast. But it was her blue eyes and those kissable lips that kept him from blinking until his eyes went dry.

Emily hadn't noticed a picture of Greg in the dining room, but there must be one sitting somewhere because she felt his eyes on her. A shiver danced down her spine as she scanned the buffet and the shelf above the archway for a photograph, but she didn't see one. The only time in her entire life that she'd had a feeling like that was in the living room the day before and in the bedroom where his picture sat on the chest of drawers. So somewhere tucked away was a picture of Greg Adams. She had no doubt about it. She just had to find it.

It might be in the kitchen. Maybe on the refrigerator door that was covered with so many multicolored sticky notes that it looked like a circus tent. Dotty said that the pink ones were recipes, the yellow ones at the top were important messages, the ones at the bottom weren't so important, the green ones were cute little sayings that she and Clarice liked, and the purple ones were… hell's bells, she couldn't remember what the purple ones were. Evidently everyone in the house had a sticky note fetish. Did she need to rush down to the office supply store and buy several dollars' worth? She'd glanced at the notes but feared that it might be rude to read through them.

"Greg! You rascal," Clarice squealed after she'd set the butter dish on the table. She dashed over to the door with her arms wide open and he picked her up and swung her around the room.

Clarice giggled like a girl. "You snuck in on us."

"I came in the front door," he said.

"Come and meet Emily," Clarice said.

Emily couldn't take her eyes off the cowboy. He was

taller than she'd thought he would be, but there was no doubt by the swagger and the drawl that he was pure cowboy, not one of those wannabes that dressed up on Saturday night in boots and belt buckles to go to the local honky-tonk with hopes of getting lucky.

The vibes coming off him were like long, warm tendrils finding their way into her cold heart to warm it back to life. She imagined it turning from blue to a nice healthy pink inside her chest. She'd barely caught her breath when he set Clarice on her feet and crossed the room in a few long strides, his hand out.

"Pleased to meet you, Emily," he said.

She put her hand in his. "Likewise."

Time stood still. The clock hands didn't move. Clarice became a statue. The sun hung on the horizon. Nothing moved.

"Nana said you decided to take the job," he drawled and let go of her hand.

"Why did you come in the front door? Where's the new bull?" Clarice asked.

In an instant, things were back to normal. At least everything but the feeling that Emily was dreaming and that she'd wake up any minute in west Texas.

Greg threw an arm around Clarice's shoulders and said, "Drank too much coffee and had to get inside in a hurry. Bull is in the trailer. I'm starving. Can we eat before we turn him loose?"

Clarice stood back and scanned him from toes to head. "I'm glad you are home. How were your folks? Emily agreed to stay on for a month."

"I've been after Nana for a year to hire someone to help her. Folks are just fine, Nana. They send their love

and hugs. Stop worrying. I am home. I'm not going back
no matter what they offer." Greg smiled.

"You keep saying that, but I still worry that they'll
offer you a corner office, a six-figure salary, and an
expense account for Italian-made business suits,"
Clarice said.

"They do every time I go down there, but I turn them
down because I love Lightning Ridge and you." He
smiled. "Supper looks good. Fried chicken is my favorite, Emily. They spoil me when I've been gone a few
days. I should leave more often."

"Bullshit!" Dotty rounded the end of the table with a
platter of chicken. "Clarice frets every time that pickup
of yours heads south. Even your notes don't convince
her that you'll be back." She set it down and gave him
a quick hug. "Now let's eat so she can go pass judgment on your new bull. I see you've met Emily. She'll
be stayin' in the room across the hall from you, so you
don't have the whole upstairs to yourself anymore."

Greg pulled out a chair for Clarice. "I stopped and
had coffee with Jeremiah. He's coming home for the
church bazaar."

Dotty seated herself before Greg could get there.
"He'd damn sure better. I'm getting homesick to see my
kid. It's been six months."

But he did make it to Emily's chair before she could
get seated. His hand brushed her shoulder, and warmth
spread from there to her heart again.

Dotty sipped at her sweet tea and explained, "Jeremiah
is my son. I got him when he was thirteen and his mama
died. I worked with her at the school lunchroom and
they were going to put Jeremiah in the foster program,

so I took him in and adopted him the next year," she explained. "Y'all best get after this food. Cold gravy and mashed potatoes ain't worth eatin'. Does he look all right, Greg? I worry about him down there in that big place doin' what he does, carryin' a gun and all."

Greg dipped into the mashed potatoes and handed the bowl across the table to Emily. Their eyes caught for a split second, then they both looked away, but not before Emily got yet another flutter in her chest. What in the hell was wrong with her? She'd seen sexy cowboys before. She'd dated sexy cowboys before. They'd kissed her and there had been a couple who had gone beyond that, but none of them sent her into a tailspin just by holding her hand in his.

That picture above the mantel didn't do him justice. In real, three-dimensional life he was so much more. His dark brown hair had been flattened by a cowboy hat with a slight horizontal indention on his forehead as further proof. His smile was genuine, and his eyes were piercing, as if they could see to the bottom of her soul and beyond. Jeremiah—they were talking about Jeremiah before Greg handed her the bowl of potatoes. She blinked several times and forced herself to listen rather than daydream.

"Is Jeremiah a policeman?" she asked.

"No, he's a private investigator. I swear to God, if I'd known he was going to go into that field, I would have never let him watch all them cop shows," Dotty said. "I thought if I sent him to college he'd change his mind. He's real good with computers, and Clarice offered him a job here, but oh, no, he had to go to the city and work at something that worries a mama to death."

Clarice put a chicken thigh on her plate and passed the platter to Greg. "Emily has taken the job I offered her. We've spent the day in the office. She's done more in one day than I could get done in a week. She's really good at organizing things. When she's not doing book work or driving me and the girls, she'll work on the ranch."

Greg forked a chicken leg onto his plate. "She don't have to do that. Y'all can find something for her to do in the house."

"I'm used to hard work, and with spring comin' on, an extra hand might come in useful," Emily said. "I've had to be inside more than outside the past few weeks and I don't mind gettin' my hands dirty."

"I'm sorry about your grandpa," Greg said.

When she looked across the table at him, his expression said that he understood her pain. "Thank you. He was sick for a long time, so it wasn't a surprise."

"But we're never ready to let go of those we love." His deep drawl was sincere.

"No, we are not," Clarice said.

"Nana, I can't wait for you to see this new bull," Greg changed the subject abruptly.

Emily understood his pain in that moment. Something had happened in his past that had been difficult to face. The death of his grandfather? A lost love?

Clarice inhaled deeply and let it out slowly. "Greg is like his grandpa. Lester was all business."

"Grandpa was a man's man," Greg said.

"Yes, he was. I loved him deeply, and we had a lot of wonderful years together, but he was not a romantic soul," Clarice said softly.

"He brought you wildflowers," Dotty piped up. "Every spring he brought you wildflowers."

Clarice smiled brightly. "Yes, he did, for my birthday. Lester loved deeply, but he wasn't one much for speaking his mind about all that folderol and payin' endless compliments, as he used to say."

Max, the ranch foreman, peeked inside the dining room from the kitchen. "Lester was a businessman. That's where Bart got his business sense. How much chicken did you fry, Dotty?"

"Enough to feed you if you want to eat, but you're going to go get your own plate," she answered.

"Good-lookin' bull out there in the trailer," Max said over his shoulder.

"See? The men on this ranch are all business," Clarice said.

"Nana, you are just as business-minded as I am," Greg told her.

Clarice passed the chicken platter back to her. "You'd best get what you want. When Max gets started it looks like a dead chicken yard by the time he's finished."

"Don't be tellin' tales on me." Max carried a plate, napkin, and silverware to the table. "Greg can outdo me any day when it comes to fried chicken."

"But not steak. I love steak, but Max could eat a whole bull," Greg teased.

"Not in one sitting, but hey, like the wise man said, a person could eat an elephant a bite at a time."

—◆◆◆—

Emily smiled at the banter. She'd loved that part of holidays and Sundays at Taylor's place most of all.

The big family and all the noise left her knowing that she belonged right there in Happy. But the sicker that Gramps got, the fewer trips they made from one ranch to the other, and she didn't even realize how much she had missed it until that very evening.

"So you have a ranch and you're on vacation?" Greg asked.

She dabbed at her mouth with a napkin. "I have a hundred acres. It used to be three sections back before Gramps got sick. It's hardly enough to be called a ranch, but it's a starting point to rebuild it. I was born on that land and it's my home, but right now I'm glad to be away from it for a few weeks."

He stretched his legs out under the table and his knee bumped hers. "Sorry about that. I've been driving all day and feel like I could stretch to the stars."

"No problem. I felt like that yesterday when I drove all the way from Happy to Sherman," she said.

Her mouth was dry so she took a couple of long drinks of her sweet tea. Greg Adams might be business on the outside, but those eyes and his smile said there was a sweet, sensitive man down underneath that tough exterior. One that had known pain and suffering as well as joys and happiness and who loved his big ranch as much as she loved what was left of hers. No one could endure the hard work of ranching without loving what they did.

"I'm glad that we've got someone to help us," Dotty said out of nowhere. "Clarice's eyesight ain't what it used to be, and that computer screen gives her headaches. When she's got a headache she's plumb bitchy. I hate computers. They're all going to fall apart one of these days and everyone is going to wish they had their old ledgers back like how we used to take care of things with an ink pen and lined pages."

"I'm not bitchy," Clarice argued.

Max filled his plate and laid a napkin over his knee. "I agree with Dotty about all this technical crap, but it's the way of the world. Can't whip it so we might as well join up with it. So tell us more about this Marvin fellow, Clarice."

"Marvin was stationed over in Korea during the war. I think they call it a conflict now, but it was a war back then," Clarice said. "I was still in high school when we first started writing back and forth. The church ladies were given names of servicemen who would like to have pen pals. That was way back before cell phones, computers, and all this other stuff you kids have today. So I started writing to him when I was a senior in high school. And then the letters stopped coming and I didn't know if he'd been killed in action or if he'd come home or what happened, until Emily brought the letters to me."

"That was before you met Grandpa, right?" Greg asked.

Clarice smiled. "I'd met Lester. We lived on adjoining ranches, but he was off to college during the time I wrote to Marvin. The letters had stopped coming long before Lester started courting me. Marvin and I might not have even liked each other in person. It's easy to make a soldier out to be a hero when all you have is words, one small black-and-white picture, and an imagination. We'll never know because a letter got lost and we both took a different path."

"Crazy, ain't it?" Max said. "After all these years,

you find out that y'all were just a hard day's drive away from each other."

"Fate," Dotty said.

"You think fate kept them apart and then brought them together again with that bunch of mail, Dotty?" Max asked.

"That's exactly what I think. Now Clarice won't go to her grave thinkin' that Marvin was a son-of-a-bitch who just used her for mail call and then threw her away," Dotty answered. "And now it's time for chocolate cake."

She disappeared into the kitchen and brought out a triple-layered chocolate cake with fudge icing.

Greg took a shower, donned gray lounging pants and a T-shirt, and sprawled out in his recliner in front of the television in his room. *NCIS* entertained him for an hour before he switched it to CMT and watched several videos, but his mind stayed on the woman who'd been dropped out of nowhere onto his ranch and was now staying across the hall from him. He tapped his fingers on the chair arm while the Pistol Annies sang "I Feel a Sin Comin' On."

"I wonder if Emily has sins in her past," he muttered.

Before his inner voice could remind him that everyone had a past, his phone rang. He pushed the remote button, checked the ID, and answered on the third ring. "Hey, Jeremiah, old man. What's goin' on?"

Jeremiah chuckled. "I couldn't leave it alone, Greg. Must be my line of business, but I'm not as trusting as you or as Clarice. There's no charge. I was only on the phone thirty minutes. Talked to several people under the pretense of vetting Clarice's new assistant girl for a job. She's pure as the driven snow. Not a stain on her anywhere. Lived on the Shine Canyon Ranch her whole life. It's not nearly as big as Lightning Ridge, but it wasn't a two-bit, one-horse operation either. She had to sell off a lot of it to keep money coming in for her grandpa's chemo, but there's still some acreage left in the ranch. Only time she was away from Happy, Texas, was when she went to college, and then she was home every single solitary weekend and worked on the ranch during summers and holidays. She's honest as God and has a reputation of a saint. She ran the ranch and took care of her grandfather, Marvin, who died last week with cancer."

"She comes off as that sort of woman," Greg said.

"Sassy or shy?" Jeremiah asked.

"Confident. She knows ranchin', but like you said today, she's got this notion that she can make a livin' on a hundred acres in west Texas. That will just barely support five cows, not a herd big enough to make a livin'. It's that sentimental stuff we talked about." Greg laughed.

"And she ain't but what, twenty-eight or so?"

"That's about right. Thanks for checking up on her, but I'm not surprised at what you found."

Jeremiah's tone changed. "Just thought you'd want to know. Don't tell Mama or Clarice. They'd say that they already knew she was bona fide, but I had to have some solid proof. Got to go. Stacy and I are catching a late dinner together."

"I wouldn't dream of telling anything. Have fun."

Chapter 3

EMILY THREW OFF THE COVERS AND SLID OUT OF BED with a yawn. Ranch work was never done, and it always, always started before daybreak. She started toward her closet and ran into a chair before she realized that she was not in her bedroom at Shine Canyon. She plopped down in the chair, turned on the lamp beside it, and put her hands over her eyes.

She'd been caught up in the moment when she agreed to this job. Gramps had said that she needed time away from ranching so she could sort out what she should do with her life. Working on a ranch, even as a glorified assistant, would put her right back where Gramps didn't think she should be. If she wanted hard work, she could do it on Shine Canyon. Staying on Lightning Ridge was pure crazy, but she'd given her word and a Cooper's word was as good as a signature on an affidavit.

She dressed in jeans and a knit shirt and unzipped a duffle bag holding all her shoes: sandals, platform heels, a pair of sneakers, and her comfortable cowboy boots. According to the television meteorologist it was forty-five degrees, so she pulled on her boots.

She needed coffee, at least two cups to even open her eyes in the morning. Why wasn't anyone up and around? It had to be close to daylight.

"Bunch of sluggards. Out in west Texas, we have to

work to make a living. We don't get to sleep until noon," she mumbled as she made her way to the kitchen.

She opened several doors before she found the coffee and filters, started a pot to dripping, and sat down at the bar to wait. The sticky notes took her attention. She knew Clarice's handwriting from the envelopes in the box and most of them belonged to her. Some had a reply at the bottom in a tight, stingy script that had to belong to Dotty. And then there were some with the same masculine scrawl as the ones on the two pictures.

We will be working on bazaar tomorrow.

No, shit!

Emily giggled.

Think up something different for us to make for the bazaar.

I need drugs to do that.

Emily laughed out loud and searched until she found the ones with Greg's handwriting. They were mostly in plain yellow and were reminders.

You promised you'd hire someone this month, Nana.

Month ain't over yet.

And another one.

Haircut on Friday.

It's about time!

They lived in the same house, talked to each other all the time. Why in the hell would they stick notes to the refrigerator? Her eyes were drawn to a yellow note from Greg in a bunch of green ones.

Glad to be home.

Her heart did a flip and she leaned over to study it more. If he was all business, then why in the devil did he participate in the sticky note campaign? Gramps would have called it a bunch of sentimental bullshit.

The coffeepot gurgled at last. While she was filling a mug she noticed the clock on the stove.

"Ten minutes to five," she groaned. She'd set the alarm wrong on the clock beside her bed. No wonder no one was up and around. It was too early.

She filled a mug with hot steaming coffee and drank it as she watched out the kitchen window for the first signs of a brand-new Texas sunrise. A rooster crowed and she could see the outline of the chicken house to the south. In the opposite direction a lonesome old bawling heifer joined in the barnyard noises.

Like she'd thought when she first awoke, ranch work was never done. She borrowed a work coat from the rack beside the back door and slipped outside. The morning air was brisk with a hint of oncoming moisture, and it was good to have eggs to gather and a cow to milk. She would have started breakfast, but Clarice had whispered that Dotty was very territorial when it came to the kitchen, and no matter what, not to interfere with her cooking.

A heifer had been penned up in the corral at the back of the barn. The old girl had a bulging udder, and a clean milk bucket waited beside a three-legged stool inside the first stall. Emily had never liked that job, but that didn't mean she couldn't squirt milk into a galvanized bucket. Some jobs were downright fun; others were just hard work. When Emily opened the door the cow bawled and headed toward the big sliding doors on the back side of the barn.

She dumped feed into the trough and the heifer had

her head in it when Emily drew the stool up to the side, leaned her head against the cow's flank, and set the milk bucket under her udder. The first few squirts made a pinging noise when they hit the galvanized bucket, but after a while it was mundane work and Emily's mind wandered back to those sticky notes. What did they do when there was no more room? Did they throw them away and start over or just take a few off at a time?

When she finished the job, she picked up the bucket, hung the stool back on the nail, and sweet-talked the heifer back outside. There was a thin orange line on the horizon, and the sun's warmth burned off a few of the gray clouds. It might be a nice day after all.

The rooster was doing his best to talk the sun up when she got back to the house, set the milk on the counter, and picked up the egg-gathering basket from a hook in the utility room. She noticed a cluster of bright yellow daffodils blooming right beside the henhouse and squatted to get a better look at them. The petals were soft on her fingertips and made her think of Aunt Molly. She adored yellow flowers of any kind. Maybe that morning Taylor was picking daffodils out in Happy, Texas, for his granny.

She was about to stand up when something cold touched the bare skin on her neck and her squeal quieted the rooster for a whole minute. She wound up flat on her back, staring at what was left of a few faint stars in the sky, with a Catahoula dog slurping right up across her chin and cheek, not stopping until he got his tongue tangled up in her hair. His tail wagged furiously, and when she tried to sit up, he put his paws on her chest.

"Hey, now!" She shoved back at him. "Cold nosing a

woman and scaring the bejesus out of her is rude. Don't you dogs up here in north Texas have any manners at all?"

When she was sitting, the dog plopped down in her lap and she rubbed his ears. "Where have you been? I didn't see you yesterday. Did you get out of the pen and go visiting the neighborhood girl dogs?" she asked.

The animal's tail thumped in the grass.

She pushed him off her lap. "Hey, I see a light in the house. That means I need to get the eggs and take them in or we might not have breakfast."

The rooster flapped his wings and set about his daily chore of waking up everyone who could hear him. She gathered thirteen eggs. Thirteen had always been her lucky number. That had to mean she'd made the right decision to stay on at Lightning Ridge.

The aroma of bacon wafted through the air and her stomach growled. She opened the back door to find Dotty staring at the milk bucket. "Girl, what are you doing up so early? Did you bring this milk in? I was wonderin' if that cow had milked herself this mornin'. What have you got there?"

She handed the basket to Dotty. "I gathered the eggs."

"Well, that's right nice of you. I was just fixin' to either go or send Greg. There wasn't enough in the fridge to make breakfast. Wipe your boots and hang up your coat on the rack over there," Dotty said.

Greg entered the kitchen through the foyer at the same time she came in the back door. He took one look at the basket of eggs and Dotty and asked, "Where did that come from? I would have gone to get them. You didn't need to get out this early."

Dotty pointed at Emily.

"I'm a witch. I knew that Dotty needed eggs so I snapped my fingers." She snapped and a loud popping noise made him blink. "And presto, a baker's dozen eggs floated down from the sky and filled that basket."

"Why didn't you snap your fingers and milk the cow?" He smiled.

"I did. You going to strain it or should I?" she asked.

"You really do know about the ranching business, don't you?"

"Most of it. Gramps made me learn from the ground up and from the time I was a little girl. I never liked milkin', but I can do it. How about you? Can you milk a cow?" she asked.

"Nana made me learn from the ground up too. I was milking cows before I was a teenager," Greg said.

"Are the children up and around already? Are they arguing?" Clarice breezed into the kitchen. She wore jeans, sneakers, and a bright blue knit shirt. Her hair had been brushed back, and her eyes twinkled.

Dotty smiled. "Oh, yeah, and I think the girl child is ahead of the boy child this morning. He's going to have to get up earlier than usual to beat her."

Emily held up a palm. "Confession. I set my alarm clock wrong or I'd still be asleep. I won't be up this early every morning unless Miz Clarice writes it into my job description, and I'm sure hoping she doesn't make me milk cows. That's my least favorite job on a ranch."

"So you aren't brownnosing?" Greg teased.

"No, sir. I like my sleep as well or better than anyone else," she answered. "Now what can I do to help with breakfast?"

"Stay out of my kitchen," Dotty said. "You got the milk and eggs. That's enough help for breakfast."

Clarice poured a mug of coffee and added two teaspoons of sugar. "Looks like I hired a good hand, right, Greg? Me and Dotty are going to be busy in the kitchen all day fixin' dinner and finger foods for the domino party tonight. Emily, you are to go with Greg. He'll put you to work doing whatever needs to be done. Greg, don't you dare make plans for the evening. Madge and Rose are both coming and we need you."

"Why?" Greg asked.

"We need an extra hand tonight. Emily is going to play and we're going to do partners," Dotty said.

"Call Prissy," he said.

"I already did and she has other plans."

Clarice sat down at the table. "We love domino night, Emily."

"Maybe Emily doesn't want to play," Greg said.

Emily looked at Greg and the heat in the room raised by twenty degrees. Did he feel it too, or was the physical attraction just on her part?

Greg tilted his head to one side. Lord, even that was sexy. What was wrong with her? Sure, it had been a long time since she'd had a date, a long time since she'd been kissed, and even longer since she'd done anything else. But Greg Adams wasn't the right cowboy for her to entertain such notions about. His roots were in Ravenna, Texas, and hers were eight hours away in Happy.

"Do you play dominoes?" he asked.

"I've played since I was a kid. Gramps loved his dominoes," she said.

"Marvin told me that he played with his grandparents when he was a boy," Clarice said.

Greg removed his glasses, wiped them clean on his T-shirt, and put them back on. "Did your grandpa let you win because you were the fair-haired daughter?"

"Darlin', I've never been called fair-haired, and believe me, I come from competitive gene stock. We don't let anyone win anything. If I won, it was fair and square. Did your grandpa let you win?" Emily asked.

"Hell, no! I was fifteen before I beat him. Thought I'd done inherited the moon and stars." Greg chuckled.

"Me too. I danced around the living room like I'd made a touchdown for the Dallas Cowboys. Do y'all play for beans or money?" Emily asked.

"Big bucks," Greg said.

"Do I need to make a trip to the bank?"

"Buy-in is fifty dollars. No bets less than five," he answered.

"Greg!" Clarice shook her finger at him.

Emily smiled. "I think I can scrape up fifty dollars. Does it have to be in bills or can I use pennies?"

Greg was on his way out of the house when Emily pushed away from a porch post. "Hey, I'd begun to think you were going to primp all day."

He tilted his freshly shaven face up to the rising sun. The light reflected off his glasses, making a halo above his head. "Did it do any good?"

"You look just like you did when you left the breakfast table, except you are now wearing boots and a coat," she said.

"Well, dammit! I thought at least I smelled better. I used my best shaving lotion to impress you." He grinned.

Her heart skipped a beat. Was he serious or was he joking? Had he felt the attraction that morning at breakfast too? If he did, maybe she'd find a note on the fridge just for her some morning.

She sniffed the air. "It's okay, but I really did like the smell of bacon better."

"Well, then I'll have to see about some bacon-scented shaving lotion. Hey, not to change this exhilarating conversation, but thank you for staying on, Emily. Nana's got a new bounce in her step this morning. I think that computerized stuff really weighs heavy on her mind. I'm hoping by the end of the month she'll let me hire someone on full-time when she sees how nice it is to have some help," Greg said.

"It seemed like the right thing to do. Gramps used to tell me that when I've done made up my mind about something and it doesn't feel right, then I should try on a different decision to see how it feels. I tried to think about spending my month on the beach, but it just didn't feel right. Then I thought about Clarice's offer and there was peace in my heart," she admitted. She didn't say a word about his pictures being a big part of the decision. Hell's bells, she hadn't even told Taylor that part, and she sure wasn't speaking it aloud right then.

"I'm glad it didn't. Now tell me, how much do you know about horses?" he asked. "I hate to ask you to do this, but the fellow who takes care of the horse barn called in sick a few minutes ago. I've got a full day lined up. I'm behind because I've been gone a week."

She didn't give him time to finish. "I love horses. I'll take care of the stables. Will I have time to exercise them?"

He pointed to a pickup truck. It might have been pea green at one time, but nowadays rust covered more than paint and it was a toss-up as to whether the green was lichen or actual paint. The tailgate was gone, and the fenders looked like they'd been whipped with a baseball bat several times.

"Hop in and I'll drive you out there. You know how to handle a stick shift?"

"I can drive anything that has four wheels," she said. "Gramps said that I had to learn to drive everything on the ranch."

"Okay, then I'll leave the truck with you and you can bring it back at dinnertime. Max can pick me up at the barn, and you'll be on your own until noon," he said. "Don't worry if you don't get the stalls all done this morning. I can help finish up after dinner. Albert and Louis both have the flu bug today. Just do what you can and we'll play catch-up later. It won't hurt the horses to go without exercise for one day."

She crawled into the passenger seat of the truck and watched him trot around the front to the driver's side. The visual that popped into her mind almost put her to fanning her face even though there was a cool breeze still blowing that morning out of the north.

Nothing made sense. She'd only known the man one day, and she'd never, not one time, had such a hot attraction to a man—any man, not just cowboys. And she had sure never envisioned doing what she just did sitting in his lap bumping along the rutted pathway at forty miles per hour.

Greg stopped the truck in front of a long horse stable and was on the phone when he slid out of the truck seat and slammed the door. "Yes, that's right. Pick me up here and we'll get busy with that." He shoved the phone back into his pocket.

She crawled out of the truck and looked at a long horse stable, not totally unlike the one that used to be on their ranch until Gramps had sold that section to Taylor.

"You got a phone? You sure you don't mind doing this?" Greg asked.

She held up her phone. "I don't mind. Keys to the truck so I can get back to the house at noon? And yes, I have a phone, and yes, I have the number to the house if I get into trouble."

"The keys are in the front seat, and thank you, Emily. I didn't plan on whoever we hired for Nana's helper to be able to do ranchin' work too."

"I'm a girl of many talents." She smiled.

"Well, this morning I'm grateful. Now, I've got a ton of business to take care of. Hopefully I'll see you at noon."

A dusty cloud followed Max's truck to the barn. He'd barely stopped when Greg got in and waved as he shut the door.

She slipped inside the horse stable, determined that she'd work her way through the emotions surging around through her body. Greg was too damned nice, and that was a fact, jack. If he'd come to Gramps with an old boot box full of letters, she would have thought he was a con man deluxe. She might have been watching too many reruns of *NCIS* and *CSI* in the past couple of years, but she would have figured he was out to get something other than closure from delivering a box of letters.

And yet, he'd accepted her on face value and his grandmother's say-so. She found a hoe, wheelbarrow, and shovel in a room so messy that she wanted to cry just looking at it. It was pitiful considering how many people worked on the ranch. Dotty said that Max and Greg always had their meals in the house but that Max had a small apartment in the bunkhouse that housed twenty permanent hired hands. Then there was another twenty who worked full-time on the ranch and lived in Ravenna or the surrounding areas. That meant a work crew bigger than the one at Taylor's place, and he'd fire someone if he found a tack room looking like this one.

On the way back to the first stable, she passed another room with a small window in the door. Peeking in, she saw a second tack room that was organized and fairly clean. The scent of clean leather and old coffee greeted her when she opened the door. The floor needed to be swept, and upon closer inspection there were a few things out of place.

According to the sign above the stall door, the first horse was Glorietta, a gorgeous buckskin mare with a dark tail and mane. Emily kissed the horse on the nose and told her how beautiful she was before she led her outside the stall and tied her bridle reins to the gate.

"Did someone clean out your stall yesterday, darlin'? This looks worse than my college suitemate's room. Surely someone as pretty as you didn't do this all by yourself," she talked as she worked.

When she'd finished scraping the last of the wet straw from the floor, she pulled the garden hose in from the end of the barn and hosed down the floor and the walls until it was sparkling clean. After that she sunk hay hooks into a small bale of hay, carried it to the stall, and cut the wire holding it together with snips. She spread it over the floor and led Glorietta back into her new clean digs.

"Now isn't that much better? You've been a good girl. I'd love to ride you, but I've got two days' work to get done in half a day to prove that I can do anything that Greg can do."

After one more kiss, Emily moved down the row to the next one. It took two solid hours to do the whole stable, including the center aisle. Her back muscles were whining by the time she wound the hose up and tossed the hoe and shovel into the wheelbarrow.

She finished the tack room with an hour to spare and remembered that the old truck smelled hot when Greg parked it, so she rolled up her sleeves and lifted the hood. It didn't take much poking around before she found the problem, but it took the whole hour to fix it.

She left a cloud of dust behind her when she braked and jumped out of the truck near the kitchen door. She hurried into the house as the clock on the mantel struck twelve times and headed straight for the kitchen sink to wash her hands. She could see across the hall into the dining room. The table was set. Max, Dotty, and Clarice all peered into the kitchen. She dried her hands on the dish towel and hurried to her place at the table.

"Sorry I'm late," she said.

Greg slid into a chair seconds before she did. "I'm late too. Got caught up with the veterinarian who was checking out the new bull."

Clarice smiled. "We had just barely got settled. Hope you like your steak medium rare. I forgot to get your cell phone number or I would have called and asked. Oh, and meet Prissy. She's been helping me to understand the computer business a little better. She works in Bonham, but she had a couple of hours this morning that she could come by."

"Pleased to meet you, Prissy. And the steak is fine any way you cook it. Medium rare is fine. Rare is fine. I like steak," Emily answered.

A woman with a name like Prissy brought images to Emily's mind of a petite little thing with big blue eyes and blond hair. But the woman who settled into a chair beside Dotty was six feet tall without the spike heels. She had brown hair and brown eyes, made even bigger and darker with lots of eyeliner and shadow. The pencil-straight red skirt barely touched her knees, and the black-and-red geometrically printed sweater dipped low in the front to reveal two inches of cleavage.

Maybe she was the one who'd started the sticky note war on the fridge. Back when Shine Canyon went computerized, Emily had given her grandfather a stack and told him to make notes about the computer and stick them to the wall above it. He had hated the notes because they reminded him of the computer, which he never did master.

Emily had the sudden desire to drag that tall woman out to the kitchen, point at the refrigerator, and ask her if she'd hauled in those notes in a wheelbarrow.

"How much did you get done? I could help finish this afternoon. Got a call from Albert and he said that he and Louis will be back tomorrow morning." Greg passed the bowl of foil-wrapped baked potatoes across the table to her. Their hands brushed in the transfer, and the heat had nothing to do with the warm bowl.

"There are two tack rooms. One doesn't look like it's been touched in years. I got the wheelbarrow, shovel, and hoe out of it, though, before I found the second one. Your horses are sweethearts. I jet-sprayed their stalls before I scattered fresh hay and fed them good. I thought about exercising a couple of them with my spare hour, but then I remembered that the truck smelled hot when you parked it, so I looked at the engine. It had a leak in the radiator. I found the little welder in the tack room. I reckon you've got a bigger one somewhere else on the ranch? Anyway, I fired it up and put a patch on the radiator and refilled it with water. Couldn't find any antifreeze, so you might want to check that since we could get another freeze before spring. Sometimes February can get downright temperamental and shove a late freeze in on us," she said between bites. "Dotty, this steak is wonderful, and the hot rolls are out of this world."

Greg's eyes were big as cow patties by the time she finished telling him what she'd done that morning. She wanted to giggle, but she bit it back.

"What? Was I not supposed to play with the welder?" she asked innocently.

"You are welcome to use whatever equipment you know how to operate," Clarice said.

"What's my job for the afternoon? Am I assistant or hired help?"

"We're still getting ready for the party tonight, so you can be hired help. We'll get into the computer business later in the week," Clarice said.

"Are there any more like you out there in Happy who might be looking for a job? You know how to drive a tractor?" Greg asked.

"I told you this morning, I can drive anything with wheels. And I don't know of anyone lookin' for a job," she said with a smile.

"You can have a choice. Rake hay or plow forty for a new alfalfa crop, or hell's bells, Emily, after the morning you put in, you might want to take a nap."

"I don't care which job I do, but I don't want to take a nap," Emily said. "It's all sitting in a tractor. Open cab? Do I need my stocking cap under the cowboy hat? Gramps always said that good hard work will cure most everything, so I reckon that's what I need more than anything these days."

"No, our tractors have good heaters and air conditioners for the hot summertime," Max said.

She looked across at him. His graying hair was cut short, and the grin that covered his face erased part of the wrinkles.

"That'll be like a vacation on an exotic island," she said. "Pass the rolls, please. I've worked up an appetite."

Clarice handed the basket of rolls to Greg, who sent them across the table to Emily. When his fingers brushed hers, she wasn't a bit surprised at the sparks dancing around the dining room.

"Thank you. One of your horses has thrown a shoe. I can fix that tomorrow after I muck out the stables if Albert is still sick." She *was* amazed that her voice was as calm as a summer cucumber and not high-pitched like a rat in a trap.

"Oh, no! Tomorrow you are driving me and Clarice

into town for our hair appointments, and then we go to Braum's for ice cream," Dotty said.

Emily nodded. "Well, since you said ice cream, I won't pout too much because I'm missing all the ranchin' fun."

"Ranchin' fun." Prissy sighed. "I never heard it called fun before."

"Gramps used to say that it's all in how you study it. It can be work or play, dependin' on how you approach it. So I take it that you don't like ranchin'?" Emily asked.

"Hate it. Hate cows. Hate the smells and hate living away from town," she answered.

Greg crawled up on the front of the broken-down tractor, opened the hood, and shook his head. Most men couldn't have done the work that Emily did that morning. She must've really cut back on her hired help and done everything herself as her grandfather needed more and more attention and money for his treatments.

Max climbed up beside Greg and handed him a wrench. "Hey, I just came from the stables. That woman is worth her weight in gold. You reckon if we drove out to the Panhandle we could find a dozen more like her? I swear she got more done than two men this morning."

"No wonder Nana likes her. She's a power horse in the office and on the ranch," Greg said.

"I'll be out at that north forty all afternoon. If you need me, holler." Max chuckled. "You might do well to pay more attention to her, cowboy. She's mighty easy on the eyes and has kissable lips to go with that work ethic."

"Hey, now, don't go getting wedding cake on your mind. She's only here for a month," Greg said.

"Clarice and Dotty are in there singing her praises."

Greg dropped the wrench and it rattled its way down to the concrete barn floor. "Dammit!"

"I don't know why you don't want to talk about her," Max said.

"Looks like I need another part for this job, and I'm not going back to town this afternoon. I'll get it tomorrow morning. I'll help you mend fence, but only if you don't talk about Emily all afternoon. I tell you, she's not interested in staying here. She's going back to Happy in a month and by then Nana will be over this trip down memory lane, and Max, I'm not going to fall for someone who lives all the way across the state just because she has kissable lips and a pretty smile," Greg said.

"I knew if I stuck around long enough I'd get you to agree to help," Max said. "I'll pick up the guys at the bunkhouse and meet you there."

Greg had barely gotten settled into his truck when his phone rang. He knew from the ringtone that it was Jeremiah.

He answered it on the second ring. "What's goin' on that you are callin' again? Not that I'm not glad to hear from you, but you never call this often."

"Wait just a minute. Don't hang up." Suddenly he was listening to a damn marching mariachi band blasting his eardrums out when he was switched over to hold.

He was about ready to hang up when Jeremiah came back. "Sorry, but that was a client and he owes me big bucks, so I had to talk to him. I did some more checkin' into Miz Emily Cooper."

"Why would you do that? You said she was clean as a whistle," Greg asked.

Jeremiah whistled through his teeth like he did when they were young. "I might come see Mama just so I can meet this superwoman. Does she wear a cape? Is she eight feet tall and bulletproof?"

"She barely comes to my shoulder. She's got jet-black hair and big, clear cobalt-blue eyes that don't match all that black hair."

"Is she bulletproof? Tell me more," Jeremiah asked.

"Hell, I don't know. I haven't shot her. Why would I? She's a hardworkin' woman. Nana likes her. You might even be losin' your place with Dotty to her, so you'd better come on home for a few days and stake out your territory before she lays claim to it. I heard that Dotty always wanted a daughter. Hell, maybe you can kiss your secretary good-bye and take up with Emily," Greg teased.

But somewhere down deep in his heart, a little jealousy reared up. Crap! He didn't have any right getting jealous over a girl he barely knew and who was only in Ravenna for four weeks anyway.

"Black hair and blue eyes? Does she look like Megan Fox?" Jeremiah asked.

"More like that woman who plays on the show that Nana and Dotty used to watch, *Hart of Dixie*," he said.

"Rachel Bilson? She doesn't have black hair and she's not blue-eyed," Jeremiah said.

"Well, give her blue eyes and dye her hair black and you've Emily. Where are you? I hear road traffic." Greg asked.

"I'm in Happy right now. Had to take a hop over to

Amarillo today on some other business, so I rented a car and drove over here to see if everything I'd learned was true. Don't be mad at me. It's the PI in me that doesn't take anything at face value. This place is not a whole lot bigger than Ravenna. Her grandpa's ranch was sold off to one of her cousins, as the old guy needed the money for cancer treatment, and it's only about a hundred acres these days, but her extended family owns more land than Lightning Ridge has."

"You sure that picture of her didn't arouse your inner love bug?" Greg asked.

"Hush, and listen. I talked to the high school principal and he said the Coopers had been here for more than sixty years. Her grandfather, Marvin, served on the school board a long time ago, and there's a picture of him in the hallway. Distinguished-looking old cowboy with bright blue eyes. I asked the lady at a local burger shop about Marvin and Emily, and according to her, Emily has wings and a halo. She said that when Marvin got cancer, Emily took up the reins and ran the ranch and took care of him too. Her cousin, Taylor Massey, helped some, but she did most of it."

It sounded like Jeremiah was slurping on a cup of coffee and then he went on, "Tell me she doesn't turn your head just a little bit and I'll tell you that you are crazy."

"What good would it do? She's only here for a month and then she'll be gone. It would be a poor business deal," Greg answered.

"Got to go. Client calling back," Jeremiah said.

Greg didn't even get in a good-bye before the line went dead. He didn't believe in love at first sight any more than he believed in Internet dating. Even though his good friend, Lucas Allen, over in Savoy, had wound up with a helluva nice woman last Christmas that he'd met over the Internet. But Lucas said it damn sure wasn't one of those crazy dating services where people can put up any old picture or say anything in their profiles. He'd met Natalie through a mutual friend that she talked to on Skype every night.

"I still don't believe in love at first sight," he declared as he crawled inside his work truck with a fixed radiator and drove out to the place where Max was repairing fences.

The tractor ran smoothly and the CD case in the cab was filled with country music. Emily wondered if they'd be playing Shoot the Moon or Chicken Foot in dominoes that evening. And how in the devil did they bet? Did they all lay out five bucks and the winner got the pot?

She whipped the wheel of the machine around and started back down the long side of the acreage when her phone rang. She picked it up from the seat and said, "Hello, Taylor."

"I hear an engine and country music. Are you on a tractor?"

"Yes, I am."

"What the hell are you doing that for? I thought they hired you to be a personal assistant," he said.

"Personal assistant wasn't needed at the house today so she's helping on the ranch. I mucked out stables this morning and I met a woman who has helped Clarice get used to computers. Her name is Prissy and I think she may be OCD and she's taught the whole bunch of these people to write every waking thought on sticky notes and plaster them to the refrigerator. There's something fishy going on with her and Dotty and Clarice. I can just feel it in my bones," Emily said.

"You did what? Are they crazy?" Taylor yelled into the phone. "Don't they have hired hands to do that kind of work?"

"I also cleaned up a tack room and fixed the radiator on an old truck," Emily said.

"Are you nuts?"

"Hard work never hurt or killed anyone," Emily answered.

"Em, darlin', if you want ranch work, I'll hire you tomorrow as ranch foreman. You don't have to take a job mucking out stables, for God's sake."

Emily shifted into a lower gear when she hit hard ground. "It's good for me to get my hands dirty. Call it therapy, and I think Gramps likes what I'm doing. I get the feeling that he is right beside me here and that he's tellin' me to stay."

"Marvin is gone, Emily. Face it, and what's this fishy thing going on?" Taylor growled.

Emily sucked air. "I have faced it. I faced it every day for five years, every morning when I went to see if he'd died in his sleep. I need this time away from Happy to get my bearings and get over his death. So don't preach at me, Taylor. And the fishy thing is just that. Prissy came to dinner and she and the ladies had these little coy looks going on. It's got something to do with Greg, I'm sure."

The click of a cigarette lighter said that he was lighting up. "Be careful, honey. I just don't want to see you get hurt."

"Anything exciting on the home front?" she asked.

"Valentine's dance over at the Franks' place next week. Melinda called and asked me to be her date," Taylor said.

Melinda came from good ranching stock. Her father, Gus Franks, owned the ranch right next to the Cooper place. Melinda got her dark hair and big brown eyes from her Latina mother. She'd be a good match for Taylor.

"Have fun," Emily said.

"You could easily be here in time to go too. Her brother doesn't have a date yet, and he's been sweet on you for years."

"No, thank you. Give Melinda a hug for me. Did I tell you we're all playing dominoes tonight?"

"You will let that sweet old lady win one hand, won't you?" Taylor asked.

"Maybe, but I won't let Greg win anything. It'll be fun to beat him. He says I have to have fifty dollars just to buy into the game, but the way Clarice scolded him, I reckon he was bullshittin' me. I may own his farm when the night is done."

"Why are you bein' mean to the cowboy? You said he was nice."

"He rattles me," Emily admitted.

"Well, shit!" Taylor swore.

"Don't worry about it."

"I'll worry even more than before. You haven't told me that a man rattled you in years, not since you were in college. That's enough to worry me. Use your business sense and not your heart. That gets you in trouble all the time. And do not put your acreage up for stakes," Taylor said.

"I wouldn't dream of it. Talk to you later." Emily laid the phone in her lap. She turned the tractor around when she reached the barbed wire fence. In a few weeks, the grass would be knee high and the cattle would be grazing in the very pasture where she plowed. It was a never-ending job, but come fall when they had the big cattle sale, they'd see the profit from all the hard work. The spring calves would be fat and would bring in maximum dollar.

"But I won't be here to see that. I probably won't even be here to see this pasture turn green. A few weeks and Clarice will get tired of talking about Marvin and I'll have outlived my usefulness. And by then I'll have the closure I want and I'll be back at Shine Canyon putting my ranch back together."

She put an old Conway Twitty CD in the player. Gramps loved Conway, especially when he sang with Loretta Lynn. He'd sit in his recliner and keep time to the music by tapping his thumb on the chair arm. She smiled at the sweet memory.

When he wasn't listening to music, he wanted to watch old John Wayne Western movies or reruns of anything that had to do with cowboys, modern day or the old guys, on television.

Those last few weeks he couldn't keep his eyes open to watch television, but he asked for music every day and the look on his face said that it took him back to another time in his life when he was a younger man. Emily wondered if his mind had been on Clarice Barton when he listened to the country songs.

Chapter 4

DOTTY PUT SIX NAMES IN A BOWL AND SHOOK IT around. "First two names are partners for the night. We're only going to run one table, so there'll be a player and an advisor. Y'all know the stakes, so we don't have to go over those. Now first name is Madge and I'm the second one. So we will be partners."

Dotty giggled. "Now who is next? I got the paper in my hand. It's Greg. Will he partner up with Rose or Clarice or maybe Emily?"

"Come on, Dotty," Greg said.

"Don't be impatient," she said. "Greg will be with…" She unfolded the paper and said, "Rose."

Emily looked at Clarice. "Guess we'll have to show them who is boss."

"In your dreams. Me and Rose can whip you all with an eye patch over one eye, can't we, Rose?" Greg grinned.

"And by candlelight." Rose nodded.

"Don't let Rose with her sweet angel face fool you," Clarice whispered to Emily. "She's mean as a hungry coyote when it comes to dominoes."

"Now you don't go telling Emily stories like that. I'm just an old lady who likes to play dominoes. It's not like I count cards." Rose had thin, wavy white hair, a round face, and a thick waist. She wore a red double-knit pantsuit that had been out of style for forty years, but somehow it looked great on her. Maybe she was an older woman who set the style rather than followed it, and by the end of summer, everyone would be trying to find vintage pantsuits.

"Y'all might as well watch from the sidelines. Me and Madge are the winners tonight," Dotty announced. "And if I win, I get…"

Clarice shot a look across the living room before Dotty could finish.

Dotty threw up both palms to ward off the dirty look. "Don't look at me like that. I wasn't going to say a fifth of Jack. Lord, if I even look at a bottle again, you'll make me go to those damned old meetings and I ain't got time to listen to folks stand up and tell me their problems. I was going to say that I was going to treat myself to one of them fancy massages when we go get our hair done this week," Dotty said, then leaned over and cupped her hand over Emily's ear. "Don't you tattle on me, but I catch a couple of meetings a month at the church. It's good for me to go to them and helps keep me sober, but I'll be hanged if they know it."

Emily pulled several bills from her shirt pocket. "Does my money go on the center of the table?"

Clarice frowned at Greg. "I told you to tell her on the way to the stables that we don't really play for money."

Emily popped him on the shoulder and stuffed the bills back in her pocket.

He grabbed his bicep and moaned. "Nana, I can't play. She's done broke my arm."

"Bullshit," Dotty said. "And if it is broke, suck it up and play with the other hand."

"Why'd you tell her that we play for money?" Madge asked.

"It was a test to see if she really thought she was any good. I didn't want a partner who couldn't hold her own. I figured if she was willing to bring money to the game, then she might not be all hat and no cowgirl."

Emily held her hands in her lap to keep from blowing on the one that had touched his arm. Dammit! How did just a simple two-second slap create so much heat? "What made you think I'd be your partner?"

"I knew they'd draw because they only set up one table tonight and you never know what the draw might do," he answered.

"You kids stop fighting. We're here to play, so hush and let's get serious about this so we can eat," Rose said and then leaned over to whisper in Madge's ear like little girls on the playground.

Emily heard something about new girl on western, but that was all she caught.

"We play for fun, but the loser has to host the next domino night. Last week Clarice lost, so she's hosting tonight. I love it when she loses because Dotty cooks when she does," Madge explained.

Madge was built on a square frame—almost as wide as she was tall. Her round face sported a weak chin, a wide forehead, and narrow-set green eyes that sparkled when she talked. She wore an orange Western-cut shirt out over her stretch jeans. Her bright orange wedge heels had enough bling on the toes to blind a person.

"You play and I'll advise, okay?" Rose asked Greg.

"You're better than I am," he said.

"That's why I'm going to advise you. Besides, I lose track of the score when I gossip, and I've got stories to tell," Rose said.

All three of the other women shot her a look and she giggled. "Some stories you tell and some you keep close for another day."

Clarice turned to Emily. "You play and I'll sit back and boss. Now what do you know, Rose, that can be shared in present company? Come on, tell us, what is it?"

Madge sat down in the chair nearest the table and started to shuffle. "You can be the silent partner tonight, Dotty." Then she leaned over, cupped her hand over Dotty's ear, and whispered something about farmers and a looker.

Dotty poured the dominoes out of a velvet drawstring bag and turned them over. "I ain't never been silent about anything. Oprah called it multitasking when she was on the television."

"Wow!" Emily said.

She'd never seen gold-plated dominoes with colored stones instead of dots.

Clarice leaned over and whispered, "It's fake gold and the stones are colored glass. They aren't real diamonds and emeralds."

"They're still sparkly," Emily said.

"Greg bought them for her for her eightieth birthday. The dominoes we play with at my house are the plain old black-and-white kind." Madge giggled.

"I thought Prissy was coming tonight. I had a computer question to ask her," Rose asked.

"Maybe I could help. I know my way around computers pretty good," Emily said.

"Thanks, darlin', but this is a personal problem and Prissy already knows all about it. I'll just call her and tell her I'm making lasagna for dinner and she'll be right over," Rose said.

"Are we here to play dominoes or gossip?" Greg asked.

"Both," Dotty and Clarice said at the same time.

Greg laid out a double six. Twelve sparkling red stones all total. Right away Rose put a six-four at the end of that and the game was on. In half an hour the table looked like a giant chicken foot. Dotty and Madge won that round. Then they went to the more complicated Shoot the Moon, and Dotty and Madge won round one of that one and Rose and Greg won the second round.

Clarice patted Emily on the wrist. "Looks like me and you are going to host and cook next week. I heard that Prissy has got a secret boyfriend. Everyone at church is just dying to know who he is, but she hasn't even told her best friends. I bet it's one of those cowboys that her granddad hired. Has she told you anything, Greg?"

Greg shrugged. "If she did, I wouldn't tell y'all since it would be in confidence."

Dotty drew her eyebrows down. "I'll ask Jeremiah. I bet he knows what's going on. He and Prissy are still real good friends. He tried to hire her to work in his business, but she turned him down. That does it for this evening. Emily is going to cook next week. Let's take this party to the dining room."

Emily glanced at Dotty, who threw up her palms and exclaimed, "Don't look at me. It's up to you to do the cooking, but you'd better not leave my kitchen or my oven in a mess. I won so I'm treating myself to that massage, and no cooking on domino day."

"We should have those little pecan pie tarts, Nana," Greg suggested.

"I'm horrible at pie crust. How about you?" Clarice asked.

Emily smiled sweetly. "It'll be a surprise. And next week, I won't *let* Greg win."

"You didn't let me win tonight," he said.

"Of course I did. You look like you'd be the type to pout if you lose, and I didn't want to put up with you whining around like a little girl all week," she teased.

Greg pushed the dominoes toward her with a grin on his face and a twinkle in his sexy green eyes. "Loser also has to put the dominoes away. I won this fair and square, so put them away, woman."

"Sure you *won*, darlin'." She patted him on the arm and winked at the ladies.

She quickly busied herself putting the dominoes away. Maybe no one else saw the goose bumps on her arms and the chills chasing down her back when she touched his arm. Rattling her was a huge understatement. That cowboy just flat turned her temperature up to the boiling point.

"Next week you will *lose* and you will cook just for teasing me about the money." Maybe words would make the ache in her body disappear. Fate wasn't being nice when she made Greg so damn sexy and then put Emily's ranch eight hours away from his land.

"You think I can't cook?" Greg asked.

"Can you?" She smiled sweetly.

Rose stood up. "There you two go again, fussing and fighting. Or do they call it flirting?" It was her turn to act like a second grade little girl and whisper in Clarice's ear.

"Y'all know that secrets are rude," Greg said.

"Now what would us old women have secrets about?" Rose giggled.

"I'm hungry," Greg said.

"Me too, and we aren't flirting," Emily said.

Finger foods were laid out beautifully on crystal platters. Slider sandwiches stuffed with ham and cheese, a vegetable tray with a scrumptious-looking dip, a fruit tray with strawberry cream cheese dip, and a cheese ball covered in pecans with an assortment of crackers surrounding it. A three-section warmer held tiny egg rolls, buffalo wings, and smoky sausages in barbecue sauce. Several kinds of homemade cookies, including oatmeal raisin, which was Emily's favorite, were stacked on pretty plates at the other end of the table.

How in the devil was she supposed to top a spread like that the next week? Maybe she should just write Clarice a note on Sunday and sneak out before daybreak on Monday. She made it to the dining room in time to hear Rose talking softly to Clarice.

"I write down what she says, but I swear I can't remember what those letters all stand for. FYI, OMG, WTF... I lost my notebook. I know one of them has a dirty word in it, but I can't remember what they are. If she don't come over tomorrow I won't be able to get on the laptop."

Rose blushed when she noticed that Emily was in the room. What in the devil were these old girls into? Had they discovered Internet dating for seniors?

—⁓—

"What a day! Gramps, I wish you were here so I could tell you all about it," Emily whispered at her reflection in the bathroom mirror.

It had gone by in a fast blur, and yet it had been the most exciting day she'd spent in years. As she brushed her teeth, she recaptured the highlights and most of them had to do with the expressions on Greg's face throughout the day.

It was only ten thirty when she crawled between the soft sheets and shut her eyes, but sleep would not come. Nothing helped! Not beating on the pillow. Not flipping from one side to the other. Not sitting up and staring into the semidarkness or imagining baby calves hopping over a low fence.

"I need warm milk. Either that or a double shot of Gramps's moonshine, and since the only jar left is on Shine Canyon, I guess it's milk." She slid out of bed, peeked out the bedroom door, and slipped out into the dark landing.

Tiptoeing down the stairs and across the foyer, she used the moonlight coming in through the windows to make her way to the kitchen. She carefully poured milk into a coffee mug, set the microwave for twenty seconds, and waited until the ding.

"Shhhh," she hissed at the microwave. She didn't want to wake up everyone in the house just because she was too worked up to get to sleep. She took a sip and decided that it needed chocolate. She held the refrigerator door open with her foot and squeezed a stream of chocolate syrup into the glass. She stirred with her finger, let the door go shut, and took a sip.

"Couldn't sleep either?" Greg asked from the shadows.

She had to swallow fast to keep from spewing chocolate milk all over the kitchen floor and cabinets. In the semidarkness, she could see that he wore light gray sweat bottoms hanging low on his hips, no shirt, and no glasses. He was so sexy that it plumb took her breath away.

The second hard swallow had nothing to do with milk and everything to do with a half-naked man right in front of her.

"Must've been all that late-night food," she muttered. "I even tried counting baby calves jumping over a rail fence."

With a flick of the wrist, he flipped the light switch. "That looks pretty good. Think I'll join you. I count calves in a pen rather than watching them jump over a fence. If I did that, I'd start worrying about catching them all."

She immediately tugged at her shirttail, but the flannel didn't stretch or cover any more of her legs. "I'll just go on back to my room."

"Stay and talk to me," he said.

The clock in the living room chimed twelve times and she smiled. "I'm not dressed to stay and talk to you."

"I got the pants. You got the shirt. Between us, we're dressed." He poured a glass of milk and added two long shots of chocolate. "Let's go to the living room where the chairs are more comfortable."

"Aha," she said when realization hit.

Fate was throwing another test at her, daring her to be alone with him.

He turned the kitchen light off. "Aha, what?"

"Nothing."

Be damned if she'd tell him that she'd figured out what fate was up to. She was being tested to see if she really did have roots on her ranch in Shine Canyon. This is what her grandfather was talking about all the time. Emily Cooper was as wily as fate, and not one thing could be thrown at her that she couldn't handle. Well, okay, maybe not dominoes, but if Greg hadn't smelled like heaven sitting right beside her all evening, and if he hadn't kept brushing her fingertips, she might have had a better chance at winning the game.

She led the way across the foyer and into the living room. Greg followed her and turned on a lamp at the end of the sofa. She set her half-empty glass on a coaster and curled up in the corner of the sofa.

———

Greg had laid his book and glasses aside when he'd heard her bedroom door open and soft footsteps padding down the staircase. He followed her to the kitchen and watched from the shadows as she heated milk. Her black hair had been set loose from the ponytail and floated in gentle waves down past her shoulders. The shirttail hem on the flannel shirt she wore curved up on the side to show fine, shapely legs.

He took a long gulp of his milk then put it on the coffee table in front of him. It did little to ease the dryness in his mouth or to still his racing pulse.

"So evidently you are not married now because you've agreed to stay on and work for Nana for a month. Have you ever been married?"

"Have you?"

"I asked first," he answered.

"It doesn't matter who asked first. I think it's only reasonable that you answer my questions too. What's good for the goose is good for the gander. You either answer mine or I don't answer yours," she said.

"Nana says that about the goose and gander all the time."

"So did Gramps. He said just because I was a girl didn't mean I didn't have to learn the ranchin' business from the ground up."

"Okay, fair enough. No, I have not been married."

"Neither have I. Why?"

"That's two questions," he said.

"You asked two, so I get two."

She turned her head slowly and her blue eyes locked with his. He wanted to kiss her, to reach out and trace her jawline with his finger; he wanted to kiss her passionately. Even if she slapped the shit out of him, he had to kiss her.

———

His eyes looked different without the glasses, softer and dreamier. Thick brown lashes rested on his cheekbones when he blinked. She reached up and touched the slight cleft in his chin.

"Are you involved with anyone?" she whispered.

He ran his left hand from her shoulder down to her hand, where he laced his fingers in hers. "Are you involved with someone?"

She barely shook her head, afraid that he'd take it as a sign to move his hand.

She wanted him to kiss her.

"I should go back up to my room," she whispered.

He nodded and tilted her chin up with his right fist. "Me too."

Neither of them made a motion to stand.

"But I don't want to." He grinned.

Oh, hell, she thought as she unlaced her hand and scooted six inches closer to him. She leaned in, wrapped her arms around his neck, and brushed a kiss across his lips.

He pulled her tightly against his bare chest, only the thin cotton of her nightshirt separating skin from skin. He deepened the second kiss until it felt like white-hot fire, silk sheets, and chocolate all mixed together. It held promises of something so wild and wonderful that it made her whole body quiver.

It ended, but it wasn't over. He brushed the hair away from her neck and moved downward to that erotic zone right below the ear and strung scorching hot kisses from there to the hollow of her neck and back to her lips.

He wrapped his arms around her waist, and she shifted positions until she was sitting in his lap. Her hand toyed with his hair at the nape of his neck, and the other pressed against his bulging chest muscle.

His hand slipped beneath her shirt and massaged her back on his way to her shoulders, then gently eased around to cup her breast. She was going to explode any minute right there on the sofa. Tomorrow morning Clarice would find the remnants of a flannel shirt and a few buttons. The rest of Emily would be scattered around the room in fine ashes.

His thumb grazed her jawbone, and his forefinger tilted her chin up for a better position, each kiss getting deeper and deeper, his tongue doing a mating dance with hers and heat building into a raging fire. He left her lips long enough to kiss both eyelids and move his hand from her breast to the top of her bikini underpants.

She arched against him, ready for his touch, wanting it. His fingertips slipped beneath the elastic. She pressed closer to him and opened up for easier access. God, she'd never been so damn hot in her whole life.

And then the microwave dinged.

She jumped like she'd been shot, and with the speed of lightning, both of his hands were gone.

"Shit!" he mumbled.

Dotty's voice floated from kitchen to den. "You couldn't sleep either? Did you check out your laptop?"

Emily and Greg scooted to opposite ends of the sofa.

"Too much excitement. We're gettin' old when a domino game keeps us up. I got out my notebook and copied it all off in a new one so I can give it to Rose. She can't do her business without the alphabet chart," Clarice said.

Greg whispered, "They're in the kitchen. I'll go keep them busy until you get back to your room."

Emily looked down at the telltale bulge in his pants and shook her head. "It would be kind of tough to cover that up. I'll wait right here for them."

"Thank you," he whispered.

She heard his bedroom door shut barely seconds before Dotty and Clarice joined her in the living room. She wanted so badly to ask them what they were doing with notebooks full of Internet lingo, but that would be prying into stuff that was none of her business. Still she would just love to see the pictures of the old men that they were flirting with online.

Were any of them as handsome as her grandfather had been?

"I figured Greg would be in here when I saw the light. Sometimes he has trouble getting to sleep," Clarice said.

"I couldn't sleep so I heated up some milk and put some chocolate in it." She pointed to the table. "That is probably his glass right there. Guess he left it when he went back to bed."

"He likes chocolate milk when he has trouble sleeping. I used to drink a little shot of Jack Daniel's before Clarice put me on the wagon. Now I have a cup of jasmine tea," Dotty said.

"That good for insomnia?" Emily asked.

Clarice sat down on the sofa beside Emily. "No, but Dotty thinks it is. Greg should have at least put his glass in the dishwasher."

"Guess none of us could sleep. I checked my emails and my Facebook site. Are y'all on Facebook? I'd love to have you as friends if you are," Emily said.

"Gracious, no! We wouldn't have the faintest idea about all that shit," Dotty said.

"We come from the age of writing letters and notes, darlin'," Clarice said. "Guess you noticed all the sticky notes in the kitchen. We get a big kick out of those. Prissy brought some when we first had trouble with the computer and she stuck them around the monitor. They kind of remind us of our younger days back before all this computer rage, so we started using them a lot."

"Well, I'll see you in the morning, then." She stood up and headed for the kitchen. It wasn't until she started up the stairs that she could breathe right again. She and Greg had damn sure lucked out that night. In five more minutes they would have been having sex right there on the sofa or on the living room floor. They'd have been so wound up in each other's naked arms that they wouldn't have even heard that microwave dinging. Thank God for microwaves! Greg would have thought she was one loose-legged hussy if she'd fallen into sex with him after only twenty-four hours.

Greg stepped out of his bedroom door and wrapped his arms around her, kissed her on the forehead, and whispered, "Your room or mine?"

Shaking her head was the hardest thing she'd ever done. "Neither. We were both saved by the microwave. When fate steps in and stops something, there is a reason."

"Damn microwave," he grumbled.

"Good night, Greg." She tiptoed and kissed him on the cheek.

She shut her bedroom door and flopped backward on the bed. She beat the pillow into submission, but something still wasn't right. Finally, she figured out that it was his picture, so she turned it around and crawled between the sheets. But sleep was still a long time coming that night.

Chapter 5

LIGHTNING ZIPPED THROUGH THE SKY IN LONG streaks, and thunder rattled behind every streak. Clarice rode in the front seat and Dotty sat right behind Emily, umbrellas right beside their oversized purses.

"Never know what it will do in February. It can put down a late snowstorm, hustle up a damn tornado, or turn off warm enough to work in shirt sleeves," Dotty said. "If it starts to rain cats and dogs and baby elephants, I promise I'll share my umbrella with you."

"Thank you, Dotty." Emily smiled into the rearview mirror.

"We're going after Rose. Thank God she don't drive anymore. Last time she got in her truck, she backed right out into the side of a police car. Totaled that car and ripped the tailgate off her damn truck," Dotty said.

"It was her fifth accident, so the insurance company canceled and no one else would insure her," Clarice said. "It was time she quit driving years ago, but she didn't have a grandson to take her truck keys away from her like Greg took mine or like Dotty's boy, Jeremiah, got hers."

Emily followed directions into Ravenna and pulled into the driveway of a little white frame place with a couple of cats lazing on the steps.

"Toot the horn. Rose primps until the last minute. She's got a crush on that old guy at Dairy Queen," Dotty said.

Emily hit the horn and Rose came right out. Emily hopped out like a professional chauffeur and opened the van door for Rose, helped her inside, and buckled her seat belt.

"Now this is real service," Rose beamed.

"See, I told you. Rose gets all fancied up to go to the beauty shop," Dotty said.

"I don't take out the garbage without putting on my makeup. Lord, I'd scare the poor old trash man plumb to death," Rose said as she took out her compact mirror and checked her lipstick one more time. "I've decided I'm having a massage today too, Dotty. I weeded all my flower beds and got them ready to plant in a few weeks before we played dominoes last night, and I'm aching all over."

"Woman, you got enough money to hire someone to do that for you. You are eighty years old, not twenty. Hire some help. There's plenty of folks lookin' for a job around here," Clarice said.

"I know how old I am, Clarice Adams, and I also know if you don't use it, it'll dry up and die, and my arms already look like bat wings, so I'm not going to just sit down and let them go to complete fat," Rose said.

"Well, shit! I ain't used my female equipment since my husband died. You think it's dried up?" Dotty asked.

Rose slapped the air around Dotty's shoulder. "Don't talk like that around Emily. You'll embarrass her. I would have been on the porch waiting, but I got a phone call from Letha who wanted to talk about Prissy… oh, turn right at the T, Emily."

Emily turned and looked over at Clarice. "Now make the next left and go a quarter mile. You'll see the arch over the gate. That's where you turn right again, and Madge will be on the porch. She still drives, but we like to take her with us on Wednesdays so we can all be together."

"We all became friends back when we were young women," Rose said.

Emily looked at Dotty in the rearview.

"Friends, hell. They are slave drivers and bossy as hell. My Johnny died five years ago and I had a lot of good old Kentucky bourbon therapy until this bunch of women interfered."

"We had an intervention," Rose said seriously.

Clarice pointed at the arch. "Yes, we did. I took charge and made her work for me, threatened to make her go to those meetings down at the Presbyterian church if she ever picked up the bottle again, and she's doing fine. Madge is waiting on the porch."

Emily hopped out of the van again and settled Madge into the third spot, beside Rose. They were cramped, but it wasn't too bad, and Madge swore she was not wiggling into the backseat, because she might miss something they said.

"Now what were y'all talking about?" Madge asked. "I was looking on the farmer's only dot…" She stopped dead and looked at Clarice.

"You mean that farmer's game thing on the Internet?" Rose asked too quickly.

Emily's ears perked right up. Those old girls were covering up something and she'd be willing to bet half her hundred acres that the next word after "dot" would have been "com."

"Oh, so you're on Facebook and you like to play the farm game?" Emily asked innocently.

"Not me," Madge said. "My grandson brought a game for me to plug into my laptop that has to do with farmin', and I was playin' with it and…" she floundered.

Clarice butted into the conversation. "We were telling Emily about our Dotty intervention."

Dotty slapped Clarice's hand. "Intervention, my ass. You should've seen them come marching into my house like judge, jury, and Jesus all in one. They poured out my Jack, yelled at me, packed my clothes, and called Jeremiah to come sell my trailer."

"Jeremiah sold your trailer?" Emily asked. She'd rather hear more about Prissy and dot com, but the conversation whipped around like the wind in a tornado.

"Yes, that rascal did," Dotty said.

"You did good with him, and he amounts to something because you raised him right. And he knew exactly what he was doing when he sold that trailer. When's he coming to Ravenna again? Y'all best call me when he does. I didn't get to see him last time," Madge said.

"He'll be here for the church bazaar. He promised, and he never breaks a promise. I got a feelin' he's got a girlfriend. He ain't just said it, but there's something in his voice that says he's happy," Dotty answered. "That rotten Greg hears from him more than I do. And I was doing just fine with my bourbon until y'all showed up with that damned interferin' shit you did."

"I'm not buying that bullshit, Dotty. You were drinkin' yourself into an early grave," Rose said.

"I would've got to that grave faster if old man Beamus hadn't died and quit making moonshine. Now that stuff was some powerful shit, and I liked it better than whiskey," Dotty said.

"Moonshine?" Emily asked.

"Walter Beamus made moonshine back in the woods," Clarice said. "Oh, Rose, I made you a new little book." She passed it over the backseat.

Emily's ears perked right up. "Prissy helping all of you girls?"

"On occasion. We hired her to help us navigate our way around our computers after we figured out that she and Greg wasn't going to... how do you kids say it? Hook up?" Madge said.

"Oh, so they dated?" Emily asked.

"Hell, no!" Dotty said. "She hates ranch livin' and he loves it."

"Emily, if you fell in love with a rancher, would you demand that he leave it and move into town and work in an office?" Dotty asked.

"You don't change what a person is. If they're a rancher at heart, they'd be miserable in town," she said.

Clarice hit the armrest hard enough that the whole van went quiet. "See there, I told y'all. If a girl is from the big city, then we shouldn't be." She stopped dead and the van went quiet.

"Were any of y'all big city girls?" Emily asked.

"Not me," Dotty said. "I come from a place down in a holler that made Ravenna look like a big city. We didn't even have indoor plumbing. I thought I'd hit the big-time when I married Johnny."

"Not me, either. I grew up in southern Oklahoma in a little area known as Russett. It's not even there anymore," Madge said. "At least it was close enough that I could go visit my folks a few times a year."

"And you, Rose?" Emily asked.

"Well, Madge and I are cousins. Our mothers were sisters. Huttig, Arkansas, isn't any bigger than Ravenna, but it was home. My folks are all gone now, so I haven't been back there in years."

"What did your mamas think when you said you were marryin' a man you'd never met?" Emily asked.

Dotty giggled. "Honey, there was thirteen of us. My mama was just glad I was leavin'."

Rose clucked her tongue like an old hen. "My mama wasn't too happy about me coming all that distance to visit my cousin, but she took me to the bus and gave me all kinds of advice on the way. She was so mad when I married a man from these parts that she wouldn't even write me a letter for a whole month. I had to take him home to meet her before I was forgiven. And then be hanged if she didn't like him better than me."

"And you, Madge?" Emily asked.

"Mama knew, but she didn't like it. Girls did things like that more in them days than they do now."

Madge whispered over the seat toward Emily, "I think Clarice has always been jealous because she didn't get to be a mail-order bride."

"I am not! Lester was a good man and we had a wonderful life," Clarice protested.

Dotty patted her on the shoulder. "Was Marvin a bad boy in his youth?"

"Not that I know of. What about your husbands?" Emily asked.

"Johnny was a bad boy. Hot-tempered. Drank too much. But oh, honey, he could flat-out set the sheets on fire," Dotty said.

"Turn right at the light and then left at the next

corner," Clarice told Emily. "There it is. The hot pink building beside that house. Shelly turned her garage into a beauty shop when her old business burned down. It used to be on Main Street. Park right out front. Thank goodness it's not raining yet. And Dotty, don't be sayin' things like that in front of Emily."

Shelly's Hair Designs was painted in purple lettering on the window sporting a zebra print valance. It hardly looked big enough to offer everything that they wanted done.

"She added on the massage and spa at the back," Clarice said. "And she's got three beauticians and two massage ladies. It's the biggest place in Bonham."

"And the most expensive," Rose said.

"Shit, woman! Quit your bitchin'. Abe squeals every time you pinch those pennies," Dotty said.

"You want to come in and get all beautified with us, Emily?" Clarice asked.

Emily shook her head. "I'll wait right here. I've got a book in my purse."

"Nonsense! Drive around and get acquainted with the town. I've got your cell phone number. When we are done, I'll call you and we'll go for ice cream," Clarice said.

The ladies disappeared into the purple magic and miracles salon. Emily waited until they were all inside before she backed the van out and drove on into Bonham. She located the library east of the town square, which she drove around three times, taking in all the stores surrounding the courthouse. If it had been a pretty sunny day, she would have copped a seat under a shade tree and read her romance novel while she waited, but the way those black clouds were rolling around, she'd probably just get settled and it would start to pour. She made a few turns and wound up in a lot beside the town's kiddy park.

She turned off the engine and reached inside her purse for the book she'd been reading and grabbed her grandfather's funeral memorial instead. The picture on the front had been taken the year she came home from college, back when he was still healthy. She wanted everyone to remember him that way, not as the withered-up guy that cancer had robbed of life and strength.

She touched his cheek in the picture and imagined him looking right at her. Tears stung her eyes, but she held them at bay until she opened the brochure. *Born January 28, 1932 ~ Passed From This Life...* she shut her eyes so she didn't have to see the date. Hot salty tears broke through the dam and flooded down her cheeks, dripping onto her denim jacket. One landed on her grandfather's nose and that brought on heart-racking sobs that echoed off the van walls. She gently laid the folder in the passenger's seat and curled up in a tight ball around the steering wheel, weeping so hard that her chest ached.

Greg startled her when he opened the door to the van, gathered her up in his arms like a bride, and carried her to a nearby picnic table. He sat down on the table, put his feet on the attached bench, and held her without saying a word. She buried her face against his chest, wrapped her arms tightly around his neck, and wept.

Lightning lit up the sky again and again, and thunder cracked through the air louder than shotgun blasts. Dark clouds held the pregnant promise of rain, a rancher's dream at the first of February. None of it mattered. The memorial said Marvin Cooper was dead, and they never lied.

The wind whipped around to the north, and the temperature dropped ten degrees and then rain came down in a torrent. Greg stood up with her still in his arms and ran to the van where he opened the front door and pushed a button to make the side door slide open. He crawled inside the wide backseat with Emily still cuddled against him.

He hit the button again to close the door against the rain falling in sheets so thick that nothing outside was visible. The skies went as dark as midnight, and the wind rocked the van back and forth. She sighed and dug her fists into her eyes like a child.

"All done?" he asked.

She shook her head and sunk back into his hard chest again. Gramps had been her anchor during storms, both naturally and those that life brought on, and he was gone. He'd never be there to guide her through the bad times that life threw at her, or laugh at her when she covered her ears during a lightning storm.

The next clap of thunder was so intense that she let go of Greg's jacket and tried to curl up into an even tighter ball. Now she had to face everything, every day alone. She had to make decisions that would affect her entire life… all alone.

"First time you've let it loose since he died, isn't it?" Greg asked.

She hiccupped. "He's gone, Greg. He's never coming back."

"It took me about a week when my grandpa died. Dad

said I should be strong because Nana needed me, so I was. And then one day I was in the horse stable and his old work gloves were right there on the tack room table where he'd left them. Still can't bring myself to go back into the tack room."

"How long ago was that?" she asked.

"Five years. I shut the door and used another room for a tack room. Louis, the guy who takes care of the stable most of the time, didn't have any desire to go back into the old one either, so it's been abandoned."

"How did he die?" she asked.

"Heart attack. He took off his gloves and dropped seconds later. If it makes you feel any better, I cried longer and harder than you did," he said.

She looked up at him. "I'm sorry."

"Me too. For both of us. They left big boots for us to fill."

‹⸺›

Her small hand felt fragile in his, as if it would break like her heart if he squeezed too hard. He swallowed the lump in his throat and changed the subject. "So did the old girls bitch and argue the whole way into town?"

He could feel the tension leaving her body slowly.

"They told me about Jeremiah. They have secrets like little school girls, and they whisper a lot."

"Jeremiah and I are really good friends. We were together a lot in the summertime when I came to the ranch. Dotty worked for Nana some back then because when school was out she didn't have a job and Jeremiah always came with her. When he got old enough, Grandpa put us both on the summer payroll.

And they always whisper and tell secrets. It's just the way they are."

As if on cue, the rain stopped, the clouds moved on to the south, and the sun lit up the inside of the van.

"Looks like the rain is over," he said.

Using the back of his hand, he brushed the last of the tears from her cheeks. "And they told me about why Dotty lives at the ranch."

"That's a good thing for her and for Nana. She needed someone to need her, and Nana needed someone to boss and keep her company. Want to go to McDonald's and get a cup of coffee?" he asked.

"I'd love one," she whispered.

"I'll drive. When the ladies call we can swing back by here and I'll get my truck." He nodded to his truck parked right beside the van.

"How'd you know I was here?"

"I didn't. I drive past here on the way to the tractor supply and saw the van. Thought you might have had some trouble, so I stopped to check."

He hit the button and the side door slid open. He swung his feet around, set his boots on the ground, and carried her around the van to the passenger's side where he settled her into the seat. Then he trotted around the back of the van and crawled into the driver's seat.

"Does it take long before the numbness goes away?" she asked.

"A while, and it's not in an instant. One day you'll just wake up and it will be filled with memories that are good rather than sadness," he answered.

"Thank you, Greg."

"You are welcome, Emily."

"The ladies told me about the intervention to stop Dotty from drinking and all about how they were kind of like mail-order brides, except Clarice," she said.

"I guess that was kind of like the forerunner of all this eHarmony.com and all that stuff today. Women wrote. Men proposed and they got married. Nowadays it's text, call, and then get married."

He parked as close to the McDonald's entrance as possible and hustled around the van to open the door for Emily. He ushered her to the counter with his hand on the small of her back.

It didn't feel right to be so sexually attracted to a man when she was grieving, but there wasn't a thing she could do about it. Her skin was tingly, her face flushed, and her breath shallow. It was a pure wonder that another lightning bolt didn't strike her dead right there under the dollar menu at the McDonald's checkout counter.

"Two coffees, one black," he told the lady taking orders and then looked down at Emily with a question in his eyes.

"Just black for me too," Emily answered.

"Did they tell you why she drank?" He carried two full cups toward the nearest booth.

Emily nodded. "Because her husband died."

He waited for her to slide into one side before he slipped into the opposite one. Their knees touched under the table, but he didn't move and neither did she.

"They'd been married more than fifty years. They never had any kids of their own. Probably a good thing since she had to work to support them both, and she did a good job of it. Worked in the kitchen at the school until she retired and for Nana in the summertime. Then Jeremiah grew up and moved away and her husband died. She hit the bottle pretty hard until Nana, Rose, and Madge took charge. Nana brought her to the ranch and put her to work full-time, and Jeremiah came home from Conroe and sold the trailer. He didn't want his momma to ever go back to that place because he was afraid she'd drink herself into the grave. He says that Nana saved Dotty's life when she gave her a purpose in life. He thinks that as long as Dotty had to provide for her husband and him that she was alright. It was when she wasn't needed that things fell apart."

"Sounds like he's a smart man."

Greg nodded. "Real smart."

<hr/>

She looked across the table and reached out her hand. "Give me your glasses. There are rain smudges on them."

He handed them across the table and she blew warm breath on each lens before wiping it clean with a McDonald's paper napkin. "There, that's better."

"Thanks. I wish I could wear contacts, but my eyes are shaped funny. I could have that surgery, but I'm a big chicken when it comes to needles, so I'll just wear my glasses." He put them back on and took a sip of coffee. "Besides, there are some things I'd just as soon not see real plain and I can always take them off."

"Too bad we don't have life glasses that we can take off and put on at will. When we had them on they'd show us what we needed to do with our lives and help us make hard decisions," she said.

He raised his coffee in a toast and nodded. "Amen!

You invent them and I'll pay for the patent. We'll make a fortune."

She touched her cup with his and they both sipped at the same time.

Yesterday they'd had a make-out session like a couple of high school kids. And today she'd mourned her grandfather all curled up in his arms during a vicious thunderstorm. If she believed in reincarnation, she'd swear that they were both old souls who had known each other in a past life.

Right then she would give half her ranch for a pair of those glasses that she'd mentioned. She'd put them on and maybe she could get a clear vision of why her grandfather insisted she take some time away from Happy, and why she felt like he was really glad that she was where she was that day.

"Earth to Emily." Greg grinned. "Your phone is ringing."

She grabbed it out of her purse and answered without looking at the ID. "Yes, ma'am. I'll be right there." She touched the screen and tossed it back in her purse.

"They must be all dolled up for the weekend and ready to go home," Greg said.

"Looks like it," she said.

"Don't expect miracles. They'll look the same, but they'll have a new spring in their step because they feel all better when they've been to see Shelly," he said. "At least it's quit raining, so it won't mess up their hairdos for Sunday. Did Nana tell you that if you live under her roof that you will go to church on Sunday morning?"

She slid out of the booth and he followed her to the door.

"She didn't, but I'm not surprised. That's exactly

what Gramps preached all the time. When I first went to college I didn't go home for two weekends just so I wouldn't have to go to church, but then I missed him and the folks at church so much that I went home the next week."

Greg chuckled.

She smiled. "You too?"

"Oh, yeah! But don't tell Nana. She thinks I just came home to raid the refrigerator and get my laundry done for free."

He drove to the park and walked with her to the van. At the door she turned around and wrapped her arms around his neck. She rolled up on her toes and kissed him hard. He tasted like coffee, smelled like a mixture of shaving lotion and rain, and the kiss came near to frying a hole in the ground.

"Thank you for helping me get through the tears," she mumbled when she pulled away.

"Yes, ma'am," he said hoarsely.

Chapter 6

ROSE WAS NOT A HOARDER. EVERYTHING IN HER HOUSE was well dusted and arranged, which made her a serious collector. A small table flanked every one of the seven rocking chairs in her living room. Each one had a fancy lamp sitting on a snow-white crocheted doily and surrounded by a matching arrangement of ceramic or china ducks, pigs, chickens, fancy miniature shoes, or snowmen. And that was just at first glance. After she'd taken a seat on the sofa, Emily noticed even more collections on shelves, two corner cabinets, and there was even a group of ceramic cats on a pretty knitted blanket under the coffee table.

The coffee table sported a long white table runner and was covered with crystal plates of finger foods: cheese and summer sausage on long toothpicks with cute little green paper fans on the ends, cookies, and crackers spread with a cream cheese mixture and topped with an olive or a tiny pickle.

A pitcher of lemonade and one of sweet tea and eight glasses waited on top of one of those antique pushcarts with three shelves. A pretty crystal ice bucket took up the middle shelf with extra paper plates and napkins on the bottom one.

Seven ladies each claimed a rocking chair, set a colorful tote bag at their feet, and pulled out their craft for the day. Emily folded her hands in her lap and watched

Clarice and Dotty's crochet hooks working in a blur as the ball of white cotton thread bounced around in their bags.

Rose was knitting just as fast as Dotty and Clarice crocheted, but evidently it did not affect her ability to talk. "Clarice, have you explained this to Emily?"

"We have our bazaar the last Saturday in February every year. We make crafts all year, meeting here at Rose's on Saturday afternoons when we can. It's not set in stone and sometimes all of us can't be here, but we try, and 'I don't want to' is not an acceptable excuse. We use the money we make to put into our fund for the ladies' auxiliary to give a scholarship to one senior girl from Ravenna. Sometimes we can give a five-hundred-dollar scholarship; sometimes we can only do half that much. But it all adds up."

Rose chimed in when Clarice stopped. "The economy isn't what it used to be. One year we gave a girl a thousand-dollar-scholarship, but folks don't come out to a bazaar and bean supper like they used to. I'd love to see the day when we could offer one of our country girls at least a two-year ride."

"Then make it a bigger affair," Emily said.

"How?" Dotty asked. "Our mommas did the bazaar before us and probably our grandmas before them. If it could be crocheted, stitched, sewn, or knitted the months comin' up to the bazaar or baked on the day before, we've done it. Folks just ain't interested in little church bazaars like they used to be."

"Offer something that people will get all excited about even during a bad economy. Ever thought about an auction in addition to all the things you make?"

Dotty looked up. "What would we auction off?"

Emily's first thought was a million dollars' worth of knickknacks from Rose's house, but she asked, "How much trouble would it be to clean up the sale barn?"

"What are we going to auction? Tractors or cattle?" Clarice asked.

"Cowboys," Emily said.

All seven rockers stopped moving and she had their undivided attention.

She took a deep breath and went on, "We did this in Happy one time to raise money for a local family when their house burned. Only we did it at the town park because it was in the hot summertime. Cowboys volunteered their time, and at that auction folks bid on the cowboys to work for them for an eight-hour day, and all the money went to the family. Raised enough for a down payment on a really nice double-wide trailer. The next week they were living in it and most of the cowboys had already worked off their debt."

Clarice clapped her hands. "I love it."

"We've only got two weeks," Dotty said.

"We could move mountains in two weeks," Clarice said. "Tell us more, Emily."

"You could have barbecue sandwiches and chips, and all the ladies could bring desserts. Charge five dollars at the door and the price includes the supper. Then anyone who wants to bid on a cowboy has to buy a ten-dollar fan. You can make those out of card stock and ice cream sticks that you get at the craft store. Put a cowboy's picture on one side of the fan and a number on the other. That makes even more money. I can print them off the computer. Most of the cowboys will have a usable picture from their ranch websites. Then put out your bazaar stuff for people to buy while they are waiting on the auction. You need a dozen or so cowboys, an auctioneer, and a bunch of tables so people can sit around and talk while they're eating and waiting and, of course, buying all your beautiful handcrafted items. More folks would be there, so more would get sold, right?"

"And the cowboys? Do they work for eight hours?" Rose asked.

"I saw a movie once where they were auctioning off really rich men in Louisiana."

"You could make the cowboy go on a date with the lady who buys him, or work eight hours if it's a rancher who wins. We could make a few posters in the office at the ranch and put them up in all the surrounding areas to draw in the single women," Emily suggested.

Clarice's smile got bigger. "I like it."

Madge raised her hand and waved it around like a little girl in first grade who knew the answer to the question the teacher had asked. "Oh, oh! I've got a cousin in Dallas who went to one of those date auctions a few years ago. This famous painter was there and she gave a painting to be auctioned, but then they auctioned the men at the party off and they had to spend the evening with whoever bought them. They could have dinner with them right there and leave with them or whatever. She said it was really a lot of fun, and it brought a lot of money."

Dotty was nodding furiously and getting into the idea now. "Only instead of a date auction, it could be a cowboy auction and we could tell... well, shit, Clarice, we're going to have to tell Emily since she's going to be a part of this. Hell, maybe she could even fill in for Prissy when we get in a jam."

"Tell me what?" Emily asked.

Clarice nodded at Dotty, and the four ladies exchanged a long look. The air was pregnant with tension while they decided what they were going to do, and then finally Dotty smiled.

"It's like this," Dotty said. "We tried to fix Greg up with Prissy when he first came to live on the ranch, but it didn't work. So we hired her to help us out and we've been lookin' for the right wife for him for more than a year. We've got her under one of them gag order things so she can't tell him."

Rose took up the conversation. "He's real busy and he don't have a lot of time to socialize, so we're helping him out. Prissy told us to tell him about these dating sites, and he laughed at Dotty when she mentioned it, so we just took things in our own hands. I've got the Western Match dating site. It's my job to be Greg an hour a day and meet all the women who think his profile is wonderful. Prissy helped me set it up, and we made a little book with all that OMG and WTF in it. I about died when I found out what some of them stand for, but God ain't zapped me dead for writing it yet. I figure it's not such a big sin if you just use the letters, and in my mind, I always say what the fizzle instead of that naughty word."

Emily gulped half a glass of tea before she came up for air. Greg would just die if he knew what they were up to.

"And I'm in charge of Christian Mingle," Clarice said. "Rose put on her profile that Greg is a rancher who is available to single women ages twenty-five to thirty-four. I put on mine that he's a good Christian man lookin' for a good woman who loves the land."

Emily felt her eyes popping dangerously open. Could eyeballs be put back in her head if they fell out in her lap?

"It's secret and nobody can know. We call each other every day and report on the women who look good to us," Rose said. "If you tell, Clarice will fire you on the spot."

"She won't tell. She's one of us now," Clarice said.

"Well, we could make her raise her right hand and put the other one on the Bible and swear to God," Dotty said.

"It isn't necessary. What is said at bazaar meetings stays at bazaar meetings, and anyone who tells, God just strikes them dead on the spot," Madge said. "I'm in charge of Farmers Only. The women who throw up their profiles when I'm Greg are supposed to know about farmin', but some of them are just flat-out lyin'. It ain't very many who I'd bring out here to meet him."

Emily was still speechless when she looked at Dotty.

"I got Plenty of Fish. Hell, I don't care if they are ranchers or Christian. We can bring them to Jesus and make them ranchin' women. I just want to have a bunch of them so I can choose which one might work as a wife."

Rose nodded toward the tea and lemonade. "Emily, would you be bartender and bring us something to drink? Now, whoever buys the cowboy gets him for the evening, right? So we'd need to have the auction at, say, six o'clock? And are we going to tell about it on our dating sites so Greg can have lots and lots of women bidding on him?"

Emily filled seven glasses and handed one to each of the ladies. Then she picked up the lemonade in one hand and the sweet tea in the other. Her hands were shaking so bad that she gripped the pitchers until her knuckles turned white.

Clarice pointed at the lemonade when Emily crossed the floor toward her. "Let's each invite our top four ladies and open the doors at four for the bazaar. Serve barbecue at five and then have the auction at six. How much do you think Greg will go for?"

"Or Mason? I can talk him into it for sure. Hey, if we find Greg a wife, then we should get Prissy or Emily to help us make a profile for Mason. We could be the marriage angels of Fannin County," Rose said.

The next lady pointed at the tea. "Oh, my nephew, Carson, has been trying to outrun one lady over in Savoy for months. I bet she'd pay big bucks to own him for the whole evening. This is a great idea, Clarice, and if we find a wife for Greg, I'd sure be tossing Carson's name in the hat for y'all four to work on next year," another said. "We'll all come about noon and help set up things, and we'll stay and help clean up afterward. I bet we can offer a two-year scholarship this year, and more folks will turn out if it's on Lightning Ridge rather than in the fellowship hall at the church."

"Hmmph!" Madge went back to her knitting. "Folks think if they walk into a church religion is going to jump out from the corners and attack them."

"Ain't it the truth." Rose nodded.

Clarice set her glass on a cute little paper coaster on

the table beside her. "I love this idea. And y'all can help set up, but the hired hands can clean out the barn and tear it all down afterward. We're too old to be hustlin' folding tables and sweeping down cobwebs. And Max can be our auctioneer—that way we won't have to be out any money paying one. He does that for our cattle sale in the fall. Doors open at four with our wares on display, and that includes the cowboys for sale. They can all be sitting in a chair in the middle of the sale ring. We won't make them stay in stalls. At five the auction starts and whoever buys that cowboy has to buy his supper. She owns him for the night. What do y'all think of that?"

"Great idea, Clarice," Emily said.

Lemonade lady followed Clarice's lead and set her glass to the side and picked up her embroidery. "Hey, y'all want to have a dance too? I got a niece I can get to play for free. She and her band gear up on Saturday night just to practice when they don't have a real job. They can practice for a crowd as well as in her barn. And Emily, let me introduce the rest of us to you. I'm sorry I didn't think to do it before now. We've all heard so much about you that we felt like we knew you, but I forgot you didn't know us. I'm Ivy. That lady working with the pink baby yarn is Edna, and the one beside her is June. We're glad you are working for Clarice. If you stay around these parts we'll have to entice you into the auxiliary. We need new blood and new ideas."

Dotty talked as she worked. "Is there some way we could make the cowboy give us money for the dances?"

"How about we don't have the auction until the end of the evening and the ladies with the fans have to pay a dollar a song to dance with them all evening?" Madge said.

"I like that. It'll make even more money." Clarice's eyes twinkled. "The auction will close out the bazaar. The cowboys all sit in the sale ring when the band starts playing and they only dance with the ladies who pay their dollar. Only the women with a bidding fan can dance with them."

"Kind of like one of them speed dating things on television, only it'll be speed dancin'." Madge nodded.

Emily returned the pitchers and sat back down. By the end of the afternoon, they'd have it all worked out and some lucky high school senior girl would wind up with a full scholarship from the ladies' auxiliary that year.

"And what does the lucky girl get who wins the bid on her cowboy? It will be too late for a date with them at that time of night," Emily asked.

"A date the next Friday night. She gets to plan it and he has to pay for it," Edna said.

Emily figured it out in her head. If the bazaar was held on the last Saturday night in the month, then the cowboy dates would be on the last day of February. She'd told Taylor when she drove away from her ranch that she'd be home by the first day of March. If she had enough money to outbid at least sixteen dating site women plus all the other ladies in the area would be the billion-dollar question.

―⁂―

Clarice was rereading one of the letters she'd written to Marvin when she heard a familiar knock on her door. Two short raps followed by three speedy ones.

"Come in, Dotty," she called out.

Dotty carried two cups of coffee on a tray into the room and set them down on the end table beside Clarice's rocker. "Reading them again, are you?"

"Thank you. After all that nibbling at Rose's place, I'm ready for coffee. And yes, I'm reading again. It's a good thing that I didn't buy a bus ticket to go see him. I was so young and naive, and he was so romantic. He could have sweet-talked me into believing anything."

Dotty settled into the corner of the sofa with a cup of coffee in her hand. "You were both young. You would have grown up and grown old together, but that wasn't what your destiny was. Mine and Rose's and Madge's was to come to Texas so we could grow old together after we lost our husbands. Yours was to marry Lester and have a wonderful son with him. Which reminds me, have you told Bart about all this?"

Clarice shook her head. "Not yet. He calls on Sunday afternoon, which is tomorrow. I'll tell him then, but only because I have to explain why Emily is here. Dotty, do you really think that everything happens for a reason?"

"Damn straight tootin' I do. It might not work out between Emily and Greg, but it was their destiny to meet to see if it would. We can like it or not like it, but when it comes down to the final period on the letter, the choice is theirs," Dotty answered.

"But Marvin and I didn't have a choice," Clarice said.

"Sure you did. You could have hunted him down in person when the letters kept coming back to you. He could have swallowed his pride and come looking for you. He had your address and knew exactly how to find you. Ravenna isn't Dallas, darlin'."

Clarice dropped the letter back into the boot box in her lap. "Kind of like two paths in the forest, right?"

Dotty nodded. "That's right, only a big oak tree had fallen across one path and you didn't want to climb over it and ruin your stockings. They were expensive in those days, remember?"

Clarice giggled like a little girl. "You always make it easy to understand."

Dotty changed the subject. "Do you remember those stockings and the garters?"

"Of course I do, and the garter belts and those little fasteners that felt like we were sitting on rocks during Sunday morning church services," Clarice said.

"I thought God had sent us a miracle when the first panty hose came out."

"He did! And now down deep in my heart I think he's sent us another one and her name is Emily."

Dotty leaned forward and whispered, "Don't say that out loud. If Greg hears you, he'll run like a scalded hound."

"It's time. He's thirty," Clarice said.

"The banister is getting dusty," Dotty said with a wink.

"Needs some kids to slide down it. We're workin' on it. Do you think Emily was jealous today?" Clarice's eyes twinkled.

Dotty slapped a hand over her mouth to keep the laughter from exploding. When she had it under control she asked, "Oh, hell, yeah, she was jealous. You got your four candidates picked out?"

Clarice shook her head. "But I'm going to decide before the end of the week. And I'm going to pick out the wildest ones of the lot just so they'll go after Greg and make her more jealous."

"You tell Greg yet that he's going to be auctioned off like a prize bull?"

"You can tell him. I've got to figure out how in the devil I'm going to tell this whole story to Bart," Clarice said.

"The hell I will! I'd rather tell Bart about Marvin as that."

―――⁓―――

The walls of the bedroom closed in around Emily. Dusk was settling early with clouds rolling down from the north. Greg had disappeared after supper. Dotty and Clarice had gone to their rooms, most likely to pretend to be Greg on their dating sites. The weather site on her laptop said that there was a cold front coming from Oklahoma and that it could dump up to two inches of snow on them. More than likely north Texas would get a layer of ice and sleet instead of pretty snow. If she'd made a different decision at the first of the week, she'd be sitting on the beach. True, it wouldn't be hot and sunny, but it wouldn't have a coat of ice on the sand.

She pulled back the curtain and looked out. Were the horses out there in the stable so far, that she couldn't see them, as restless as she was?

Gramps always said that when something was troubling the soul, even when a person had no idea what was doing the troubling, that good old hard work would bring it to surface. She'd mucked out stables at midnight, stacked hay in the barns in the middle of the night, even scrubbed the kitchen floor lots and lots of times, trying to make sense of the antsy feeling.

There was no way she was going to scrub the floor at Lightning Ridge. It would offend Dotty if she found

Emily on her knees working on an already clean floor. Or else Clarice would think she was crazy and send her packing. The thought of leaving Lightning Ridge put a painful catch in her chest.

She tried reading, but that didn't work. She turned on the television and it bored her. She checked the clock. Only fifteen minutes had passed since she first came up to her room. Lord, it was going to be a long night if she didn't find something to do.

Finally she put on her boots and work coat and slipped out into the hallway, down the stairs, out the back door, and to her truck. She remembered the way to the horse stables, and there was always leather that could be cleaned in the tack room.

The north wind rattled through the bare mesquite branches and seeped through her coat, chilling her from the inside out as she ran from truck to stables. A few horses snorted as she passed their stalls, but a quick check said their stables had been done that day and were in good shape. Down the center aisle she could see a sliver of light coming from under the door of the old tack room. Had she left it on when she returned the wheelbarrow and shovel? That was days and days ago.

She peeked inside the window and there was Greg sitting at the old weathered table in the middle of the room. She rapped on the window and waited for him to look up. He motioned her inside, so she opened the door.

"What are you doing here?" he asked.

"Had trouble sleeping and thought I might find some good hard work to wear me plumb out. What are you doing here?" she asked.

"Making peace."

She pointed. "Is that your grandpa's saddle?"

He nodded.

"You should be whupped for letting it get like that." She removed her coat and gloves and rolled up her sleeves, stuck her hand down in the bucket of water beside the saddle, and brought up an extra cleaning sponge. She squeezed out most of the water and then rubbed in the saddle soap until it was lathered up.

He fished a second sponge from the bucket and started working on the stirrup leathers. "I couldn't make myself come back in this room until tonight. And I told the hired help not to touch his saddle when they took things from here to the new room."

"I'm surprised it's in as good a shape as it is." She made sure she got soap into all the nooks and crevices of the saddle. "I would have expected it to be dried and cracked."

"He'd treated it before he put it in the closet over there. He rode the day before he died," Greg said.

She gave the saddle a once-over and then picked up a dry rag to wipe all the excess lather away, then stood back and looked at it again. "Where's the oil sponge?"

He tilted his head toward cabinets on the left side of the tack room. She quickly found it and poured a generous amount of oil into one of the old sponges. He did the same and together they rubbed enough into the leather to make it just slightly damp. Their fingers got tangled up and the touch of his warm, wet fingers brushing against hers shot delicious shivers through her veins.

"And now the conditioner," he said.

Did that bit of hoarseness in his voice mean that he was affected as much as she was? She looked across the table and their gaze met, but he quickly blinked and picked up a couple of clean rags.

She started the final step while he conditioned the stirrups and then he joined her, rubbing the conditioner all over the saddle. The air in the tack room reminded her of the way it felt right before a tornado struck out in west Texas. Everything would suddenly go so still that it was downright scary. The next sound would be an electrical crackle in the air like power lines falling. And then all hell would break loose.

The hair on the back of her neck prickled. The stillness was eerie and the quietness deafening as she waited for the storm to hit. The air fizzed around them. She wanted him to say something, anything to fill up the weird emptiness in the room, but he just stared at the saddle.

The fabric of his thermal knit shirt stretched across his chest and biceps. He'd pushed the sleeves up to his elbows to keep from getting them wet, and the dark hair on his arms was plastered against his skin. His fingers were long and his hands broad, like a working man's should be.

Emily had never wanted to touch a man more than she did at that moment, but the timing wasn't right. His thoughts were on his grandfather, not the woman in front of him.

Finally, he cleared his throat and said, "Thank you."

"Gramps used to say that hard work would help a person figure through their problems," she said.

"Grandpa said the best way to get to know a person was to work along beside them." He smiled.

"Couple of wise old men, weren't they?"

"Wonder what they would have thought of each other, what with them both loving the same woman at different times in their lives?" he mused aloud.

"Shows they both had good taste in women." She smiled.

"Guess it does. Want to go for a moonlight ride?"

"Horses or four-wheeler?" she asked.

"Four-wheeler. Easier to get out and put back and we wouldn't have to rub it down or saddle it up," he said.

"You sure you're ready to leave this room? Want some more time alone? I can go on back to the house."

He picked up his cowboy hat, settled it on his head, and held the tack room door open for her. "I'm good now, and I really need some company."

Her heart floated. Lord, it was good to be needed again, even if it was just for company. Until that moment, she hadn't realized the big hole her grandfather's passing had put in her heart simply because she was alone in the world.

───※───

The warmth of Emily's body snuggled up against his back chased away the chill of the night air whipping around the speeding four-wheeler. At times the dark clouds shifted and stars popped out from behind them, but it didn't take long for the clouds to cover them up again. The headlights on the four-wheeler showed a path that was little more than tire tracks and dead grass, but Greg knew exactly where he was going. He'd been there so often that he could have driven there blindfolded in the pitch-black dark with no lights at all.

When he braked in front of the old log cabin, Emily hopped off and clapped her hands together to warm them. Even with good lined leather gloves, they felt numb.

"What's this?" she asked.

"Grandpa's old hunting cabin. I haven't been up here since he died either. Thought I might as well do up the evening right and get it over with," he said.

"Are you going inside?" she asked.

"If you'll go with me. I haven't been inside since… well, you know. The hired hands come up here during deer season and stay a few days at a time whenever they want to, but…" He let the sentence dangle.

"Looks like the perfect place to set up a moonshine still back here in all these trees. No one could spot the smoke or smell it," she said.

He raised an eyebrow. "Moonshine?"

"Gramps kept one going on his place until he got sick. His dad made it during Prohibition and they used the money he made to buy the ranch out in west Texas. That's why it's called Shine Canyon Ranch. Gramps and I stilled off one batch every fall. Stump liquor, he called it," she said.

He stepped up on the porch and opened the door. "And did you like that moonshine, Emily?"

"Not particularly. It burned like pure fire going down, but I sampled it with him and we always used it for a New Year's toast."

He picked up a box of matches and lit an oil lamp. The cabin was a sixteen-foot square with bunk beds on one side, a broken-down sofa facing a fireplace in the center, and a table with a few pots and pans and mismatched dishes on the other side of the room. Behind the sofa was one of those old red tables with chrome legs and four matching chairs.

He removed his hat and hung it on a nail beside the door. "Want to set up a still?"

"Oh, no! Not me! I could make a batch, but Clarice would throw me off the property if I led her fair-haired boy into temptation." She sat down on the sofa and pulled her coat tighter around her body. She wondered just what those sixteen women would look like and what he'd do when he figured out that they thought they'd been chatting with him for all those months.

"I'm not fair-haired, but she might get mad at us if Dotty got into the 'shine. It's cold in here. Let's build a fire."

"But then we'd have to stay until it went out. Did you come up here to hunt?"

Greg sat down on the other end of the sofa and patted the place beside him. "Every single year. We stayed for three days and went home the evening before Thanksgiving. Grandpa said that gave the women folks time to cook and fuss around in the kitchen without us underfoot and it gave us some time to eat beans out of the can and chocolate cupcakes whenever we wanted."

She sat but kept a foot of space between them. One touch would kindle a fire that could only be put out one way, and as much as she wanted to be tangled up with him under the quilt on one of those bunk beds, her heart said the timing was still wrong.

"You hunted with your grandfather. I made 'shine with mine. Two different men altogether, but I think they might have liked each other."

He stole glances at her while they sat in comfortable silence. He'd never brought another woman to the cabin, but if he had, he couldn't imagine a single one of them waiting patiently for him to bury his ghosts and say good-bye to his grandfather.

"Good memories," he said finally.

"That's all we got when they are gone."

"You ready?" he asked.

She turned toward him. "When you are. I'm not in a hurry if you need some more time. And all this brought back memories of my grandfather. We didn't have a cabin, but we did have a campsite."

He stood up and held out his hand. "Emily Cooper, you are one in a million."

She put her hand in his and let him pull her up. "That could be a compliment if I'm the best gold piece in a million. But it could be something altogether different if I'm one in a million when they measure cow patties."

He chuckled. "You do have a way with words."

He pulled her close to his chest and tipped her chin up with his knuckles. His lips were cold, but the kiss was pure red-hot fire that heated her from the core of her heart all the way to the tips of her fingers that were splayed out on his chest. She could hear his heart thumping in unison with hers. She wasn't sure how he managed it, but suddenly his gloves were gone and his bare hands cupped her cheeks, fingers making lazy circles on her temples as he deepened the next kiss. She opened her mouth to grant him entrance and pressed closer to him. She jerked her gloves off and dropped them on the floor so she could feel the skin on his neck. Who knew that fingertips could be an erotic zone?

"God, Emily," he said.

"I know," she said.

He made the first move to step back and said, "We'd

better get going. One more of those and we'll never leave this place."

"Oh?"

"There wouldn't be anything left but ashes in the morning." He grinned.

"I bet the ashes would be hot for a long, long time." She smiled back.

He retrieved her gloves and kissed her fingertips before he put them back on her hands, then he picked his up from the sofa and jammed his hands back into them. "Ready?"

"No, but I expect we'd better leave anyway."

Emily hugged up close to his back, her arms around him and her cheek against the rough texture of his work jacket. The roar of the four-wheeler engine was nothing compared to the noise of her heart thumping against her ribs. The first flakes of wet snow peppered against her face as Greg braked and brought the machine to a stop just inside the lean-to on the side of the sables.

"Looks like we are going to get in on that storm like they said. It always happens on the weekends when help is short. You going to be up for moving cattle or feeding tomorrow morning?" he asked.

Weather! How could he be talking about the damn weather when all she could think about was hot kisses, wild sex, and more hot kisses?

"Miz Clarice says that I'll be driving her and the ladies to church," she said.

"Not if this keeps up. When it snows or ices the preacher calls off church. He lives outside of town and he doesn't drive in the bad weather. It only happens about once every two or three years at the most, but I'd be willing to bet that tomorrow is slick enough that there won't be services," Greg said.

"If we don't go to church, then, yes, of course I'll help. Time to go now or…" She let the sentence hang.

"Guess we'd better," he said.

They walked side by side, hands brushing, but neither of them made the first move to grasp the other. He opened the truck door for her and hurried to his own truck, hopped inside, removed his Stetson, and brushed the snowflakes from the brim before putting it on the passenger seat beside him. He waved for her to go ahead of him, so she started the engine and turned on the windshield wipers. The snow had gotten serious and the wind had picked up. The swirling snow made a black-and-white kaleidoscope in the headlights, but Emily was so deep inside her own thoughts that she didn't even appreciate the beauty.

She parked, hopped out of the truck, jogged up on the porch, stuffed her gloves and stocking hat into her pockets, and hung her coat on a rack inside the kitchen door. Greg had parked out front and she heard him stomping the snow from his boots on the porch before he came in through the front door.

Greg met her in the foyer. He'd hung up his coat and hat and left his boots by the hall tree. He traced her jawline with his forefinger, then tipped her chin up and brushed a sweet kiss across her lips.

Dotty yelled, "Hey, Greg, come on in here. Prissy stopped by."

Emily's phone rang and she smiled up at Greg. "Bad timing. Be there in a minute." She fished it out and said, "Well, hello, Dusty, darlin'. No, it's not too late to call.

It's only eight o'clock. I've missed you too. I'd love to go to the Valentine's party with you…"

———∽∾∽———

All the passion turned to instant jealousy in Greg's heart and soul. Dammit, anyway! She'd said she wasn't involved with anyone, so who in the hell was *Dusty, darlin'*?

"Do I hear you out there too, Emily? Come on in and have a cup of hot chocolate with us. Prissy came by this evening to help me with a computer problem," Clarice said.

Emily whispered something and shoved the phone back in her pocket.

"Hi, y'all." Prissy smiled. "We were just talking about the Valentine's party. Want to go with me, Greg?"

"Oh, I have a date for the party," he said.

"And who is that?" Clarice asked.

"Just someone that I really, really think a lot of," Greg said.

Prissy smiled. "Well, rats! I thought we could go as friends so we wouldn't be all alone. If you've got a date, I'm not going. Thanks for the sweet tea, Miz Clarice. If you have any more trouble with that pesky site on your computer, just call me."

Greg's phone rang and he dug it out of his hip pocket. "Okay, okay, I'm on my way."

He hung up and said, "Max needs me to come to the bunkhouse and help him fix the hot water tank down there. See y'all later."

"Glass of sweet tea?" Clarice looked at Emily.

"I'd love some, but I really should return my cousin's call. She called to ask me to go with her to the

Valentine's party out at Happy and I left her hanging. I don't want to make that long drive. Thank you, though. See you in the morning for church?"

"Madge already called. No church tomorrow, so I guess you are on your own," Clarice said.

"I promised Greg I'd help him with feeding if we weren't going to church," she mumbled.

Blast her promises all the way to hell! She didn't want to spend the morning with Greg in dozens of feeding lots full of cows in the cold weather when he had a date with another woman for the Valentine's party. He'd kissed her and he'd told her that he wasn't involved with anyone. How could he not be involved if they were going to something as big as a Valentine's dance together?

Dammit! How in the hell can things get so complicated in such a short time? Shit! I sound like Dotty.

Chapter 7

"SORRY ABOUT THAT," SHE APOLOGIZED WHEN DUSTY answered the phone.

There was no answer, so Emily thought she'd lost the connection. "Dusty?"

"Sorry, I was... I wish you'd come on home where you belong, Emily. I don't want to tell you bad news on the phone."

"What bad news?" Emily went to the window and pulled the curtain back slightly, just in time to see a cute little black sports car with its headlights lighting up the snowflakes. "Crap!" she mumbled.

"What did you say?" Dusty asked.

"It's not you."

"Someone out there in that godforsaken part of the state has upset you? Well, what in the hell are you still doing there? You know how to drive in bad weather. Come home and we'll go up to the Golden Spurs in Amarillo and have a drink."

"I've still got eighteen days to think about things," she said.

"Well, think how damn far you are from home, Emily. Taylor wants that land, but we all want you to come back, whether you ranch or work somewhere in town. You can live in your house even if you sell the rest of the ranch to Taylor. You are family and it's your home until you die if you want to live there. We miss you, girl."

"I miss all y'all too, but I don't want to talk about that tonight. Now what did you say about bad news?"

"I don't know how to tell you gently, so I'm just going to spit it out. Bill died."

She sat down in the rocking chair with a thud. "When?"

"Found him this morning."

Tears ran down her cheeks. Bill had come to the farm as a puppy. A big old yellow teddy bear of a dog of mixed breed that tailed behind Gramps everywhere he went. Bill rode in the truck passenger seat with his head hanging out the window when Gramps went into town. If Gramps went to the barn, Bill walked right beside him and waited patiently for him to finish whatever he had to do. He was more than just a pet, though. Gramps had trained old Bill to be the number one dog, the one that he sent in last when a wild bull or cow wouldn't get its sorry ass back to the herd.

"Taylor was too big of a sissy to tell you, but he's standing here with his hand out for the phone now," Dusty said. "Y'all can talk while I get my clothes ironed for church in the morning. I wish you were home for another reason. I want to borrow those black platform heels you bought last month."

"They're in the closet over at the house. I didn't bring them with me. Go get them," Emily told her favorite girl cousin, Taylor's youngest sister.

"We buried him out behind the barn and made a wood cross with his name painted on it," Taylor said.

"Thank you," she whispered.

She should have been there. If she hadn't left, Bill might have taken up with her and he wouldn't be dead. He had never liked Taylor, wouldn't even let him scratch his ears. Poor old boy probably thought she'd died too.

"Are you still there?" Taylor asked.

"I'm still here," she said.

"You know I will," he said softly.

"You still taking Melinda to the Valentine's dance?" she asked to keep from sobbing.

"I am still here, Em."

"Don't forget to take her a pretty corsage and dance the last dance with her. Good night, Taylor." Emily ended the call before he could say anything else.

She heard Greg's footsteps coming up the stairs, heard him pause at her door, and held her breath, but he didn't knock. The sob that caught in her throat and hung there was not because of a woman, not even if she was just his friend.

The weeping was for old Bill, a big yellow dog. She clamped a hand over her mouth to keep it from escaping. Greg would think she was a big crybaby if he caught her crying twice in one day. When she heard his bedroom door shut, she buried her face in the pillows and let it all out.

As usual, Emily awoke the next morning long before daylight. She could almost see the aroma of coffee swirling around the bed and beckoning her down to the kitchen. She dressed in work jeans, boots, and a thermal shirt and frowned at her reflection in the mirror as she brushed her teeth. She pulled her dark hair up into a ponytail and picked up her weathered old cowboy hat as she followed her nose to the coffee.

Dotty was in the middle of a monologue tirade and didn't even notice her when she poured a cup of coffee.

"I damn sure will not tell that hussy that she can come to the bazaar. She's crazier than an outhouse rat high from smokin' too much funny weed and drinkin' old Beamus's moonshine."

She stopped long enough to slide a pan of biscuits into the oven and stir the sizzling sausage. "She's not invited. I swear to God, she'd best not show up here."

Emily sipped at her coffee.

"I need to call Madge and Rose. We need to compare notes. I bet that floozy done showed up on their sites too, and if she did, they need to be warned that she's a stripper in a hoochy-kooch bar. I guess we'd best go out to the barn and sharpen up some shovels."

Emily swallowed quickly to keep from spewing coffee all over the spotless floor. "Dotty!" she said.

"What?" She turned away from the stove. "When did you get here?"

"Been here a while. Need some help?"

"With breakfast or the shovels?"

Emily giggled. "That's what y'all gals get for pretending to be Greg. What does this floozy know?"

"Too damn much. I'm the best Greg among the four of us. Those other three don't even know how to talk like a bad boy, but I was married to one so I know," Dotty snorted. "And she lives in Dallas so she could drive up here in a couple of hours, and she said that she'd figured out that he owns Lightning Ridge and she's coming up here to see him and that's going to spoil the whole auction."

Greg's inner alarm didn't go off that morning, so he was awakened by a click and the radio weatherman announcing that north central Texas was in for a late winter storm that had already dumped three inches of snow on the ground through the night. Another inch would fall that morning, the temperatures would hover around freezing through Monday, and then on Tuesday the cold front would move out, the sun would shine, and the snow would melt by Valentine's Day on Friday.

He hit the button on top of the clock and slapped a pillow over his head. Prissy had sure enough caught him at a bad time when she showed up. After the emotional day with Emily and then finally facing the tack room and the cabin, he'd been drained. Then that cowboy, *Dusty, darlin'*, had called.

He wasn't a sentimental person; even Nana said he was like his grandpa. He was all business, so what in the hell was going on in his heart? He'd never felt like this before, and it was unsettling. From the time he graduated high school he'd had a goal in mind and gone after it with determination, perseverance, and without looking back one time. He was going to be a rancher like his grandfather, and he was going to run Lightning Ridge so well that when he was old and gray, it would be twice the ranch it was when he took over the reins.

By the time he'd gotten back from the bunkhouse, Emily was up in her room returning a phone call, according to what Dotty told him.

"She told me she wasn't involved with anyone. What was she doing making out with me and kissing me if she's calling him darlin'?" he grumbled all the way to the bathroom.

He dressed quickly in soft faded jeans, two pairs of socks, and boots and a denim shirt over a thermal undershirt. The aroma of breakfast food and coffee mingled together led him from his bedroom, down the stairs, and to the kitchen.

Clarice and Emily were at the table sipping coffee, and Dotty was mumbling about something as she pulled biscuits from the oven. A cold blast of air swept across the floor as Max came through the back door.

"I thought I smelled sausage. The cook at the bunk-house is making pancakes and I'd rather have sausage gravy this morning, as cold as it is. Got to have some-thing to stick to my ribs if we're going to get all these cattle fed with the help we've got today." Max pulled a plate from the cabinet and helped himself.

"I'm helping y'all since there's no church today," Emily said.

"We'll take all the hands we can get." Max nodded.

Greg dropped a kiss on Clarice's forehead. "Good morning, Nana."

He poured a cup of coffee and sat down at the table. He looked across the table at Emily and willed her to look at him, but she didn't.

"Since you have a date for the Valentine's party and I always go with you, I decided to have my own date this year," Clarice said.

"Why would you think I have a date?" he asked.

"You said so last night when Prissy asked you, so I've made other plans."

Max's fork stopped midway from plate to mouth. Dotty turned around so quick that the kitchen towel draped over her shoulder went flying. Emily looked up and into Greg's eyes.

"Hell, I was just kidding. Who is your date?" Greg shifted his stare to Clarice.

Marvin, the old teenage love, was one thing, but to replace Grandpa with a local man was quite another. For her to be seen with a man at the Valentine's party would be opening up a fifty-gallon drum of gossip that would have her remarried at the age of eighty by the end of the summer.

"Emily is going as my date," Clarice said.

His green eyes darted from Clarice to Emily, registering in an instant the look of pure shock on her face.

"Emily is going to Happy to a Valentine's party out there with some cowboy named Dusty," he blurted out.

"I am not. I told Dusty that I didn't want to drive that far. What gave you the idea that I was going?" Emily asked.

"You said that you'd love to go with *Dusty, darlin'*... remember?"

"And then Clarice called us into the study and I called Dusty back and said that I wasn't going. And for your information, Dusty is Taylor's sister, not a cowboy. She's my cousin and we often go to parties together."

Damn!

The day couldn't get any worse.

Clarice patted Emily's hand. "Well, you can just go stag because Emily is my date this year. I checked the weather. It's going to clear up by Wednesday and we'll go over to Tressa's in Sherman to shop. The party is Friday night, so we'll be okay. I saw the cutest little red number over there last time I was there and you'll look lovely in it. I'm thinking of buying a white pant outfit trimmed in red sequins and we'll be the belles of the ball."

"But..." Emily started.

"As my assistant, you *will* be my date. I need someone to drive me, and for the first time in his association with this ranch, my grandson made me believe that he wasn't taking me, so he can live with his cute little lie." Clarice's eyes twinkled.

Dotty picked up the towel and tossed it on the cabinet.

"Well, that's just great!" Greg jumped up and turned his back to the table and loaded a plate with biscuits and sausage gravy. Max was right; he'd need some good hot food to stick to his ribs if he expected to make it through a long cold morning of feeding cows.

"So?" Dotty asked. "Who was on your mind when you told that lie?"

"I was talking about Nana. I always take Nana. It's a standing tradition for us to go to the Angus parties together," Greg answered.

Max finished eating about the same time that Greg sat down. He carried his plate to the sink, rinsed it, and put it in the dishwasher. "Thanks, Dotty. That was wonderful. Just like you used to make in the lunchroom for breakfast when we were kids."

Dotty smiled for the first time that morning. "Glad you liked it."

Emily stood up. "I'll go with you and help."

"Would love to take you along, but I done got Louis ridin' shotgun with me this morning. You can go with Greg. Besides, he's got that pasture full of the wild cows to move today, and he's going to need all the help he can get." Max grabbed his coat from a hook. When it was buttoned up, he crammed his hat down on his head and waved over his shoulder.

"Helluva day to be moving the wild bunch," Clarice

said. "Emily, you got any experience with cows that carry a wild gene?"

She nodded. "Gramps had a pasture full of them. I never understood why he'd keep them around when they kept reproducing more calves with that gene. Then that first year after I finished college and came home to take care of him, I learned real quick that they were throwing the best sale calves we had. They might be wild, but by golly, they grew off thirty percent faster than the other calves and they weighed in heavier every fall. Plus, they'll herd up and circle around the calves to protect them from coyotes and cougars. They are fearless and we seldom ever lost a calf to wild animals."

Clarice nodded. "That's exactly what we've discovered. Lester kept them away from the other cattle, though, because he didn't want the gene bred into the prime stock. They do a good job of filling out the sale bill and bringing in the revenue, but if someone is buying for breeding stock, they usually don't want a wild gene in the mix."

"Sounds like Gramps," she said. "Y'all use dogs?"

Greg nodded her way.

Emily swallowed hard and said, "Dusty called last night to tell me that Gramps's number one dog, Bill, died yesterday. He was old so it wasn't unexpected, and I guess he just didn't want to go on without Gramps. I loved that old boy. The ranch won't be the same without him."

Greg reached across the table and laid a hand over hers. "I'm so sorry. I can't image losing Coolie, the number one dog on the Lightning Ridge."

"Thank you, Greg." She pulled her hand free, pushed

back her chair, and carried her plate to the sink, keeping her back straight and stiff the whole time.

She didn't fool Greg one bit. He could feel her pain, and he would have felt the same way. It seemed like he'd known Emily his whole life, like they'd grown up on adjoining ranches right there in Ravenna.

Chapter 8

MOVING WILD COWS IN WEST TEXAS INVOLVED TAKING the dogs out to the flat acreage, gathering up the critters, and herding them through a gate into an adjoining pasture. In Ravenna, it was a whole different story.

Emily's coat was buttoned up and scarf tucked in. Gloves warmed her hands, but the cold north wind slung the wet snow against her bare cheeks with enough force to make them sting. Greg had let the dogs out of the boxes on the back of his truck and they stood between them, waiting for the signal.

"Number these dogs so I know who to send after that rangy old bull first," she yelled over the sound of the wind rattling the bare tree branches like bones of an old skeleton.

"You think they'll listen to you?"

"I've been working with dogs my whole life."

"I'll stay here in case they balk at a stranger."

She stooped down, looked each dog in the eyes, and then kissed him on the top of the head. "We'll do fine, Greg. They like me."

"Like is one thing. Respect and obey is another. Max trained them and I can work them, but we're the only two people on the ranch that they'll listen to."

"They'll listen to me, I promise. I know dogs like I know ranchin'," she said.

"Oh, yeah?" His tone was as cold as the wind swirling around them.

She rubbed her gloved hands together to generate a little more warmth. "Did someone piss in your gravy this morning? You've been distant all morning. What's your problem? Bad day or mad? And if I'm at the center of your mood, then what did I do wrong?"

He leaned against the truck fender. "Maybe we're talkin' about you thinkin' you can make a workin' ranch out of a hundred acres. Maybe we're talkin' about the fact that you aren't going to be around here much longer and Nana is going to be so sad when you leave."

"I can make a ranch out of a hundred acres and I'll be sad when I leave too, but my roots are on Shine Canyon. Now are we going to bring those wild heifers up from the mesquite, or are you trying to start an argument because you are mad about something else?"

Greg pointed as he talked. "Okay, give it your best shot. Blister is number four. Angel is three. Merlin is two, and Coolie is the number one dog."

Four new dogs in her world.

Four new people.

She tapped Blister on the head and pointed. The dog took off in a dead run while the others waited, every muscle quivering as they sat patiently waiting for the signal that it was their turn.

Blister circled the bull, yapping at its heels until it finally started moving. Trouble was, it lowered its big head and charged straight toward Emily. She held her ground and when the bull was inches from her, she twisted one leg to the inside just slightly. He turned and headed back to the mesquite thicket with Blister right on his heels.

It was an old trick that her father taught her and

Taylor. He said it was kin to bull fighting without the red cape, and she'd just proven it for the first time for herself. Her heart raced and her chest hurt from holding her breath, but she'd never tell Greg that she'd been too damn scared to move.

She whistled shrilly. Blister ran back and sat down at her feet. She grabbed him between the ears and kissed him before she pointed at Angel. "Go on, baby girl, and show these boys how it's done."

Angel was a red heeler and her stance said that she was a no-nonsense girl. She crouched low, growled, and then took off with a yip, disappearing into the thicket. In a few seconds there was a ruckus that sounded like the bull was trying to uproot the trees. Then the old boy trotted out with Angel snapping at his heels and joined the herd.

"I'll be damned." Greg chuckled.

"Are they all herded up now?" she asked.

"No, there's another pocket of them about halfway out toward the far fence. I'll go open the gate and take Blister with me to get them moving if you want to drive down there and work some more with the dogs," he answered.

"I don't need to drive. I can walk that far," she said.

"There's about forty of them down there. You better take Coolie," he said.

"You take him with you. I just need Angel and Merlin. I don't like to see the cattle lose an ear or have a bloody lip in this kind of weather. And that's why Coolie is the number one dog. He takes care of the matters when nothing else works, right?"

Greg nodded. "Be careful. That bull scared the hell out of me when he charged you."

"Me too. I almost broke and ran," she admitted.

"So what was your dog's name that died? I know you probably told us, but I forgot. I'm sorry," Greg asked.

"Bill was our Coolie. We only sent him in when the bull was too stubborn to work with the first three. They'll miss him on the ranch," she said.

It wasn't until she was walking away with Angel and Merlin at her heels that she realized she'd said that *they* would miss him on the ranch, not *we'll* miss him. It was a slip of the tongue. Emily was going home to Shine Canyon. She and Gramps had so many memories there that they'd both be happy doing what they could to build it all again.

Angel gathered up the rest of the strays in a few minutes, and when Emily turned Merlin loose to help, they worked together to keep them moving toward the gate on the far side of the pasture.

"That all of 'em?" Greg yelled.

She held up her right thumb and watched his lips move as he counted them when they went through the gate into the next pasture. She snapped her fingers and Angel and Merlin had a race back to the truck where they hopped up on the tailgate with Coolie and Blister and waited for Greg to open their cage doors.

Grace, in all its forms, deserted her. She took a step backward, stepped in a gopher hole, and boom! Snowflakes were falling in her wide-open eyes. Greg bounded off the tailgate of the truck and knelt beside her, jerking his gloves off and checking the pulse in her neck.

"I'm not dead," she gasped.

"Then blink."

"Look!" She tried to point toward the front of the truck, but her hand wouldn't move.

A low guttural growl set the dogs to barking so loud that Greg looked at them instead of under the truck at the bobcat stretched out not five feet from Emily's outstretched hand.

"Bob…" she whispered.

"I thought your dog's name was Bill. Why are those dogs carrying on like that?"

"Cat…" she said.

Finally Greg understood what she said and tilted his head. He slipped an arm under her shoulders and one under her legs, picked her up, and carried her to the passenger's side of the truck, whistling as if nothing was the matter.

Either the man was crazy or he was a bobcat whisperer.

He opened the door, set her inside, and then jogged through the snow to the driver's side, got in, revved up the engine, and the bobcat ran out toward the mesquite trees.

"Whew!" He wiped his forehead. "I was scared that thing would take a swipe at my legs. Never saw one that big around these parts. If you hadn't seen it we might both be scratched and bitten all to hell."

"It's a good thing we got the cows and calves moved out of here or we'd have lost one by morning." That feeling of helping, of being needed, washed over her again, warming her soul from the core of her body to her outer skin.

She'd done it again: said *we* instead of *you*. Guilt slammed into her heart like a baseball and she mentally apologized to her grandfather for the slip.

"Are you okay?" he asked.

"I'm fine. The snow flat-out covered up that gopher hole."

"Want me to take you home?"

Home?

Where was it? Happy or Ravenna?

"I'm fine. I'm not hurt. Let's just get back to work so that when we go home we can get warm and not have to come back out in it today."

Greg's eyes locked with hers. "If you're sure."

"I'm sure. That big old bull with his horns didn't scare me like that cat and his growl." She managed a weak laugh.

―――

"We really need to talk," Greg said.

"Nothing to talk about."

"Yes, there is. I lied about that date and it wasn't right," he told her.

"Greg, everything happens for a reason, and I think that Dusty calling me and you thinking it was an old boyfriend was just the big curve that said for us to slow down. Things were going too fast. Yes, you are sexy as the devil. Yes, I'm attracted to you. A woman would have to be blind not to be. We have ranchin' in our blood and we have common interests, but I'm going home to Happy in a few days. It's where my roots are. We shouldn't start something that is just going to bring us pain when I leave," she said.

"But what if it's what would make us both happy?" he asked.

"It can't. My roots are in west Texas. Yours are here.

There's eight hours between the two," she said. "Tell you what, we'll slow down and give it a week, until after the Valentine's party, and then talk about it again."

He sighed and adjusted his glasses with his thumb. "And then what?"

"Then we reassess and see if a week without the kisses and the almost sex has made us rethink the attraction. Now, are we takin' the dogs home and bringing out the hay?"

"We'll take the dogs home, but Max is bringing the hay. We're going to load up the cubes and feed thirty lots of cows today. They need more than hay in this kind of weather," Greg said.

She held up her fingers. "Thirty lots. Four lots per truckload. If we hustle we can be done by dinner, right?"

He shook his head. "Hopefully there won't be a lot to do after dinner. Tomorrow, we'll be working with a full staff, so you won't have to help."

She cut her blue eyes across the cab of the truck. "Do I make you nervous, cowboy?"

"Am I making you nervous talkin' business sense? You know I'm right about it takin' more than a hundred acres to make a ranch," he shot right back.

"You don't make me nervous, and honey, if my heart is in it, I could make a ranch out of five acres. It's all about how much heart you put into it. Let's talk about something else. Where did you go to high school? I didn't recognize that tassel in the picture."

He drove slowly over the icy path toward the ranch house. "I went to high school in Houston, where my folks lived all my life. Dad hated ranching and he went to work in an oil company in Houston right out of college. They worked in the same firm and now they are partners in it. But in the summertime they let me come to the ranch. Nana wanted me to be a part of her and Grandpa's lives, and it sure saved a lot of hassle with nannies or sitters. Dad hated ranching, but Nana always said it skipped a generation, because I loved every bit of it."

"So it's your ranch now?"

"No, it's not mine yet. It will be mine when Nana thinks I've learned enough. I started at the bottom rung when I came to live here permanently. She said I had to learn it all before she handed it over to me," he said.

He was glad that the conversation had steered away from *Dusty, darlin'*, even if that was a girl cousin. "What about you? You live on the ranch your whole life?"

"From birth. And I couldn't wait to get away from it. I was going to be a lawyer or maybe an engineer. By the time the second college semester rolled around, I'd changed my major to business agriculture. It didn't take me long to realize where my heart was."

He parked in front of the dog pens. "There's no need for you to get back out in the cold. I can put the dogs in the pens and drag their boxes off by myself."

——~~~——

She didn't argue, since she was just barely able to feel her cheeks, and even through two pair of socks, her toes were tingling with the cold. She wanted to tell him about the old gals' interference in his love life, but that little bout with the bobcat said maybe it was a warning. God would strike her dead in a horrible way if she told anyone what went on behind the closed doors of the bazaar meetings.

Greg finished the job and hurried back to the truck. "This is crazy. We didn't have weather like this in December. I bet the thermometer has dropped ten more degrees, and that wind can cut right through jeans."

The blast that followed him into the truck told Emily that he wasn't exaggerating one bit. "Better the wind than a bobcat's claws. We'll work fast so we can snuggle up close to the fire."

He wiggled his eyebrows. "Snuggle?"

The desire to kiss him was so strong that she almost lost her resolve, almost forgot all about anything but Greg and always having him by her side. "Remember what I said, Greg Adams."

He was sexy even when his lips were blue with cold and his glasses were fogged over. His grin shot the temperature in the truck cab up, and it was her turn to swallow a groan. He drove straight to a barn, backed the truck in, and shook his head when she started to open the door. "These are fifty-pound bags of feed. I'll load them."

"I'm not a wimp. I've been tossing bags of feed for years. I'm going to help." She got out of the truck and headed toward the stacks of cattle cubes. The brand was the same that Gramps bought and griped about every time he had to resort to using it to supplement the hay. It didn't come cheap, but then things that were worth anything were costly.

When they had loaded the feed, Greg drove through blowing snow out to a lot at the back side of the ranch. "We'll start back here and work our way toward the front of the place. Max has already been here with the hay, so he's a few steps ahead of us. Hard to believe in this kind of weather that it's almost spring, isn't it?"

She nodded and inhaled the warm air inside the truck one more time before hopping out when he parked. Winter was supposed to be on its way out of the country in February, not hanging on like an old love to a relationship that had died long before.

"Crap," she mumbled. Every single thing that happened circled her thoughts back around to Greg.

She crawled up in the bed of the truck and handed feed down to him. He wasted no motions as he slit the tops open with his pocket knife, snapped it shut, and shoved it back in his pocket before picking up the bag and dumping it in the feed trough. It didn't take the cattle long to leave the big bale of hay behind and wander over to the feed trough.

"Look at them go after it," he said.

"To the cows, hay is steak. That stuff is chocolate cheesecake," she said.

"That your favorite dessert?"

She shook her head. "I like it just fine, but it's not my favorite."

"What is?"

It was on the tip of her tongue to say that he'd do just fine for dessert and she'd take it before dinner, after supper, or even for breakfast. She wasn't even particular about where. It could be in the hayloft, in a nice warm bed, or in the backseat of his truck. But she was the one who'd laid out the rules. A whole week and then a big party where lots of pretty women would be all dressed up and flirting with Greg. And that would be nothing compared to the bazaar auction.

"Well, what is your favorite dessert?" Greg dumped the final bag into the trough and tossed the empty bags in the back of the truck.

She jumped over the side, landed square on her feet, and beat him inside the cab. "I guess it would be pecan pie with ice cream. Or maybe chocolate sheet cake like my grandma used to make when I was a little girl. What is yours?"

"Peach cobbler and Dotty's cinnamon rolls right out of the oven when they're so gooey and hot that you have to blow on them before you can take the first bite."

Gooey.

Hot.

First bite.

Damn! Those words put pictures in her mind that shouldn't be there, visions that would make a sailor blush and a cowboy kick at the dirt in embarrassment. But by damn, it would sure enough warm her up.

Whoa, girl! She brought her thoughts to an abrupt halt.

"What are you thinking? It looks like you are fighting with yourself or an imaginary person. You seeing ghosts or something?" Greg chuckled.

"You might say that. Tell me more about the Valentine's party. Clarice and Dotty are all excited about going shopping for it, so it must be a big deal, but Dotty says that wild horses couldn't drag her to the thing. Rose and Madge are going, so why isn't she?"

"We belong to the North Texas Angus Association and they have a few parties a year. Sometimes they do a Valentine's party; sometimes not. This year they're having one. It's not a sit-down dinner but a dance with an open bar and refreshment table. The guys wear their Sunday getups, usually a jacket, and the ladies get all dolled up. Rose and Madge were married to ranchers, so they are still honorary members. Dotty wasn't, and it's hard to explain, but she wouldn't go if she could. She doesn't like big parties like that," he said.

"But she's all excited about the bazaar party."

"That's different. It's got to do with the church. That puts it in her ballpark." He parked at the next lot. "Ready to fight the cold again?"

"Might as well be. Don't want the cows to starve. Guess we could move them all into barns and take the baby calves in the house." She grinned.

"You tell Dotty that." He laughed.

Just before noon, they met Max and Louis, who drove up with a load of feed. Max hopped out and yelled, "Go on to the house. We'll get this one since we're loaded. When we got to the end of the line with the hay, we started working our way back with the feed. We get this one done and it's finished for the day, thank goodness. I can't feel my fingers anymore. Who would've thought we'd have this kind of weather in February? It ain't normal."

"Thanks! You'll get no argument from me. Louis, come on to dinner with him. Dotty will have enough to feed an army today. She's making tortilla soup," Greg hollered back.

Louis waved over his shoulder and nodded.

"Looks like we get to call it a day after all," Greg said.

"The snow is coming down harder. Maybe the weatherman was wrong," she said.

"Emily…"

"Greg…"

They both started at the same time.

"You go first," he said.

She didn't hesitate. "You ever think that maybe you should think of settling down?"

He turned on the windshield wipers and looked at her. "You askin' me to marry you?"

"No, sir," she said before she turned and looked out the window.

Chapter 9

TANGY TORTILLA SOUP SERVED WITH WARM, FRESHLY made corn tortillas tasted good after spending the day out in the blowing snow. But what tasted even better to Emily was the hot, freshly fried sopapillas. She made a hole in piping-hot, cinnamon-dusted Mexican bread and was in the process of filling it with honey when Dotty announced that she and Clarice would be working on their bazaar projects that afternoon.

"Speaking of which…" Clarice looked at Emily. "Did you tell Greg?"

"Tell me what, and pass the sopapillas," he said.

"That's way above my pay grade." Emily picked up the platter and handed it his way, their fingertips barely touching in the transfer. She let go before he had a good grip, and it took both of them doing some fancy juggling to keep from dropping the platter on the floor.

Clarice tucked her chin down and looked up at Emily. "Then I'll give you a raise."

Greg looked at Max. "What are they talkin' about?"

The older man shrugged. "Don't know what is going on, but if it's above Emily's pay grade, then I'm not sure I want to know."

Emily caught Clarice's eye and mouthed, "How much?"

Dotty nodded slightly and said, "Okay, okay! The

new plan for the bazaar this year is that we're having it at the ranch on the last Saturday in this month."

Greg cut a hole in the top of the Mexican pastry and picked up the honey jar. "In the house?"

Emily took a sip of sweet tea. Thank goodness they weren't talking about the dating sites. She'd have to have more than one raise and pay grade jump to tell Greg that story. "We're having it out in the sale barn. The homemade things will be displayed on tables. Folks will buy a ticket at the door for five dollars and they get supper, dancing, and visiting for their money. Dinner will be barbecue sandwiches and chips. The ladies will provide desserts."

"Y'all must be plannin' on sellin' a bunch of crafts and barbecue to do that." Greg smiled.

"Go on." Dotty nodded at Emily.

"You can tell the rest." She fidgeted.

Sometimes the bearer of news got strung up in the nearest pecan tree with a length of rope.

Clarice snapped her fingers. "You have been promoted and it's now within your pay grade. Tell him about the auction."

"We are having a cowboy auction. It goes like this…" She went on to tell about how the bachelors would sit in the middle of the floor and have to dance with the ladies who paid for a bidding fan and put up their dollar a dance.

By the time she got to the part about the auction itself, Greg was shaking his head emphatically.

"You didn't put my name on one of those chairs, Nana? Please tell me that you didn't." His words were to Clarice, but his eyes didn't leave Emily's face.

"Yes, I did. You have the number one chair and right next to yours is Mason Harper, and Louis, you get the number three chair," Dotty said.

Louis grinned and nodded. "My pleasure, ma'am. There's a couple of chicas that I've been flirting with. It'll be fun to see what I'm worth."

"Max?" Greg asked.

Max was not smiling one bit when he asked Clarice, "I'm auctioneering for it, right?"

She nodded. "You can have a choice. If you want to auction, you can. If not then we'll get Rose's nephew and you can be a dancin' cowboy."

"I'll auction," he said quickly.

Greg groaned. "What happens if I'm bought?"

Clarice smiled. "There is no *if*. You will bring a good sum to put into the scholarship fund. Just think of it this way—a lot of my prized bulls might not want to leave Lightning Ridge, but I can't keep them all and they go to the sale in the fall. Tell him what happens, Emily."

"You will have a date on the next Friday night. The lady gets to plan it and you have to pay for it. The ladies pay a dollar for each dance and then they will bid on whichever cowboy they liked best. Think of it as speed dating on your toes," she said.

"I bet he goes for big bucks," Louis said. "There's all kinds of women who'd like to chase him right up to the altar by summertime. I wonder why it is that brides always like to choose June for their wedding. Oh, well, it don't matter because from February to June is long enough to plan a wedding. Who are you bidding on, Emily?"

"I might give your chicas a run for their money." Emily winked.

Louis had thick dark hair, big brown eyes, and a round face. He was still young enough to blush and had thick dark eyelashes that most women would commit homicide to have.

"I'd rather see you give all them women after Greg a run for their money," he said.

"Why?" Dotty asked.

"I'd hate to take orders from some of the women around these parts," Louis said honestly.

"Dammit! I'd have to marry the woman for her to get to boss anyone on this ranch, and that ain't happening! I do have a say in who I marry, don't I?" Greg asked.

"I'm not so sure. A chica tells me she's going to marry me, I'd be afraid to tell her no. She might slit my throat in my sleep," Louis teased.

Dotty poked Clarice on the arm. "Looks to me like we're going to have a real lively sale."

Emily pushed her chair back. "Y'all don't need me for the afternoon, then?"

Clarice shook her head.

"If you change your mind, call me on my cell phone. I'm going out to take some nature photographs," she said.

Clarice looked at Greg.

"Don't look at me. I'm not going to take up knitting for your bazaar. I'm doing my part in being a worthless bull that you are selling off," he said.

"None of my bulls are worthless. Some are just keepers and some aren't. I'm only selling you for one Friday evening, so stop your whining. Think of it as…" Clarice giggled.

"As stud service," Dotty finished for her.

Jealousy, pure and simple, swept through Emily like

a Texas wildfire. She didn't want Greg going to bed
with another woman, and yet she'd been the one to put
the "slowdown" on their relationship.

"I'm going to drive into Bonham and pick up another
load of feed. We'll need twenty more bags to get us
through tomorrow. Then hopefully it'll clear off for the
year," Greg said.

Clarice and Dotty each claimed a recliner in the den and
pulled a ball of white cotton thread and a number-ten
crochet hook from their tote bags.

"Don't know why in the hell we make these. Folks
won't pay what they're worth, and the young girls
don't want them on their tables and chair backs.
They're too lazy to dust them, much less keep them
starched," Dotty grumbled.

"Let's make snowflakes instead. I can do one in an
hour, and I betcha they'll sell better," Clarice said.

"Why didn't you think of that before? We can sell
them as snowflakes or sew a feather in them and say
they are cowboy dream catchers," Dotty said.

Clarice kept crocheting. "I like that idea. We'll starch
them heavy, and instead of a feather, let's sew one of
those little buttons shaped like a boot that we bought last
time we were in the hobby shop. And we can put a jute
twine hanger on them. Did you decide on your four?"

Dotty nodded. "Yes, I did, and I already invited them
and started talkin' up the sale and how it would be so
nice if they bought me... I mean Greg... so we could
have a real date. Betcha we can turn out a dozen of
these this afternoon and it'll be something no one else is

doing. What are we going to do if he falls for one of the women we've been rustling up for him?"

Clarice laid her crochet down and whispered, "Emily won't let that happen. She's in love with my grandson. I can see it. But if Emily runs out of money and can't bid anymore, I'll get Rose to buy him and then give him to Emily afterward."

Dotty giggled like a little girl. "Sounds like fun to me. We haven't been this naughty since way back in high school. Emily and those dating sites kind of put a bounce back in our lives, didn't they?"

———

Emily drove to the stables, took a four-wheeler out of the shed, and slung the strap to a camera over her shoulder. She was going to take lots of pictures to show Taylor and Dusty when she went back to Shine Canyon.

The wind still rattled the limbs of the low-growing mesquite trees and the crooked scrub oaks, but the snow had finally stopped falling. Emily pulled her stocking hat lower over her ears and set out to the back of the ranch where the cabin was located. Maybe it would be remote enough that she could capture some really good pictures of deer, bunnies, or even a covey of quail.

She parked in the same spot that Greg had and started around the cabin, when she saw the deer herd right at the edge of the woods, not twenty feet ahead of her. She sat down on the back porch and held her breath as she slowly brought the camera up to eye level. The buck was an old man, sporting a rack that couldn't be covered with a bushel basket and several scars on his neck and body. A dozen does nosed about in the snow looking for green grass, and four fawns with spots still shining milled about their mother's long, spindly legs.

She let her breath out slowly and snapped a dozen times before the buck sniffed the air and spotted her. He bounded back into the woods with the does following him and the little fawns right behind them. She stood up slowly, looking around to see if there were any more surprises. A cottontail rabbit lit out from the edge of the porch in a blur, but if she'd tried to catch a picture, it wouldn't have been anything but a streak of light brown fur.

Cold crept through her coat and her toes were numb within an hour, but she had more than a hundred amazing pictures of mistletoe covered in ice, a bright red cardinal pecking at the snow, a robin searching for worms, and a litter of bobcats tumbling around with each other while a mother watched from under the low branches of a cedar tree.

"Are you the same one that I saw, or was that the poppa and he's off eyeballing one of our calves?" she whispered softly.

Our calves? Was that a slip of the tongue or a manifestation of the way she really felt? Or maybe her brain was frozen and thought she was back at Shine Canyon. Even though the snow had stopped, the wind was still bitter and there was firewood stacked up against the back of the cabin. She'd build a fire, make good strong campfire coffee, and get warm inside and out before she went back to the ranch house.

The kindling was wet, so it took several tries before she finally got a flame started with the last matches in the box. She let out a whoosh of pent-up air when it caught.

"Better put matches on a list to bring up here or the next person will have to rub two sticks together. Now surely there is coffee and a pot in here somewhere. Dammit! I hope that the pump isn't frozen." She talked to herself as she started by grabbing the handle of the pump and working it for a full minute before clear, cold water came gushing out into the dishpan below it.

She found an old blue granite pot shoved back in the corner, removed her gloves to keep from getting them wet, held the pot up to the edge, and caught enough water to rinse it out, flushing out two dead spiders and a couple of flies. She rinsed it three times to be sure that it was clean before filling it.

Gramps always used a heaping cup of grounds when he filled the pot, but since she'd only filled it half-full, she measured out enough for that amount and hung it over the fire. Then she squatted in front of the blaze and held her hands out to warm them.

"I wish you were here, Gramps. I'd tell you about Clarice. I like her a lot. And you could help me sort out this thing I have for Greg. There's something in my heart for him and it's more than just a sexual attraction. I can't leave Shine Canyon. I just cannot do it," she said and then leaned back against the worn old sofa to let her thoughts wander.

Every single song on the country music radio station reminded Greg of Emily. Something she said. Something she did. The way her head leaned to the left when she was thinking. Her walk. Her good common sense even when he didn't like it. He would have much rather let the relationship keep going in high gear than put the brakes on it.

Nana liked her. She and Dotty were already playing matchmaker between them, and Jeremiah had checked her out. She was the real deal, but west Texas was calling her name. If she would just think with her head instead of her heart she'd know that he was right. He leaned against the fender of the truck as the guys at the store loaded the fifty-pound sacks for him.

"You sure are quiet today," Buster said.

"Just thinking," Greg said.

"'Bout having to unload all this or that pretty girl out at the ranch? I heard that Miz Clarice done hired a brand-new assistant girl and that she's real pretty."

"Maybe I'm thinkin' about both," Greg said.

Buster tossed the last feed bag on the truck. "My aunt told me that y'all are plannin' a big ranch party and the ladies from the church are puttin' it on. She says there's goin' to be dancin' and you're goin' to auction off cowboys for dates with the women. What do I have to do to get my name in the pot to be auctioned off?"

"Call the ranch and tell my grandmother. She'll be tickled to put you down. You sure you want to do that? What if some old woman buys you and you have to go out with her and buy her dinner and all that?"

Buster's eyes twinkled. "I'm hopin' that some pretty little thing will just fall head over heels in love with me."

"Well, good luck with that. Ranch number is in the book," Greg said.

He left the radio on and the pickup door open as he unloaded the feed. When he finished he headed off toward the back side of the ranch. Maybe he'd light a fire and make a pot of coffee in the cabin and think about his grandpa some more. Or maybe he would sneak in a quiet afternoon nap on the sofa and not think of anything at all.

He parked behind the four-wheeler and sighed. He'd wanted to come up there to think, not listen to hunting stories from Louis or Max or anyone else who was out to flush a covey of quail. He might as well dash in, shoot the bull with them for a while, and have a cup of coffee. From the scent in the air, they already had a pot going.

He crawled out of the truck and ran across the yard, up on the front porch, and swung the door open to find Emily sitting on the floor with a cup in her hands and a smile on her face.

"Welcome home, honey. How was your day?" she teased.

He shed his hat, shoved his gloves into his coat pockets, and hung both hat and coat on nails beside the door. "Day went fine. You make plenty of that coffee? How was your day, darlin'?"

"My day was great," she said.

"I love campfire coffee," he said as he poured a cup and took a sip. "Good Lord, Emily, this would make one of those energy drinks look like lemonade."

"Good, ain't it?" she said.

He sat down beside her and leaned back against the sofa. "What put you in such a good mood?"

She shrugged. "I like where I am today. I like my life. I like my memories, and even though I miss Gramps, it's okay. I'm always going to miss him, just like I'm always going to miss my dad. They wouldn't want me to whine around and carry on, and besides, this is damn good coffee on a bitter cold day. And I saw a whole herd of deer, and I got the pictures to prove it."

The second sip didn't try to melt all the enamel off his teeth like the first one did, so he gave the third one a try. It wasn't bad at all.

"You buzzing yet?" she asked.

"Almost!" He grinned. "It's just about strong enough to give me a peyote vision."

"Didn't know you had Indian blood."

"Grandpa had a little bit, but I was remembering an old Western that I saw years ago."

"Did you see the size of that chicken?" She quoted a line from an old Western movie, *Young Guns*.

"I'll never forget that line in the movie. This coffee comes pretty close to giving me visions of chickens that big too. Did you watch it with your grandpa?"

"More than one time. He loved *Young Guns*, and I swear he knew the dialogue almost line for line. He always said that if coffee wasn't strong enough to wake you up that you might as well drink water. Have you gotten over Clarice loving my Gramps when she was young?" Emily asked.

"No. Maybe. I don't know yet. It's okay for me to have loved and lost in my lifetime, but I've always thought Nana had wings and a halo and loved only Grandpa."

Emily laughed out loud. "Kind of hard to visualize grandparents being young and hot in lust, isn't it?"

He snarled his nose. "That's just wrong to talk like that."

She laughed again. "Honey, human nature is the same, no matter where the place or the time. Back in caveman days, the men lusted after the women and they still do. And believe me, the women lusted after the men too, and they still do."

"Want to go into that with more detail?" He grinned.

She shook her head. "Well, cave women did some lusting too, and that's all I'm going to say about that. I found a deck of cards over there on the kitchen table. Want to play some gin rummy this afternoon while we drink this coffee?"

"Oh, Greg Adams, darlin', where are you? I heard you were back here all alone." A thin, tinny voice called out from behind the front door.

Emily jerked her head around and narrowed her eyes into slits. "*Greg, darlin'*. Don't you be fussin' at me over Dusty no more."

"I have no idea who that is," he whispered.

"Let me in, you sexy devil. I drove through ice and snow, but we can sure warm each other up. I found you and your big old ranch and I like what I see," she said.

Greg went to the door and cracked it just enough to see outside.

Emily peeked out from behind the curtain. Oh, sweet Jesus, that was the stripper that Dotty had been fussing about.

"Look what I brought just for you." She whipped open her long denim duster to reveal nothing but red thong underbritches and a low-cut red lace bra.

What in the hell had Dotty told her when she was playing at being Greg?

"Open the door. It's cold out here and I've driven a long way. It's been long enough to go without us meeting each other," she said.

Emily raced from window to door, stepped in front of Greg, and threw the door wide open. "Who in the hell are you?"

"I might ask you the same thing," the woman said. "I'm the one that intends to show Greg a good, good time. I can learn to love the little baby cows."

"You bastard," Emily slung over her shoulder at Greg. "I'm going to take a hammer to that damned computer. You promised me when I got pregnant that you'd never put your picture on those damned porn sites again."

Greg's face registered pure shock.

"You are Greg Adams who owns this whole big Lightning Ridge Ranch? I saw your picture on the website when I searched out the ranch." The woman snapped her duster shut and held it tight with her hands.

"I am Greg Adams," he said.

"But he doesn't own this ranch. I don't know where you got your information," Emily said.

"PlentyOfFish.com. I knew it was too good to be true. It's creeps like you who ruin it for us. I hope you do tear up his computer and then take that hammer to his head," the woman said before she marched off the porch, crawled into a late model red car, and drove away.

"What in the hell was that all about?" he asked.

"Some crazy woman that thinks she met you on a dating site. Haven't you ever heard of PlentyOfFish.com?"

"Hell, no, and I don't do dating sites, and if someone has put my picture on there as a joke, I'm going to shoot them," he said.

"Well, you are welcome."

"For what?" he asked.

"I saved your ass again."

"Again."

"Admit it." She poked him on the arm. "You need me to save you from sorrow, bobcats, and now wanton hussies."

He finally grinned. "Okay, I need you to save me. I'm admitting it. But Emily, I don't have my name on a dating site."

"Well, evidently someone thinks that you are on one."

"And whoever did it, I bet it was that ornery Buster down at the feed store. He was entirely too friendly today. I'll get him later, but I'm not going to let it spoil my day right now. Let's play strip poker." His eyes glittered. "If I can't partake of the wanton hussy, then surely we can partake of some strip poker."

"After the Valentine's party I'll play poker with you. I will take all your clothes and make you walk home naked and barefoot in the snow." She'd gotten off easy that time, but the ladies had better be a hell of a lot more careful. She might not be there the next time to run interference for them.

"Rummy it is," he said.

He shuffled the cards and handed them to her to deal. When she had her cards fanned out before her, he said, "I remember the first time I played in this cabin with my grandpa. I'd been playing with the guys at the bunkhouse and thought I was unbeatable. Didn't know that they'd let me win a few times just to keep me happy. How did that woman know where to find me?"

She studied her cards. "Gramps and Daddy never ever let me win. I was fifteen years old before I ever won a game. It was just before Daddy got killed and I did a victory dance all over the living room floor. Some of the guys at the bunkhouse probably saw your truck drive by and figured you were coming back here. If she stopped and asked they would have told her."

It wasn't a lie, so God shouldn't be sending that big mother-of-all-damned-bobcats to tear her limb from limb.

Greg glanced at his cards and then looked back at her. "I guess so. If I had whoever told her about me, I'd string them up by their toenails. After I figured out that the guys had let me win, I wished they hadn't. Gramps asked me if I'd teach him to play. Of course, he whipped me soundly several times before I figured out that he knew all about the game. Has anyone ever told you that your eyes are mesmerizing, Emily? You could walk into a bank and rob it with nothing but your eyes."

"I might give that a try if there's another drought year. I'd hate to borrow money against the ranch. Stealing it might be a better alternative. And for your information, darlin', that is one of the best pickup lines I've heard in a long time. And Miz Clarice said you weren't a romantic."

"It's the truth. I'm surprised that some old cowboy hasn't already proposed just to get to wake up every morning to look into your blue eyes."

He wanted to reach across the space and run a thumb down her jawline, cup her chin in his palm, and lean in for a kiss. He wanted to watch those pretty blue eyes snap shut just before his lips found hers. More than any of that, he wanted to make wild, passionate love to her on the deerskin rug in front of the fire.

"You are a charmer as well as a businessman. Speaking of which, I wonder how much that woman intended to charge you for her services or if she was out to marry you and get the whole ranch?"

"Just speakin' the truth, and honey, she said she could learn to like baby cows, remember?" he answered.

"Are you trying to throw me off my game?" she asked.

He laid a hand over his heart. "You hurt me right here, accusing me of such a dastardly deed as throwing you off your game. Honestly, Emily, you could be a runway model."

"Yeah, right. I'm too short and my hips are way too big," she argued. "I'm just a plain old ranchin' woman looking forward to dancin' all night at a party."

His heart felt like a rope had been tied around it and a three-hundred-pound cowboy was on each end, pulling with all their might. He didn't even like to think about the other cowboys dancing with Emily, but what could he do? They'd be lined up like hot little kids in front of a snow cone stand, just waiting to dance with her, especially since Clarice was her date.

—◆◆◆—

Neither the heat from the fireplace nor the excellent hand she'd been dealt had a thing to do with those hot little sparks landing everywhere around her like multicolored bits of fire. Greg's denim work shirt was unbuttoned to show the oatmeal-colored thermal shirt underneath. Never before had a thermal undershirt fallen into a sexy category in her world. A tiny little patch of chest hair had snuck out at the neckband, and she had to grasp her cards tightly to keep her hands from reaching out to see if it was as soft as it looked.

"Maybe I will dance with all the pretty girls there while you are dancing with the cowboys. Does that make you jealous?" he asked.

"Damn straight. Can't you see the green glow coming off me? And I bet there's going to be a hell of a lot more girls there than cowboys," she said. At least sixteen more than there would have been without the dating sites.

"Don't tease me, Emily."

She looked over the top of her cards right into his eyes. "Who says I'm joking? I will be jealous. That's the gospel truth according to Emily Cooper, who does not blaspheme for fear of being zapped into a pile of ashes on the spot. High-octane coffee loosens the tongue more than moonshine, don't it?"

His gaze drew her past the lenses of his glasses and into the depths of his heart.

"It does, and I'm going to be jealous too," he admitted.

"Good. I'm glad. Now let's play cards and drink coffee while we enjoy a perfectly wonderful afternoon together in this cabin."

"Will you come back up here with me next week after this party is over?" he asked.

"Are you asking me on a date, Mr. Adams?"

"I am." He nodded.

"Then my answer is yes, if you don't find someone who takes your eye at the bazaar auction."

Chapter 10

CLARICE AND DOTTY WERE IN THE KITCHEN HEATING up leftover soup and stuffing slices of chicken, lettuce, tomatoes, and picante sauce into flour tortillas, making sandwich wraps for supper, when Emily got home that evening.

"Shut the door, child. That cold wind is chillin' my feet," Dotty said.

Emily hurriedly pulled the door closed and sniffed the air as she hung up her coat and hat and removed her boots. "Something sure smells good. Is that onions and peppers?"

"Louis made his famous picante sauce this afternoon. We made wraps for supper to go with the leftover soup," Clarice said.

"Did you get any bazaar things made?" Emily peered over Clarice's shoulder at the soup pot. "You are going to have to start putting sticky notes on the cabinet doors. That refrigerator is completely covered."

"Yes, we did get bazaar things made," Clarice said. "We've got one more week and then we'll take down the notes. We do it once every six months. We love those little notes. They spice up our days."

"What do you do with them when you take them down?" Emily asked.

Dotty giggled. "We put them in a shoebox. This will be our second one. Then we put the box on the attic. They're like them things they bury in the ground and then dig up. Someday, in a hundred years, there will be a family in this house who will find all that shit. By then sticky notes will be a thing of the past and they'll think they've found some big history thing. Hell, by then they won't even need computers. Everyone will just get one implanted in their big toe and they can send their thoughts without even typing or writing. Fingers will disappear and that'll be a damn shame because they're pretty damned useful for other things. And to answer your question, we made cowboy dream catchers," Dotty said.

"And I even know what you meant when you said OMG!" Clarice beamed.

"Can I see one of the dream catchers?"

"They are in there in the den. I made four and Dotty made five, but she used the center of the doily she'd been working on yesterday, so she didn't really do more than me," Clarice pointed out.

Emily peeked around the corner to see where Greg was and whispered, "That woman, the stripper you met on the dating site, showed up, Dotty, and she wasn't wearing anything under a denim duster but underwear. I had to pretend to be Greg's wife to get her to leave."

"What woman?" Clarice asked.

"I'll tell you all about it. Follow me, Clarice. Did he figure anything out?" Dotty tilted her head toward her apartment.

"No, I fixed it," Emily whispered.

"You go on in there and look at the dream catchers with him and I'll explain to Clarice. I knew that damned old hussy was up to no good." Dotty grabbed Clarice's arm and led her out of the kitchen.

Emily crossed the kitchen, went through the dining room, and across the foyer to the den. Greg was already there looking at the dream catchers with amusement written all over his face.

"How many folks do you think will really buy these?" He chuckled.

"I'm buying several and putting them up for next year's Christmas presents. Taylor will hang it over the rearview mirror in his truck, and Dusty will put hers on her vanity. We all believe in dreaming. Don't you?" She held one up in the air.

"I don't dream. I believe that you make your own future and dreams have little to do with business," he said.

"How sad."

"Why would you say that? Aren't you plannin' on takin' what's left of a ranch and turning it around to be a big working business? That's not dreams, and it's not fate. It's sweat, hard work, and lots of business savvy."

"I believe that paths are laid out before us. If we travel down one it will take us to a much different future than if we took the one right beside it. Yes, it takes work and business smarts, but we make the choices that are laid upon our hearts. And we work with what we have in the way of intelligence and soul for that day. It's our choice, but we do have to live with the consequences."

Dotty stuck her head in the door. "Supper is ready. We're eating off the bar tonight so y'all can stand in here and admire the pretty things or come eat. It's your choice."

"See, it's our choice, but we have to live with the consequences of what we decide. We can go eat and not be hungry, or we can stand here and look at all this hard work and starve to death." Emily laughed. "I'll be right there, Dotty. I've got to go wash up first."

"Beat you up the stairs," Greg said.

"What's the winner get?"

"Kissed," he said.

"Not this week, cowboy," she said.

"What if, because you've slowed us down, our relationship takes off like a hound dog chasing a coyote? What if we find that the slowing down didn't do anything but fan the flames so they are even hotter?" he asked.

"We'll go down that path when the road forks," she said.

Emily dipped out a bowl of soup, set it on a plate, and added two chicken wraps. She carried it carefully to the table and sat down just as Greg found his way back to the kitchen. He'd changed into clean jeans and a knit shirt that stretched across his muscular chest. She caught a whiff of fresh shaving lotion and swallowed hard. In her mind's eye, she could see the path forking right up ahead of her. One way led to Shine Canyon, the other right into Greg Adam's arms.

She blinked several times to clear her mind and studied the two older women at the table. Dotty was dressed in a red sweat suit with a picture of kittens on the front, and Clarice wore jeans and a red flannel shirt with an embroidered picture of a kitten on the pocket.

"Y'all like cats?" she asked.

Dotty looked at her with a blank expression.

Clarice smiled. "We both love cats, but it's just a coincidence that we are both wearing them on our clothes today. This is one of my favorite shirts for cold days because it's worn and soft. Dotty's son sent her that outfit for Christmas, and since he's coming for the bazaar this year, she figures she'd better wear it a lot so it will look worn. Jeremiah fusses at her if she's putting things up for good."

"Is Jeremiah going to be on the auction list?" Greg asked as he sat down right beside Emily.

"Hell, no! He ain't a cowboy. Working on this ranch when he was in high school taught him right quick that he did not like cow shit and working out in the cold or heat," Dotty said.

God was punishing Emily!

Either that or the devil loved her.

Maybe it was both because they'd put the biggest of all temptations right beside her. She wanted so badly to touch Greg, to take off his glasses and kiss his eyelids, to trace his lip line with her fingertip. It would be so easy to give in to what she'd been fighting all afternoon up at the cabin. All she had to do was lean over six inches and her shoulder would touch his. She could reach under the tablecloth and lay a hand on his thigh and no one would even know.

She didn't have to do either.

He leaned to his left to reach for the bowl of picante and the chips and his whole left side stuck to hers like they were both magnetized and were fused together. Dotty and Clarice would have to call the Ravenna Volunteer Fire Department to bring the Jaws of Life to get them apart.

"I love kittens. Do you?" Clarice was asking when Greg moved away from Emily and she could think sanely again.

"Oh, yes. I always wanted one, but Gramps was

allergic to cat hair. We had barn cats, but I couldn't bring them inside. I named them all, and when I was little, we had funerals when one died. After he got sick, Gramps confessed that he didn't always tell me when one died because he hated to see me cry," she said.

Bless Clarice's heart! Emily could hug her for taking her thoughts away from Greg. Even unfortunate kittens were better than what she'd been thinking.

Then, be damned, if Greg didn't decide that he needed more chips, and there he was plastered to her side again. She looked over her shoulder only to find his face close enough to kiss and his eyes boring into hers. It was a wonder her hot breath didn't fog his glasses right over.

"We aren't allergic to cats in this house. Greg, next time you find a litter about ready to wean in the barn, you bring one in for Emily. What color do you want?" Clarice asked.

"Green," she whispered.

"Sorry, darlin', we don't have green cats." Clarice giggled.

She gulped and quickly said, "I mean green-eyed. I want one with those pretty green eyes. Other than that, I don't care about color. I like them all. Orange, black, calico, any of them."

The sizzle was practically audible in the distance separating them as he straightened up in his chair again. "There's a litter out in the barn now. The momma's been hissing at them, so I started giving them dry food last week. Want to go out there and pick one out after supper?" Greg asked.

It was on the tip of her tongue to say yes, but she shook her head. "I can't."

"Why?"

"I'd get attached if I did and I'd cry when I had to leave it behind," Emily said honestly.

"When you leave you can take it with you. There's always plenty of kittens around here in the springtime," Dotty said.

"And there's another reason," Emily said. "If there's a litter, I'd feel sorry for the ones left out in the cold. You pick out one for me, Greg, and I'll be happy with it, even if it doesn't have green eyes."

"Okay, I'll see what I can do. It'll have to use dirt in a box until we can get to town and buy a litter pan," he said.

"There's still half a bag of litter in the pantry and an old plastic dishpan that she can use," Clarice said. "Remember Smoky?"

"Holy shit, Nana! That was fifteen years ago. You sure that litter is even still good?" Greg said.

"Holy shit, Gregory!" Dotty roared at her own joke. "Litter ain't got no expiration date on it. It's just for cats to scratch in, not to eat!"

Clarice explained, "Greg was fifteen and a little gray cat got thrown out in the grocery store parking lot. Nothing doing but we bring it home. We bought litter and a pan and food and the whole nine yards, but Smoky hated being in the house. He whined and carried on until we had to put him outside. We had a lot of gray kittens for the next ten years and then he disappeared and we started getting less and less gray ones."

Greg chuckled. "I think he's got a great-grandson out there in the barn. One of those that I saw tumbling around with his siblings was solid gray. I'd forgotten about old Smoky, but I do remember what a big boy he grew up to be."

"Oh, yeah, and evidently quite the mama cat's idea of a good father," Clarice said.

After supper, when he disappeared out into the darkness, Emily wished that she would have said that she would go with him. She had never had a pet that was allowed in the house, and she'd passed up the opportunity to pick out her favorite. So she just paced the kitchen floor and looked out the window at the end of every loop around the table.

Dotty had gone to her room to watch television.

Clarice was in her apartment reliving her past by reading letters again.

Max and Louis hadn't come back to the house after lunch.

Did people on the outside of a birthing room feel like she did as they waited for the first cries of a newborn baby? She peeked out the window toward the barn and squealed when she saw the lights go out. That meant that Greg was on his way back with her kitten. She rubbed her hands together. What would it look like? Hell, at this point she didn't care if it had yellow or blue eyes or even one of each and was the ugliest critter ever born to a mama cat.

He opened the back door and his hands were empty. Her heart dropped to the floor and tears welled up behind her eyelashes. She swallowed hard. She would not weep over a damn kitten that she'd never even known.

"Couldn't catch one, huh?" she finally said.

"Nope." He grinned.

It wasn't funny, not to her. But then he couldn't know how much she really wanted a pet her whole life. A kitten. A puppy. Just something that would love her and she could keep in the house but preferably a kitten.

He reached into the deep pockets of his coat and brought out a squirming ball of yellow fur. "Its eyes are blue like yours."

She reached for it. "You are mean to tease me like that. Oh, look, it likes me. Is it a boy or a girl? I have to know, so I can name it."

"I didn't tease you, darlin'. I couldn't catch one, but I could catch two because they were playing together. Besides, if I brought one in the house, it would whine and cry. Two will be playmates and sleep together." He pulled out a smoky gray one with the greenest eyes she'd ever seen.

"Oh!" she gasped. "Will Clarice mind me having two?"

"You could have probably brought in the whole litter. But these were the only two I saw, so they are what you get."

She hugged them both up under her chin, petting and talking in a high-pitched voice to them. "Oh, you are the prettiest babies in the whole world and we're going to get along so good. You can sleep in my room, yes you can, and you can play chase under my bed, and I'm going to love you so much."

"They are both boys, which will mean a trip to the vet when they are four months old or you'll have problems with them marking their territory in the house," he said.

She held them up and pursed her lips as she looked at the yellow one. "You look like a miniature lion, so you are Simba after the critter in *The Lion King*. And what is your name if yellow boy gets an important name like Simba? You are one chubby little fellow. Help me, Greg."

He shook his head. "Oh, no! I'm not naming cats for you."

"Fat Boy. If you don't help me this boy will go through life as Fat Boy." She giggled.

"Bocephus," he said quickly.

"Perfect, and Hank Williams Jr. appreciates it, I'm sure."

"I'm surprised that you even knew that was Hank's nickname."

"Hey! I'm like the song Tammy sang about being country when country wasn't cool, so I know who Hank is and his nickname. I know his father and his history. Gramps loved Bocephus and it fits my boy cat just fine. So the boys are Simba and Bocephus. I like it. Will you bring the litter and the pan up to my room? I'll put it on the tile in the bathroom so it'll be easy to keep swept up when they scratch it out on the floor," she said.

She carried the wiggling fur balls and he followed behind her with a blue plastic pan, half a bag of litter, and two bowls: one for water and one for the jar full of dry food he'd fetched from the big bag in the barn.

Clarice and Dotty peeked around the corner of the hallway leading to Clarice's little apartment, where they'd been hiding all along.

"Look at them, taking their first babies up to the bedroom. Simba and Bocephus. I like that. We sure dodged a bullet when that hussy showed up here, but I told y'all Emily would keep our secret. She even did better than keeping it, she helped us. We need that girl on Lightning Ridge," Clarice said.

"Don't be gettin' your hopes too damned high, old girl. It might not pan out. She thinks with her heart and he thinks with his head. It ain't going to be easy," Dotty whispered.

"Listen to them giggling. There's nothing like baby kittens to bond a couple, now is there? I remember our first house cats when Lester and I married. We used to get so tickled at the way they walked all sideways and cocky. And Dotty, it might not work out, but it won't be because I didn't do everything in my power to make it happen."

Dotty poked her on the arm. "You've got everything you ever wanted except Marvin, but I'm tellin' you, if you have a heart attack because she leaves, I'm going to die with you. Losing that sumbitch husband of mine wouldn't be as tough as losing my best friend. Might as well just go on and die with you as I drink myself to death."

"You are full of shit, Dotty!" Clarice said.

"Why, Clarice Adams, such talk comin' out of your mouth! You been hangin' around with me too long. Let's go to my room and make some of that microwave popcorn that tastes like damned old Styrofoam and break out a bottle of cold Pepsi to celebrate our new grandcats." Dotty grinned.

"When we go to Walmart this week, we'll buy blue baby blankets and cute little collars," Clarice said.

"You know what that makes us, right?"

Clarice raised an eyebrow. "What? Grandmas?"

"Hell no. If they'd have gotten dogs we would be grandbitches. They got kittens so we are grandpussies."

"Dotty!"

She put her hand over her mouth and giggled. "That

old floozy that showed up at the cabin don't have a thing on us."

"You are horrible."

"Yes, I am and proud of it. When we go to Walmart I'm going to buy one of those tree things to sit in the corner of the den for our grandkitties to climb on while we are babysitting them. You know she's not going to leave them all alone up there in her room while she is out working with Greg on the ranch. Like I said before, we can't go countin' the chickens before they are hatched, but I do believe we might have worked some magic with our kitten shirts today." Dotty looped her arm into Clarice's and they tiptoed to Dotty's room.

"And we didn't even know that she liked cats when we wore them," Clarice whispered.

Chapter 11

EMILY PUSHED THE COVERS BACK AND LEANED OVER the side of the bed to watch the kittens chase each other and fight with the fringe on the chenille bedspread. When they tried to climb the side of the bedspread, she swept them up into her arms, kissed them on their cute little foreheads, put them back on the floor, and watched her step on the way to the bathroom. They fought with her toes, and then Simba chased Bocephus behind the potty and into the corner.

"Sing to him, Bo. He's mean as a lion, but you can tame him with your singing." She laughed.

As if the kitten understood her, he started to meow pitifully until his brother bounded out of the corner and they rolled on the floor, chewing on each other's tails and ears until they grew tired and fell fast asleep on the rug.

"It's amazing how you do that," she whispered. "One minute you are fierce and mean as rattlesnakes, and the next you are sleeping like sweet little babies."

She'd barely finished brushing her teeth when her cell phone ringtone said that Taylor was calling. She had to dig the phone out of her hip pocket, and her jeans had been tossed into a dirty clothes hamper. She finally picked up on the fifth ring.

"Good morning. You are calling early. Is everything all right out there?"

"You sound chipper before the sun is up," Taylor said.

"I've got cats. A gray one named Bocephus and a yellow one named Simba. And they are so cute. If I didn't wake up in a good mood with them around, there would be something severely wrong with me. Simba is the alpha male like a fluffy miniature lion, and Bocephus is gray and slick and he's the lover, not the fighter."

"I sneeze when I'm within twenty feet of a cat," Taylor said.

"You and Gramps both. You'd think y'all were blood kin instead of shirttail kin."

"You can have a kitten now if you want it. I can't come see you if you do, but you can still come see me. You'll have to shed all your clothes and take a shower before you come in the house, but it can be done," Taylor said.

"You are full of shit, Taylor Massey. You should see them. They're sleeping like two little fur balls on the bathroom rug right now. A minute ago they were trying to tear each other's ears plumb off." She laughed.

"Nothing about a cat is cute. They're just overgrown rats with fluffy tails and more meat on their bodies. I'll get you a puppy if you'll come home tomorrow. You can even keep it in the house. I'm not allergic to dogs, just cats," he said.

"I'll keep fifty cats in the house if I want to. It's my house and I'm bringing Simba and Bocephus home with me. Dotty said I could," she said.

"Hey, don't go all Rambo on me." Taylor laughed. "I didn't call to fight with you."

"I'm sorry," she said.

"I really would get you a puppy, two if you want,"

Taylor said. "I won't even make you take a shower before you come in my house. I'll just send Dusty out with one of those sticky rollers to run all over you," Taylor teased.

"You probably aren't even allergic to cats. What you are allergic to are those damn cigarettes," she fussed.

"Leave them cats out there and I'll have two big old fat puppies waiting for you," Taylor said.

"Good night, Taylor." She hung up without arguing any further.

Simba woke up, yawned, and sat down at her feet, looked up, and started to purr so loudly that Bocephus came to check on his brother.

When she picked them up, they immediately snuggled down together in her lap. "Puppy, my ass. I might have a puppy, but only if y'all like it."

<hr />

Clarice looked up from her morning newspaper when Emily made it to the kitchen the next morning. "Good morning. Did the new kittens keep you up?"

She headed straight for the coffeepot. "No, it was pretty quiet all night. I didn't even hear snoring. What's on the agenda today?"

"The cleaning ladies come on Monday. They missed last week because they were off to a family reunion. Three sisters, so when one is gone, they all are. They'll be here all day. We'll be working on our bazaar stuff. I'd planned for us to go into town and shop today, but I've put it off until Wednesday," Clarice said.

"You can help Greg feed again this morning and we'll take care of the new babies," Dotty said. "Bring the litter pan down to the utility room. We'll have to get another one when we go shopping in a couple of days, so we don't have to keep moving it."

Emily took a deep breath. "It's two kittens. Greg brought in a gray one and a yellow one. We named them Bocephus and Simba."

Dotty clapped her hands. "Of course not. Now we won't fight over who gets to hold the baby."

Clarice winked at Dotty on the sly. "I get the gray one."

"We'll just see about that. I bet they both like me better than you, anyway. I had cats in the house the whole time Jeremiah was home. Lord, that boy drew strays to his side like a red flower draws a hummingbird. If there was a stray within forty miles, he'd find it and come totin' it home. If we'd been twenty minutes later getting to the grocery store that day, the gray cat Greg rescued would have gone home with us instead of you," Dotty said.

Greg yawned and dug at his eyes with his fists as he headed for the coffeepot. "I hear the talk of the morning isn't on the bazaar or that date auction y'all cooked up, but it's on the new kittens."

"We're babysitting while y'all feed this morning. We don't want them to get lonely. And besides, the cleaning ladies are coming. The vacuum might scare them," Clarice said.

Greg filled a mug and carried it to the table. "I peeked in at them. They're ferocious attack cats. They'd tear that vacuum up if it came at them. They told me they were going to practice learning their fighting skills with y'all's crochet thread this morning."

━∾━

After breakfast, Greg and Emily donned coats, hats, and gloves and were on their way out the back door when Max yelled at them from the cab of his truck. "I've got plenty of help for feeding this morning, but Albert called in a while ago. Now his wife is sick and Louis has gotten a second dose of it, so they're both staying home."

Greg groaned. "I guess that means we'll do the stable duty until he gets back."

"Horses get all skittish around most strangers, but they liked Emily and they'll tolerate you." Max chuckled.

"You mind?" Greg asked Emily.

"Work is work and it's all got to get done on a daily basis. When we get done, can we exercise the horses?"

"Not can. Have to. Albert usually recruits a hand or two to help him with that part, but they'll all be busy today. I hope this is the last of winter. Spring is busy, but it's routine busy. Snow in February is a bitch."

Emily crammed her cowboy hat down over a stocking hat that had been pulled down over her ears and crawled inside Greg's truck.

"Hey, cowboys open doors for their ladies," he said.

"Hey, today I'm hired help, and I've been opening my own doors since I was old enough to reach the handle. And darlin', I'm not your lady," she said.

He got into the truck and drove toward the stables. "What are you, Emily?"

She hesitated for a minute. "Your friend."

He wiggled his eyebrows. "With or without benefits?"

"We'll cross that path when we get to it. The one we are on right now leads to the stables," she said.

Paths.

That word kept popping up in everyone's conversations.

Nana saying that she chose the path when Greg had said, "Nana, just think if y'all had the technology that we have today, Marvin could have texted you or emailed you and it wouldn't have gotten lost the way it did."

"No, thank you. There is something about a letter that you can hold in your hands even after sixty years and still experience the emotions that you felt that day. An email doesn't have the same feel. Now go on to bed and let me get back to living in the past. It's a good place for me to visit on these cold evenings. And Greg, the path I wound up on led me to a wonderful life. I wouldn't have you if I hadn't traveled down it," she had said.

Emily kept talking about the paths behind them and the ones ahead of them and being careful to choose the right one.

It seemed that every time he poked his head in Nana's door these past weeks, that box of letters was close to her. *Something about a letter that you can hold in your hand, even sixty years later.*

The idea appeared like a cartoon bubble above his head and he knew exactly what he was going to do that evening before he went to bed.

Emily bailed out of the truck the second it stopped. She jogged to the long building, sucking icy cold air into her lungs and wondering if they'd freeze before she could even see one horse. The wind whistled through the center aisle, creating six-inch-tall tornadoes with loose straw strewn about the concrete floor. She didn't stop until she'd loaded a wheelbarrow with a small rectangular bale of straw, a shovel, and a bucket of feed and pushed it to the first stall.

"You get right at it, don't you?" Greg followed her lead.

"Got lots of work to do, and these horses are eager for a little exercise. Come on, Star Baby, we'll get your apartment all cleaned while you eat your breakfast and then we'll go for a gallop out in the snow. It'll be melted off tomorrow, so you'd best enjoy the feel of it on your hooves. This will most likely be the last that you see this year," she talked to the big black stallion as she led the horse out into the center aisle, tied him to a center post, and draped a full feedbag over his neck. She stopped long enough to pet him and kiss him right between the eyes.

"Your cats will be jealous," Greg called out from the other end of the stable.

"Not if you don't tell them."

"I won't have to say a word. They'll smell the horse on your lips when you kiss them," he said.

She giggled and ran the blade of the shovel under the dirty, wet straw and tossed it into the wheelbarrow. Would Greg taste horse on her lips if he kissed her right then?

They worked stall after stall and finished at mid-morning before he said another word. When he did open his mouth it was just to say, "Time to saddle up. It'll take right up to dinnertime to get them all ridden even fifteen minutes each."

"What are we doing after our noon meal?"

"You can do whatever you want. I've got some errands to run in town. Want to go with me?"

"No, I want to ride each horse longer than fifteen

minutes. If we aren't done by noon, you can run errands and I'll ride the rest of them. And Greg, I don't need a saddle. I can exercise them bareback."

"Not Star Baby. He's wild as the March wind," he said.

She led him out into the center aisle and crooned into his ear a minute before she hiked a boot on the rungs of a stall door, held his reins, and mounted. "There, there, pretty boy. We'll ride free and wild like horses were supposed to be ridden. See you in half an hour, Greg. We're headed up to the cabin and back."

"Well, damn!" he exclaimed as he hopped on the bare back of Wild Bill and rode after her. It had been years since he'd ridden bareback and though exhilarating, it took every bit of his concentration to stay put and not slide right out onto the frozen ground.

She rode with wild abandon, hanging on to her hat with one hand and the reins with the other, giving the feisty horse all the speed and power that he wanted. She'd be rubbing him down for a good thirty minutes when they got back to the stables. But it was a beautiful sight to watch the way that she and the horse connected and became one on the ride to the old cabin. She had slid off and was giving him a handful of grass that she'd found in a spot where the sun had melted the snow when Greg rode up into the yard.

"You planning on riding back at that speed or walkin' him back?" he asked.

"Whatever he wants to do is fine with me. This is his exercise program, not mine. I'll rub him down good. He loved being set free," she said.

Greg slid off Wild Bill to let him catch his wind. Emily had said a week, but that was her rule, not his. He marched over to her side, put a hand on each shoulder, and kissed her passionately. She tasted like cold morning and coffee mixed together with just a hint of breathlessness.

"Think about that while we are getting through this helluva long week. Better not wait too long or he'll get chilled." Greg hopped on his horse, turned Wild Bill around, and started back toward the stables. He hadn't gone five feet when he lost his balance and slid right off the side, landing in the cold wet grass.

Emily hopped off her horse and ran back to him. "Are you hurt?"

He sat up and dusted off his jeans with his hat. "Just my pride. You are right, ma'am. I do need you. I could have laid here and died."

She rolled up on her toes and kissed him on the cheek. "Since you didn't die, I bet my horse can beat yours back to the stables."

Greg hopped back on and gave Wild Bill all the rein he needed to race. Both horses were sweating and both riders were gasping when they reached the stables. Emily slid off Star Baby's back and immediately started rubbing him down, talking to him the whole time.

Greg did the same with Wild Bill, only instead of talking he listened to Emily. Her voice set easy on his ears, as his grandfather used to say about Clarice's. Marvin had never heard Clarice say a word. He had words on paper, but never a voice to go with it. At least Greg knew Emily in person and had heard her voice and felt her lips on his.

What would happen if one man had it all?

"What are you thinkin' about so hard?" Emily asked.

He turned around to see her hanging on the other side of the stall, arms crossed and her chin resting on them.

"The perfect woman," he said.

"Which is?"

"I'm not going there," he declared.

He took two steps forward and stopped just inches from her nose. His face was on the same level with hers, and he wanted to kiss her so badly that his body ached with desire. Her blue eyes softened, and she licked her lips.

His willpower weakened, but he got control of it seconds before his lips found hers. "I'm starving," he whispered. "How about you?"

Her eyes popped wide open. "Yes, I am, but we've got time to exercise two more horses before noon."

He didn't say that he was starving for her kisses, her touch, and the way he felt when she was next to him. For someone that had only been in his life a short while, she'd sure found a way past all his bachelor defenses, his good solid business sense, and smack to the core of his heart. A place that scared him senseless since he'd prided himself on thinking with his head and not his heart.

***

After supper that evening, Greg went straight to his room, leaving Emily in the den with Dotty, Nana, and the kittens. She'd exercised horses until noon and could hardly wait to get back to the stable to ride more in the afternoon. He would have rather been riding with her, but Max needed more veterinarian supplies. It didn't matter if there was snow on the ground or if it was over a hundred degrees—when it was time to work cattle, then it had to be done. The ranching business changed little from one year to the next, and it took a dedicated woman to understand it the way Emily did. As determined as she was, he had no doubts left that she could turn a hundred acres into the biggest ranch out there in west Texas if she set her mind to do it.

The whole day he'd thought about what he would write to her. He sat down at his desk and pulled out a sheet of ranch stationery. That night he would pen a letter in his own hand, not type out a message on his laptop and print it.

The first attempt landed in a wadded-up ball close to the trash can. The second followed it. By the third, he was about ready to give up, and then he heard her talking to the kittens on her way to her room.

He picked up the pen again and wrote,

Dear Emily, I cannot ever remember writing a letter to anyone in my whole life, so this is a first and suddenly I'm tongue-tied…

With the sound of her voice lingering in his head, he reached up and touched his lips to see if they were still as warm as when he'd kissed her out there in the cold weather. He went on to write three pages before he closed with a heart symbol and his signature. He looked it over and understood why his grandmother had such an infatuation with those old letters. There was something very personal, very heartfelt, romantic—if he could face that word—about putting words on paper.

He put it into an envelope and addressed it: Emily Cooper, Lightning Ridge Ranch, Across the Landing from Greg Adams.

He laid it on the desk and stared at it. He should tear it up into pieces so small that no one could ever put it back together.

"Not after all the time I put into it," he whispered.

He picked it up and padded barefoot across the landing. He could hear her singing and water running, so she had to be in the shower. Before he lost his nerve, he slid it under the door and went back to his room, picked up the remote, and turned on the television.

Emily wrapped a towel around her head and one around her body. The kittens were busy attacking something over by the door, but she figured it was one of her white socks. She dried her hair, ran a brush through it, and wiped the water droplets from her body before donning a pair of flannel pajama bottoms and a tank top.

Bocephus growled at Simba, grabbed the sock, and was on his way under the bed with it when Emily realized that it was an envelope, not a sock. It took crawling on her knees and chasing him down to take it away from him. When she saw her name she figured it was a cute little invitation from Clarice asking her to the Angus party. Who else would be writing a note?

She took it to the chair, turned on the lamp beside it, and settled down to read whatever it was. She giggled when she saw the address, but it wasn't until she opened the letter that she realized it was from Greg.

She read it five times before she held it to her chest

and went searching through her suitcase for a pen and paper. All she had was a spiral notebook that wasn't nearly as fancy as his letterhead stationery, but it would have to do for that night. Maybe when she and the ladies went shopping she could find some decent stationery… if anyone still sold it.

"And a whole pad of sticky notes," she mumbled.

She wrote with a sharpened yellow pencil because she couldn't find a pen, not in her suitcase or in her purse.

Dear Greg, what a lovely surprise to find your letter. It's your first letter to write. It's my first to receive. I've gotten cards but never a personal letter, and it touches my heart. I've never written a letter to anyone either, so this is new territory for me…

She went on to tell him how much she loved the kittens and how much it meant to her that he brought them to her, what a wonderful time she had that day riding the horses, and how much she liked Lightning Ridge. When she finished she realized that she didn't even have an envelope to put her note inside, so she folded it neatly and wrote on the outside: Greg Adams, Lightning Ridge Ranch, Across the Landing from Emily Cooper.

She looked both ways before she slipped out of her room. There was still light showing under his door, so she gave it a shove and hurried back to her room where she read his letter twice more before she went to bed.

Chapter 12

GREG WAS SITTING ON THE BOTTOM STEP OF THE STAIR-case the next morning when Emily started down. His green eyes twinkled when he looked up at her.

"I liked it. There's something so personal about it. I think I understand Nana better," he said. "So the snow is almost melted and the roads are clear. Are you assistant or hired hand today?"

"Don't know for sure until I ask Clarice," she said. "Ready for breakfast?"

"Yes, ma'am." He stood up, shook the legs of his jeans down over his work boots, and crooked his arm.

She tucked hers inside the loop, and he covered her hand with his. "I'm already looking forward to tonight," she said.

"Me too." He smiled down at her.

The desire to kiss him was so great that she had to blink and look away.

"Well, look who's up and ready to get on with the day." Dotty grinned.

Clarice was dressed in ironed jeans, a light blue shirt, and a red blazer. Dotty wore jeans and a dark green sweater. It looked like they were going Christmas shopping rather than Valentine's party shopping.

"I guess that by the way you two are already all spiced up that we're going to town today," Emily said.

Clarice looked up from her morning newspaper. "We

are, but you've got plenty of time to eat. Tressa doesn't open until nine. We're picking up Rose and Madge on the way. Tomorrow we're having our hair and nails done in Sherman, so you belong to us two days in a row."

Greg poured two cups of coffee and set one in front of Emily. "Dominoes tomorrow night or not?"

"Oh, speaking of dominoes tomorrow night, I asked Prissy to join us," Dotty said.

"Why? Don't we have enough people to play?" Greg asked.

Dotty raised a shoulder in a shrug. "Truth is I need her to help me with a computer problem, and since she's going to be here anyway, she can stay and play with us."

Clarice put down her newspaper. "We'll set up two tables and we won't play partners like last time."

"Oh!" Emily gasped.

They all three looked her way.

"I flat-out forgot that it's my job to cook. We won't take all day doing the shopping, will we?"

"I've got some secrets that I'll share," Dotty whispered. "I won't cook for you, but I do have a few quick recipes."

Greg's phone rang and he answered it while the ladies went on with their conversation.

Clarice patted Emily on the hand. "Dotty could prepare a meal good enough to feed a king in under an hour. She's that good."

Greg put his hat and coat on. "I'm going to the bunkhouse. That damned hot water tank is on the blink again. I guess it's time to buy a new one."

Emily waited until he was out the door and said, "I hate not telling him what's going on with Prissy and what y'all are doing. I feel like a traitor."

"But we want him to have a whole bunch of women to pick from. Think of it as a business. We've done the preliminary interviews. Now he can get down to the serious shit," Dotty said and then changed the subject. "Clarice, are we going to put Simba and Bocephus in solitary confinement for the domino night?"

Clarice smiled. "Of course not. Madge has indoor cats and so does Rose. Prissy don't like cats, but she's not allergic to them."

Clarice whispered into Dotty's ear, "Well done, old girl. You sidestepped that real good. Now she'll worry all about them women she has to compete with. Did you really invite yours yet?"

"Oh, yes, I did. A little competition never hurt anyone, did it? OMG, you don't think she'll shoot one if they get too close to him, do you?" Dotty grinned.

"FYI, I hope not! Now here is our golden chariot with our princess driving. Let's go do some major retail therapy, as Rose calls it," Clarice said.

They picked up Madge first that morning. And when they reached Rose's house, she wasted no time hustling out to the van.

"Ivy just called me and said that Prissy was coming to domino night. Which one of y'all is having trouble with your machine? Emily, can you help out? He's going to catch on before the auction. I just know he is and then we'll all be in trouble," Rose rambled.

Madge finally clamped a hand on her shoulder. "Hush and stop your carryin' on. Even after that thing with the stripper, we're okay. Emily took care of it."

"Turn right here and then park at the first sign of a place. Parking is limited down in this area of town," Clarice said.

Tressa's Dress Shop didn't look like such an exclusive place from the outside. Wedged between a doctor's office and a shoe store, it had two display windows, with mannequins dressed in casual attire on one side, and on the other a mannequin in a party gown seated at a tea table. It reminded Emily of an old movie setting instead of a modern-day dress shop. Inside she picked up the first tag and blinked half a dozen times. It did not change the handwritten numbers one bit. She might pay a hundred bucks for a fancy pair of jeans for the fall ranch sale, but six hundred dollars for a little black dress was just plain crazy.

A gray-haired lady came from behind the counter and gave Clarice a hug. "Miz Adams, I'm so glad to see you. It's been a while. I bet it's time for the Angus Valentine's party, right? And this is the young lady you called me about yesterday. I do believe you sized her just right."

Tressa's gray hair was pulled back into a tight little bun at the nape of her neck. Bright red lipstick had bled into the wrinkles around her mouth, and crow's-feet had settled around her green eyes. She folded her arms across her big chest and eyed Emily critically.

"The red one isn't the right one, Miz Adams. No, ma'am. Everyone else will be wearing red or white. This one needs to stand out, and I got just the right dress in yesterday. It's definitely one of a kind." Tressa went to the back room and returned with a long dress on a hanger.

Run, run, run, Emily, played through her mind as she looked at the ugliest pale blue dress she'd ever seen. Emily would look like she was wearing her Nana's nightgown.

"Some dresses are hanger dresses. Some are not." Tressa removed the plastic bag and shook the dress out. "It was designed for a short lady like you, and she decided at the last minute that she wanted something in red. She didn't have your eyes or hair and would have never pulled it off like you will. She had a bit too much flesh on her back and thighs and this requires absolutely nothing under it."

Emily checked for the price tag when she got to the dressing room, but there wasn't one. She muttered as she removed her jeans and boots about not paying more for the ugly bit of blue silk than she would a decent pair of jeans with bling on the pockets. She pulled off her bra and her underpants but left her white boot socks on and stretched them up to her knees. There was a clip in her purse so she twisted her hair up in a messy French twist and secured it with the black toothed clamp.

"Well, here goes nothing," she said as she put the dress over her head and let it shimmy down her naked form.

"Oh, my God, it feels like cool water against my skin. It really is a nightgown." She smiled. And then she turned around to look at herself in the three-way mirror. Tressa was a genius. The subtle silver threads woven into the shimmering blue silk picked up the light every time she moved. Thank God there was a built-in bra because Tressa had been right about not wearing anything under it. The faintest panty line would show and even a touch of cellulite would shine through like Christmas tree lights.

The back draped from the shoulders to the waist in soft folds, and the walking slit up the back seam went from the floor to four inches below her fanny. She was totally in love with the dress, and if she had to sell the ranch to Taylor to pay for it, she had to own it.

"Come on out here and let's see," Clarice called from the other side of the door.

Tressa pointed. "Right up here on the bride's stand so I can really look at it. Yes, it's perfect on you."

The round stand surrounded by mirrors was much better than what was in the dressing room, and Emily fell in love with the dress all over again.

"Them socks ain't goin' to cut it, girl. We'd better look at some shoes too, Tressa," Dotty said.

"I thought I'd go barefoot or wear my boots," Emily teased.

"As near barefoot as possible. You do not want to draw the eye to your feet, but you want the men folks to ache to touch your bare arms and shoulders. You want them to imagine what could be under that dress," Tressa said.

Emily felt the heat rising from her neck and circling around to her face, but there wasn't a blessed thing she could do about it.

Clarice smiled and nodded. "What have you got, Tressa?"

Madge giggled. "This is more fun than Barbie dolls."

"Shit, woman! We're all too damned old to have ever played with Barbie dolls," Dotty said.

Tressa left and returned with a shoebox. "Size six, right?"

"How…" Emily started.

"Honey, I've been in this business almost fifty years. I can tell every one of you what size you wear, what size your bra is, and your shoe size. They weren't ordered to go with the dress, but I think that's what it needs." She opened the box to reveal silver slippers with flat soles and no bling.

They looked so plain that Emily was disappointed until Tressa jerked off her socks and slipped them on her feet.

"See, they won't hurt your feet when you dance and they won't jack you up to be even an inch taller. You need to play on your petite size and femininity, and most especially your mesmerizing blue eyes. You should not be wobbling on heels so high that you look like a clown on stilts at a circus. Shoes should enhance, not overpower."

The woman was a genius. Emily wanted to adopt her.

"Jewelry?" Rose asked.

"Diamond ear studs. Nothing dangling, and have her hair done in an upsweep that will show off the back of the dress. Maybe a pretty but small clasp in all that dark hair would be nice. Nothing overpowering. The dress will carry the evening," Tressa said.

"She can borrow my studs," Clarice said. "Corsage or not?"

"Are the other women wearing flowers?" Tressa asked.

Clarice nodded. "They usually do."

"Then you shouldn't. You don't want to be like everyone else, darlin'. You want to stand out as the exotic flower among the weeds." Tressa smiled for the first time.

"Do you take credit cards or checks?" Emily asked.

Tressa patted Emily on the wrist. "For you, neither.

This one is on the house. I have owed Miz Adams a favor for twenty-five years that she would not let me repay. Please allow me to do this in return for something she did for me."

When they were in the van and the gorgeous dress was hanging in a special garment bag, Emily looked over at Clarice and asked the question, "What was this favor?"

"It was nothing." Clarice's cheeks turned bright red.

Rose held up her hand like a second grader. "I'll tell you. In the early nineties, with the arrival of all the cheaper stores, Tressa was either going to have to fold or go to cheaper clothes off the rack rather than one of a kind. She went to the bank for a loan, but they said that she was a bad risk."

Clarice raised a shoulder. "I liked her things and we need a place like she runs in the area. If we wanted something really outrageously nice, we had to go to Dallas."

"So Clarice bankrolled her," Dotty said.

"And she weathered the storm and paid me back every single dime," Clarice said. "Now the favor is really paid in full. You will be lovely at the party, my child."

"I would have gladly paid for it."

Madge tapped her on the shoulder. "We all have to learn how to receive as well as give, darlin'. Consider it a lesson with benefits. Now let's go to the Catfish King and eat lunch. Then we'll go to Walmart and have a good time there. I hear you got two new cats. I love their names."

—◇◇—

"What in the hell are you so upset about? You've done nothing but fuss and fume like an old woman all damn day," Max asked.

"Women! Something is going on and I can't put my finger on it," Greg said.

"Understanding all that rocket launching shit down in Houston would be easier than understanding the simplest of women. What have they done anyway?"

"Whatever they are up to, I know Dotty and Nana are in the middle of it. And Emily might be and that's what makes me so mad. It's got something to do with that woman who showed up at my cabin. I'm still mad at Louis for telling her where to find me," Greg said.

"What could they be up to? Lord, Greg, they're four old women and the youngest one of them is eighty years old. And Louis says that he had no idea what she wanted to see you about."

"Something fishy is going on. Why don't you come to the house and play dominoes with us? You'll see what I mean. There's all these little sly glances and whispers, and Prissy is in on it too."

"A conspiracy? Are you losing it?" Max laughed. "Just date Emily and if they are up to something, she'll have to tell you because she'll be your girlfriend."

Greg punched him on the bicep. "Who said anything about dating Emily?"

"I can see the way you look at her, and I can damn well see the way the sparks fly between the two of you. Makes me wonder if the universe put things in motion…"

Greg held up a hand. "You sound like Nana. So what if I'm attracted to Emily. I've been attracted to lots of girls."

"Yes, you have." Max grinned.

"And I didn't get the itch to marry one of them," Greg pushed on.

"No, you didn't."

"So let's just get back to work and drop it," Greg said.

"Sounds like the right thing to do, but do you really want me to come to dominoes or not?"

Greg grinned for the first time all day. "Yes, I do."

———————

Emily fished her brand-new stationery with matching envelopes, along with a whole package of sticky notes, from her Walmart bag. She'd chosen stationery that had a picture of horses running across the top of the page and a horse head on the corner of the envelope. It didn't look all sexy and inviting, but it reminded her of the way she'd felt when she let Star Baby run to his top speed the day before. She'd looked forward to stable duty again that day, but the experience in Tressa's made up for the disappointment when Albert and Louis returned to work that morning.

She opened a package of ten-for-a-dollar ballpoint pens, pulled one from the plastic wrap, and wrote, "Dear Greg," but then she didn't know what to write next. He'd written and she'd responded. It was his turn to write. That's the way it worked in the old days and it should be a rule.

Bocephus crawled up into her lap, turned around a couple of times, and curled up in a gray ball. Simba chased shadows thrown onto the carpet by the sunrays filtering through the lace curtains.

It was early. She should go back down to the den and visit with Clarice and Dotty as they worked on their cowboy dream catchers, maybe even offer to do the starching job when they finished each one. But she wanted to tell Greg about her day and how much fun she had going to lunch with the ladies.

He'd been so quiet at supper that she wondered if he even thought about writing another letter, especially that soon. From the dates on the letters from Clarice, she and Marvin hadn't written every day there at first. Toward the end the letters had been postmarked more frequently.

A movement in her peripheral vision caught her attention. When she turned her head, she saw that Simba was attacking something he had tucked into his tummy area and was kicking at it like he intended to kill the wicked thing.

She jumped up so fast that poor little Bocephus went tumbling from her lap to the floor, but she got the letter before it was ripped to shreds. She picked the gray kitten up, returned to her chair, and read,

> *Dear Emily, I miss you when you aren't here on the ranch. Just knowing you weren't in the house made me lonely. I'm beginning to see why Nana spends so many hours reading her letters. I've read yours a dozen times…*

She picked up her pen after she'd read through the first letter again. Handwritten letters took on a whole new meaning. They were much more than a text message or even an email. They were two people in a vacuum that no one else could ever hack into. She read through the letter again before she started writing,

> *Dear Greg, Spending the day with the ladies was an experience that words can't describe. They were so much fun, but I have to admit,*

*I missed riding the horses and cleaning the
stables, and I missed you.*

She didn't tell him that everything from the gorgeous
dress to little snippets of the conversation with the ladies
brought something about him to mind. Or that her breath
had caught in her chest when she sat down at the dinner
table beside him and his thigh brushed against hers.

Chapter 13

DOTTY CLAPPED HER HANDS TO GET EVERYONE'S attention. "Okay, ladies and cowboys, here's the way we're doing things tonight. We've got eight players so we're going to run two tables. No partners tonight, just straight-out playing. At the end of the night we'll have a loser from each table, so we'll toss a coin to see who hosts next week's game. I've got eight names on paper slips in this bowl. I'm going to divide them evenly. First bunch will sit at this table right here." She tapped the one in front of her. "Second will take the second table over by the fireplace."

Clarice held up a palm. "Before we start, I want everyone to know that Emily lost last week and that she did her own cooking. Dotty offered to help and so did I, but she said that it was her loss and she'd do her duty. And you are in for a treat." She pointed to a tray at the end of the table. Emily had really enjoyed cooking "armadillo toes"—the bacon and cheese wrapped around the jalapeño coated the mouth and kept the heat at a minimum, and she knew her pecan floozies were a mouthwatering treat. Both were among her grandfather's favorites.

"And," Dotty held up a hand to hold off the applause, "my kitchen is clean and my oven is spotless, so Emily is welcome to cook in my kitchen anytime she wants to."

Itchy heat started on Emily's neck and crept to her cheeks as they all applauded. A quick look around the room netted her a wink from Madge, a big smile from Max, a brief nod from Greg, and a smile from Prissy.

"Maybe you could teach me how to cook," Prissy whispered.

"Don't let all that fanfare fool you, ma'am. I'm not all that great. I just made something no one else has," she whispered back.

Dotty picked out four papers and said, "Rose, Clarice, Madge, and I will play right here. Guess that leaves the rest of you—Emily, Max, Greg, and Prissy—to play at that table. No fists, as little cussin' as possible, and no bloodshed. Loser at both tables is up for next week's host. Coin toss will decide the real loser."

She raised her voice and held up her fist. "Now play dominoes! I always wanted to say that."

"Well, ain't I the lucky one," Max whispered to Greg. Prissy sighed loudly.

"Something wrong?" Emily asked.

"Nothing anyone can fix but me," she said.

Greg and Max seated Emily and Prissy and then settled into the remaining chairs. Max turned the dominoes upside down and shuffled them. Greg gave each player seven and the game began.

"Where's the gold ones?" Emily asked.

"My dominoes. My table," Clarice said. "You can lose just as well with black and white ones, my child."

Prissy finally smiled. "We really should go to lunch sometime, Emily. I could use an opinion from someone who doesn't know me so well."

"We'll give you our opinion," Rose raised her voice.

"You know me," Prissy said.

Prissy was on Greg's left, Emily on his right, and Max across the table from him. Greg was frustrated about something and it showed in his lack of attention when he made a horrible play. He kept looking at Max and nodding toward the table where Rose and the ladies were whispering.

They were most likely comparing each of their four names to be sure there were no duplications, but it didn't take a rocket scientist to know that Greg was catching on to them.

"That was sweet," Emily said as she played off a double deuce and bit back the giggles.

Greg kept his eyes on his dominoes. "My mind was somewhere else."

"Well, get it in the game." Max laid down a trey-deuce off of Emily's six-deuce.

"Ouch!" Emily said. "Prissy, you just stomped my toe."

Prissy threw her hand over her mouth. "I'm so sorry. My legs are so long and I really didn't know that was your toe. I was just trying to get comfortable. I hate being this danged tall."

"Well, then give me some of that height," Rose said. "I was lookin' at that weight chart in the doctor's office and if I was five feet eight inches I wouldn't be a pound overweight."

Emily scooted her chair as far to the left as she could and moved her legs to one side in such a way that her knees were against Greg's thigh.

"I said I was sorry," Prissy pouted.

"You are forgiven, but I'm not taking any chances of you getting my other foot. I intend to dance all the leather off a brand-new pair of shoes at the party on Friday." Emily smiled.

"Oh, are you going with Greg?" Prissy asked.

"No, she's going with me," Clarice answered. "Y'all going to play dominoes over there or keep fussin'?"

"Play dominoes," Emily said.

Greg looked at Prissy and said, "Your turn. What has Dotty had you working on today? She said something was haywire in her computer."

Prissy studied her dominoes for a full minute. "Just a glitch in a game she likes to play." She put down a domino that would be a bitch to play off of and laid her hand on Greg's wrist. "What's wrong with you tonight? Your mind is off somewhere else. Are you going to have to cook next week?"

"Hey, Prissy, did you know that Tommy Randolph is leaving your grandpa's ranch?" Max asked. "I'm having coffee with him in the morning at Braum's to discuss what it would take for him to come work for me."

The woman's face lost all color and her pretty red lips made a perfect circle as she sucked air and jerked her hand away from Greg's wrist. "Tommy would never leave my grandpa's ranch."

"He might if I make him a good offer. We were talking last week and he said that things were getting kind of sticky over there. I had the impression that it had to do with a woman, but that's his personal business and I don't pry. He's been working on a ranch for more than ten years, and I think he'd train up to be foreman quality, so I'm going to offer him a sweet deal," Max said. "Your turn, Greg."

Greg was more careful that time. He studied the

table and his hand before he played. "I'd love to recruit Tommy for Lightning Ridge. That man can tear down a tractor and put it back together faster'n greased lighting."

Clarice called out across the room, "Hey, did I hear Tommy Randolph's name over there? Offer him fifty percent more than he's making and tell him we'll give him his own trailer. He can step into your place when you retire, Max."

Prissy inhaled deeply and let it out slowly.

"So you grew up with cows and barbed wire like the rest of us?" Emily asked. Poor girl looked like she was about to faint dead away and Emily sure didn't want Prissy falling on her other foot.

Prissy fiddled with the multicolored scarf around her neck. The browns and turquoise colors blended beautifully with her ecru-colored sweater and dark brown slacks.

"I grew up in town. I hate the smell of cows and anything to do with a ranch. But going to Grandpa's ranch doesn't mean I have to wear boots and a hat and look like a man." She clamped a hand over her mouth. "I'm so sorry. That came out wrong. I didn't mean you look like a man."

Max put out a domino. "I'm not stealing Tommy. Your grandfather's been a good friend of the family here on Lightning Ridge for years, but if the guy is feeling like he needs a change, I'm willing to give him one. He'll just find another ranch if we don't take him on, and I'm not getting any younger. Man can do a lot worse than working as a foreman on a ranch. Your older brother is the foreman at your grandpa's ranch, so that position is going to stay in the family. Tommy don't have much room for advancement over there."

"Ryder is happy working with Grandpa," Prissy said. "What about when Greg has children? What if one of them wants to be a foreman?"

"I reckon that's at least twenty, thirty years down the road if he had one next year. By then Tommy will be ready to hand over the reins to him or her," Max said.

Prissy laid out a domino. "What do you mean him or *her*? A woman could never be a foreman. She can be the wife of the owner like Grandma, but a foreman? Come on, Max. I wouldn't want my daughter to be out walking in cow manure in her high heels."

"I own a ranch and I suppose you could say I've been the foreman of it for the past five years. And I wear scuffed-up cowboy boots and an old mustard-colored work coat and a Stetson when I'm out there shoveling crap out of horse stalls or working cattle. Woman does what a woman has to do," Emily said.

"Ain't that the truth," Prissy said softly.

A tinny version of "Hillbilly Bone" caused everyone in the room to look toward the fireplace. It wasn't Emily's ringtone, and Greg wasn't jumping to grab the phone either. Max looked at the other table and all four women shook their heads.

"That will be mine," Prissy said. "Excuse me. I'll have to take it."

"Hillbilly Bone" was hers? That made no sense at all. She wore custom-made clothes and had her hair done in Dallas or maybe even New York City. Who in the hell would she give a ringtone like that to?

She turned her back to the tables and whispered only a few words. Emily made out "right now?" and "I don't believe it," but the rest was just mumblings covered up by a crackling fire and conversation at the other table.

She shoved the phone in her purse and in a couple of long strides was back at the table. "I'm so sorry, but I have to leave. Nice seeing y'all, and maybe I'll play again another time. Sorry I missed out on your cooking, Emily. And about that lunch, maybe next week?"

"Wonder who that was?" Max asked when she was out of the room.

"I'd guess that it was Tommy," Emily said. "Now let's get serious about this game."

She moved her legs back under the table. No way could she concentrate with Greg touching her, and she'd be damned if she cooked two weeks in a row.

Chapter 14

"WHO IS THAT EXQUISITE CREATURE?" MASON HARPER set his scotch down with a thud on the shiny bar top.

Greg turned around on the bar stool and his mouth went as dry as if he'd been sucking on an alum lollipop. He downed the beer left in his longneck Coors before he could speak.

"Well, I'm going to find out right now." Mason stood up and brushed the shoulders of his Western-cut jacket.

"That would be Emily Cooper, my mother's assistant and the new girl at Lightning Ridge," Greg said.

"Well, hell! Like the old saying goes, if it wasn't for bad luck, I'd have no luck at all."

"And what does that mean?" Greg couldn't peel his eyes away from her in that blue dress. It looked like she was wearing cool water the exact same shade as her eyes.

"It means that I'm not so far from Ravenna that I don't hear the gossip. And I've been left out in the cold again because you've done beat my time."

"You didn't hear wrong." Greg took a deep breath. Several cowboys had already headed toward Clarice and Emily, no doubt angling for an introduction.

Mason smiled. "Come on, cowboy. You can introduce me to Emily just in case she decides she doesn't like you."

―∿―

Emily was aware of exactly where Greg was sitting when she walked in the door. He was dressed in black creased jeans that stacked up just right over his shiny black boots. His silver belt buckle was embossed with the Lightning Ridge brand. Flashes of a white shirt showed behind the lapels of his black Western-cut jacket. Her mouth was so dry that she craved just one sip of that longneck Coors he was holding.

Clarice introduced people to her so fast that she'd never remember any of the names. She'd shaken hands with dozens of cowboys and as many ladies when suddenly someone turned up the heat in the Denison Country Club about forty degrees. She felt Greg's hand on her bare back exactly one second before she looked past his glasses into his green eyes and realized that it was the sexual energy between them that had caused the sudden rise in temperature and that it had nothing to do with the thermometer.

"Emily, this is my friend, Mason Harper. He's got a ranch called Bois D'Arc Bend over near Whitewright and a set of twin girls that look like angels but are living proof that looks can be deceiving."

She extended her hand. "Pleased to meet you."

Not a single spark flashed between them even though he was as tall as Greg and had gorgeous big brown eyes and a killer smile.

"Pleasure is all mine. How are you this evening, Miz Clarice?"

"I'm fine, thanks for asking, Mason. You should bring the twins over to our ranch sometime. I bet they are half-grown by now," she said.

"They would love that, I'm sure, and they are growing up faster than I like," he said.

Mason waved at a couple across the room and headed in that direction. "Oh, there is Lucas and his new bride. Did you hear that they got married over Christmas? Baby's already on the way. His grandfather and daddy are happy as piglets in a fresh wallow."

Greg slipped an arm around Clarice and one around Emily. "So can I tell everyone that you two lovely ladies are my dates tonight?"

"I'm Clarice's date. You'll have to ask her," Emily said.

Clarice patted their shoulders. "I'm going to talk to Natalie. Yes, my grandson. I'll relinquish my date into your hands until the clock strikes midnight. Then you are driving home alone and my date is driving me home in the van. That's your punishment for telling us that you had a date."

The band kicked off with a slow two-stepping song, and Greg held out his hand. "May I have this dance, ma'am, even if you aren't my date?"

She let him lead her to the middle of the dance floor. The singer did a fine job of Toby Keith's song "You Shouldn't Kiss Me Like That," and Greg was an expert dancer, one that she could easily partner with for the rest of the night.

The lyrics said that he had gotten a funny feeling the moment that her lips touched his. Greg pulled her closer and looped both of his hands around her waist. She reached up and wrapped hers around his neck and laid her head on his chest. His heartbeat was strong and steady, but it beat faster when he started singing softly in her ear. The words said that everyone was watching them and thinking that they were falling in love and that they would never believe that they were just friends.

She leaned back and looked up at him. "Do you think everyone thinks that we are falling in love?"

"I imagine they are."

The male singer stepped aside, and a lady in tight-fitting jeans and a red satin shirt took the microphone. She sang a slow Lorrie Morgan song, and Greg brought the dance down to a slow country waltz. The lyrics sunk deep into Emily's soul, but she didn't hear them, just felt the spirit of the melody as her heartbeats blended in unison with Greg's.

"Please be my real date," he whispered.

She barely nodded.

"Is that a yes?" he asked.

"Okay, but if Miz Clarice needs me to get her some punch or another shot of bourbon, you'll have to take the backseat for a little while," she teased.

He tipped her chin up with his fist and brushed a sweet kiss across her lips. "That's just so everyone in this room knows that we are together tonight."

"Branding your territory, are you?" she asked.

He grinned.

She tiptoed and kissed him long, hard, and passionately. "Now all those hussies staring at your cute little ass will know that you are branded for the night too."

"Whew!" The grin widened. "Let's get out of this place and find a motel room."

"I don't do sex on first dates," she said. "And besides, two kisses are probably all that Clarice wants to explain for one night."

"You really think my ass is cute?" he asked.

"If I didn't I wouldn't have said it," she answered.

"Well, darlin', I think all of you is downright sexy as hell tonight. That dress looks like moving water," he said.

She smiled. "Why, Greg, you are romantic at heart, but I bet you say that to all the girls."

"Never said it before. Never saw anyone that could take my breath away like you do," he said.

The night was over too soon.

It lasted until eternity and beyond.

How both could be the truth was a complete mystery, but that's the way Emily felt at midnight when the party ended. She drove Clarice home in the van, but she could see the headlights of Greg's truck in the rearview the whole way home.

Home?

When did that happen? Two weeks ago, her ranch out there in west Texas was home. A grown, responsible woman did not make a change in her thinking like that in such a short time. Not even after a Cinderella evening when she had been transformed into the belle of the ball.

Home?

Gramps used to say that home was where the heart was. That was scary as hell. Her heart should be out there in the flat country, not in north Texas rolling hills country, tangled up in mesquite and scrub oak.

"You sure are serious and quiet," Clarice said.

"So are you," Emily said.

"I was thinking about Marvin. I danced lots of times at Angus parties with my Lester. He was a good dancer and a wonderful man and I adored him. I never got to dance one time with Marvin. Tell me, Emily, did he like to dance?"

Emily slowed down as she drove through Ravenna. "He loved to dance. He and Nana used to dance around the living room floor, and sometimes he'd dance with me after she was gone."

"I suppose it's come about from reading those letters again, but I wish I'd danced with him, held him, and kissed him like you did Greg tonight. I wish I had that memory, even if it hadn't worked out and fate declared that I would marry Lester." She sighed.

Emily reached across the console and patted Clarice's hand. "Gramps felt the same way about you. He adored Nana, but his past was unsettled."

Clarice leaned over and kissed Emily on the cheek. "Thank you for tonight, Emily. You made my grandson happy, and that made me happy."

Emily's smile lit up the van. "He made me very happy tonight."

Clarice got out of the van and made her way up the steps, opened the front door, and disappeared inside the house. Emily drove the van around to the detached garage and parked it. She grabbed her weathered old work coat from the backseat and slipped her arms into it when she got out of the van.

"That sets off the whole look," Greg said from the shadows.

"It's cold."

"Tough as nails on the outside. Soft and gentle on the inside," he said.

"You got it, cowboy," she answered.

He took a step forward and she did the same. Somehow the distance between them disappeared and she was in his arms. His lips were on hers, his tongue making love to her mouth, and she was floating somewhere between the garage and heaven.

His hand slipped inside the coat and massaged her bare back as he deepened the kisses even more. She leaned in, giving way to the fire that had been building all evening as they danced. His fingers inched their way down inside the back of her dress.

"My God," he groaned.

"What?"

"If I'd known you didn't have anything on under that dress, I would have busted out my zipper. I had to think about cleaning horse stalls to keep from having a problem as it was," he whispered.

"This zipper," she said as she laid a hand just below his belt buckle.

"I thought you didn't do sex on first dates," he said.

"I'm not totally inflexible, Mr. Adams," she said.

"Oh, I bet you are very flexible."

"Your truck or the van?"

His hand cradled her neck as his lips came closer. "Two nice bedrooms in the house."

"Not with Clarice and Dotty in listening distance," she mumbled between scorching hot kisses.

He scooped her up in his arms and carried her across the garage floor to a door on the other side of his truck. He opened it and she pulled away from his lips.

"What is this? In a closet? Is it big enough?"

"Trust me, Emily."

He carried her up a flight of narrow stairs to an attic

room with a sloped ceiling. A twin-sized bed shoved up against the wall with a small table beside it was the only furniture in the whole room. He laid her down gently on a handmade quilt and stretched out beside her.

"You feel so good just lyin' here beside me," he whispered hoarsely.

She slipped up a hand in the narrow space between them and shoved his jacket down over his shoulders. He helped her and tossed it across the room, then slowly removed her coat and threw it in the general direction of his jacket.

A window above the bed made a picture frame for a big lovers' moon sitting in the middle of twinkling stars on a midnight blue background. The light of the moon sharpened the angles of his face. She reached up and traced his lip line, then his strong jaw.

"Your touch brings those stars out there into the room with us." His deep drawl sent warmth through her veins.

"I know. You do the same to me."

"I've wanted to touch you all week. Even just your hand or your cheek. Keeping my hands to myself has almost driven me insane."

She unfastened his shirt, one button at a time, kissing his muscular chest as she bared it.

He pulled her even closer and slipped the dress up over her head. "My God, you are beautiful."

"I believe that's a cliché line from an old movie."

"I don't give a damn where it came from, it's the gospel truth, Emily. You are stunning." He teased her with strings of kisses starting at her lips and going to that tender part of the neck right below her ear before he moved down to her breasts, her ribs, and her belly button. She trembled and arched toward him when he went even lower.

"I'm going to catch plumb on fire if you don't get on with it."

"I'm already on fire, and I don't want to have sex with you, Emily. I want to make love to you," he said. "Protection is…"

"I'm on the pill. We don't need anything else."

She pushed the covers back and straddled his waist and unzipped his jeans. "Is this an eight-second bareback bronc ride, or is it an hour-long horse ride up to the cabin and back?"

"First or second time?"

She giggled. She had trouble pulling his belt from the loops, so she left the sides hanging as she freed his erection from the tight jeans. "Help me get rid of all this packaging. I want the present, not the jeans it came in. And darlin', if I'd known that you were commando, we would have snuck out of the dance and locked the bathroom door."

"We call it going cowboy, not commando." He kicked his jeans and boots off in one easy motion.

"I call it downright damn sexy."

"Cold is not my friend." He chuckled.

She slipped her warm hand around his erection and said, "This help?"

He returned the favor, running a hand up her inner thigh until he reached the place that had her wiggling and moaning in less than a minute. "It's been a while, Emily. Would you be terribly disappointed if the first was a bronc ride and the second was a trip to the cabin?"

"And the third time can be…" she panted.

He covered her mouth with his and slid into her with a long, hard thrust. She groaned and worked with him, rocking at the right time to bring them both the most pleasure. He took her to breathtaking heights half a dozen times and then backed off before the thrusts finally became shorter and faster.

"God, that feels so good. I think this is a trip to the cabin instead of an eight-second ride," she panted.

"I never knew anything could feel like this." His drawl was deep, hoarse, and hungry.

"Me either," she moaned.

"Ready?"

The moonlight shifted so that she could see his eyes change from sexy to soft and dreamy. She managed to nod, but she didn't have the breath to answer.

He slipped his hands under her bottom and with a dozen fast and furious thrusts, he brought her right up to the biggest climax she'd ever known.

"Wow… all to hell!" The words came out in a high-pitched squeal when she could catch enough breath to force them out of her mouth. She floated toward the window, toward the big lovers' moon and the stars, and then she fell back to the narrow bed with a thump that knocked the breath out of her all over again.

Would it be a total sin to stay in the attic and live there forever with him, doing nothing but making love like that until she died? She had never felt such raw passion in her entire life.

"I've never…" he said.

"Never what?" She inhaled deeply and straightened her legs.

He pulled the edge of the quilt around them, making

a tight-fitting cocoon. She thought that she'd burned up every nerve in her body, but when he kissed her inside that quilt, desire shot through her like white lightning through an IV.

She buried her face into his neck and whispered, "I still want you."

"Good, because it's a long time until daylight."

———————

Dotty met Clarice in the kitchen the next morning. The coffee was already made and Clarice had turned on the oven for biscuits. She poured two cups and handed one to Dotty.

"We'd best make a big breakfast. They'll be starving."

"Already planned on it. They came in the back door quiet as mice about an hour ago. She was carrying her dress because I heard him say something about not getting it all dirty. It was well worth the money, wasn't it?"

Clarice giggled. "Now, Dotty, you know that dress was payment for a favor."

"Yes, and I know that favor was paid back ten years ago and the diamond studs in Emily's ears are the payment. I was there when Tressa handed them to you and told you how much she appreciated you bankrolling her."

Clarice carried her coffee to the kitchen table. "You got the memory of a damned elephant."

"Long as I don't get the elephant's big nose or big gut to go with it, I ain't complainin'. Van or truck?"

"Attic," Clarice said.

"Shit! I forgot all about the attic."

"Lots of memories up in that attic."

Dotty pulled a package of bacon from the fridge. "Want to share?"

"Now, Dotty, you know I never was one to kiss and tell."

"You ain't no fun at all. Won't let me read them damned letters and won't tell me about the attic. Is that pretty log cabin quilt still on the twin-sized bed up there?"

"How'd you know about that?" Clarice asked.

"I don't kiss and tell neither." Dotty giggled.

"You didn't!"

"I did. Remember, darlin', I was here in Ravenna a month before I got married. I met you right here on this ranch at a picnic. Johnny was working for Lester's folks back then."

Chapter 15

BOCEPHUS WAS CURLED UP ON HER FANCY DRESS, AND Simba was sleeping soundly on her coat when Emily awoke the next morning. She picked up the gray cat first and brushed a couple of hairs from the dress before hanging it inside the special garment bag in her closet.

"You are a good boy, yes you are. You didn't even snag my gorgeous dress." She crooned as she set him on the bathroom vanity and brushed her teeth. He swatted at the water then shook his foot so hard that droplets landed on the front of her faded chambray work shirt.

"Good boy just ended," she said. "But if you had to be a bad boy like the singer you were named for, I'm glad it was in the bathroom and not tearing my dress. I had the most amazing night, Bo. We danced and danced and we…" She blushed at the memories.

Bocephus looked up at her and meowed.

"I can't wipe this grin off my face. That should tell you something, but I'm not telling you what happened. You are much too young to hear such things said out loud."

The kitten flopped back like a baby when she picked him up, purring and blinking at her as if begging for more of the story. She laid him on the chair and he flipped over, jumped down, and attacked Simba, biting his ears and tail until the yellow kitten woke up.

It wasn't until she was getting dressed that she saw

the envelope with the scratch marks and frayed edges tucked under her coat on the floor. The smile got bigger when she picked it up and wider yet when she opened it to read one word.

Amazing.

She put the letter back into the envelope and pulled open the drawer of her nightstand where she'd stored the other two, and there was the little red velvet box that held Clarice's diamond studs. Emily touched her ears and groaned as she removed the earrings and put them into the box.

Dammit it all to hell on a splintery old shovel handle. She had to face Dotty and Clarice that morning, and she had less than two hours of sleep and a grin that she couldn't erase. What in the hell was she going to do? They'd know the minute they looked at her that she'd had sex. It was written all over her face. She'd hock her pickup truck for a lemon to suck on right then.

The kittens bounded out of the room the minute the door was opened and chased each other down the stairs, rolling and tumbling from one step to the other. Emily's feet were like lead. She couldn't face them and yet she had no choice. It was worse than the time she came home from college after her first experience with sex. She had dreaded facing Gramps, but all he talked about that weekend was the big cattle sale.

Too bad there wasn't a cattle sale going on at Lightning Ridge.

She went straight to the table where Clarice was sitting. "Thank you so much for loaning these to me. Tressa was right. They were the perfect jewelry."

"Good morning. Clarice says that the dance was a big success," Dotty said.

"Well, look here. The boys are joining us this morning. Good morning, Bocephus and Simba. I bet Dotty has enough bacon fried up that you could share a piece this morning."

"I'm not sure those two get bacon this morning." Dotty pointed at the refrigerator. "I think they punished you for leaving them last night."

Sticky notes had been shredded up as far as two little kittens' paws could reach. The little rascals had no sense of conscience because Simba crouched like a big yellow lion, wiggled a few times, and made a dive for a flapping note that still hung on to the refrigerator door. He reminded Emily of a squirrel bouncing from one tree limb to the other as he used the sticky notes to claw his way to the cabinet top. He snagged a piece of bacon, landed on his feet when he jumped off, and growled at Bocephus.

Emily slapped a hand over her mouth. "Oh, no!"

Clarice reached down and grabbed an end of the bacon and played tug-of-war with the kitten until she'd broken a chunk off. "Now, Bo baby, this is for you. Simba has to learn to share."

"I'm so sorry," Emily said.

"It's time to clean them off and start all over anyway," Dotty said. "But we've got to work on training the boys to stay off my cabinet."

"Yes, ma'am. I don't think they're going to get bacon for a week, and they have to stay in my room for a week too. Come on, boys, you are in big trouble," Emily agreed.

"That's too harsh," Clarice said. "No bacon

tomorrow, but you'll be punishing me and Dotty if you don't let them come out and play."

"I'm making ham and eggs tomorrow," Dotty said.

"Shhh! They don't know that." Clarice giggled.

Max stopped in the middle of the kitchen floor. "Looks like a tornado hit y'all's refrigerator."

"Hurricane Simba and Tornado Bocephus," Emily said.

"Give them an extra piece of bacon. They deserve it after demolishing that ugly thing."

That tingly, breathless feeling told Emily that Greg was close.

"Your boys had a party last night, Greg. Dotty cleaned up the mess on the floor, but she left the rest for y'all to see," Clarice told him.

"Want me to peel them all off and wash down the front of the fridge?" he asked.

"Hell, no! I've saved all the little pieces and I'll put those," she nodded toward the refrigerator, "in the shoe-box with them. We've already written the date on the outside and Simba and Bocephus's names. When the future generations come upon them, they'll know what year the boys came to live with us."

"Did you punish them, Emily?" Greg grinned.

"They don't get bacon tomorrow," she answered.

"You hear that, boys? Enjoy that treat this morning because you don't get any tomorrow. Hey, big news isn't the cats trying to shred the sticky notes. Louis left me a text message," Greg changed the subject.

"Is he sick? Do I get to help with the horses this morning?" Emily asked.

"No, he's on his way right now. But Prissy and Tommy eloped to Las Vegas. Her grandpa is having a double-wide hauled in for them to live in, and Prissy will be living on the ranch. Guess that she figured out that she was about to lose the best thing ever."

Dotty shook her head from side to side. "The heart will have what it wants or else it will wither up and die."

"Speaking from experience?" Max asked.

Dotty pointed to the food on the bar. "Damn straight, I am. Now fix plates and eat. This ranch don't run itself, and you got to make hay or plow or whatever the hell needs done while the sun shines and all that shit."

"What are my jobs today?" Emily looked at Clarice.

"You are working with Greg this morning. We're going to work on bazaar things. Come Monday morning we'll start getting the barn ready for the big affair, so this is our last weekend to work on our projects, and this afternoon we've got to get things caught up in that office. Payroll and important business things." Clarice winked.

Greg brushed past her on the way to the coffeepot and for just a brief second, his fingers touched hers. When she glanced his way, he mouthed the word, "Amazing."

--~~~--

Emily really wanted to ride bareback with the brisk pre-spring wind blowing her ponytail and the sunrays warming her face, but Albert and Louis were already out in the stables. That left two jobs: walking the fence row on the back side of the ranch or running errands in Bonham.

Max handed her a piece of paper. "Here's the list. I'm glad Clarice hired you, Emily. I hate running errands like this."

Greg blew her a kiss from behind Max's back, and a

vision of the two of them in the attic room materialized
so real in her head that her cheeks started to burn. She
whipped around and made a trip back through the house
to ask Clarice and Dotty if they needed anything from
town before she left.

Clarice nodded. "I need another package of buttons
or charms if you can find them from the craft section at
Walmart. Anything that has to do with cowboys—boots,
hats, lassos, or horseshoes. And we also need twenty
pounds of sugar. That way we can get busy on the
banana bread and pumpkin bread on Monday without
fear of running out of sugar," Clarice said. "Oh, and this
afternoon we really will work on the payroll. Boys like
their money on Saturday night. Then you need to catch
up on the entries for the past week, both for the incom-
ing bills and the cow information. They've been doing
all kinds of vet work this past week, so there's a stack
an inch thick on the cows. And then I want you to look
at the four ladies I've picked out to invite to the auction
and get your opinion on them."

"Looks like I've got a full day." Emily's cheeks were
no longer fire-engine red, but now her soul had turned
bullfrog green with jealousy.

Dammit! In the haze of long-lasting afterglow, she'd
forgotten about all the women who thought they were
talking to Greg Adams on the dating sites.

"She's a slave driver, I tell you, she is," Dotty said. "I
have to cook and crochet until my hands bleed, and then
I have to be Greg and talk to the women like a man."

"Oh, hush; it's better than drinking yourself to death,"
Clarice said. "Take the van, Emily."

The door up to the attic beckoned to her when she

was in the garage. She eased it open and tiptoed up the steps. Maybe she'd dreamed the whole evening. Maybe it hadn't happened at all and all that dancing had made it very vivid. Maybe the single word on the letter from Greg that morning had been concerning the good time they'd had at the Angus party.

When she reached the top, there was Greg stretched out on the bed.

"Good morning, beautiful," he said.

"It was real, wasn't it? It was so wonderful I thought it might be a dream."

He patted the bed. "I know exactly what you mean, darlin'. I couldn't resist coming back to make sure when Max said we needed to take a roll of barbed wire in case we see a break. We've got about ten minutes."

"With or without clothes?" she asked.

He popped up off the bed and shucked out of his coat and boots so fast that it was a blur. "Damn, it's cold up here. We really should get us one of those little space heaters."

"It'll be warm in a few seconds," she said as her jeans, shirt, boots, and underwear all joined his in a pile beside the bed.

He grabbed her around the waist and fell onto the bed with her in his arms. She grabbed a handful of hair and brought his mouth to hers. "Don't waste time on foreplay. I've been hot since you walked into the kitchen this morning."

He propped up on an elbow and kissed her long and lingering, and yet gentleness and sweetness were mixed in with the passion. "I hate that this has to be a quickie. I like to play and cuddle afterward."

She rolled over on top of him and in one swift motion and wiggle of the hips planted him inside her. "Me too, but if you don't put this fire out, I'm going to be real bitchy all day."

He flipped her over so that he was on top. "Well, darlin', we can't have a bitchy woman on Lightning Ridge, can we? After curfew tonight, we'll meet here again for the real thing."

"Yes, sir."

⁓

"Is the van backing out of the garage yet?" Clarice asked.

Dotty leaned closer to the kitchen window. "It's Greg's truck, and now it's the van."

"Fate brought her to Lightning Ridge and that's the whole reason that Marvin and I ever wrote to each other in the first place. The stars weren't lining up for us but for our grandkids," Clarice said.

"All that fate stuff is a load of shit, Clarice Adams. What would you have said about any other girl who went to the attic with Greg last year? Anyone who he's dated in the past seven years he's been on this ranch?"

Clarice's eyes twinkled. "I might have nailed that door shut and booted her off the ranch. But that was last year and this is different. He's been here seven years." She clapped her hands. "That's my lucky number, Dotty. I swear, it's the stars all getting lined up perfect."

"Don't matter who all is convinced. What matters is if he is, and it has to go beyond what's going on in that attic, don't it?"

⁓

Greg was running on less than two hours' sleep, but he couldn't force the grin off his face. Emily was amazing both on the ranch and in bed, and just thinking about her kept him in semi-arousal all morning. That night he planned to take candles to the attic and maybe a couple of beers.

"For a man who danced until midnight, you sure got lots of energy this morning. I figured you'd come up with something that would put you in the house so you could sneak a nap this morning," Max said.

Greg slapped his thigh. "Must be too tired from partying all night for my mind to be working. You said the fence needed checking and I just did what you said without even asking questions."

"We'll be done by noon. Clarice mentioned yesterday that she and Emily would be working on the computer this afternoon. I guess they could probably use your help."

Greg shrugged. It was too new, too raw, and too passionate for him to talk about, even to Max, who'd been like a second father to him.

Father!

Greg's dad had said not to tell Nana he and his mother were coming to the bazaar because it was a surprise, so there hadn't been any talk about it and in all the excitement he'd forgotten to even mention it to Emily.

His parents would meet Emily!

His hands were suddenly sweaty inside his leather work gloves. His mother wouldn't like Emily because she was a ranching woman. Nancy Adams had held out hope ever since her son moved to Lightning Ridge that he'd get his fill of dirt and cows and move back to Houston.

Greg wiped sweat from his forehead.

"It's not that warm. You must've drunk a lot at the party and it's working its way out of your system." Max chuckled.

"Guess so," Greg said.

"You didn't answer me about Emily. You like her or not?"

"I do," Greg answered. "But she's determined to go back to Happy. If she had a lick of business sense, she'd realize that she can't do the impossible."

"Like what? I thought she could move mountains and walk on water," Max said.

"It's not possible to run enough cows to make a living on a ranch the size of hers, especially out in west Texas," Greg answered.

"You don't believe that, and that's what makes you so mad. If she set her head to do it, she could turn a garden plot into a profitable ranch."

"I don't have to admit it though, do I?"

Emily got back to the house right at noon. She'd been to the feed store to drop off a payment, to the bank to make a deposit, to the tractor supply to pick up some more veterinary supplies that they had to unpack and mark up before they'd sell them to her, and had stood in line forever at the Walmart store. To have more than twenty checkout counters and only two checkers was downright sinful. She would have zipped through a self-check counter, but none of them were working.

She hoped that Greg had come in from the back forty at least for dinner so she could see him. It wouldn't be as good as getting to sneak off to the attic or even snag a couple of kisses in the den when no one was looking, but it would have to do. Until he was ready to announce that they were dating, if that's what they were doing, she intended to keep silent.

Dating?

Or was it just sex? Which did she want it to be?

"In the dining room. We're just sitting down to eat," Dotty called out when Emily entered the house.

"I'll be right there soon as I wash up," she yelled back.

She could hear Clarice talking, but something wasn't right in her tone.

Dotty wasn't using a single cuss word and Greg sounded strange.

Shit!

The preacher had come to dinner and Emily was wearing her work boots, a chambray shirt, and faded jeans. She quickly ran her fingers through her hair and redid her ponytail. Bocephus came slinking around the corner with Simba right on his tail. Both of them crawled low on the ground and their eyes were wary. Could a preacher get into heaven if cute little kittens were terrified of him?

She stopped long enough to pet the kittens and whisper reassurances in their ears and did not wash her hands afterward. Maybe she'd even touch the preacher's hot roll instead of passing him the bread basket. Sorry old sucker anyway for scaring her two kittens. Now they were hiding under the kitchen table and peering out around the chair legs.

"You get lost in there?" Max called out.

Even his voice sounded different, and nothing rattled Max.

"On my way," she said.

Everyone turned to look at her when she entered the room—Clarice, Dotty, Max and Greg, and Taylor.

"Surprise!" Taylor said.

Her breath caught in her chest. Her feet were glued to the floor and she couldn't move.

"Taylor!" she squealed.

He pushed back his chair and hugged her tightly. "I'm here to surprise you, and I think I just did it." He led her to the table with his arm around her shoulders.

She was glad that there was a chair nearby and doubly glad that it was right beside Greg instead of across the table from him.

"I'm so tickled to see you but… oh, my Lord, you've got bad news?"

Taylor flashed a beautiful smile. "No, darlin', no bad news. I would have told you right up front if that was the case. I bought a bull a month ago from a breeder in Blue Ridge, remember? I know I told you about it. Blue Ridge is less than half an hour from here, so I came by to see you while I was in the area, and I'm glad I did. A greasy old burger couldn't measure up to a feast like this one."

Color returned to her ashen face. "Did you leave Happy in the middle of the night?"

"Drove halfway yesterday. Wanted to pick up the bull, check on you, and get home by midnight. I hate leaving a big old bull on a trailer overnight," he answered.

Greg laid a hand on her leg and the tension eased out of her body. No one had died. Everything in Happy was fine. Taylor, her favorite boy cousin, was right there at the table with her.

"I know you remember the bull. We looked at his lineage online just before Marvin passed. What surprised me is that he's tame as a…" Taylor went on, "I was going to say kitten, but I really hate cats. The bull is as gentle as a lamb."

"Emily has two kittens," Dotty piped up.

"I know. She told me," Taylor said.

Emily helped her plate but didn't pay any attention to the food. "So your plan is to drive all the way to west Texas tonight? Clarice, couldn't he put the bull in a holding pen and spend the night? That way he could get an early start in the morning."

"We've already invited him," Clarice said.

"And I do thank all of you for the offer, but after dinner I'll head back to Happy. I've put in longer hours than this lots and lots of times. So have you, Em," he said.

"I'm willing to lose a little sleep for something I enjoy," she said.

That got her a leg squeeze under the table.

Talk went to bulls, ranching, and whether or not it would be a good year for the hay, and dinner was over way too soon.

Taylor pushed back his chair and said, "Miz Dotty and Miz Clarice, that was an excellent meal. I've eaten too much, and believe me, I will be braggin' about it when I get back home. Walk me to the truck, Em?"

She laid her napkin on the table beside her plate. "Of course, but I sure would feel better if you'd stay the night. We haven't talked nearly enough."

"I'll be home by bedtime and the roads are clear."

"Please stay one night. It's like a dream that you are

even here, and you didn't even get a tour of the ranch," she begged when they were out of the house.

"Remember, I'm holding down my ranch and yours. I just wanted to surprise you," he said.

"Well, you sure did that. I thought I was dreaming. I wish you would've brought Dusty. She would have put up a fit to stay at least one night and we both know you can't refuse her," Emily said.

"The surprise was only part of the reason I drove out here. The bull could have waited another month, but I wanted to meet this Greg fellow and I came prepared to hate him, but I didn't and now I'm scared that you might stay here. The way he looks at you is downright—" He stopped.

She leaned against the cattle trailer. "What?"

"You've been like a sister to me and Dusty both," he said. "At least promise you'll come home and tell us in person, not do it with a phone call."

"What in the hell are you talking about? I'm coming home, cowboy. This is a vacation, and folks come home from vacation," she said and quickly changed the subject. "Did you take Melinda to the Valentine's party last week?"

Taylor chuckled. "I did and we hit it off really good. I'm not lookin' at her like that cowboy in there looks at you, not yet anyway, but I did ask her out again."

Chapter 16

GRAMPS USED TO SAY THAT PEOPLE WERE FOOLS IF they set their plans up in stone because God had a wicked sense of humor, then he'd go on to tell stories about how his plans had been thwarted. Emily remembered several of those stories as she carried her two kittens up to her room that evening.

She'd offered to go with Max and Greg when they got the call that their fence had been cut and there were at least fifty head of cattle wandering up and down the road, blocking traffic. That would be using the word "traffic" very loosely, since there might be two or three pickup trucks driving down the road from Ravenna toward Lightning Ridge in a day's time. But once out of the pasture, cows roamed, so there wasn't anything to do but go herd them back into the pasture and fix the fence by flashlight power.

That meant a long, long night, no playing around in the attic, and she didn't have a blessed thing to do that evening. The kittens must've put in a hard day of play after Taylor was out of the house because they went right to sleep.

Emily took a shower, washed her hair, did her nails, and picked out a dress for church the next morning. She would most likely be driving the ladies, and Greg would sleep in if he fixed fence all night long.

Her phone rang at ten thirty, and she picked it up without even checking the ID.

"Greg?" she asked.

"No, it would be Taylor. My bull is safe and sound, and the cows are already ogling him like you did Greg. Thought I'd let you know," he said.

"I did not ogle." She sighed.

"Oh, yeah, you did. I've never seen you look at a man like you do him. He might be the one, whether I like it or not."

"I'm glad you are home safe, but I'm still mad at you for not staying the night. I could use some company. The cows got out and Greg is fixing fence and my cats are asleep," she said.

She heard the sound of a cigarette lighter and rolled her eyes toward the ceiling.

"And I'm glad I came on home, because if I was there, I'd be fixin' fence with the men folks, not sittin' in the living room talkin' to you, darlin'. That's what visitors do when there's work that needs to be done. You know that. Good night," he said.

"You tell Dusty that you had dinner with me?" She hung on to the conversation.

"No, I did not. I don't want to listen to her cussin'." He laughed. "I'm hanging up now."

The phone went completely silent and she sighed. Less than a minute later she heard a jingle and looked down at her phone. There was a text from Greg. Fence is fixed. We're herding them in through a gate down the road. Be late getting home. See you tomorrow morning. Dinner in Sherman after church?

She tapped in a message with her thumbs. Are you asking me on a date?

Yes, came back instantly.

I'd love to, she typed in.

A smiley face icon appeared with one eye slid shut in a wink.

The standard preacher's sermon lasted half an hour and she really tried to listen. But with Greg's whole body pressed up against hers in the short pew, the preacher could have been reading straight from *Fifty Shades of Grey* or one of the sequels.

From what she'd heard and read about the book, she figured her mind was leaning a whole lot more toward the "Grey" book than it was toward the Good Book that morning. One good romp and a ten-minute quickie in the attic had set her hormones into a tailspin, and all she could think about was kissing Greg and his hands on her body.

She was an adult, not a sophomore in high school, but that morning she did not get the message from the birth date on her driver's license that she was a grown-up now or from Taylor, who'd reminded her quite emphatically and often that they were adults.

Finally, the preacher wound down and looked out over the congregation.

"Some of you may have heard the good news, but I'll tell it again. Prissy Landers and Tommy Randolph were married this weekend in a private ceremony in Las Vegas. We all expected that when Prissy got married, it would be right here in her own church, but they didn't want a bunch of fanfare, so they eloped. However, the ladies in the church are having a reception for them on Wednesday night at seven and everyone is invited.

We'll look for all y'all to be there. Clarice Adams is one of the hostesses, so if you have questions, call her. Now Everett Dempsey will please deliver the benediction."

Every head bowed and Everett's big booming voice said "Our Father." The preacher tiptoed down the aisle, his head bowed reverently. The old guy took a while, but when he finally said, "Amen," the Lord had been thanked for everything from the day and the wonderful spiritual sermon to the green grass beginning to come up after the snow and the sunshine.

"Praise the Lord," Dotty mumbled next to her.

Emily looked over her shoulder.

Dotty said from the side of her mouth, "I thought we were going to starve plumb to death before he got his praying done. Remind me to never invite that man to supper. I hate cold mashed potatoes and gravy."

"Madge has invited us to have dinner with her," Clarice said as they waited for the congested center aisle to clear out. "We're going home with her and then she'll drive us to the ranch later this afternoon. We're going to talk about the final touches for the bazaar next week. Y'all want to come along?"

Greg shook his head. "Emily and I have a date. We're going over to Sherman and having a nice quiet dinner and maybe take in an afternoon movie."

Clarice raised both eyebrows halfway to heaven. "A date?"

"Is it all right?" Emily asked.

"Are you over twenty-one?"

"Oh, stop the sh… sh… stuff, Clarice. You almost made me cuss right here in church. God… d… dang it! See there, I almost did it again. They're grown. They can go get a hamburger and watch a movie without asking me or you," Dotty said. "I swear cussin' is even harder to give up than good Kentucky bourbon."

"I'm over twenty-one," Emily answered.

"Then I reckon you can date my grandson," Clarice told her.

Greg laced his fingers in Emily's and led her toward the pulpit, through the choir entrance, and out the back door.

"We'll go to hell for sure if we don't shake hands with the preacher." She giggled.

"By the time Nana and Dotty get to the front of the line, he won't remember who all he shook hands with. How about Chinese for dinner?" He helped her inside the van and leaned across to fasten the seat belt for her.

"How about takeout?" She kissed him on the cheek when he finished.

He took time to really kiss her, gently, then deeper, and then with so much hunger that she could feel her whole insides starting to hum. "Takeout where?"

"There's a big backseat." She tilted her head back. "Or a nice attic at home."

"Too many windows for the backseat. Too far to get back to the attic. But I know just the right place to take our Chinese takeout dinner. I looked forward to meeting you in the attic all day yesterday and felt cheated last night."

"Me too. And I didn't have a letter under the door this morning," she said.

"Did Marvin and Nana write every day?"

"Not at first."

"Have I told you that you look beautiful today? That

dress is the same color as your eyes. What color underwear are you wearing?" His eyes glittered like stars in a midnight sky.

"Who says I'm wearing any?"

He groaned. "God, Emily! I'm glad I didn't know that in church."

"They are blue and so is my bra." She giggled. "And yours?"

"None. I told you about going cowboy."

Her gasp was ever so slight, but he heard it and pointed a finger at her.

"Gotcha!"

The trip took less than twenty minutes and the takeout was ready in ten minutes. It smelled scrumptious in the backseat, but she wanted something else much more than she wanted food.

"Where to now?" she asked.

"See that sign right up there?"

"The car dealership?"

"No, the one beside it." He pointed to the hotel sign.

"Oh, yes, sir."

Signing in was a breeze. He carried the bag with their food and stopped at the vending machine room on the way and bought four Cokes.

"Is that enough?" he asked.

"Might have to come back. We could get very hot and thirsty," she said.

Flirting had never been so much fun.

The room was at the far end of the hallway, and when they were inside, he set the food and drinks on the desk, turned around, and picked her up like a bag of chicken feed—butt up, head dangling down his back, giggles bouncing off the walls, dress flipped up to reveal two almost-naked, well-rounded cheeks with a string up the middle and the barest of silk at the top of the thong.

He kissed the cheek closest to his lips before he tumbled her onto the big, soft king-sized bed and landed on top of her. "You've got a very kissable ass, Miss Emily Cooper."

"So glad you think so. I grew it just so you could kiss my ass." She laughed.

"Ah, you are a smart-ass."

"Make up your mind, cowboy. Is it kissable or smart?"

He pulled off his glasses and laid them on the night-stand and rolled to one side, keeping her in his arms. Lying on the bed put them on the same playing field, but still she felt herself tiptoeing when his eyes shut and his lips found hers in a scorching kiss that almost set the sprinklers in the ceiling into action.

He carefully undid every tiny button down the front of her dress, laid it back, and kissed her bare tummy, moving downward until he reached the thong. He grabbed it with his teeth and removed it slowly down her legs to her ankles, over her toes, and tossed it over his shoulder without ever touching it with his fingers. Then he started back up, tasting and kissing until she was moaning and arching her back.

She sat up, shimmied out of her dress and bra, and threw them at a chair, then pushed him back on the bed. Taking her time undressing him, she made sure he was panting every bit as hard as she was before she strad-dled his body and leaned forward, her breasts brushing against his chest hair.

Damn! She meant to turn him on to the boiling

point, but that soft chest hair was doing a number on her desire button. She was near to exploding when she found his lips. She tasted the last remnants of the morning coffee and caught a whiff of the aftershave that put her squarely in the middle of the hottest desire she'd ever known.

He rolled with her and together they took their pleasure in each other's bodies as if they'd die if they weren't completely sated before the day ended. His mouth never left hers until they both cried out in a loud whisper at the same time, "Now. Right now."

Afterward he pulled the edge of the snowy white comforter up over them and kissed her eyelids. "There are no words. Amazing doesn't even cover the way I feel when I'm with you. I feel complete and whole."

"Mmmm," she said.

Taylor might be right. Maybe she did ogle!

Greg awoke in the middle of the afternoon to the sound of the shower running in the bathroom. He rolled out of bed, padded naked and barefoot through the open door, and pulled back the shower curtain.

"Water is nice. Dive right in." She grinned.

"Don't mind if I do," he said. "Could I wash your back, ma'am?"

"And my front and anything else you want to touch, but not right now. If I don't get food pretty soon, I'm going to wilt and pass on to the other side of eternity," she said.

"Chinese is cold by now, darlin'."

"I don't care if it's moldy. I'm going to eat it, drink

two Cokes, and then we will get our money's worth out of this room before we have to go home."

"You'll wear me plumb out. I'm not a teenager." He chuckled.

"Couldn't prove it by me." She patted his bare butt and stepped out of the shower. "I'll get the food out and the table set."

"I didn't see a table," he said.

"Of course you didn't, sweetheart. You are the table."

"You are not eating Chinese off my stomach," he said.

It was her turn to point and say, "Gotcha."

He grabbed at her, but she stepped to the side and wrapped a big white towel around her body, tucking the end in above her breasts.

Even with water dripping off her, a hotel towel around her, and all her makeup gone, she was still gorgeous.

Chapter 17

THE RAIN STARTED ON MONDAY MORNING WITH A CLAP of thunder that sent both kittens skittering under the nearest chair. It hit with wind and a force that blew it so hard against the kitchen windows that Emily thought there could be a tornado pushing it. But by the time breakfast was finished it had slowed to a gentle drizzle coming from solid gray skies.

"I'm glad we've got a barn to get ready for the party," Max said at breakfast. "We'd have cranky hired hands if they were all holed up in the bunkhouse with nothing to do. I'll call Louis and tell him that we'll meet them there in ten minutes."

"Want to come along?" Greg asked Emily.

"No, she's my assistant again today," Clarice said.

Greg pushed his coffee cup back. "You are going somewhere in this weather?"

"We're going to the office. Computer work is backing up. Emily is going to work on that," Clarice answered.

Dotty refilled her coffee mug. "Thank God! Clarice gets plumb bitchy when she has to poke numbers into that stupid machine all day. That computer shit ain't for us old dogs to have to learn. That's the reason I don't want a new cook stove. New ones ain't got nothin' but fancy buttons. Give me five knobs any day of the week rather than a bunch of push buttons."

Emily would have far rather been in the barn as

inputting data into the computer, but that was as big a part of ranching as cows, hay, and plowing. Work always came before play. Sometimes work was play; sometimes it was plain old work.

"It will take her at least three days to get done. Then Thursday and Friday all of us bazaar ladies will decorate the barn and she's going to help with that. She is my assistant all week. You've got lots and lots of help who can clean out a barn," Clarice said.

Emily picked up the kittens. "I'll see y'all at dinner-time. The boys and I will be in the office if anyone needs any one of us."

Dotty slammed a dish towel down on the bar with enough force that it popped almost as loud as the thunder. She glared at Clarice until the woman finally threw up her hands and said, "What?"

"You've gone and ruined it. Just when they were gettin' on so good, you put her in that damned office for a week and send him to clean out a barn. How in the hell are they supposed to find any attic time or even thirty seconds to steal a kiss? What is the matter with you, Clarice Adams? Have you lost your damn mind?"

Clarice smiled.

"I'll slap that grin right off your face and leave a big smear of lipstick all the way to your ear when I do it," Dotty fumed.

"Remember when you were a little girl and you played with your little friend all day on Saturday and then went home with her after church on Sunday?" Clarice asked.

"What the hell has that got to do with anything?"

"On Monday, what did you want to do?"

"Play with my friend some more, but Momma wouldn't let me." Dotty clamped a hand over her mouth.

"Because familiarity breeds contempt?" Clarice asked.

"Words right out of her mouth; I swear you even sounded like her."

"They need some time apart to want to be together. They might not even realize it, but I do. It's less than ten days until her vacation time is up. There's just flat-out not time for them to spend any of it fighting. So they need to yearn for each other and want to be in each other's arms so badly they can taste it."

Dotty nodded very slowly. "They will fight some-time. You know that, don't you, Clarice? You and Lester fought. Me and my husband were professional at fighting, but oh, honey, the making up was so hot that the fights were worth it. Sometimes I started one on purpose just so we could have makeup sex."

Clarice giggled. "Any smart woman knows how to do that. They can fight, but only after she decides that she wants to stay on Lightning Ridge. When she sells Marvin's ranch to Taylor she won't have a place to run to when they have their first big one."

"Forgive me for doubting you." Dotty held out her pinky finger and the two old ladies locked their fingers together, counted to three and let go, clapped three times, and then went back to work.

Emily found a letter under her door on Tuesday. One short page talking about getting the barn cleaned out and how much he missed having her by his side. Even if he couldn't hold her or make a quick trip to the attic, he liked knowing that she was close enough he could see her. It was a bigger job than they'd thought since they'd stored hay in it until the fall sale and would sure enough take every waking hour until Wednesday. Maybe they could meet on the steps or in the living room late tomorrow night, even if only for a few minutes to cuddle.

The noise of a truck engine took her attention to the yard. There was Max and Greg, wearing slickers the same color as the sky. Greg looked up at her window and blew a kiss her way and then he was gone. She didn't even know if he realized she was looking out.

After breakfast she went straight to the office. She found Simba asleep on the keyboard and Bocephus sorting through the basket of paper, sending it flying all over the floor. She grabbed the gray cat by the scruff of the neck, gave him a toy mouse to play with, and carefully moved Simba to the rocking chair.

She hit the enter button and Christian Mingle popped right up, which meant that Clarice had already been in the office that morning and had forgotten to log out of the site. Emily had the cursor on the "log out" button, but she couldn't force herself to hit the enter key. Just what did Clarice say to make those women believe that she was truly Greg? How did an eighty-year-old woman convince twenty- and thirty-year-old computer-savvy women that she was a cowboy?

Curiosity won the battle playing out in her head. She opened up the chat window and her eyes got bigger, bigger, and bigger until she thought for sure they'd pop

out of her head and Bocephus would bat them around
the floor like marbles.

Tonya: What kind of man are you?

Greg: I like to be in total control.

Tonya: Ohhh, I like a man like that. Shall I bring the leather?

Greg: Honey, if you want to ride on our first date, it can
    be arranged.

Tonya: Ohhh, I'd like to ride. I'll bring the leather and a whip.

Greg: No whips. I like a rough ride, but I'm not into whips.

Tonya: So you are a down-to-business-type man?

Greg: Yes, ma'am. I am a businessman. My grandmother
    and her friends are having a church bazaar at Light-
    ning Ridge ranch on Friday night. Why don't you join
    us and I'll show you just how much I enjoy getting
    down to business.

"Dear Lord," Emily gasped.

She had to look away from the screen to blink. And
that's when she saw the sticky note with four names
attached. Tonya was one of the four.

"You are in for a big surprise, Tonya. You're speaking
one language and the person playing Greg in this picture
is speaking another. I'll have to be on my toes for sure if
I'm going to protect him that night," she whispered.

She started to go into the chat room with the next woman, but Bocephus made a running dive for the basket of paper under the desk, reminding her that she had a lot of work to do before the auction on Friday night. She'd already read enough to know that poor old Greg had best put on his tallest boots because he was going to be wading through some serious shit.

—∿∿—

After supper Greg yawned and declared that Clarice had better give him and the guys more than a week's notice if the bazaar was going to be held at the ranch every year. "That barn was a complete mess and cleaning it up for a fancy bazaar is a lot different than getting it ready for a cattle sale. I'm tired, so I'm going up to my room and catching up on emails. See y'all tomorrow morning."

"Don't forget that tomorrow night we've got to be at the church for the reception," Clarice said. "Y'all knock off work at four. Supper will be an hour early so that Dotty, Emily, and I can get down to the church to help decorate. We're on the hostess list."

"You are the hostess, Clarice. I didn't volunteer. Did you, Dotty?" Emily asked.

"Oh, yeah, I did, and I put your name down too. We are all three hostesses. And Madge and Rose, and about seven or eight others. You might as well learn that business as well as dominoes and ranchin' and takin' care of that computer shit," Dotty said.

Emily grumbled under her breath all the way up the stairs to her bedroom, where she shut the door. Jesus couldn't even make her smile, so the kittens didn't have a chance in hell of putting her in a better mood.

She shed her boots and jeans, ran a tub full of water, and sunk down in it. Hostess, her ass! Prissy would be floating in her new bride status, flashing either a gold wedding band or a set of diamonds and gloating. Emily hadn't even planned on going to the damned old reception and now she was a hostess?

In her fretting she didn't hear anything until she looked up and there was Greg sitting on the edge of the tub. He leaned forward and kissed her hard on the lips.

His chest was bare, his hair still wet, and his plaid lounging pants rode low on his hips. He wasn't wearing glasses, and he had a heavy five o'clock shadow.

Bocephus was in one arm and Simba in the other.

"The babies were crying at the door," he said.

His smile erased all her grumbling. He set the cats on the floor and Bocephus attacked the toilet paper, rolling off two feet before Greg could grab him and put both of them out in the bedroom. He shut the door and picked up the shampoo from the vanity.

"Sit up and lean your head back. I'll wash your hair," he said.

"You look like a Greek god," she whispered.

"Greek gods had blond curly hair." He filled a plastic glass from the vanity with bathtub water and poured it gently over her hair.

"Mine don't," she said.

The cool shampoo sent chill bumps up her naked back, but when his fingers began to work it through her hair, the chill turned hotter'n the devil's pitchfork.

"I missed you so bad these past two days."

"Me too," she whispered.

The kittens set up a howl on the other side of the door, sending one little gray paw and one yellow one under the door to wiggle around and beg for forgiveness. Greg ignored them until he got her hair washed and rinsed then said, "Don't go away."

She heard him sweet-talking to the kittens as he put them out on the landing. Then he was back, had lathered up the washcloth, and was running it up her thigh, her stomach, and around her breasts.

"This water is about to start boilin', and what if…" she whispered.

"Nana and Dotty are in the kitchen making starch for their doodads, and they haven't climbed the stairs up to this floor in more than a year," he said.

"They've got ears like bats, Greg. They can probably hear us whispering."

She stood up and he wrapped a towel around her, scooped her up in his arms, and carried her to the recliner. He sat down and she snuggled against his chest. The masculine scent of men's soap and that smell that belonged solely to Greg Adams stirred desire and lust together.

"We can't, not in the house," she said.

He chuckled. "We can sit here with both of us nearly naked, but we can't have sex?"

Dotty's voice got louder and louder as she climbed the steps. "Okay, okay, Simba. I'll take you back up to Emily. I swear you are the biggest crybaby. Bocephus is happy as a lark playing with his toys in the kitchen."

"I told you," Emily muttered and jumped up.

She grabbed Greg by the hand and pulled him into the

bathroom with her, shutting the door behind them just as Dotty knocked on the door frame.

"Hey, Emily, you in here?" Dotty called out.

"In the tub," she yelled.

"I brought this whining cat up here. I'll put him on the recliner and shut your door."

"Thank you," Emily yelled.

"I'll bring Bo up when he gets tired of playing," Dotty said.

"Just holler and I'll come get him," Emily said. "No problem. I don't mind. More than a year, huh?" she whispered to Greg.

He nuzzled the inside of her neck. "I guess you were right. They do have ears like bats."

His warm breath shot a stream of scorching fire through her veins.

Emily hopped up on the vanity.

His eyes went all soft and his lips found hers in a kiss that steamed up the whole bathroom. He laid the towel back gently and cupped her bottom in his hands.

They fit perfectly that way, but still, when he slid into her, she gasped. She wrapped her arms tightly around his neck and enjoyed the sensation of a hard surface under her butt and a broad chest against her breasts. It was her first experience with vertical sex, and she floated over the moon.

It ended in a rush with her digging the tips of her fingers into his back and burying her face in his neck. She wrapped her legs firmly around his waist and he carried her to the toilet, put the lid down, and sat down with her in his lap.

"Wow!" he said.

"I know, but I already feel guilty, Greg. We shouldn't. It's disrespectful in Clarice's house," she whispered.

"Hey, Emily, I'm putting Bocephus in here too and shutting the door. He's not happy without Simba," Dotty yelled.

"Thank you," Emily managed to holler, but even in her own ears it sounded breathless.

"Good night," Dotty said and the door slammed shut.

"Neither one of them have been up here in months. I've felt like something fishy was going on for days. Now I know it," Greg said.

"I tell you, they've got my bedroom bugged or else they speak cat language and those two boys told on us," she told him. He knew something was up and the ladies would be lucky if he didn't find out exactly what it was before the auction.

She stood up and turned on the shower above the tub. "Come on. We'll take a fast shower, get dressed, and go sit on the steps. I don't think that's sinnin', is it? And Greg, darlin', that was surreal."

He put a finger on her lips. "It was, wasn't it? I missed talking to you today. Somehow texting just isn't the same. So, yes, let's sit on the stairs."

———

It was after eleven when Clarice and Dotty came out of the kitchen and noticed the kittens fighting with a catnip mouse on the bottom step. Dotty frowned and said, "I took them critters up to their bedroom. How'd they get out?"

"They can't make up their minds if they want to be with me or with y'all," Emily answered from halfway up the staircase where she leaned against the banister.

"Y'all are up past your bedtime, aren't you?" Greg asked.

They didn't fool him one bit. They'd stayed up late just to check on him and Emily. They'd both pushed them together until he said they were dating, and now they worked at keeping them apart. Didn't Nana realize that she was playing the game backward?

Clarice narrowed her eyes at him. "I thought you had a lot of emails to take care of."

"Took care of all my stuff and heard Emily giggling at the kittens, so I came out here to see what was so funny. We've been talking," he said.

Clarice sat down on the second step from the bottom. "About the auction? Who are you bidding on, Emily?"

"Oh, do I get to bid? I didn't know the hostesses got to bid."

"Of course you get to bid. All unmarried women who buy a ten-dollar bidding fan get to bid. You are going to buy a fan, aren't you?"

"Haven't decided. Who are you bidding on, Clarice?" Emily asked.

"I'm bidding on Max," Dotty said. "I promised him that I'd buy him so that he wouldn't have to be nice to some middle-aged woman trying to sweet-talk him into bed."

"If you'll pass those two wildcats up to me, I'm going to put them to bed. Tell y'all what... if I dream about Greg tonight, I'll bid on him at the auction. If not, then I'll stand aside and let all the other single girls have a chance at him," Emily said.

"Good night, ladies." Greg blew kisses to them

all and disappeared into his room. He picked up his glasses and pen and started to write. His phone signaled a text message.

Emily had written: *I need a letter tonight so badly*.

He wrote back: *Yes, ma'am. Dream about me. Please dream about me*.

His pulse quickened as he thought about standing on the bidding block and watching her raise her fan to outbid the other women. He wanted to belong to her. He wanted for the whole area to know that they were together, and he wanted her to stay on Lightning Ridge forever.

He'd dreamed about her since that first night. Sometimes it was sexual and he awakened to find a pillow lying next to him and not Emily. Sometimes it was sweet, like the one last night when they'd been lying on the quilt from the attic in a field of wildflowers. She wore the pretty blue dress that she'd worn to church and she was barefoot. They pointed out the shapes that the big white fluffy clouds made in the sky like two little kids. Their bodies didn't touch, but their hands were laced together.

He looked down at the ranch stationery and wrote,

Dearest Emily, I dream of you often. Last night…

Chapter 18

For a town the size of Ravenna, the church fellowship hall was huge. The hostesses on the decorating committee had done a fine job of turning it into a lovely reception, complete with yards and yards of frothy white tulle and lots of pretty pink roses—silk for the most part, but then Valentine's Day had just passed and that had probably wiped out the stock of real flowers for the whole state of Texas.

Emily remembered a line from the old movie *Steel Magnolias*, when the mother of the bride had said that the whole church looked like it had been sprayed down with Pepto-Bismol. The bride had argued that her colors were pink and bashful!

To Emily, there wasn't anything pink and bashful about it. It really did look like a coating of Pepto-Bismol. The multitiered cake was even topped with pink satin roses.

"What is my job?" Emily asked Clarice.

"You will hand the bride the gifts when she is ready to open them. She'll sit in that chair under the canopy with Tommy right beside her. You'll hand them to her. One of her friends will write down who gave the present and what it is so that she can write proper thank-you notes. And then you will take the present to the display table and arrange it real pretty so that all us fussy old women can make the proper noises about them after they're all opened," Clarice answered.

"It's a shitty job, but somebody has to do it," Dotty whispered out the side of her mouth.

Emily loved Dotty.

"But why can't one of her other friends do that?" Emily asked.

"Because it is a hostess's job," Clarice said. "Just think, someday you'll be sitting under the canopy and opening presents."

Emily shuddered. She might get married someday, but she damn sure did not want a reception that resembled a high school prom.

Dotty patted her on the shoulder. "Words aren't even necessary."

Yep, Emily loved Dotty.

"When do my duties start?" Emily asked Clarice.

"When the bride and groom get here, they'll make the rounds and visit for a little while, then they'll open presents and after that we will serve refreshments. Tonight it's wedding cake and a chocolate groom's cake, plus an assortment of tiny little cheesecakes that Rose makes for these occasions and punch, lemonade, and coffee," Clarice said.

"So I've got time to go to the ladies' room?"

Clarice touched her arm. "Sure you do."

The ladies' bathroom had been recently redecorated and still smelled like paint and wallpaper paste. Emily had hoped it would be a one-potty room with a lock on the door, but no such luck. There were three stalls, double sinks on one wall, and an old-fashioned vanity with a velvet bench already pulled out and waiting for the ladies to check their makeup in the three-way mirror.

She sat down with her back to the mirrors and heard

a noise. Her feet rose off the tile floor six inches as she checked every available corner for a mouse. God, she hated mice. Even the little white babies in the pet store gave her a case of hives.

Bocephus and Simba had better be good mousers or she would throw them out in the barn so their less fortunate siblings could teach them what cats did with those scary critters. She didn't see a thing but heard a whimper coming from the last stall.

"Hello," she said softly.

"Go away," a voice answered.

Emily lowered her feet back to the floor. Thank God it was a woman in distress and not a mouse who might run up the side of her cowgirl boot and fall down inside to touch her leg. She'd have to throw a two-hundred-dollar pair of boots in the trash if a damned old mouse touched them.

"Are you okay?" Emily whispered.

"No."

"Can I help?"

A movement made Emily lean forward. Two white satin high-heeled shoes were visible. "Prissy?" she asked.

"What?" the voice asked.

"It's Emily. Open the door and tell me why you are crying."

"Emily? Really?" Prissy asked.

"In the flesh, cowboy boots and all, but I did wear a dress so I don't look too much like a man," Emily said.

Another sob.

"You're going to be a mess for your reception if you don't stop caterwaulin'," Emily said. "Come out here and let's talk."

She sounded like a sick calf, one that was about half-dead and the other half starving. Emily tried the door, but it was locked from the inside. If she died in there, she was on her own. Emily wasn't going to kick in the door or drag her body out into the church sanctuary for someone to try to resuscitate her. She was responsible for Tonya and all those other women on the online dating service, not to mention all those sticky notes that were starting to accumulate again on the refrigerator.

Prissy's face showed above the stall before anything else could be seen. Emily figured she'd look like hammered rat shit after all that blubbering, but other than a little makeup mishap, she looked like a runway model in her cute little white brocade dress with long sleeves.

"If someone comes in the door, I'm going right back inside," she declared.

Emily pushed the vanity bench in front of the door and sat down on one end. "I reckon if you'll sit right there, it would take a couple of good strong cowboys to budge that door."

Prissy sat down and leaned forward, elbows on knees, head in hands. "I made one hell of a mistake, Emily. I hate living on a ranch. I'm not a rancher's wife. I don't like boots and I hate cows. And there are presents in that room and a freakin' cake and Tommy is about to bust the buttons off his shirt and I don't want to be married to a rancher."

"And the whole place looks like it's been sprayed down with Pepto-Bismol," Emily said.

Prissy raised her head and sniffled, but a smile did

tickle the corners of her mouth. "I remember that show very well. Julia Roberts said that her colors were bashful and blush. It was the only thing about the whole movie that I hated because I absolutely hate pink. It's what petite little girls wear, not giants like me. Why would they put up all that fluff and pink, gawdawful pink, for my reception? Not one person asked me if I even wanted a big foo-rah! Hell, didn't going to Vegas let them know that I didn't?"

She inhaled deeply and went on, "I've always liked brown, with maybe a little yellow, and I never liked lace. Momma let Grandma give me this gawdawful name and then dressed me in pink dresses and satin hair bows until I was old enough to rebel."

The corners of Emily's mouth turned up in a grin. "Probably, but you got to admit pink bows do go with your name, right?"

"Oh, hush. With a name like Emily and your size, you didn't have to worry about a freakin' thing."

Someone tried the doorknob and then hollered, "What's going on in there?"

"Sorry, we've got a problem. Potties won't work for at least ten minutes. Use the men's room right across the hall," Emily called out.

"The hell I will," Dotty's voice was clear. "Emily Cooper, open this door."

"We've got a bride crisis, Dotty. We'll be out in ten minutes."

"You'd better be. There's a bunch of old women in there drinking coffee like camels after a long march through the damn desert and they'll be hunting a potty in a few minutes. Old women have thimble-sized bladders," Dotty said.

Emily threw an arm around Prissy's shoulders. "We're on limited time. Fix your makeup while we talk."

"I'm not going to the reception. I'm going to file for an annulment tomorrow morning. Tell them to give the presents back. I don't need fourteen gravy boats," Prissy said.

"You are going to grow up," Emily said sternly.

"Don't you talk to me like that."

"If you feel this way then why in the hell did you marry Tommy?" Emily asked.

"I love Tommy," Prissy answered.

Emily pointed at the mirror and the small evening bag slung over Prissy's shoulder. "Then why are you going to annul the marriage?"

"You wouldn't understand. You like the ranch," she said.

"What do you do for a living, anyway?"

"I'm an accountant and I take care of all the family business from an office in downtown Bonham," she said. "It's really a house that Daddy bought years ago and remodeled into an office."

"You going to keep working?" Emily asked.

"Of course."

"And you love Tommy, right?"

Prissy nodded.

"You will be at the ranch an hour in the morning and a couple of hours in the evening. You'll be in your own house and you probably won't have to look at a cow except at the fall cattle sale, which you probably attend every year anyway, right?"

"Of course," she said again.

"Then what in the hell is your problem? Suck it up!

Tommy loves ranchin'. He'll be the one on the ranch all day. You'll be at work," Emily said.

"I thought I could talk Tommy out of it even after we were married, but he's not budging. I wish I would have fallen in love with Greg." Prissy carefully retouched her makeup in the mirror above the sinks.

"Greg is a rancher, in case you haven't noticed," Emily said.

Prissy stopped what she was doing and stared at Emily. "Greg won't be a rancher forever. He's just playing at it. His momma and daddy want him to come back to Houston and work in the firm with them. It would be easy to convince him to leave Lightning Ridge."

Emily pushed the bench back in front of the vanity and sat back down on it. "When you heard that Max was going to offer him a job, it scared you. And then Tommy called you. His ringtone is 'Hillbilly Bone,' isn't it?"

Prissy applied lipstick and asked, "How did you know?"

"Did he give you an ultimatum?"

She nodded. "He said he was leaving the whole damn state if I wouldn't marry him that weekend."

"How'd that make you feel?"

"My stomach hurt. My heart hurt. I couldn't breathe. It was horrible."

Emily put her hand on the doorknob. "Even more horrible than the pink reception?"

Prissy frowned and then nodded slowly. "I do love him and I don't have to be on that ranch all day. What was I thinking? I'm just so scared. Thank you, Emily."

Emily hugged Prissy. "You are welcome."

A gentle knock on the door was followed by a man's voice. "Prissy, darlin'?"

Emily swung the door open. "We were doing some last-minute touch-ups. Hello, Tommy, I'm Emily. Y'all give me two minutes to get into the fellowship hall and then make your entrance."

She heard Prissy say, "Tommy, I love you so much," as she did a fast walk toward the pink reception.

Emily was quiet on the way home that evening and went straight to her room when they arrived. Dotty and Clarice didn't tarry for even a minute in the den. Their bazaar things were boxed and ready to take to the barn on Friday, and they'd vowed that they were taking a monthlong break before they started on the next year's sale items.

Greg showered, changed into lounging pants, started a letter to Emily, and tore it up after the first paragraph. Something wasn't right. He could feel it in his heart with every single breath.

Finally, he went out onto the landing and sat down on the top step. The kittens bounded out of the door, which had been left open a crack, and attacked a toy mouse with a jingle bell attached to its long tail.

In a few minutes Emily joined him, brushing past him without so much as a sweet little kiss and set-tling on a step a fourth of the way down the staircase. He stretched his leg out and touched her bare arm with his toe. Her skin was as soft as silk sheets, and that idea conjured up visions that put him into semi-arousal instantly.

"You've been awfully quiet ever since you disap-peared and barely made it back before Prissy and Tommy showed up."

"She was in the bathroom having a meltdown, threatening to have her marriage annulled."

"Why?"

"It happens."

"Is that what you've been thinking about?"

She shook her head and told him what Prissy said about him getting tired of ranching. "Is there any truth in that?"

"Hell, no! I hate that kind of hustle and bustle. I'll never leave the ranch, especially not for a woman."

When she smiled his heart floated. "Not even one that has sex on a twin bed with you?"

"Are you asking me to?"

"Hell, no!" she said just as emphatically as he had. "If there was a chance you wanted to live in the city, I'd break this relationship off right now. I wouldn't ever want to be an anchor on your ass."

He rubbed his chin. "So we are in a relationship?"

"What would you call it?"

"Relationship sounds fine to me."

"We've known each other less than three weeks and in a few more days there will be eight hours between us. You think we can survive a long-distance relationship?"

"You think that time or distance has anything to do with it?" He completely ignored the question about long distance.

She scooted up one step. "I'm walkin' in virgin territory. It's all new to me. I don't know if it's crazy to feel like this after such a short time. Maybe it's just plain old physical attraction and lust."

"Hot lust, sweetheart. There's nothing plain about what goes on between us."

She moved up another step and he moved down one. He put a leg on either side of her and draped his arms around her neck. She leaned back against his broad chest and sighed. "I like listening to your heart beat."

"Your hair smells wonderful. Like wildflowers and roses all together in a bouquet, but that's just you," he said.

"What is *just me*?"

"You are cultivated roses when you are in public, but when we are alone together you are wildflowers growing free out in the pasture. It's a pretty heady combination, Miss Cooper."

She looked over her shoulder. Her blue eyes would charm the horns off the devil. He wanted to be looking into them when he drew his last breath at the age of ninety.

———

Emily wiggled out of his embrace and held out her hand. "Hold me in the recliner again. I need to feel your arms around me."

She left the door wide open so the cats could come in if they wanted, and if Dotty or Clarice snuck up on them, they wouldn't catch them doing something that would bring embarrassment to the ranch.

He sat down in the recliner and she curled up in his lap. He reached for the lever on the side and got comfortable. She fit in his arms like she belonged there forever, her head resting on his chest, one hand behind his neck, and one splayed above his shirt pocket.

"Now what?" he asked.

"Just hold me, Greg."

It would be like this when they were too old to enjoy each other's bodies anymore. The house would be quiet except when the children brought the kids and then the great-grandkids home from hopefully nearby ranches.

She'd fallen in love with Greg. Plain and simple. In less than three weeks she had lost her heart and soul to someone who lived all the way across the state.

Maybe he hadn't gotten as far as she had, but that was okay. She wasn't going anywhere and she would give him all the time he needed. He was sleeping when she looked up at him. His arms held on to her tightly even in his sleep and that was a good sign, wasn't it?

Using his rough tongue, Bocephus licked up across her cheek and woke her at three o'clock in the morning. She squirmed out of Greg's embrace and finally worked her way up from the recliner.

"Hey, did we go to sleep? Is it morning?"

"Almost," she said. "You can thank Bo for waking us up. Go on over to your room and get a couple of hours of comfortable sleep."

He stood to his feet and cupped her face in his big hands. The kiss was a mixture of passion and sweet, full of fire and gentleness. She leaned into it and locked her arms around his waist.

When he broke it off, she took a step back. "Good night, Greg."

He leaned down and kissed her right between the eyes.

She pushed him toward the door. "Go before I do something stupid like beg you to go to bed with me."

He touched her face once more, tracing the outline

of her lips with the tip of his forefinger. "Good night, Emily. I love you."

He was gone before she was even sure she heard him right.

Chapter 19

By seven thirty on Friday morning the pasture to the side of the sale barn had begun to look like a used car lot. Trucks from the hired help and the bazaar ladies, vans, cars, and even a 1970 vintage Volkswagen bus was parked out there.

Clarice and Dotty told Louis exactly where to set the first table, then Madge chose three strong cowboys, led them to the hippie bus, and made them carry boxes upon boxes of food into the barn.

"It's too early to bring in food," Emily said.

Rose flipped a checkered cloth over the eight-foot table and started unloading platters of cookies and finger foods, all the while shaking her head.

Dotty moved around to the back side of the table and began helping. "This isn't for the bazaar. It's for all the folks who'll be working all day at putting the bazaar together. The work that goes on before takes longer than the party lasts, and we never pass up an opportunity to bring food in this neck of the woods."

Clarice leaned in from behind Emily and whispered, "The boys work twice as hard if they're well fed."

"And the women gossip twice as much," Rose said.

"We handle things the same way out in west Texas. Whose VW is that?" Emily pulled a plate of pecan sandy cookies from a box.

"Mine," Madge said. "And yes, I was a hippie, and

yes, I still would be if I wasn't an old woman. And I picked out four of the wildest women on my site for Greg. I hope that at least one of them lands him."

"Hell, Madge, don't let age stop you. And your wild women ain't got a chance against my list," Dotty whispered as she scanned the room.

Madge pointed at her. "You ain't got a chance against my girls."

"Quit your fightin'," Rose said. "I've got the whole bunch of you bested."

The tingle on the back of Emily's neck said that Greg was somewhere close by. While the ladies bantered she scanned the room. Cowboy hats and jeans were everywhere, but none of them fit Greg's description.

Her senses were never wrong.

He had to be hiding in the shadows. She very carefully looked from corner to corner, and back again. Still no Greg, but she could feel his gaze undressing her like he did that morning at the breakfast table.

Finally, she looked up and there he was leaning over the buyer's balcony. He pointed to the right and then crooked his forefinger. Without saying anything, she slipped away from the arguing ladies and found the door leading up to the balcony. He met her at the top, slipped a hand under her knees and one under her arms, and carried her to the top bench.

When he sat down, she locked her arms around his neck and laid her cheek against his chest. "What are you doing up here?"

He buried his face in her hair. "Hiding out and waiting for you."

"Clarice will find us," she said.

"I know, but we've got a few minutes. I wanted you to know that I meant what I said last night. I was wide awake when I said it and I meant it."

She leaned away from his broad chest and locked gazes with him. "Are you sure?"

"Want me to get out the megaphone and yell it from the banister so everyone in the barn will know? Yes, I'm sure." He pulled her back into his embrace and his lips met hers in a passionate, scorching hot kiss that convinced her even more than his words. "You don't have to say it right now. I'm a patient man, and I can wait until you feel it in your heart."

She'd had relationships of one depth or the other in her lifetime, but it was the right time, the right place, and Greg was the right man. Everything lined up so perfectly that it scared her. God would throw the wrench in the gears; she just knew he would.

"I'm wide awake now and so are you, so I'm going to say it again so you won't have any doubts. I love you, Emily," he whispered.

"I love you, Greg," she said. "And just for the books, I'm not saying it because you did. It hit me just seconds before you said it, but I thought…"

He hugged her tightly. "You thought I was half-asleep."

"Greg Adams." Max's voice bounced off the walls of the barn, and Emily's soul came close to leaving her body.

Greg pulled her back into his embrace. "He's playing with the auctioneer's microphone."

"Greg Adams, wherever you are, your nana says she needs you to find her. She's the lady in the red shirt and a chocolate chip cookie in her hand," Max said.

"Guess that's our cue," Emily said.

"I'd rather stay up here and make out with you all morning."

She tilted her head toward the narrow bench. "We'd have to stack up like cord wood. This isn't even as wide as the attic bed."

"I'll gladly take the bottom so you don't get splinters in your pretty little butt. But they'd bust in on us and ruin the moment. Maybe we'll go into town for ice cream tonight?"

"Do they have ice cream in the vending machine at the hotel?"

The ringtone coming from his shirt pocket said that Clarice was serious about finding him. Emily pulled the phone out and handed it to him.

"I heard Max. Probably half the county heard Max. I'm on my way," he said.

Emily was close enough that she could hear Clarice's voice. "Jeremiah says that he got tied up and can't make it today, but he will definitely be here tomorrow evening. And Emily, we need you to work on some signs when you get finished kissing my grandson."

"Yes, ma'am." He chuckled.

"Dear Lord," Emily gasped.

"We're dating, darlin'. And that means kissin' is allowed right along with holding hands, even in Nana and Dotty's world. Let's go work on signs and set up tables."

When they were halfway down the stairs, Dotty yelled across the barn, "Y'all stay out of Madge's van. Her motto when she first bought that thing was that if the bus was rockin', don't come knockin'." Dotty laughed.

———

Clarice air slapped Dotty. "You'll embarrass her."

"They're kissing? Did I hear you say they were kissing?" Madge asked.

"When did all this start?" Rose pushed Madge to the side so that she could be closer to Clarice.

"Shhh! They're close enough they can hear us, and yes, they were kissing and they are now dating." Dotty shushed them all.

"What about the dating site women?" Rose asked.

"Not a thing," Clarice whispered then motioned for Emily. "You have such beautiful handwriting, I'd like for you to sit down at this table and make a name placard to go on each of the chairs. Here's a list of the names and there's paper, pens, crayons, glitter glue, and a whole box of sticker things."

"I could probably do a better job on the computer," Emily said.

"We want it handmade, not computer generated," Rose told her.

Greg let go of her hand and kissed her on the cheek. "I'll see you later. If I don't go help Max move that round pen, he'll pick up the microphone again."

"It's true, Emily?" Rose sighed.

"What?" Emily raised an eyebrow.

"You are dating Greg. That makes me so happy. To think that Marvin's granddaughter and Clarice's grandson… oh, it's a fairy tale. But, oh no! How are you going to handle all the women we've invited here tonight?" Rose gasped.

"We'll deal with them. Can't undo what's been done,

and maybe they'll get into a bidding war and really bring in a lot of money for the scholarships," Emily said.

Clarice put her head in her hands. "You are going to have to buy up every dance ticket, and dear Lord, you have to buy him or one of those women will tell him, and now that he's fallen for you, he'll be so mad at us."

Emily patted Clarice on the shoulder. "It's all right. I'll take care of it. But I do have a question."

"What?" Dotty barely whispered.

"Do any of you know what it means when someone says they'll bring the leather?"

"Of course, it means that they want to ride horses and they'll bring their own saddle. Greg loves horses. I was hoping you'd look at that site this morning when you sat down at the computer. I'm worried that I didn't invite the right four," Clarice answered.

Emily smiled and leaned across the table. "In today's world, ladies, leather means bondage, as in she will tie him up and spank him if he wants and she'll be wearing leather underbritches that are real skimpy and a leather bra. And what she's intending to ride is not horses."

"Oh, my sweet holy Jesus," Rose said.

"Holy-damn-shit." Dotty actually blushed.

"So how many ladies are bringing leather?" Emily asked.

Clarice held up two fingers. Dotty held up four.

Madge said, "One of mine likes leather and one is expecting a very wild ride that will blow her mind. Please tell me that *blow her mind* doesn't mean some kind of drugs."

"Rose?" Emily asked.

"I'm just trying to remember what all I said when I

was Greg. I think I might have given the impression that I could show her such a good time that… oh, my! I was talking about taking her to a rodeo and I can't even say the words."

"Well, it ought to be a right lively auction for sure." Emily laughed.

"You will dance all the dances with him, won't you?" Clarice asked.

"No, ma'am. But I will do my best to dance the last one and everyone knows whoever gets the last dance is the one that takes him home. Now tell me more about that VW bus out there." She quickly moved the attention to Madge.

"Oh, honey, things went on in that bus that will live on in memories. You'd never believe it if we did tell you." Madge blushed.

"Oh, yes, I would. That's why it's still running and bringing stuff to the church bazaar—so it can hear tales about what went on when it was in its prime, right?" Emily raised a dark eyebrow.

Dotty answered, "That's why we keep bringing things to the bazaar. We're trying to buy ourselves a ticket into heaven. The VW is to remind us that we got a lot of work to do yet. Now, young lady, you sit right down here and put those cowboys' names on these plaques. We're going to make them hold them in their laps so the women folks can see them real good. You better make a bunch with Greg's picture and name on them. Now tell us, how long have you known that you were fallin' for Greg?"

"I'm not saying jack shit. I've got plaques to make," Emily said.

Clarice pointed at Dotty. "You are a bad influence. You've got her cussin'."

Dotty grabbed Clarice's finger and held it tightly. "You might have made me stop smokin' when I adopted Jeremiah and stop drinkin' when Henry died. But I'll be damned if you make me stop cussin'. It's all I got left."

"And I'm going to grow up and be just like her," Emily teased.

Clarice pulled her finger free and said, "Well, shit!"

A lone candle burned on a weathered old wooden feedbox beside the bed. Long lashes rested on Emily's cheekbones as she slept nestled in the crook of Greg's body after a bout of scalding hot sex. He shouldn't be sneaking out to the attic with her; they should be sleeping together in his bed in the house. But she would have none of it, saying that it was disrespectful to Clarice. She'd felt guilty about the two-minute quickie in the bathroom and said that they couldn't even do that anymore.

Doubts plagued him as he stared at her as long as he wanted. Maybe she loved him but she wasn't in love with him. There was a vast difference in the two, and he'd proven it a couple of times in the past. He had loved but he'd never been in love before Emily.

He'd never believed in that instant falling in love that his friends talked about. No woman would ever rein in his heart to the point that he couldn't think of anything but her all day long. Lust did that and when it finally played out, then the relationship died. But it had happened and he understood being in love as opposed to simply loving.

—₥—

The moon was gone from the attic window when Emily awoke. The candle was still burning, but the first sun rays of the day gave enough light that she could study Greg's face as he slept. In the depths of sleep his face was softer, the angles less pronounced, but his lips still belonged to a masculine cowboy. Thick dark lashes rested on his cheekbones, and the effect was sexy as the devil, but she liked for his eyes to be open.

She liked the way he looked at her, that instant flash of heat that she got when his eyes went all soft and dreamy just before he kissed her. She stretched until her lips were even with his and woke him with a series of burning kisses.

"Good mornin'," he mumbled.

"It is morning and we probably need to go in the house before Dotty gets to stirring around. I love waking up with you," she said.

"Me too," he said.

He framed her face with his hands. "Emily, I'm in love with you. I want you to understand that."

"I do," she said.

"There is a difference in saying that I love you and being in love with you."

"I know, Greg," she whispered. "My heart was in love with you before my mind was willing to say that I loved you."

"Just so you know and never doubt it," he said.

"Then why this serious mood?"

"I just have to say what is on my heart or it'll blow up." He slapped her playfully on the fanny. "Are we going to go to the house or move in together here in the attic? Your call."

She wiggled out of his embrace. Her bare feet hit the cold linoleum, and she quickly stomped on her boots without pausing to put on socks. She grabbed an oversized T-shirt and pulled it over her head, picked up her flannel lounging pants, and slung them over her shoulder.

Greg crawled out of bed, stretched, and dug his glasses out of his boots. "Oh, my, you are even more beautiful when I can see you as well as touch you," he said.

Emily pointed to the bed. "You are a charmer. At first I thought you were going to be a cold businessman. But I was wrong."

"I think I was before you came into my life," he admitted.

"And now you are a hot cowboy charmer." She smiled.

A hell of a lot of women were showing up that night expecting more than a charming cowboy. She wondered if they'd have a suitcase packed plumb full of leather goods to tease him with.

He picked up the corner of the quilt. "This thing must have magical powers."

"It's like me, darlin'. Just a plain old quilt that promises red-hot sex. No magic. No leather. No whips. Nothing kinky."

"Thank God." He chuckled. "Plain old red-hot sex is what this cowboy likes. That kinky shit ain't for me."

"Tell me, darlin', how many times have you had to wash this quilt before I came along?"

He jerked a gauze undershirt over his head. "I've

only slept on it with one woman and that's you. Never was in the attic with another person except Jeremiah, and we weren't up here for sex."

"Well, thank God for that news. What were you up here for?"

"Well, for starters we smoked our first cigarette up here and decided after we turned green that smoking was not for us. We chewed our first Copenhagen tobacco up here, and believe me, it only took one time. And when I snuck my dad's *Playboy* magazines out of the house the summer we were fifteen, we wore out the pages up here until one day they were gone. Dotty or Nana, neither one ever mentioned them, and believe me, we didn't either." He pulled on his jeans and boots.

She dressed hurriedly in the denim skirt she'd worn to supper that night. "That sounds like me and Taylor and the barn. Only he never shared his magazines, just his cigarettes, which he never quit, and his daddy's tobacco, which neither of us ever used again."

He opened the door. "The joys of childhood."

"I could live in the attic. It's got all we need. A bed and a candle." She sighed.

"What about the kittens?" he asked.

"The boys would be cramped. The big house has so many corners and things to hide in. Simba practices his lion maneuvers every morning. Poor old Bocephus doesn't even know what hits him."

"Then I guess maybe we'd better not move in together if there's not room for the children." Their hands were laced together as they crossed the yard and went into the house through the kitchen door. "You forgot something, darlin'."

She stopped and turned, but his hand kept traveling. His grin was pure mischief. "I don't feel underbritches."

"Oh, no! They're probably tangled up in the quilt."

"Which I plan to sneak into the house and toss into the washer and dryer this afternoon. I really don't mind commando."

She wiggled free of his hand before it got an inch higher, because if it did, they wouldn't make it back to the attic room or to breakfast that morning.

Emily took a quick shower, dressed in jeans and a sweatshirt for the morning's work, and laid out a nice sweater and fancy jeans to wear to supper that evening.

"Hey, you decent?" Dotty rapped on the door.

"Yes, ma'am. Come right in," she yelled.

Dotty carried a cat in each arm. "They were whining for you. What's that?" She pointed at the outfit on the bed.

"I'm trying to decide what to wear this evening. Jeremiah will be here in time for supper, right?"

"Oh, he wouldn't miss a chance to sit up at the table with family and good food. We'll be busy out in the barn getting last-minute things ready, but I've got his favorite enchiladas made and ready to heat and a Crock-Pot of beans brewing. It won't take but a minute to put some jalapeno corn bread in the oven." Dotty sat down in the rocking chair with both cats still in her arms.

"I want to look nice. He's Greg's best friend," Emily said.

"Stop worryin' about what to wear. Men folks is all business for the most part. And honey, I got a feelin' that he's bringin' home a woman to meet me, so he's not going to know if you've got on jeans or that fancy dress that you wore to the party with Clarice."

"A woman." Emily frowned.

"He said he had a surprise, and one time when I called him a woman answered. I'm old but I'm not stupid, and it's time for him to settle down. Oh, and her name is Stacy," Dotty said.

"How did you figure all that out? Maybe a woman answered because he was on a date. That doesn't mean he's bringing one home to meet you," Emily said.

"At three in the morning?"

"Dotty! What were you doing calling him at that time?"

Dotty giggled. "To see who would answer."

"What excuse did you use?"

Another giggle. "The electricity had gone off in the night and I didn't have my glasses on when I reset the clock. Good one, ain't it?"

"Dotty, you are a bad girl." Emily smiled.

"Yeah, but I found out what I wanted to and now I won't die with a heart attack when he brings her home to meet me," Dotty said.

"So does Stacy work in the business with him?"

"Stacy has been his secretary for six months." Dotty set the kittens on the recliner. "Breakfast is ready. But let me tell you right now, when they get here, he's sleeping in the room next to Greg and Stacy will be next door to you. I won't have them sleeping together in my house."

Emily couldn't fight back the blush, so she hung up the shirt and moved hangers around in her closet so that Dotty couldn't see it.

"They aren't about to get away with something that we won't let you and Greg get away with. And one other thing, there's extra quilts in the linen closet if it gets cold in the attic." She winked and hurried out of the room.

Bright scarlet filled her cheeks. They knew about the attic and they weren't making a noose to hang her from the nearest oak tree. Did that mean Clarice wouldn't throw a fit if the relationship took another step?

Chapter 20

EMILY'S CHEEKBONE HAD A STREAK OF GOLD GLITTER glue smeared across it like war paint. A dot of purple glitter the size of a quarter was right between her eyes. It was all over her hands and her ratty old work shirt. Her jeans were faded and her hair pulled back in a ponytail. She checked the clock and figured she still had an hour before Jeremiah and his girlfriend, if Dotty was right, would show up. That would give her plenty of time to finish the last cowboy's name and grab a quick shower, wash her hair, and dress to be presentable.

She'd just finished putting a heart instead of a dot on top of the *i* on the last cowboy's name when she heard Greg yell from across the room, "Jeremiah, you are early!"

If only Emily had asked to see a picture of Jeremiah, her jaw might not have dropped. She'd pictured him as tall, dark, handsome, like Greg, only maybe wearing a three-piece suit and dark sunglasses. But the man that Greg grabbed in a man-hug was short, slightly round, and almost bald. The woman standing beside him wore high heels, skintight jeans, and a denim jacket with enough bling to blind a person. Her hair was black with blond steaks and cut short in a spiky 'do. Her eyes were almost as black as her hair, and her skin had that slightly toasted tone that comes from one Latino parent.

Jeremiah's deep booming voice carried all the way

across the barn and shocked Emily as much as his looks. It went with that image of the tall, dark, handsome private investigator.

"Meet Stacy, my girlfriend," he said.

"Jeremiah!" Dotty hollered from the back of the barn. When she reached his side, Jeremiah wrapped his arms around her and picked her up off the ground.

"Put me down, you crazy kid." Dotty laughed.

He might be short, but he was strong as a horse if he could pick Dotty up like that. By the time he released his mama, Clarice was by her side to get her hugs. "It's so good to have you home. What do you think of our idea for the bazaar this year?"

"Greg told me all about it. Y'all might raise enough with this auction idea to put two girls through school. I want to introduce you both to my girlfriend, Stacy. She is my secretary and keeps me organized." Jeremiah looked at her like he could eat her up right there in front of everyone.

Emily didn't even realize that Greg was beside her until he grabbed her hand. "Come on, darlin'. I want to introduce you to my best friend."

She wanted to crawl under the table and hide, but there was nothing to do but stand up straight, ignore her messy appearance, and put on her brightest smile.

"Jeremiah and Stacy, I want to introduce you to Emily," Greg said.

Jeremiah stuck out a hand. Everything about him might be generic, but when he smiled the whole room lit up. Lord, with that grin he could probably ferret more information out of someone than a tall, dark, and handsome cowboy ever could.

"Pleasure to meet you, Emily. I've heard so much about you. Greg has emailed dozens of pictures, but I pictured you taller. But there's room in this world for us short people too, right?"

Stacy smiled at Emily with a friendly, down-to-earth smile that made Emily like her on the spot. "I hope so. If not then we'd best go on and forget about the party."

"You are both so right. We make up for height in power and determination for sure," Emily answered.

She would deal with Greg later. Just when had he taken pictures of her? Oh, Lord, hopefully not in the attic while she was sleeping.

Emily shook Jeremiah's outstretched hand. "I'm glad to finally meet you. I've heard lots of stories."

Jeremiah cocked his head to one side. "About the cigarettes?"

"My lips are sealed," Emily said.

Then she held out her hand to Stacy. "We'll have to find time for a visit before the day is done."

"Looks like y'all got this under control, so I'm going to take Stacy up to the house so we can get unpacked before supper. I'll tell you stories to curl your hair later, Emily," Jeremiah said.

Greg threw an arm around Emily's shoulders. "Dotty won't let him out of her sight the whole time he's here."

"You got that damn straight," Dotty said. "I'll ride up to the house with them and get the enchiladas going for supper. That way I can get to know Stacy better and tell her some stories that might curl *her* hair."

"All done with your chores?" Greg asked Emily.

Emily nodded. One more hour and she'd have looked presentable. And she'd agonized all day over what she would wear to supper, whether she'd make an entrance or just slip into her chair unnoticed.

"Then let's go to the house too. By the way, darlin', you are cuter than Bocephus or Simba with that glitter on your face." He leaned down and kissed her on the tip of her nose.

"I look like crap. And his girlfriend is gorgeous. I felt like a country bumpkin beside her," she said.

"Then crap is beautiful. Nana, we're going on home. See you at supper. Are Madge and Rose stayin' with us?"

"Yes." Madge nodded. "Dotty made enchiladas. Ain't nobody in the county can make them as good as she can."

Greg waved over his shoulder and led Emily out to the truck. He opened the door for her, buckled her in, and then kissed her hard, his tongue teasing hers until she forgot all about how she looked. When the kiss ended he strung softer butterfly kisses over her face, spending extra time on the streak of bright red glitter.

"Now it's on your lips." She giggled.

"Yes, it is. We match, so we're a couple. Jeremiah liked you even if you aren't all dolled up in your best boots. I like you, so it doesn't really matter anyway, but now you've met the whole bunch of us... almost."

She gasped. "Almost?"

"Well, Momma and Daddy will be here for supper too. They're flying in from Houston in Dad's little plane to surprise Nana. Nana has a place out in the pasture fixed up for them to land."

She threw her head back on the back of the seat and shut her eyes. Her breath caught in her chest and panic set in. Meeting Jeremiah was one thing. Meeting Greg's parents… well, shit! And if that sounded like it came straight from Dotty… well, so be it.

"They won't bite and you do have time to polish your best boots," he said as he shut the door and went around the front of the truck to his side.

"My boots are polished," she said when he started the engine.

"Then you don't have a thing to worry about."

"Put yourself in my shoes. Would you worry if you were about to meet my parents even if your boots were shined?"

"Yes, ma'am! I'd be shakin' in them boots. But I love you, Emily. And they will too. They'll see that you make me happy and love you for it." He laid a hand on her knee as he drove.

She had changed clothes six times and her bed looked like one of those overfilled boxes at the back of the Goodwill store. She filtered through the pile one more time, but nothing looked right to wear when she meet Greg's parents. Now she remembered why she'd squirmed out of most relationships before she had to meet the parents and family. It was downright nerve-wracking.

Bocephus thought the clothing pile was better than a mountain of fall leaves. He stuck his nose in the waist of her jeans and crawled down the leg. It reminded her of those pictures of snakes trying to digest a small animal, only her jeans didn't keep Bocephus. He stuck his nose out of the bottom of the leg and meowed at her. Simba was the lion, sneaking up on a pearl snap with his tail high and the fur on his back standing straight up. When he pounced, there wasn't a pearl snap in all of Texas that didn't shiver.

But nerves kept her from enjoying the kittens' antics. She finally decided on her best pair of jeans even though the bling on the pockets wasn't anything compared to Stacy's, and a fitted knit shirt with long sleeves. Her boots were indeed shiny, and she'd taken time to apply makeup and to use the curling iron.

She took a deep breath and opened the door to find Greg sitting outside on the top step. He'd cleaned up, but he hadn't dressed up. His jeans were soft and hadn't seen the benefit of an iron; his chambray shirt hung open and covered a snowy white T-shirt. He pushed his glasses up on his nose and smiled.

"You are gorgeous tonight. I thought maybe we should make our entrance together. Mom and Dad got here about half an hour ago. I heard Nana squealing, so I knew they'd arrived, but I haven't been down to see them yet." He stood up and crooked his elbow.

She'd never loved him more than she did that moment. He waited for her. Now that was a cowboy worth keeping around forever.

"They're in the den. Dad likes a cocktail before dinner," Greg whispered.

"Does he know about my gramps and Clarice?" she whispered.

"Nana told him a couple of days ago, so he knows."

"Well, look who is finally joining the party," Jeremiah said from the other side of the room.

Stacy had removed her jacket but looked the same otherwise. She had a cold beer in one hand and waved with the other one. "Where's the glitter war paint,

Emily? I liked it." Her tone and her expression said that she was as nervous as Emily.

Emily smiled. "We can always go down to the barn and get it if things get too tough."

Dotty's long bony forefinger shot up in the air in a blur. "Don't you be stealin' her away. We haven't even started getting to know each other. Jeremiah wouldn't even leave us alone a minute, so we still have lots to discuss and I get her first."

"Fuss at me when I don't come home. Fuss at me when I do. Damned if I do. Damned if I don't." Jeremiah smiled.

Clarice pointed at Bart and drew her eyebrows down. "Speaking of kids not coming home. It's been two months since I've seen you two and that was only for half a day at Christmas. You should have told me you were coming for the bazaar. I would have made your favorite foods."

"That's why we didn't tell you. You've been busy enough with this bazaar without cooking even more," Bart said.

A blond-haired lady with brown eyes crossed the room and held out her hand toward Emily. "I'm Nancy Adams, Greg's mother. I'm glad to meet you, Emily. And Mama Clarice, we'll do better, I promise. This time we are staying two nights."

Emily shook her hand briefly and then Nancy let go and hugged her son tightly. She whispered something in his ear that made him smile even bigger, but Emily couldn't hear the words.

"Which barely makes up for Christmas," Clarice said.

Bart chuckled. "The road runs both ways, Mother. You could come to Houston."

"I get claustrophobic in big places. All that traffic and all those people give me the hives," Clarice said. "Besides, I'm old and you are still young."

"Clarice Adams, you aren't ever going to be old, so you don't get to play that card," Emily said.

Nancy smiled and winked at her. "I see why you hired this girl. I bet she keeps you all on your toes."

"Yes, she does," Dotty said.

"Emily, this is my dad, Bart. I'm sure you figured that out already," Greg said.

There was no doubt that Bart was Greg's father. He was an older model of the same man, same green eyes, and same wire-rimmed glasses. Bart was thirty pounds heavier and two inches shorter. Instead of jeans and a Western-cut shirt, he wore soft relaxed-fit khaki slacks, loafers, and a three-button baby blue knit shirt.

"I understand you own a ranch out in west Texas," Bart said as he shook her hand firmly.

"Yes, sir, I do. Not very big right now, but it's still home."

"Lot of flat land out there. Great place to land a plane. You can see for miles and miles."

"It's a little different than the land around here. It's all dirt and sky and not many trees, but ranchin' is ranchin', and when it's in your blood, it's about all the same," she said.

"That's what my son and my mother tell me. It must've bypassed my bloodline. It's all right to visit the boonies, but I wouldn't want to live here. Can I make you a drink?" he asked.

"I wouldn't mind having a beer like Stacy is having. In the bottle is fine," she said.

"Yes, sir, son, she's a rancher all right." Bart laughed.

Later that night Emily cuddled up next to Greg on the single bed in the attic and inhaled deeply. "You washed the quilt. It smells like fabric softener."

"I made an excuse to leave the barn for a while and got it in the washer and dryer without anyone even catching me. I wonder how many other lovebirds have been up here in this attic."

"I can't picture Clarice…" she started.

He slapped his hands over his ears. "I don't want to picture that. I'm one of those fellers that think their parents and grandparents didn't do those things."

She giggled. "Come on, Greg! They were all young like us at one time. They had raging hormones too! And they liked cuddling and kissing. I betcha that's why there's still just a twin-sized bed up here instead of a big old king-sized one. They liked being close as much as we do."

"Em… i… ly!" he drug her name out. "I don't want to think about that."

The giggling stopped.

She sat straight up in bed and clamped one hand over her mouth and the other against her forehead. "My underwear?"

"Oh, no! I must have left them in the dryer," he said.

She fell back on the bed with a loud moan. "What are we going to do?"

"Momma was talking about doing laundry before she went up to bed. She'll find them for you," he said.

"She'll know and she'll hate me and I thought maybe that she was going to like me. We've got to sneak down there and get them out before someone finds them, Greg. They'll throw me to the coyotes in the morning."

"Well, I've gotten kind of used to having you around and I wouldn't want the coyotes chewing on your cute little ass." He reached across her and picked up the black lacy underpants from the table. "Just kiddin'!"

She slapped him on his broad chest and grabbed at them. "God, you scared me so bad. What if your mom really had found them?"

"She wouldn't know they were from the attic. She'd just think you didn't get them out when you did laundry. Nobody knows we come up here. It's our secret," he said.

Emily eased back down and put her head on his chest. Nothing that went on at Lightning Ridge would ever be a complete secret, but Greg didn't need to know what Dotty had told her earlier.

She tossed the underpants back on the table and shifted her position until she was lying on top of him. His body was hard and tough but felt oh so right underneath her naked breasts, tummy, and legs. She traced his masculine jawline with her forefinger and he groaned.

"You turn me on with nothing but your hands." He wrapped his arms around her tighter and nuzzled his face into the soft crook of her neck.

"You turn me on with nothing but your kisses," she whispered.

He flipped her over and kissed her softly at first, then deepened the kiss, turning sweet into a raging fire of desire that begged for satisfaction. Her hands roamed over his broad back and lower to his hips and thighs until she ran out of reach. She'd never realized before that moment that there were erotic zones in the tips of her fingers, and just touching his body turned her on almost as much as him touching her… almost.

He kissed her lips, eyelids, tip of her nose, neck, and every other part of her body he could reach as he settled on top of her and found his way inside her body, uniting them. They began a steady rhythm, working together until they were both frenzied. She nipped his neck and then backed off. His mother would hate her if he showed up with a hickey. But even that fleeting notion going through her head couldn't take away the heat. Not until he looked down into her eyes and asked without saying a word; not until his mouth found hers as they tumbled over the top together; not until he'd rolled to the side and wrapped his arms around her, letting the afterglow of something wonderful warm them from the inside out; not until then did the heat subside inside her body.

"I love you," she panted.

"I love you, darlin'."

Just before she fell asleep, she wondered what happened next in the relationship. She'd never gone this far before, never said the words, never felt the love in her heart. Now what?

Chapter 21

THE BAND WAS SET UP AND READY. DOTTY HAD DONE A quick head count and there were more than a hundred people in the barn, so that meant more than five hundred dollars was already in the fund. They'd sold twenty fans at ten dollars each, so that was even more. And now the band was ready to start playing and the ladies with the fans stuck in their hip pockets had bought tickets.

"It's time." Dotty pointed at the chairs. "Greg, go take your place."

Greg pushed back his chair. "How many tickets did you buy, Emily?"

"I got a fan but no tickets. They were sold out by the time I got to the end of the line to buy some. You're on your own, cowboy," she said.

The grin that had been on his face all evening faded. "You are kidding, right? Women have been coming up to me all evening saying that they're so glad that I invited them and I don't know who in the hell they are. I just smile and say that I sure hope they're having a good time."

Jeremiah sucked in a lung full of air and let it out slowly. "I'm glad Mama didn't put me up there to auction. And believe me, those women sure know you, so don't be playing dumb. Several of them have cornered Stacy. Those two over there in the leather jeans and cowboy boots," he nodded toward the bar, "they made Stacy blush. And that's not an easy thing to do."

"Do you know what in the hell is going on?" Greg asked Dotty.

"Just enjoy having so many adoring women around you," she answered.

Greg groaned. "What in the hell have they done, Emily?"

Max had an empty beer bottle in one hand and was on the way to the bar when he stopped and said, "Looks like this might be an annual affair, so you guys who don't like being on the auction block might be thinking about finding a wife by this time next year. I'm on my way to get another beer. Auctioneering will dry me plumb out if I'm not well hydrated."

Greg planted a kiss on Emily's forehead. "Next year I think it should be reversed. Us cowboys get to buy the fans and the tickets and the cowgirls have to sit in the chairs up there in the sale ring."

"Now that's a damn fine idea. Every other year we'll turn it around. My granny always said that turnabout was fair play," Dotty said.

"Can I have your attention, folks?" the band's lead female singer said.

All conversations ceased and everyone looked toward the stage.

"We are going to start playing, and I understand it's time for the cowboys who have chairs reserved to come right on up here and take their places. Ladies, look at your tickets and see who you've bought the rights for this first song."

An even dozen cowboys took their seats and held glittered signs in their laps. Cowgirls started the stampede from the bar and the far corners to look at the cowboys.

"I've got to go relieve Ivy at the bazaar table," Dotty said. "Look. Nancy picked up two baby stocking hats and a pretty pink baby blanket."

Emily blushed and Nancy waved. "I heard that, Dotty. One of the secretaries at the firm is having a baby girl."

"Oh, I thought you were looking ahead at being a grandma." Dotty took Ivy's place behind the table and straightened the items that had been rifled through. "This whole thing was Emily's idea. She thinks of everything. It was her idea to sell the tickets and to put names on the front and numbers on the back. There could have been a stampede if she hadn't. Might have been fun to see the hair pullin' and bitch slappin' though. She figured out that if the cowgirls just put a dollar in a jar, there could be catfights over which cowboy they wanted to dance with, so they had to buy tickets with the cowboy's name on them. If they get caught dancing without a ticket they get a bazaar fine and have to put ten dollars in the jar."

"It makes me sad," Nancy whispered.

"That the women would flock around your son? Look at all those girls lining up to dance with him."

"No, that the chance of him coming back to Houston to work in the firm is getting slimmer by the minute, and it doesn't have a thing to do with all those women. It has to do with Emily Cooper," Nancy whispered as she picked up several of the cowboy dream catchers. "I love these. Who made them?"

"Clarice and I did, and you better get as many as you want because they're going like hotcakes."

Nancy smiled. "How many tickets has Emily really got in her pocket to dance with my son?"

"Not a single one. For one thing, Rose bought up the last five while Emily was helping us fix up the home-made table. For another, she says that she wants to dance with the other cowboys to see which one she's going to bid on," Dotty answered.

A frown replaced Nancy's smile. "That's crazy. I figured she'd buy all his tickets and then bid on him too. She does love him, doesn't she? Or is he going to get his heart broken?"

Dotty leaned forward and whispered, "What if he did?"

"I'd hate to see him in pain," Nancy said. "But it might make him realize that he should come on back where he belongs. He's thirty and it's time for him to get established in the company if he's going to make partner by forty."

"He was born a rancher," Dotty said.

"I know that, but a mother can hope for a change."

Dotty reached across the table and patted Nancy on the hand. "I wanted Jeremiah to go into ag-business in college so he'd stick around here. Clarice had already said that she'd make a job for him at Lightning Ridge, but be damned if he didn't have his heart set on being a private investigator. Ain't no room in Ravenna for that kind of job. So I had to suck it up and accept it. He's happy. That makes me happy. You be happy for Greg wherever he settles or you'll be miserable."

"I'm not you, Dotty," Nancy said.

"He's a cowboy, darlin'. And he loves it. And them two kids were made for each other. Emily knows what she's doin' tonight, and when it comes down to the final moment, she'll realize that she can't stand for another woman to have him even for one date."

"If he's in love with her or falls in love with her, they'll settle down right here forever," Nancy whispered.

"I think that part about falling in love has already happened." Dotty gave Nancy's hand another pat and moved to the end of the table where several women had gathered to look over the display of knitted scarves.

———⁓———

Nana was so excited about all the money coming in for the scholarship fund that Greg would bet his brand-new boots that it really would be a yearly affair from then on, and by damn, next year he was going to be married.

"Whoa, cowboy," he mumbled.

He caught sight of his mother and Dotty having a visit at the table where the ladies had spread out all their sale items. It looked like she was buying a baby blanket.

What would his and Emily's children look like? Would they have her gorgeous blue eyes and dark hair?

Sons? Would they be cowboys or would it skip the next generation and he'd be a grandfather before a child was born into the family who loved the land as much as he did? No, he and Emily's genes were rooted in ranching enough that their sons would be cowboys for sure.

Daughters? He kept the groan inside, but when he thought of teenage daughters as pretty as Emily, he vowed that he would nail the door shut to the attic room above the garage. And he'd keep a shotgun beside the front door to scare off the boys.

Prissy dragged Tommy over to the table and spoke to Nancy before picking up several things and handing them to Dotty. Tommy pulled out his billfold and paid while Dotty put the purchases into a bag.

Greg wiped his brow, leaving a few flakes of sparkly glitter in the wake. Tommy wanted children, lots of them. Greg wanted children, lots of them. Sweet Jesus, what if Prissy's daughters grew up to fall in love with Greg's ranching sons?

Now that is one scary as hell idea, he thought.

"Ladies, choose your partners. We're off and running with a good old country two-step from Sara Evans in exactly two minutes."

The lead guitar picker hit a couple of chords, and two dozen ladies with little red tickets showed up at his chair. "He's mine. He invited me personally to this party. Tell them, Greg. Tell them that Tonya is the one who brought the leather and intends to go for a wild ride later tonight. Tonya is going to buy Greg, so the rest of you can just stand back. I don't even need any of those damned old tickets. He's promised every dance to me."

"You're full of shit, woman. And he wouldn't invite you when he invited me. Tell her that I'm the one you've been cyber-dating on PlentyOfFish.com."

"I've been doing what?" Greg said, his mouth dropping open.

A whole passel of women jostling in front of him, blondes to redheads to brunettes and every size imaginable, looked like they were about to put up their fists and start a brawl right there in Nana's bazaar.

A cute little blonde pushed her way to the front of the line. "PlentyOfFish.com. That's not where a good Christian man would be hanging out on cyberspace. He wouldn't even look at that site. He and I met on Christian Mingle. Look at me. There's no way you'd forget this." She did a sweeping motion with her hand from head to toe.

"You can both kiss my ass. You've got the wrong Greg Adams. We met on Farmers Only and I'm here at his personal request. I'm a ranching woman and that's what his profile said he's interested in." A tall redhead bullied her way right up to him and laid a long, passionate kiss on his lips. "You said I was supposed to save a kiss for you, so let's dance."

Tonya pushed her to the side and the woman turned around with her fists up. "You want some of this? I might be a Christian, but I don't put up with being pushed around."

Emily yelled, "Enough!" and the crowd of women parted like the Red Sea to let her through. She held up a hand. "I'm sorry, ladies, but there's been a big misunderstanding. Someone has put Greg's profile on several sites without him knowing it. Only the women who have tickets can dance with him tonight. There's a number on the back of your ticket, so check them."

"Tickets? No one told me I had to buy tickets. He said I was guaranteed every dance with him," Tonya said.

"Well, shit! I drove a hundred miles to this shitty affair," one woman said.

"Hell, honey, I flew from Wyoming."

"I came from Kentucky," another said.

"I'm sorry again, ladies. You might as well have a good time while you are here, and there's still some tickets for the other cowboys if you want to dance. And you'll all have a chance to bid on Greg at the auction if you want to come back in a week for a date," Emily said.

"Emily, you want to explain what's going on here?" Greg said behind her.

"Later," she whispered over her shoulder.

"I'm on my way to buy up every ticket there is for the Mason cowboy," the little blonde said.

"You're going to have to beat me," the tall redhead told her.

They all ran for the table where Rose was selling the last of the dance tickets faster than greased lightning.

That left two women standing in front of Greg. The closest one giggled. "You got him first, Montie. I didn't realize they were numbered. Mine has 2 behind his name, so he's mine next. Don't wear him out or whisper promises that you can't keep in his ear. I can't believe someone actually had those hussies believing that Greg was on a dating site. Lord, anyone that knows him would know better than that."

Greg stood up and laid his glitter sign on the chair. Montie wrapped her arms around his neck and plastered her body so close to his that her breasts were crushed flat against his chest. "Darlin', I brought my checkbook and I fully well intend to have a date with you next week. I've already booked a hotel room in Dallas and told them what to order for room service. You just bring lots of energy and your credit card to pay the bill."

The song ended and a tall blonde tapped Montie on the shoulder, held up her ticket, and took her place with Greg. He looked out over her shoulder to see Emily waving at him. A trip to the courthouse was looking better by the minute.

The blonde in his arms smiled at him. "I don't think you remember me, darlin'. I'm Mallory and I was a freshman when you were a senior. I met you right here in this barn that summer at the Fourth of July party and fell in love with you. I will own you when they do the auction. Daddy said I could spend up to five hundred dollars because it's a good cause."

He and Emily hadn't discussed money. He'd just assumed that she would bid on him, but he couldn't see the fan in her hip pocket and she had to have one to bid.

"Are you listening to me, Greg Adams?" Mallory asked.

"Yes, ma'am. And if you buy me, what are your plans for a date?"

"I'm cooking at my house. I'm making your favorite."

"And that is?" he asked.

"Fried chicken, hot rolls, mashed potatoes, gravy, and chocolate cake for dessert. I know everything about you except how good you are in bed, but I will find out that night, darlin'. I intend to feed you every bite of supper before we slip and slide around on satin sheets. You won't lift a single finger or fork on our date, and honey, I will be naked except for a see-through, black lace apron," Mallory whispered.

Nana would have a heart attack if she knew what she'd unleashed with her idea of a cowboy auction. Were all the other cowboys getting erotic play-by-plays of their upcoming Friday night dates?

"And if you don't win a date with me, who else are you bidding on?" Greg asked.

"Second choice is Mason. Third would have been Tommy, but Prissy done stepped in and stole him, so my third choice is Coleman."

Greg chuckled. "Mason has twin daughters."

Mallory giggled. "Darlin', I'm just buying him for a night, not forever. I'm damn sure not taking on those two girls. They'd put a shrink in a mental hospital."

"My turn." A short redhead stepped into Greg's arms on the third song. "Hello, Greg."

"Fiona," he said stiffly as he wrapped his arms loosely around her waist.

"Been a while."

"It has," he said.

"I'm not bidding on you, but I did want one dance with you just for old time's sake. I'm sorry about the way things ended. I didn't mean to hurt you," she said.

"It's in the past. Don't worry about it." He swung her out, twirled her, and brought her back to his chest. "We still dance pretty damn well together, don't we?"

"Honey, we never had a problem in that area or in bed. I just didn't like playing second fiddle to a bunch of damn cows," she said.

At the end of every song Greg looked out over the crowd to see if Emily was coming toward him. It wasn't until the sixth song that she said something to Clarice and started across the dance floor. He smiled at her and she winked, but when she reached his side, she brushed her fingertips against his and kept walking. He turned his head and saw her hold up a ticket to dance with Mason Harper.

Mason flashed a brilliant smile and held open his arms. It looked like Greg might really have to marry Emily so that neither of them would be on the auction block next year.

"What did I do wrong?" he mumbled.

"Not a thing wrong in my eyes." His next dance partner looped her arms around his neck. "I like a good slow dance. It lets us get up close and personal. And I love this speed dance dating idea, honey. Now tell me what we're going to do if I buy you and we go on a date."

"You get to plan it. I just pay for it," he said.

"That's right. Shall we go fishing or quail hunting? I like either one, and afterward we can go up to that hunting cabin y'all got and cook whatever we catch or kill."

"And?" he asked.

"And lock the doors and play all kinds of games," she whispered seductively.

"How did you know about the cabin?" Greg asked.

"Been up there with Louis a few times. I'm going to bid on him tonight if I don't get you. He's really the one I'm after, if you want to know the truth. Had my eye on him for over a year, but he's a hard one to catch, but I figure if he thinks you and I are at the cabin then he'll get jealous enough to ask me the big question," she said.

"But..." Greg stammered.

"A woman's got to do what a woman's got to do." She laughed.

Greg wondered if that's why Emily was dancing with Mason Harper. No, not his Emily. She was as forthright and honest as sunshine. She was not manipulative, or was she?

The song ended and Emily disappeared completely as another woman took her turn with Greg. After an hour, the band leader announced that there were only five more dances left and then the auction would begin.

No one came forward to claim Greg, so he returned to his chair, sat down on the glitter sign before he realized what he was doing, and hopped up—but it was too late. His whole butt was covered with sparkles. Would that make him worth more at the auction? Three songs later, the singer announced that there were only two more songs and he looked up to see if anyone was coming his way. Emily was nowhere to be seen.

Every other chair was empty and he had to admit, he felt lonely, sitting there all alone. The other cowboys waved and winked. The ladies smiled at him, but Emily was gone completely.

"Last song, ladies," the singer said. "We're closing out the evening with a song by Josh Turner."

Greg sighed and then someone tapped him on the shoulder from behind and a ticket appeared in front of his eyes. He tipped his head back and looked up into Emily's dancing blue eyes.

"I had to pay Rose a helluva lot for this ticket, so you owe me this dance, cowboy," she said.

He was on his feet in seconds. "Rose?"

Emily grabbed his hand and led him out onto the dance floor. "She says she owes it to you for being such a good domino partner. She bought the last five so you could have a rest before the auction, but she'd only sell me the one for the last dance and she threatened to sell off the other four to the cyber-women if I didn't pay what she wanted."

He wrapped her up in his arms and whispered softly, "Thank you for saving the day with those women. If Louis did this I'm going to fire his sorry ass tomorrow morning."

"It wasn't Louis, and you are welcome."

"What would I do without you to save me? And who is it if it's not Louis?"

"Let's just enjoy the dance, darlin'. We'll discuss this later, and remember, I love you," she said.

The lyrics to the song said that he was her soul mate

and he'd love her until the end of time. Emily listened to him sing with the singer and tears filled her eyes.

"We really are soul mates." He brushed a sweet kiss across her lips. "Please tell me you aren't going to let someone else buy me at this auction. I can't go out with another woman feeling the way I do about you."

She looked up at him and he brushed the tears from her cheeks.

"Why are you crying?"

"I'm scared, Greg. I love you, but where can this go?"

He kissed her eyelids. "Like you said before, we'll cross that path when we get to it. I never thought I'd say this, but Nana is right. She and Marvin had that time with the letters so that you and I would get together. It's crazy but true. I thought I was a solid businessman, but I swear I'm getting a romantic streak like Nana."

"And now," the singer said into the microphone when the last drumroll ended the dance. "The time has come. Max is going to auction off the cowboys, so ladies, y'all get your fans out of your hip pockets and turn the numbers around so he can see them. Miz Clarice says that the cowboys are to pick up their signs and bring them up here to the stage. That way everyone will know exactly which cowboy they are bidding on."

"Time to get on with it. Are you bidding on me or throwing me out to the bobcats?" Greg said.

"Soul mates don't need to ask questions like that." She rolled up on her toes and kissed him on the cheek. "Now go get that sign that I worked so hard on. I wouldn't want to bid on the wrong cowboy."

Max picked up the microphone and said, "Ladies, take a long look at these old hardworking cowboys. Your money is going for a good cause and these guys will be yours for a whole evening come next Friday night. There's an even dozen of them, and I'm not letting a single one walk out of here for less than fifty bucks. So that's the starting point for Greg Adams. Now somebody give me fifty… do I hear fifty… come on now, ladies, fifty…"

He talked fast and furious and nodded when a fan at the back of the room went up. "Now sixty… do I hear sixty… I've got fifty… somebody… I see sixty, let's go for seventy."

"Five hundred dollars!" The red-haired lady who'd kissed him raised her fan. "He's mine, ladies, so why mess around with chump change."

Max wiped his brow with an oversized red bandanna he pulled from his hip pocket. "Now that's a serious bid, ladies. I've got five hundred… do I hear six hundred… six hundred, anyone… going, going…"

"One thousand dollars," another woman said. "Sorry, darlin', but I bet my daddy's got more money than your daddy."

Max wiped his brow again, making a dramatic show of it. "Okay, now we're getting real serious. I've got a thousand dollars. Does the little lady who jacked up the bids to five hundred have anything to say about that?"

Max went on. "I've got a thousand dollars. Do I hear eleven hundred? Come on, ladies, this is prime cowboy. Someone give me eleven hundred. Going… going…" He had the hammer raised to hit the podium.

"Two thousand dollars," Emily said.

"Two thousand one hundred," the short cyber-blonde yelled.

"Two thousand two hundred," the redhead shouted.

"Two thousand five hundred," Tonya yelled above the noise.

"He's mine. Three thousand dollars," the redhead said.

"Five thousand," Emily raised her voice. "And, darlin', my daddy didn't put a cap on what I can spend, so if y'all want to stay in the game, then you'd best get out your checkbooks and prepare to write a lot of zeroes."

She hadn't planned on spending one cent over a thousand dollars, but by damn, that hussy was not going to spend a single minute with Greg. Besides, Emily rationalized, it was tax deductible, for a damn good cause, and she hadn't spent a single dime of her money on a vacation.

"Well, Miz Emily, with the number thirteen on her fan, has given me a five-thousand-dollar bid. Anyone out there going to top that?" Max asked. No one said a word or even fluttered their fan. "Then Greg Adams goes to Emily Cooper. You can make out your check to the Ladies' Auxiliary Fund and give it to Dotty, or I understand that she does take cash. Go on and get off the stage, Greg. Now we've got Mason Harper up for bids, and I'm starting at fifty dollars."

"Five hundred dollars," the blonde said.

The crowd parted for Greg to get to Emily. He picked her up and swung her around several times before he set her back down.

"I love you," he whispered.

"I hope so, because I've got a helluva date planned for Friday night." She laughed.

"Want to tell me where and what so I can be prepared?"

"Oh, no! It's a big surprise, darlin'."

He slung an arm around her shoulder and was walking toward the door when Nancy stopped them.

"Girl, I was so mad at you for not dancing with my son until the last song that I could've wrung your neck," she said.

Emily smiled sweetly. "A cowgirl always goes home with the cowboy that she dances the last song with, even if it costs her the next year's calf crop. And I knew what I was doing. If they all danced with him, then they'd bid high, and this is for a good cause."

Nancy hugged her. "Well, next time you could let me in on your plans so I won't waste energy being mad at you. And what was that deal with all those women in front of him one minute and arguing over who got to dance with him?"

"A bunch of dating site women who thought he invited them to the party," Emily said.

Nancy looked up at her son. "Are you on a dating site?"

"Hell, no! Someone played a big joke on me," he said.

Nancy glanced at Dotty and Clarice, who were whispering behind their hands and then back at Emily, who slid one eye shut in a sly wink.

"I see," she said.

Dotty and Clarice plowed through the crowd and had a group hug with Greg and Emily. Clarice whispered in her ear, "Darlin', I've already paid the five thousand to the fund. I'll declare it as a charitable donation on the ranch taxes."

"But…" Emily started.

"It was worth it, believe me," Clarice said. "And if

you ever tell a soul that I paid for it, I'll take a pecan switch to you."

"Yes, ma'am, and thank you. Can I take him away from here now that I own him?" she asked.

"I expect you are both old enough to go to the house without a chaperone," Nancy said.

Greg hugged his mother. "Well, I don't know about that, Mama. You think you'd better go with us?"

"Oh, I think Emily can protect you." Nancy laughed.

"Sold for two thousand dollars to Fiona. Mason Harper, you are now owned by Fiona next Friday night," Max said.

Mason reached over and took the microphone from Max. "Thank you, Fiona, for buying me and not letting me stand up here like a worthless old bull. I'll look forward to Friday night. You mind if I bring the girls with us?"

Dotty laughed so hard that she had to wipe the tears from her cheeks. "I'd give another two thousand dollars to get to go with them if he does."

Clarice hooked an arm in Nancy's. "I'm telling you, Emily did good when she came up with the auction idea. We're going to be able to help more than one girl through her first year of school."

Greg grabbed Emily's hand and led her out of the barn. When they were both inside the cab of the truck, he cupped her face in his big hands and kissed her with so much sweet passion that she felt like a boiling pot of pepper jelly.

"I love, love, love you."

"Maybe you'd best save that until you hear what next Friday is going to cost you," she said.

"Darlin', I will not complain one bit."

It was midnight before the rest of the family left the barn and went to the house. Clarice couldn't remember the last time she was so tired or so exhilarated. They'd raised over fifteen thousand dollars that night, more than they'd made in the last ten years all put together. Next year would be even better because the word would get out about what fun everyone had had. And they had sold out every single homemade item on the tables, even the leftovers from the years before.

The lights were still on in the kitchen and the smell of coffee met them at the back door. A chocolate cake waited on the table and mugs were set out on the bar.

"Emily! Bless her heart," Dotty said. "That cake is still warm."

Bart threw an arm around his mother's shoulders. "It's one of those like you used to make when you didn't have much time, Mama. Remember when I'd come home from school with half a dozen friends and you'd throw one of those together? We'd eat it hot right out of the oven and put away a couple of gallons of milk."

"I remember." Clarice smiled.

"Where are those lovebirds?" Jeremiah asked. "I hardly had time to talk to either of them this evening. It's not fair that they get private time and me and Stacy don't."

Dotty poked her head around the kitchen door and motioned. "Shhh. Be quiet or you'll wake them."

Six adults tiptoed through the dining room, across the foyer, and into the den. One lamp burned at the end of the sofa where Greg was stretched out with Emily wrapped up in his arms, her back to his chest.

A gray cat and a yellow one were both curled up at their feet.

"She's good for him, Bart," Clarice said.

"I can see that," he whispered.

"Ain't they cute?" Stacy sighed.

Jeremiah drew Stacy close to his side and whispered, "I believe those two are soul mates."

"Soul mates with half the state of Texas separating them here in a week. Someone needs to tell them that they need to be together forever," Dotty asked.

"They'll figure it out on their own," Nancy said. "Now let's go eat chocolate cake. I might like her after all if that cake is as good as Mama Clarice's."

Chapter 22

THERE WAS NO ROOM TO WIGGLE IN THE CHURCH PEW, so Emily had to sit still, but every single nerve in her body tingled. Greg's right arm was thrown around her shoulders and his thumb made slow circles on her upper arm. Even through the sleeve of her sweater, his touch was pure fire. His left arm stretched across his lap and held her hand: bare skin on bare skin, which was even hotter than her arm.

The song director told them to open their hymnals, and Greg's hands left her body, but their hands touched as they shared the book. Words came out of her mouth, but the picture in her head had nothing to do with praising God for all his wonderful works.

The preacher took his place behind the podium and started his sermon. She looked right at him but didn't see his pretty red tie or his gray hair. The movie in her head played on and she and Greg were the only two stars in a little attic room with a twin bed in the center. Any minute a sharp crack of lightning could zip down through the beams, crossing the ceiling and frying her right on the spot for her thoughts, but she couldn't stop them any more than she could stop breathing.

Greg leaned to his right just slightly and whispered, "Have I told you that you are gorgeous this morning?"

"Shhh." If she looked at him, he'd be able to see what she was thinking.

He squeezed her hand and brushed a kiss across her cheek. "You are, and don't shush me. Are you thinking about the attic?" Greg whispered.

His warm breath created ripples of goose bumps from her neck to her toes.

"Are you?" She pulled her hand free of his and laid it on his thigh right above his knee. The quiver in his leg said that her touch did the same thing for him that his did for her.

"You aren't playing fair," he whispered.

The temptation was great, and she could not fight it. If she was going to see the trees, she had to get out of the forest. She'd learned to love the forest and she didn't want to leave, but she had no choice. Her head needed to be clear as a bell when she made the decision lying heavy on her heart.

Technically, she had five more days, a date with Greg on Friday night, and then before midnight on Saturday she had to be back at Shine Canyon. That was the plan she'd agreed to on her grandfather's last day on this earth.

"We'll ask Bart Adams to give the benediction this morning. It's always good to see him back in Ravenna for a visit. But first, I've got to mention that last night's bazaar was a big record breaker. The ladies are pleased to announce that they'll be offering scholarships to more than one area girl this year. Now Bart, if you will, please," the preacher said.

Jeremiah hugged everyone including Emily. "After that dinner Mama made, I should take a nap before I leave."

"It's only an hour and a half home and I can drive if you want to sleep," Stacy said.

"You could be eating like this all the time," Dotty said. "And you'd look a hell of a lot better. I swear to God, you've lost weight."

Jeremiah left Stacy with Emily and hugged Dotty one more time. "Mama, you aren't supposed to swear on Sunday or tell lies either. I've gained five more pounds since Stacy has been cookin' for me."

"I'm the mother. God don't tell me when or where I can cuss, so you can't either," Dotty said.

Nancy and Bart pulled their suitcases out onto the front porch. Clarice followed right behind them, fussing the whole way, "I hate it when everyone leaves at the same time. I hate good-byes, and I wish you'd come more often."

"But that would just make more good-byes." Bart chuckled.

"Maybe I wouldn't hate them so bad if I knew you were coming back in a week," Clarice said.

Nancy hugged her. "We'll do better. I promise."

"I'm holding you to that promise," Clarice whispered. "But you don't fool me. If you do come more often it will be because you've finally given up on Greg coming back to Houston."

Bart picked up both suitcases and carried them to Greg's truck. "Come on, son. There's not a bit of need in dragging this good-bye stuff out. Drive us out to the plane and we'll get on our way."

"You hate good-byes just as much as the rest of us," Greg told him. He grabbed Emily's hand. "Come with us, darlin'. We'll take a ride after we get these old folks on their plane."

"Hey, who are you calling old?" Clarice fussed.

"Not you, Nana. You'll never be old, but Momma and Daddy might be getting too old to fly. They might need to build a house up here and stay a few weeks at a time when they come around," he said.

"I'll get with a contractor next week," Clarice teased.

Bart waved over his shoulder. "Better wait until I retire, Mama. And then I wouldn't live here all the time. If I had to be away from the hustle and bustle of the city I'd die."

A few minutes later, Emily leaned against the truck fender and watched the small plane as it soared into the white clouds and got smaller and smaller until there was nothing but a small dot.

"I hate good-byes too," she said.

Greg slipped his arm around her waist and drew her close to his side. "We all do. There's always the possibility that it will be the last time we see someone and that's scary. You are shivering. Let's drive to the cabin and make a fire."

There was no place on the ranch, other than the attic, that she'd rather spend her last day there, so she nodded. How would she ever drive away from Lightning Ridge? Just thinking about it created a lump the size of a basketball in her throat. How could she ever tell Clarice, Dotty, and most of all, Greg, good-bye?

She was quiet all the way to the cabin and curled up on the old sofa when they were inside. Greg tucked a quilt around her and set about building a fire. If he would have joined her on the sofa, the sparks doing backflips off the walls would have warmed the whole place up, but the second he left her side she was cold.

He wasted no movements or matches. When the blaze was going, he made a pot of coffee and hung it on the andiron to boil.

She lifted the edge of the quilt and he snuggled down inside with her, his hands slipping under her shirt to warm on her bare skin.

"My folks liked you a lot," he said.

"Did they say that?"

He shook his head and then buried his face in the crook of her neck. "Not in words but in actions. And you?"

"Loved them all, especially Stacy. She'll be good for Jeremiah."

"Nana says that Rose charged you fifty bucks for that ticket?" He laughed.

"Hey, anything worth having costs something, whether it's money or something else," she said.

Time was even more valuable than money, and she'd be giving up several days to go back to Shine Canyon, but it had to be done. She had to be absolutely sure about the ranch and about Greg.

"Kiss me," she said.

"Gladly." He tipped up her chin and kissed her ever so sweetly, then deepened it into something hotter and more passionate.

They were used to the cramped space of the twin-sized bed in the attic, so it wasn't hard to adjust from sitting to lying on the sofa. He removed his boots and hers and then his lips found hers again. His hands moved over her body as if they were finding brand-new territory for the first time. He loved that Emily was a new experience every time they made wild passionate love or even sweet quickie love. Nothing was familiar;

everything was exciting and fresh, from her kisses to the way her body felt beneath his hands.

"I love the way your body feels next to mine," he said.

"You make me hotter'n blue blazes just by touching my hand in church. When I'm snuggled up to you, I'm just a big pot of boiling desire."

With one swift motion she unsnapped his shirt and teased his nipples to aching nubs on her way down to his belt buckle. Passionate kisses got deeper and deeper as she deftly undid his belt and zipper. Her hand was like silk when it circled his erection, and his groan sounded hoarse even in his own ears. He'd never given up complete control of his body to another woman, but Emily was special. He was in love with her and wanted to spend the rest of his life with her beside him.

She arched against him and he thought that he would explode before they even got naked, but she moved her hand upward to rest on his chest.

"Darlin', I think we'd best come out of the rest of these clothes," he whispered.

She jumped up and her clothes were blurs as they flew through the air to land behind the sofa. "It's still cold, so you'd better hurry," she said as she dove back under the quilt.

His jeans and shirt joined her things and he lay on top of her, his erection hard against her belly. He made love to her lips, tongue, and mouth in scorching kisses that left her panting.

"I'm so, so ready," she whispered.

"Are you sure?"

"Oh, yes," she gasped as she wrapped her legs around his middle.

He started a rhythm and she rocked with him. Nothing had ever felt so right in his whole life. Emily was his soul mate and he fully well intended to write her a long letter that evening and tell her so.

His mouth covered hers in a string of kisses and she arched her back against him, giving herself to the red-hot fire and forgetting about saying good-bye the next morning. As always, her toes curled when she heard him say that he loved her, and she found a sweet release seconds before he did. In a few swift shuffling moves, they were wrapped in each other's arms on the narrow sofa. Her head rested on his chest and she bit back the tears. She could never tell him good-bye… not ever.

He kissed her good night at the top of the stairs that Sunday night. One last wonderful sweet kiss that she'd take with her. Both Bocephus and Simba were curled up in the recliner on their fluffy blue blanket when she got out the stationery and ink pen and started to write Clarice a note first. She told her that she needed to go back to Shine Canyon to settle both business and her heart. The next note was to Dotty, and she begged her to take care of the kittens while she was away.

The third was the hardest. *My dearest Greg*, she started and then ripped the page into shreds. Writing good-bye was just as difficult as saying it out loud.

She heard his movement on the landing, and an envelope slid into her room from beneath the door. She picked it up and held it against her chest, much like Clarice had done with that sixty-year-old letter the first day Emily had come to Lightning Ridge. She couldn't read it, not before she'd written her letter.

She tucked the letter inside her purse and picked up

another piece of stationery. The words flowed from her mind to the paper, along with several tears that turned some of the words blotchy. She could only hope as she sealed the letter and kissed the back that he would understand the desperate need she had to go back and settle the past before she could go forward into the future.

She kissed the kittens at a little after four. It took two trips to take her suitcases down the steps. Before she carried them out to the truck she went to the kitchen and plastered the top of the refrigerator with sticky notes that all said, "I love Greg Adams!" and had little hearts drawn in all four corners.

When the sun came up in her rearview mirror she was already a hundred miles away from Ravenna on her way back to Happy, Texas. On the west side of Wichita Falls, she pulled over at a rest stop, used the bathroom, and got a free cup of coffee. She reached in her purse for Greg's letter from the night before and pulled out her grandfather's funeral memorial for the second time.

"Okay, Gramps, tell me what you've got on your mind," she said.

She waited, but nothing came to her mind.

"Are you telling me to turn around and go back?" she asked.

Her phone rang and her soul came close to leaving her body.

"Hello?" she said cautiously without checking the caller ID.

"Mama said that you left the ranch. What in the hell is going on, Emily? I thought you and Greg were solid as concrete." Jeremiah said.

"I left a letter to each of them explaining what I was

doing. I've got to settle the past before I can face the future. I love Greg, but I've got to get rid of the baggage. It's not fair to him to take on my problems. I'm trying to take care of it."

"You sure?" Jeremiah asked.

"Both of us need a few days to be sure that this isn't all just something of the moment. He might not realize it, but he needs it as much as I do."

"Lust instead of love?" Jeremiah's voice softened.

"Yes, sir."

"What do you want me to tell Greg?"

"I wrote him a long letter. He knows what I need and he'll do it. And I left sticky notes on the refrigerator."

"Then I'll just listen to him whine like a little girl. And I heard about the sticky notes already." Jeremiah finally laughed.

"Greg might be lonely just like me, but he won't whine," Emily said.

"Hurry up and figure it out. Mama and Clarice miss you as much as he does and it's only been a few hours."

"I will. I promise."

"Besides, you've got a date on Friday night, remember? And Clarice paid a hell of a bill for you to go on that date."

"How'd you know that?" Emily asked.

"I'm an investigator, remember. Get home by Friday, Emily."

"Home?"

"It's not to me, but it is to you. Call me when you arrive to Shine Canyon and I'll let Mama know. She worries about the people that she loves." Jeremiah didn't say good-bye; the line just went dead.

Emily looked down at the memorial folder in her hand. "Guess you answered that question loud and clear, didn't you, Gramps?"

Chapter 23

THE HOUSE WAS CRAMMED WITH MORE THAN SIXTY years' worth of furniture and memories, but it was still empty when Emily pushed her way inside with a suitcase in each hand. She set them down in the living room and went straight for her grandfather's bedroom. The hospital bed still sat beside the window and the drapes were open. The rug beside it had a few tufts of yellow hair, and there at the end was a dog food dish half-full of dry food covered in ants. She cussed all the way to the back door where she tossed the food out into the yard for the birds.

It wasn't quite noon, but she was starving, so she went to the kitchen and opened the refrigerator. It hadn't been touched since she left. Mold grew on leftovers. The milk was soured and smelled horrid. She pulled off her jacket, rolled up her sleeves, and pulled the garbage can in from the utility room.

She had a container of something green in her hand when her phone rang. She tossed container and all in the trash, reached in her hip pocket, and answered on the third ring.

"You home yet?" Stacy asked. "Jeremiah is out on a case and he told me to call. Dotty is driving us both crazy."

"I'm at Shine Canyon cleaning out the fridge. Want to come on over and help me? I'll give you a beer as soon as the job is done. It hasn't been touched since I left and believe me, you'll need a beer to get the taste out of your mouth," Emily said.

"Good enough for you, running off like that without saying good-bye to the family. I'll let Dotty know. She's called me six times this morning. I can't get a damn thing done and she cries when she mentions the sticky notes. What's that all about?" Stacy asked.

Emily explained what the refrigerator looked like when she got there, what it looked like when the kittens shredded the flapping notes, and how she'd covered the top of it with new notes before she left. "I hate good-byes. It was the best I could do," she explained.

"Fix it so you don't ever have to say another one and I will be calling to check on you every day. I've never seen Jeremiah so troubled or worried about his mama. He's worried that she or Clarice will have a stroke over you leaving. Drink a beer for me," Stacy said and was gone before Emily could answer.

She picked up a container of her grandfather's favorite picante sauce with a layer of white mold on the top. "Damn, Gramps! I thought this stuff would last forever. I've never ever seen it go bad," she said.

When the refrigerator was clean, she carried the trash outside to find that the cart had not been taken out to the road since she'd left. It smelled even worse than the refrigerator. Thank goodness the trash man ran on Tuesday. She made a mental note to load it up and take it out to the edge of the road before dark.

The freezer netted her one frozen pizza that she popped into the oven. While that cooked, she pulled her luggage back to the room that had been her home since she was in a crib. It felt every bit as empty as the rest of the house.

"Hey, where are you?" Taylor's voice echoed down the hall from the living room. "Hoyt called and said that he saw your truck."

She met him in the narrow hallway. "I'm right here. You could have at least cleaned out the refrigerator, Taylor."

"Didn't think about it. Been busy on my ranch and that didn't leave a hell of a lot of time to be doing women's jobs," he said.

She poked him in the chest. "Women's jobs! If we're dividing jobs, then I guess I don't need to haul hay or work cattle since that's a man's job."

He backed up into the living room. "Hey, don't get all pissy with me. I was just stating facts."

She brushed away a tear and he grabbed her in a fierce hug. "Let's start over, okay? I'm glad you came to your senses. Those were nice people but not our kind. If you need any help call me and I'll send someone. Sorry you found a mess. We've been busy and I didn't think about cleaning up."

Not our kind. The three words rattled around in her head, replaying over and over again.

"I'll be back in a little while to help you. I promise, but I need to step out on the porch and call Melinda. She's expecting me at her place in fifteen minutes."

"Go. I'm fine." She stepped back.

"Are you sure? I don't mind staying," Taylor said.

She pushed him toward the door. "Go. I'm a big girl and I've got a lot of things to think about before I start working in the house. Tell Melinda hello for me."

"Okay." He grinned.

"Not our kind," she whispered when she heard his truck pull out of her driveway.

What was their kind and what was our kind? What was the difference?

"Not our kind?" she raised her voice and repeated the phrase.

The timer on the stove dinged and she opened the oven door to the smell of pepperoni, cheese, and spices. "Does our kind eat frozen pizza, Taylor? I didn't eat it once on Lightning Ridge. Is that what makes us different?"

After she'd put away half the pizza and washed it down with a bottle of Coors beer, she picked up her purse and slammed the back door on her way out. Her daddy used to punish her when she slammed the door in anger. She had to come back inside and go out, shut it gently, and repeat the process ten times. She went back inside the house, shut the door without a sound on her way out, and said, "That's for you, Daddy."

—⁓—

Clarice looked across the kitchen table and said, "She wouldn't have left all the notes if she wasn't planning on coming home."

Greg swallowed a baseball-sized lump when he looked at the multicolored notes on the fridge. He picked up the platter of fried chicken, put a wing and a leg on his plate, and passed it to Max. "If she's not here Friday evening, I'm going to Happy and I'm taking Bocephus and Simba with me. And don't throw away a single one of those notes. I'll put them all in a boot box and put them in the attic when she's home."

Max chuckled. "And what good will two tomcats do?"

"She's got to miss them, so maybe if she knows she

can't have them unless she comes home, she'll come to her senses," he said.

Dotty exhaled loudly. "Patience, Greg. It's a good thing she's doing. Right, Clarice? And besides, where did this streak come from? I do believe your words were that a ranch didn't need a lot of sentimental shit. It needed good business sense."

Clarice felt Dotty's eyes on her. "Why are you looking at me?"

"Explain to him about jitters," Dotty said.

"You explain." Clarice blushed.

"I didn't do it. If I had, I might not have done it, but I didn't. You did. So explain to Greg," Dotty said.

"You're talkin' in riddles, Dotty. What was it you didn't do that you might have done?" Max asked.

Clarice kicked Dotty under the table. "Must be the effects from all that liquor that she put away all those years ago. It does fry the brain cells."

"Don't you kick me, woman. I'll kick you back," Dotty said.

"Now it's getting interesting." Max laid his fork down. "I've never see you two argue over anything."

"Nana?" Greg asked.

Clarice glared at Dotty.

"If you don't tell, I will. It'll make him feel better."

Clarice shoved a fork full of potatoes into her mouth and held her hand over her mouth when she said, "I'm not sayin' a word."

"Okay, then I'll tell what happened. It was two days before her wedding date. She showed up at my house with bride jitters. I'd gotten married a couple of months before that and my husband actually had a job in those days. He was working nights at a sawmill place down in Bonham. So I was alone and here is Clarice looking like hell on my front porch, crying her eyes out."

"Why?" Greg asked.

"Because women do that," Dotty said. "They get scared and they worry that they'll make the wrong decision. And Clarice was ready to call off her wedding right then and run away so her parents wouldn't be embarrassed and she wouldn't have to face Lester's sorrow."

"You understand any of that?" Max asked.

Greg shook his head.

"It must be a woman thing."

Greg pushed back his chair. "I'm going upstairs to write a letter. She didn't say that we couldn't write."

"Real letters? On paper?" Clarice asked.

"Oh, yeah. We've been writing to each other all month," he said.

"I think that it's time we talk about putting the ranch in your name," Clarice said.

"Why now?" Greg asked. "We were talking sticky notes and letters, not deeds."

"Because you are finally realizing that it takes more than business sense to love a ranch like you should. It becomes part of your heart and soul like a real person, and I think you have gotten to that point."

"Just because I..." Greg started.

"Yes, just because you..." Clarice smiled. "When you open your heart to one thing, the door is open, period."

"Hard to explain the way it works, isn't it?" Greg said.

Clarice laid a hand on his arm. "Business requires explanation. The heart doesn't care about that. It just knows love."

"And pain," Greg said.

—◦◦◦—

Dotty handed Clarice a cup of coffee and sat down on the other end of the sofa. "I thought he'd stop worrying if he realized even his nana had to get away for a little while and figure things out."

Clarice patted her on the knee. "I know. It's a woman thing. I hope they have a dozen daughters and he has to deal with them. I hope at least one comes to him just before her wedding with the jitters. Then he will remember and understand."

A grin erased all the wrinkles in Dotty's face. "How'd they get the letters to each other? I'm the one who gets the mail, and I didn't see any letters."

"So they have secrets other than the attic," Clarice said.

"They pulled the wool over our eyes," Dotty said.

"I'm glad that I didn't marry Marvin. If I had, we wouldn't have this in our old age."

"God saved the best until last, didn't he?" Dotty grinned.

"I believe he did. Why would they write real letters when they've got all that texting and email stuff at their fingertips?" Clarice said.

"Wouldn't you just love to see those letters?"

—◦◦◦—

Emily hugged up to Greg's back, slipped an arm around his body, and snuggled in close to him. They'd have to get up soon so that they'd be in the house before Dotty started breakfast. She hoped that Dotty would make pancakes and bacon.

"Coffee," she whispered. "Wake up, darlin'. I need coffee."

She inhaled deeply but didn't get even a single whiff of anything. Not bacon or warm maple syrup or even coffee. But hey, it was a long way from the kitchen, across the backyard, and to the attic. Her eyes popped open to see the sun rising out the window. She jumped out of bed and grabbed her boots.

"Greg," she yelled over her shoulder. He had to wake up right now so they could slip into the house before Dotty made it to the kitchen.

Then she realized that she was in her bedroom on Shine Canyon, not at Lightning Ridge. And that she'd been hugging a pillow and not Greg. She threw the boots all the way across the room and stomped her bare feet so hard that the pictures on the wall shook.

"Dammit! Dammit!" she screamed at the walls. "And I bet there isn't coffee brewing or pancakes either." She slapped the pillow so hard that it rolled off the bed and landed on the floor.

She pulled on a pair of socks and padded to the kitchen. The bread was molded, but there was a box of English muffins in the freezer and if she shaved the hard edges off the cream cheese, what was in the center was still good. The coffee had been kept in the fridge so it wasn't too stale.

One second she was chewing on an English muffin and the next Taylor was in the kitchen pouring a cup of coffee. He startled her so badly that she dropped her muffin and had to do some quick fumbling to catch it before it hit the floor.

"Did you knock?" She gulped.

"Why would I? I've never knocked on the door in my whole life."

"Have you even been in this house since I left, other than last night for thirty seconds?"

"No, I haven't, and don't you be giving me any grief about last night. I told you I'd stay," he answered. "Why would I be in the house if you weren't here, Em? I checked on things but you are home now. Things will go back to normal."

"I'm going to town as soon as I finish breakfast. I'm going to the cemetery and from there to Amarillo," she said.

Normal her ass! If this was normal, she didn't want any part of it.

"I figured you'd want to get right back into the groove of work around here. There's pastures to be plowed, and if you're going to have cattle, you need to go to the sale up in Amarillo tomorrow and buy a few head. Are you going to raise Angus like always or switch over to another breed? Why are you going to the cemetery?"

"Because I'm going to see Gramps. Taylor, we need to talk, since you are here. Sit down and listen to me."

He sat down at the table and cocked his head to one side. "You aren't home for good, are you? I had my hopes up, but you aren't staying, are you? Well, you're damn sure going to tell Dusty. She's off on a three-day thing with her job, but I'm not telling her. You have to do it."

"Taylor, you are a good man and Lord knows this ranch wouldn't have survived without you these past years. I love you…"

He grinned.

"But…" she stammered.

"No buts. You love me like a brother and you can't

bear to move off and leave me and the rest of the family, can you?" he asked.

"I do love you like a brother, but I love Greg too. And his ranch is over there and so is his family and they've become like family to me and I love them and this is so damned hard. My roots are here and I want to make this work again for Gramps."

He reached across and touched her hand. "I know, Emily. I knew when I saw you with Greg. I feel the same way about Melinda and I understand. But you can't blame me for not wanting to let you go."

She jerked her hand free. "You can come see me anytime you want."

Taylor's eyes twinkled. "And you'll come home for some of the holidays?"

"Of course I will. But a good brother would have taken out the garbage and cleaned the fridge."

"That's why a good brother needs a good wife. I hate those kinds of jobs even worse than I hate cats. You didn't bring those miserable fur balls with you, did you?"

She shook her head. "No, they're at home whining for me."

He smiled. "I believe it now, cousin. You just said they were at home. You didn't say back there or on Lightning Ridge. You said at home. Now to the important part of today—are you cookin' breakfast?"

"Hell, no!"

"Well, shit! I'm going to the bunkhouse then. They're making sausage gravy and hot biscuits. Want to go with me?"

She shook her head. "Thank you, but no thanks."

"Em, I'm really glad that you've come back for a few days." He stood up and laid a hand on her shoulder. "Go on to town and do whatever you need to."

One more shoulder squeeze and he disappeared out the back door, leaving his dirty coffee cup on the counter.

"Oh, yeah! Big brother who can't even rinse out a coffee cup," she said. "Gramps, why did you die and leave me in this mess?"

Her first stop was at the cemetery. The rectangular sign at the entrance said that the cemetery had been there since 1912, more than a hundred years before. She drove right to the family plot and got out of the truck.

The grave had sunk, but someone had brought in sand and a rake. The old flowers from the funeral had been removed and there was a really nice wreath on a tripod in front of the tombstone. The folks who'd put the stone up when Nana died had come back and put the dates on it, and the first sprigs of grass were spouting on the top of the grave.

"I guess big brothers are good for something." She smiled.

She propped a hip on the edge of the tombstone and studied each grave. To the left of Gramps and Nana's stone was one with his parents' names and on the right was the one with Emily's dad and mom. There was no more room in that area. If she came back to Happy, she and her family would be buried somewhere else in the cemetery.

"Is this my sign?" she asked.

And that's when her phone rang.

"Hello," she said.

"Hey, girl, where are you? I hear birds," Stacy said.

"Jeremiah wants to know how things are going and believe me, I do too."

"I'm at the cemetery. Things are going just fine. I wonder why my great-grandparents only bought six lots."

"Probably that's all they could afford or thought they'd need at the time. Or maybe it was to tell you that when those folks were gone, it was time for a change."

"I miss Greg," Emily said.

"Well, halle-damn-lujah! I can't wait to tell Jeremiah. He says that Greg went upstairs to write you a letter last night. A real, honest-to-God letter on paper and put into an envelope. I don't have one of those from Jeremiah, so I'm jealous as hell. Oh, and Jeremiah laughed his ass off when Dotty told him about those old gals pretending to be Greg on a dating site. He made me hack into the sites and you should have heard him roar when he read what they'd written. It was like two worlds colliding and neither really knew the lingo of the other one."

"Oh. My. God," Emily said breathlessly.

"Don't you dare tell them that I hacked into those sites."

"Does Greg know?"

"He does now. Jeremiah told him and he understands that you saved his ass at that auction. That was the funniest sight I've seen in a long time. You and I are going to be good friends, girl. Got to go now. Talk to you later."

Emily plopped down on her grandfather's tombstone. "Gramps, it's been a crazy world. I'll tell you about the dating sites later, but right now I want to tell you about the letters. We've been writing real letters like you and Clarice wrote. And I've got the last one he wrote in my purse. I've already just about read all the words off it."

She settled more comfortably on the tombstone and

said, "I do miss Greg and it's only been a little over twenty-four hours since I left. Gramps, I don't want to disappoint you. I love Shine Canyon. I know that your folks worked so hard on the ranch and that Daddy did and you did. How can I walk away from my inheritance? But I can't ask Greg to walk away from his, either. Tell me what to do, Gramps."

"Mornin', Miz Emily," a voice said right behind her.

She jumped up so fast that she got a head rush and had to hang onto the tombstone for support. "Amos, you scared me."

The old man's mouth turned up in half a smile. "I heard you too. It's okay, child. I talk to him too. We was friends from the time we was just kids, went to the service together, and wound up right here in Happy when we got home. His folks moved and I married a girl from here, but you know all that."

Emily nodded. "I'm glad that you come to visit him and I'm real glad that you came around when he was sick."

Amos shrugged. "He'd a done the same thing if the cancer had got hold of me. He'd tell you to follow your heart, Emily. Marvin loved that ranch, but he wouldn't want it to hold you back if your heart is somewhere else. Now get on out of here and let me have a turn to visit with him."

"Thanks, Amos." She hugged him.

"You are very welcome. Taylor will do just fine with Shine Canyon. He kind of reminds me of your dad. If your momma had birthed a child before you he might've been just like Taylor."

Yep, an older brother, she thought as she made her

way back to her car. She'd asked Gramps for help and he'd sent it. First in the form of a phone call from Stacy and then from an old friend, Amos. She knew what to do now, but it didn't make it any easier.

She drove to Amarillo to the small law firm that her family had used her whole life. When she walked through the door, the secretary jumped up from behind the desk and hugged her tightly. "Ray is out to lunch with a client. Let's go to Olive Garden and get some soup and salad."

"I'd love to," Emily said.

Edna worked in Amarillo, but she lived in Happy, went to the same church as the Coopers, and had at one time been interested in Emily's dad. She drove across town to the Olive Garden and when they were seated she wasted no time in saying, "Okay, girl, what is going on? You've been gone a whole month. Did you go to Florida like Marvin told you to do?"

Emily shook her head and told Edna the whole story while they ate lunch. "And now I'm two ways about the ranch. I don't want to let Gramps down but…"

Edna reached across the table and laid a hand on Emily's arm. "Marvin would want you to be happy, and it sounds like fate has been workin' overtime for more than fifty years, darlin'. A ranch is just dirt no matter where it is. If it isn't home, then that's all it'll ever be. But a ranch shared with someone you love is a home. You've got a lifetime ahead of you. Does that cowboy love you?"

"He says he does."

"Looks to me like all that's left is the paperwork," Edna said.

Chapter 24

SHE CHECKED THE MAILBOX FIVE TIMES ON WEDNESDAY, but there was no letter from Greg. Stacy said that he'd written to her so where was it? Surely it wasn't stuck in the bottom of a mailbag somewhere between Ravenna and Happy. That couldn't happen twice in the same family, could it?

Until that letter arrived, she couldn't make the final decision to sell Taylor the rest of Shine Canyon. On Thursday morning she was having a bowl of junk cereal for breakfast when someone knocked hard on the door. It startled her so bad that she dropped her spoon and it scooted halfway across the floor. She wrapped her grandfather's plaid robe tightly around her body and opened the door.

"Mornin', Miz Emily. Got a letter here that you have to sign for." He held out a small pad with a pen attached with a cord. "Right there in the box, please."

She scribbled her name and handed it back. He put a letter in her hands, and her heart skipped a full beat when she saw the return address. It was from Greg Adams in Ravenna, Texas.

"Thank you. I would have come into town to get it if you would've called me."

"No trouble. I had a couple of deliveries to make out this way. Rumor has it that you aren't stayin' in Happy. That true?" he asked.

"Still thinkin' about things."

"Well, we'll miss you if you go."

"Thanks again," she said. She should invite him in for coffee since he'd always spent a few minutes with Gramps when he brought the mail. On some days the mailman and Amos were the only people outside of Taylor and Emily that Marvin talked to.

"Got to go. Miz Blackstone has been callin' every day about her package. It's something that her grandson has sent and he's over in France. She says that it's one of those fancy French scarves and she wants to wear it to a weddin' this weekend. You did hear that Gracie Caldwell is marrying Teddy Green, didn't you?"

Emily shook her head. "Lot happens in a month, don't it?"

"Yes, it does. Hope you enjoyed your trip to Florida though. Marvin told me he was sending you away for a month. I was surprised to see you home a few days early. Guess home always calls to the heart, don't it?" He spun around and was halfway back to his mail truck before she could do anything but look at the letter.

"Yes, sir, it surely does," she finally said as she shut the door. She sat down in Marvin's recliner and held the letter in her hand for a full minute before she opened it and read:

My darling,

I'm abiding by what you asked even though not seeing you, not hearing your voice, not being able to kiss you are the hardest things I've ever endured…

She inhaled deeply. "Okay, Gramps, you've sent enough messages. The decision is made and home does call out to the heart, but it doesn't make it easier to say good-bye to the past."

———~~~———

Greg awoke on Thursday morning with Bocephus on the pillow next to him and Simba sharing his pillow. "Good mornin', boys. The house sure seems empty without her, but I'm not giving up hope and neither should you."

He crawled out of bed, threw open the curtains, and looked down at the backyard. The place where she parked her truck even looked lonely. He dressed in work jeans and tugged a thermal shirt down over his head before he checked the USPS tracking number that they'd given him at the post office.

"Hey, guys, the letter has arrived," he yelled across the room at the cats that were chasing each other from one end of his bed to the other. "She's got it in her hands right now. God, I miss her so much."

When he reached the kitchen, he grabbed Dotty around the waist and danced across the floor with her. "The letter arrived," he singsonged.

"Have you lost your mind, boy? What letter? The mailman hasn't come yet," Dotty said.

"My letter. The one I wrote to her. It took me two days to get it just right and I sent it by registered mail and they gave me a tracking number and it got there this morning. I wasn't takin' chances on it getting lost like that one did from Marvin to you, Nana." He stepped back and poured himself a cup of coffee.

"And what did you say in this letter?" Clarice asked.

Greg smiled. "Can I read that last letter that Marvin wrote to you?"

"Hell, no! That's private," Dotty answered for Clarice.

"Then y'all don't get to read mine."

———∾∾———

Emily poured the rest of her cereal in the trash can, got dressed, and called Taylor.

"You cooking this morning?" he answered.

"No, but we could go to IHOP in Amarillo," she said.

"You sure?" he asked.

"Blueberry pancakes with maple syrup, western omelet, and hot biscuits and gravy," she said.

"I'll pick you up in ten minutes," he said.

Emily picked up the letter again and read it. When she got to the second paragraph, it took two hard swallows to get rid of the lump in her throat.

> *Bocephus and Simba have slept with me since you left. Poor little boys keep sneaking back into your room and meowing for you. I know exactly how they feel. I sat in your chair all evening that first night you were gone. Your perfume still lingered in the room. I'm glad I found the sticky notes before anyone else got up that morning. I touched each one and told myself that you would come back. I need you in my life, Emily Cooper.*

"Hey, you ready? I'm starving," Taylor yelled through the door.

She shoved the letter back into the envelope and dropped it in her purse.

"I'm ready," she said.

She hopped into his truck and fastened her seat belt. "What kind of plans you got for today?"

He fired up the engine and headed toward town. "What a rancher does everyday. Work the land, the cattle, and hope that by fall there's enough profit that I can do it again another year. What have you got in mind?"

"I thought maybe you might like to buy a ranch, or the last of what was left of a pretty big spread at one time." She smiled.

"You sure? I thought once you slept on it and went to the cemetery you might still change your mind."

"I'm more sure than I've ever been about anything in my life," she said.

"How about you just lease it to me with intent to buy in one year? I don't want you to get out there in that forsaken part of Texas and change your mind. We can close up the house and it will be waiting right here for you and I'll take care of the land like it was my own until you come back."

She shook her head. "No, Taylor. I want a clean break. If I change my mind, I'll put my money into something else."

Taylor laughed. "You're in love for real, aren't you? You went out there with intentions of staying one day and flat-out fell in love."

"Yes, I did. I talked to Ray already and he has two sets of papers drawn up. You don't have to pay for the whole thing if you don't want to. You can pay me in installments like a banknote, only with no interest. It's up to you."

"You know it will become part of my ranch and my brand. It won't be Shine Canyon anymore. Does that bother you?"

"It's yours."

Taylor stomped the brake and left a cloud of dust behind the truck. When they came to a stop in the middle of the dirt road, he turned toward her. "The ranch has been Shine Canyon since your great-grandparents bought it, Em. Don't you have any feeling of family?"

She wiped a tear from her eyes. "My momma and my daddy and my grandfather are all gone. Gramps kind of saw something that made him send me away for a month and I want to think it was a vision of the way things should be, Taylor. It was Buffalo Draw when Gramps's folks bought it from the previous owners. A name is just a name and a brand just a brand. Add it to your ranch like Gramps wanted you to do," she said stoically and vowed that the tears were over and done with.

He took his foot off the brake and drove to the paved road that would take them into Amarillo. "I understand and I'm sorry I yelled at you. Will you promise to come home for the Fourth of July?"

"I promise, but only if I can bring Simba and Bocephus with me, and I won't have my boys around cigarette smoke."

"Then keep your scrawny, bony ass out there. You're not bringing no damn cats in my house," he teased.

She rested her hand on his shoulder. "We're both getting a good deal. I know that you'll love the land and I'm going home to a family who loves me."

"You saying we don't?" he said hoarsely.

"Hell, no! I'm just sayin' that you don't have to worry

about me, Taylor. I will be loved. Hey, there is one jar of moonshine left. Let's have a toast when we get home?"

Taylor smiled. "Sounds like just the right thing to do. And FYI, darlin' cousin, my shirt pocket is empty. Melinda asked me how I'd feel about my daughters smoking and it set me to thinkin'. I put my first patch on this mornin' and threw the rest of my pack out the truck window."

"Bless Melinda's heart." Emily smiled brightly.

———

Greg kept time with his thumb on the steering wheel as he listened to the country music station on the radio.

"Emily will be home by Friday night. She paid a lot of money for a date with you," Max said from the passenger's seat.

"What made you think of that?"

"I'm psychic. I can read your mind. Every song reminds you of Emily, doesn't it?"

"Guess it does. I love her, Max. I told her and she left without telling me good-bye. I was so angry and upset that morning, but then I read her letter and saw all those sticky notes and I understood that she had to go back before she could go forward."

"What if she asks you to leave Lightning Ridge and move to her ranch? Her roots are there even more than yours are here. She was born right there and raised on that ranch. She's never lived in another house, Greg. Your roots aren't nearly as deep as hers," Max said.

"It's going to work out between us. I know it is. This is her home now. I just feel it in my heart and soul, Max."

"I hope so, son. I really, really hope so," Max said.

The papers were signed and now the hard part was before her. With a critical eye she walked through the house. Everything held a memory. How could she leave anything behind? Taylor had said that she could store what she didn't take in one of the barns, but she'd decided on a clean break. She had twenty-four hours to decide what was the most important. But first she had to make one more trip.

She pulled on a jacket and headed toward the barn. She sat down beside the wooden cross with Bill's name on it. "I'm so sorry, old boy, that I wasn't here for you. If you hadn't gone on to be with Gramps, I'd have taken you with me. You'd like Coolie, but he wouldn't like you because you'd put him in second place. There won't ever be a number one dog like you, just like there won't ever be another Gramps."

Taylor sat down beside her. "I'll take care of his grave. I promise he won't ever be forgotten. And Em, I promise to take care of the family plot at the cemetery, too. I've been taking care of other members of the family for the past few years, so it won't be any trouble to keep two looking good. And I promise there will always be flowers on Uncle Marvin's grave at the cemetery."

She brushed tears from her cheeks. "And you'll call me every now and then to let me know what's going on out here."

"I thought you wanted a clean break," he said.

"That don't mean I don't want to hear."

He squeezed her hand. "Of course I'll call. And you'll let me know how things go with the four-eyed cowboy."

She jerked her hand free and slapped him hard on the arm. "Don't you call him that. I think he's sexy with those glasses."

Taylor grabbed his arm. "You've broken it and now you have to stay and work for me until it's healed."

"Stop your whining. You aren't hurt and I wouldn't work for you one day."

"Afraid I'll make you muck out horse stalls. Speaking of which, are you taking Dream Boy or are you going to sell him to me?"

"You might have bought the ranch, but my horse and the trailer that he rides in belong to me," she answered.

"He only takes up half of that trailer. Why don't you use the rest, as well as the back of your truck, to get all your junk out of my house?" Taylor's grin said that he was teasing.

"Sounds like a good idea to me. Go bring it and a couple of good strong men that don't have broken arms to the house and we'll get started."

She turned back the covers in her dad's bed that night. She still hated good-byes, so after she and Taylor had a toast with the moonshine, she'd told him that the next morning she would load Dream Boy and drive away without any hugs, kisses, or even waves. He'd kissed her on the forehead and told her to call if she got into trouble and to remember that she always had a home, a job, or a place if she wanted to come back to Happy.

The minute her head hit the pillow that night panic set in.

What in the hell had she done? This was her home.

It was where her momma brought her home from the hospital. She'd kissed her first boyfriend out behind the barn after the sale the fall that she was thirteen. Gramps had drawn his last breath in the room across the hall from where she was curled up on the bed where her daddy spent his last night on earth.

She jumped out of bed and started pacing on the cold floor. She pulled the curtains back and there was a big moon hanging in the sky. Was Greg looking at the same moon?

The clock made a ticking noise as it clicked off the night. Twelve thirty. An eternity later it was twelve thirty-one. Time had sped by so fast when she and Greg were in the attic room wrapped up in that old quilt together; how could the same time be so slow that night?

She flipped on the light and pulled the letter from her purse.

She touched the letter as she read it until she got to the final paragraph, when she whispered the words aloud:

If you feel the same way about me, then meet me at the front porch swing on Friday at three o'clock. I'll be the one on my knees with a ring in my hand. I love you, Emily Cooper, and I'll spend the rest of my life trying to show you just how much. It wasn't in the cards for Nana to be a mail-order bride, but I'm asking you to be mine.

She folded the letter, kissed it, and put it back in her purse. She flipped out the light and the darkness erased every single doubt in her mind. In her dreams she had gray hair and a cane. Greg's glasses were thicker, but he was still her handsome cowboy. And they held hands on the front porch of Lightning Ridge as they watched children playing with a litter of yellow and gray kittens in the yard.

Chapter 25

MAX TOOK THE SUITCASES OUT OF THE BACK OF THE van and carried them inside the hotel. Stacy met him inside the door and whispered, "Do they know?"

He shook his head. "Best kept secret in all of Fannin County."

Stacy hugged Dotty. "I was afraid you'd back out. Jeremiah is away tonight and tomorrow on business, and I thought this would be a wonderful time for us to get better acquainted. If he gets back in time, he plans to join us for supper."

"Clarice wanted to back out, but I made her keep her word and here we are. We both need a change of pace from that quiet house. Since Emily left, it's like a morgue. Lord, girl, this is one damn fancy place."

Stacy raised her hand and a bellboy came right over to take their bags to their room. "First thing we're going to do is go to the spa. We'll be there until suppertime."

"A real spa with massages and the whole works?" Clarice asked.

Stacy threw her arms around their shoulders. "Yes, a real one complete with mud baths. We're about to sink ourselves into three tubs full of wonderful mineral-enhanced mud and rest in it for one hour while aroma-therapy candles burn around us."

"That'll be my cue to leave. Ain't no way you're going to talk me into sinking my body in a tub full of mud," Max said. "I'll be back tomorrow at noon to get y'all. Have fun."

"Looks like we're in your hands for twenty-four hours." Clarice smiled. "I always wondered what it'd be like to soak in one of them tubs filled with warm mud."

Stacy led them through the lobby and down a hallway toward the spa. "When you leave you're going to be relaxed and making reservations to come back in a month."

"Maybe by then Emily will be home and we can bring her." Clarice sighed.

"I would love that. I really did like her. I think we could be good friends." Stacy ushered them into a waiting room where a receptionist looked up and raised an eyebrow.

"We have appointments for the afternoon. Stacy Mendoza," she said.

"Yes, ma'am, with lunch, right?"

Stacy nodded. "And a bottle of champagne with that."

The cute little receptionist smiled. "If you ladies will follow me, we'll get you into robes and ready for your mud baths."

"I'm hungry as hell," Dotty whispered.

"Lunch is served on the side of the tubs. You're going to love it," Stacy said. "Miz Dotty, you take this changing room. See, there's a towel on the hook. Clarice, this one belongs to you."

When Stacy was in her cubicle, she called Jeremiah and asked, "News?"

"The eagle is ahead of me, flying east with a full load. I'm going to veer south when we get to Wichita Falls."

"Eagle, my ass! The phones aren't bugged. And,

darlin', you'd better be at this hotel in time for supper. I'm not sleeping without you. I told your mama that you might be coming to eat with us and her whole face lit up. She'll be delighted."

"Yes, ma'am. Will you be the one in a sexy black nightie thing?"

"No, I'm the one in a red lacy nightie thing, and if you make eyes at a woman in a black one, I'll have to scratch her eyes out."

In the next cubicle over, Dotty pulled out her cell phone and called Clarice. "She's on her way home," she whispered.

"Well, praise the Lord. I knew she wouldn't leave us for good. Are you really going to get in a bathtub full of mud or can we plead sick and go home?"

"They need tonight, so we'll play along with their plan and yes, we're going to sink our sagging asses down in the mud bath." Dotty giggled. "It's going to happen, Clarice. We're going to get her for our very own."

Greg sat on the porch for all of two minutes before he began to pace back and forth from one end to the other. A cool breeze ruffled the tree limbs, but he didn't feel a thing through his denim jacket. There was a different story going on in his heart. Was this the way that Marvin felt? Did he rush to the bus station every day to see if the westbound Greyhound had brought Clarice to him? Did he declare every thirty seconds that he'd never marry if he couldn't have the woman he wanted?

Max called at fifteen minutes until three and said he was on the way home. Clarice and Dotty were at the hotel with Stacy and it looked like they were in for an experience. "Mud baths! Can you believe it? They're actually going to sink their bodies into a tub of mud, Greg. Women! Fuss at us if we get muddy working cattle on a rainy day and they go get in a tub of mud to beautify themselves. Don't make a bit of sense to me. Did she get there yet?"

"No, but it's still early and she might have gotten into traffic," Greg said. "I'll wait until four before I call her."

"And then?" Max asked.

"I'm getting in my truck and going to Happy to beg," Greg answered.

At two minutes until three he raced upstairs to the bathroom. "I can't meet her with my legs crossed. I should've known better than to drink a whole pitcher of sweet tea while I've been waiting."

Simba and Bocephus met him halfway up the stairs and he had to slow down or trip over them. He grabbed them up in his arms, put them in her bedroom, and shut the door.

Emily got tangled up in construction work for twenty miles between Wichita Falls and Henrietta. She found herself in a long line of one-lane traffic with concrete barricades on either side of her truck, a semi behind her, and a man with a cell phone stuck to his ear in front of her. The speed limit said fifty-five miles per hour but up ahead of the fellow talking on his phone was a big vintage Caddy going thirty miles per hour.

She had slept later than she'd planned and then even though she'd forbidden anything to do with good-byes, the whole crew at the ranch had lined up beside her truck for farewell hugs. She left with tears streaming down her face and pulled over a mile down the road to get herself under control. Now she was half an hour behind the schedule of arriving at the ranch in good time and there was a slow-moving Caddy in front of her. Was fate telling her this was not a good decision?

"No!" She slapped the steering wheel.

And boom, the traffic started flowing, two lines opened up, and she pulled out around in the left lane and passed everything in sight, including the slow-moving Caddy.

Statistics said that cops didn't stop anyone going four to five miles over the speed limit. That day stats were wrong. The arresting officer gave her a warning instead of a ticket, but it set her back fifteen more minutes.

It was two minutes after three when she parked in front of the house. Louis came running around the house with his hand held out. "Miz Emily, I'll take your truck keys and go take care of your horse. Looks like a fine animal, but I'm not supposed to stand around and yak."

She grabbed her purse and tossed the keys to Louis. The truck was already on its way toward the horse stables when she looked down and saw the bright yellow sticky notes on the sidewalk marking the path up the steps and to the front door. Each one had one word on it and she read as she walked. Welcome. Home. My. Darling. I. Missed. You. So. Much. I. Love. You. I. Need. You. I. Want. You. In. My. Life. Forever. The door sported dozens upon dozens of sticky notes making a big heart and on each one was written: Greg Loves Emily.

She reached out with one finger and rang the doorbell.

She heard footsteps and then the door opened.

Greg looked so good when he opened the door that she wanted to throw herself in his arms, but they weren't open.

"Can I help you?" he asked.

"I'm supposed to meet a sexy cowboy on this porch at three, but I got tied up in traffic and I'm a little late. Is he here?"

He stepped out onto the porch, dropped down on one knee, and held out a red velvet box. He snapped it open to reveal a square-cut sapphire surrounded by sparkling diamonds and said, "Emily Cooper, I can't imagine living without you in my life. I love you. Will you marry me?"

He slipped the ring on her finger. "The sapphire reminded me of your eyes. The diamonds reminded me of the stars sparkling in the sky from the window in the attic room. I love you."

Tears flowed down her cheeks. "Yes, yes, yes. It's perfect and I love it almost as much as I do you."

He stood up slowly, wrapped his arms around her, and kissed her with so much hungry passion and promise that it fairly well took her breath away. "I love you, Emily. Promise you'll never leave me again."

"I promise. My heart couldn't take that much misery two times without dying. I think I started falling in love with you the first time I saw your picture with that sticky note attached to the side of it. I know I did when you showed up in the dining room that next evening, and I love the notes on the sidewalk and the door," she said.

He swept her up in his arms and started inside the house.

"Be careful. I don't want a single sticky note

destroyed. They'll go into my very first box to go in our attic," she said.

When he started up the steps, she gasped, "Not here, darlin'. Let's go to the attic."

"Nana and Dotty are gone until tomorrow. Jeremiah and Stacy came to our rescue. I thought we'd make a trip to the courthouse tomorrow morning and when they get home we can break the news to them. But believe me, there will be one of those receptions at the church within a week, so get ready for it."

"Small price to pay if I never have to say good-bye again. After you make wild passionate love to me, we could go to the courthouse today," she whispered.

A sticky note heart, done up in pink, adorned the headboard of his bed. On every single one were three words: She said yes!

He laid her on deep blue satin sheets that matched the color of her eyes. The curtains were drawn and dozens of lit candles threw out soft light. He pulled off his glasses, stretched out beside her, and drew her into his arms. "Tomorrow is early enough. I don't want to share you with anyone, not even a court clerk or judge today."

She smiled as his lips found hers. Someday she'd tell her green-eyed daughters that she was a mail-order bride and maybe she'd let them look at her letters all tied with a pretty red bow even if she didn't let them read a single one of them. But right then she just wanted to cuddle up with Greg and know that she was going to spend every day for the rest of her life with him.

Dear Reader,

This book has a very special place in my heart. About fifty years ago my best friend, Karen Garrison, was dating a boy who was in the Army. He was sent to Germany and they wrote to each other every day. Airmail stamps cost eight cents in those days, and it took a week to get from Germany to Tishomingo, Oklahoma.

In one of her letters he sent a picture of a group of several of his new friends, and I picked out the one I wanted. She got the address from her boyfriend, and I wrote the first letter. Brazen hussy I was, even back then. About a year later she received an engagement ring in the mail, and her boyfriend came home for a couple of weeks. They got married and she went back to Germany with him.

Meanwhile, I was still writing to the fellow I had picked out in the picture and another year went by. One day a lovely proposal and an engagement ring came in the mail. I got on a Greyhound bus and went to Pennsylvania to meet him. We were married six weeks later, and folks said it would never last. That was forty-seven years ago and we're still together.

So now when people say they have found this brand-new dating program on the Internet, I just smile. Husband and I were the prototypes for that program! And I have a whole big stack of letters plus a proposal right there on paper to prove it.

Emily Cooper, in *The Cowboy's Mail Order Bride*, is on a mission. When an old letter is found stuck to the inside of a sixty-year-old mailbag that's been stuffed into an antique desk at the Happy, Texas, post office and taken back to her grandfather, well, a can of worms is opened up. Grandfather makes her promise to deliver not only that letter but a whole box of letters that he'd received from a woman who was not her grandmother.

Now she's taken the letters home to Ravenna, Texas, and history is about to be made.

Enjoy the ride!

Thanks again to the Sourcebooks staff who continue to help me turn my ideas into books. Thanks to my agent, Erin Niumata, who continues to sell my works and believe in me. And thanks to every one of you who continue to read my books.

I hope that Emily Cooper, with her sass, and Greg Adams, with his sexy swagger, steal your hearts.

Until next time,
Happy Reading!
Carolyn Brown

*If you love Carolyn Brown's
hot cowboys, then read on for an
excerpt from her heartwarming
and hilarious women's fiction.*

The Red-Hot Chili Cook-Off

Coming soon from Sourcebooks Landmark.

Chapter 1

SOME MEN ARE JUST BORN STUPID. SOME DON'T GET infected until later in life, but they'll all get a case of it sometime. It's in their DNA and can't be helped.

Carlene could testify with her right hand raised to God and the left on the Good Book that her husband, Lenny, had been born with the disease and it had worsened with the years. Proof was held between her thumb and forefinger like a dead rat in the form of a pair of bikini underwear. They damn sure didn't belong to her. Hells bells, she couldn't get one leg in those tiny little things. And they did not belong to Lenny, either. Even if he had become an overnight cross-dresser, his ass wouldn't fit into that skimpy pair of under-britches, not even if he greased himself down with bacon drippings.

They were bright red with a sparkling sequin heart sewn on the triangular front. They'd come with a matching corset with garter straps and fishnet hose. Carlene recognized them, because she'd designed the outfit herself at her lingerie shop, Bless My Bloomers. They belonged to a petite, size-four brunette with big brown eyes who had giggled and pranced when she saw herself in the mirror wearing the getup.

Carlene jumped when her cell phone rang. The ring tone said it was Lenny, but she was still speechless, staring at the scrap of satin in her hand.

She dropped to her knees on the carpet and bent

forward into a tight ball, her blond hair falling over her face. She felt as if someone had kicked her firmly in the gut and she couldn't breathe. In a few seconds she managed a sitting position, wrapped her arms around her midsection, and sucked in air but it burned her lungs. The noise that came forth from her chest sounded like a wounded animal caught in a trap. Tears would have washed some of the pain away but they wouldn't flow from her burning green eyes. Finally, she got control of the dry heaves and managed to pull herself up out of the heap of despair. Dear God, what was she going to do?

The brunette who'd bought the red-satin outfit had told her that she and her sugar daddy were going to Vegas, and she wanted something that would make him so hot he'd be ready to buy her an engagement ring. What was her name? Bailey? Brenda? No, something French, because Carlene remembered asking her about it. Bridget…that was it! Bridget had been to Vegas with Lenny. On how many other trips had he taken a bimbo with him and how many of them had been ten or fifteen years younger—and a size four, for God's sake?

In seconds, the phone rang again. She picked it up and said, "Hello." Her voice sounded like it was coming from the bottom of a well or, maybe, a sewer pipe.

"Carlene, I left my briefcase in my office. I slept on the sofa to keep from waking you since I got in so late last night. Bring it to me before you go to work, and hurry. There's a contract in it that I need and the people will be here to sign in ten minutes. I'll hold them off with coffee until you get here."

No good-bye.

No thank you, darlin'.

Not even a please.

Did he talk to Bridget like that?

Anger joined shock and pain as she dropped the panties back in the briefcase and then removed the little card she'd made for him to find that morning. She'd written that she was sorry she had fallen asleep before he got home and that she'd make it up to him that night with champagne and wild sex. She stood up, straightening to her full statuesque height of just a couple of inches under the six-foot mark. Damn that sorry bastard to hell. How could he do this to her?

Ripping the note into confetti-sized pieces and throwing them in the air did nothing to appease her anger. Dozens of questions ran in circles through her mind. Had Lenny brought his twenty-something-year-old bimbo to her house for a romp on her bed while she was at work? Did that sorry sucker have sex with his mistress at noon and then with his wife that same night? Just how long had the affair been going on, anyway?

Among them all came one solid answer. She was not living in the same house with a lying, cheating, two-timing son of a bitch. She was leaving his ass and nothing or no one could convince her to stay another night under the same roof with him.

Five Red-Hot Chili Cook-Off trophies looked down from the mantle at her. She picked them up one by one and hurled them across the room. Not one of the damn plastic things broke, which made her even angrier, but she didn't go to the garage and get a hammer to work them over. Instead, she turned into a feverish packing fiend. In less than half an hour her van looked like an overflowing Salvation Army donation hut. Clothing and shoes were stuffed into the back like sardines. Plastic grocery bags filled with items from her dresser drawers were stacked in the backseat, and the briefcase sat right beside her on the front seat.

She gave it looks meant to fry holes through the leather, but it just sat there as cool as Lenny. Damn his black soul to hell for all eternity. She hoped that he was given a place sitting naked on a barbed wire fence and every time he fell off the devil shot him with a cattle prod.

From their house in Cadillac, Texas, to Lenny's car dealership in Sherman was exactly seven miles and she made it in a little less than five minutes. If it hadn't been for good brakes on her van, she would have plowed right through the plate-glass windows and rammed into that pretty brand-spanking-new red Corvette in the showroom. Some days started off bad and got worse as they went along.

Tears begged to be turned loose but she blinked them back. Be damned if he'd see her cry or reduced to a heap on the floor, either. It might happen, but he wouldn't bask in the glory of seeing it.

Her hands shook and her jaw ached from clenching her teeth. She took a deep breath and pushed open the door of her van, remembering to grab his briefcase before she slammed the door shut. Her bravado left when she looked through the window and caught sight of him through the glass windows in his office right off the showroom floor. Her stomach churned and nausea set in again. Could a person love and hate someone at the same time?

Her legs felt like they were filled with steel when she

pushed open the glass door and headed toward Lenny's office. He looked up from behind his desk and with a flick of his wrist motioned for her to come on in.

She was still staring at him trying to figure out whether to beat him to death with the briefcase or just set it in the middle of the floor and get the hell out of there before she started weeping, when she saw a movement in her peripheral vision.

"Well, hello!" Bridget appeared from behind the Corvette parked just inside the doors. "It's good to see you again."

Either the woman did not know Carlene was Lenny's wife or she was a fool who'd caught an acute case of stupid from Lenny Joe Lovelle. Either way, she was crazy as hell and didn't value her hair or eyeballs. Anyone with two sane brain cells in their heads could see that Carlene Lovelle was a time bomb with a lit fuse.

Bridget's eyes twinkled and she lowered her voice to say, "The red outfit drove my sweet sugar daddy right up the walls. Honey, we had the honeymoon suite and we didn't hit the blackjack tables one time all weekend. He didn't even leave to go to his business meetings. We spent the whole two days in that big round bed or else in the heart-shaped hot tub. It was our five-month anniversary and he said that he got luckier in that room than he ever did at the gambling tables. I'll be back in to buy something else for the sixth month. We're going to Florida to celebrate my twenty-second birthday as well as our anniversary. I'm thinking naughty nurse so get the bling out and I betcha I get my ring on that trip. Oh, and guess what else? We are both members of the mile high club now."

Carlene plopped the briefcase down on the hood of the Corvette and wished that she'd bought one of those shiny metal ones for Lenny's birthday instead of one made of soft kid leather. Hell, if she had a metal one, she really could beat him to death with it, but that fancy leather thing wouldn't even leave bruises.

Bridget's eyes widened out to the size of saucers when she saw the LJL initials on the top of the familiar case and had trouble staying in their sockets when Carlene popped it open. Right there on the top of a big manila envelope were the red panties.

Using a pen with the car dealership logo, Carlene picked up the underpants and threw them at the woman. Then she dumped documents, pens, sticky notes, and everything else in the briefcase onto the tile floor and stomped holes in the papers with her spike heels.

Bridget caught the scrap of red satin and all the color drained from her face. "What are you doing with my panties? And why do you have Lenny's briefcase? Who in the hell are…oh, my, sweet Jesus!" She slapped a hand over her mouth. The panties hung on her pinky finger, and it looked like she was trying to swallow the evidence.

Carlene picked up the empty briefcase and lobbed it like a rocket toward the window between her and Lenny. It lost momentum and didn't even crack the glass but it made him drop like bird shit behind his desk.

"I…I…" Bridget stammered.

Well, praise the Lord, her vocabulary now had two vowels. Maybe by the end of the day, she could add a consonant or two and be able to speak in whole sentences again.

Lenny must've jumped up as fast as he dropped

because suddenly he was beside her. "My God, Carlene, what in the hell…oh!" He stopped dead.

His eyes darted from Bridget to Carlene. "I can explain. Bridget, honey, tell Uncle Sam to close the deal with Mr. and Mrs. Reynolds. He'll have to reprint the contracts. And would you please clean up this mess before anyone sees it? Carlene, we'll go discuss this over some coffee in the lounge."

Then he proved just how damned stupid he was by reaching out and touching her shoulder as if he could charm her into forgiveness. Well, Lenny Joe Lovelle wasn't charming jack shit out of her that morning, and it would be a cold day in hell before she ever forgave him. Even Alma Grace, with all her religion and praying, would agree that the Good Book did not condone adultery or fornication—even though it didn't mention skimpy under-britches.

She doubled up her fist and landed a good right hook in his left eye. He went down on his knees and yelled, "Why in the hell did you do that?"

"Because you touched me, you son of a bitch. If you ever lay a hand on me again, I will snatch you bald-headed and then start on your bimbo over there," she yelled.

Shit! Had she really raised her voice right out in public like that? Carlene Carmichael Lovelle was a lady who did not air her dirty laundry, but dammit, he'd broken her heart, twisted it up into a pretzel, and now he was acting like it was nothing. She glared at him, hands on hips and back as straight as steel.

Bridget instinctively covered her hair with her hands, the panties now looking like dangly earrings as they floated down from fingertips to shoulders.

He stood up and narrowed his eyes. "Come on, Carlene, we have to talk."

"You can talk to my lawyer."

He laid a hand on her shoulder and smiled. "Darlin'…"

She slapped him with her open hand hard enough to put a blaze of red on his cheek, but he didn't drop to the floor. "Dammit, Carlene. You are making a scene."

"A scene. You want a scene? I'll give you a damned scene that a sugar daddy can appreciate." She placed the toe of her high-heeled shoe on the bumper of the Corvette and marched up across the hood, leaving dents that looked like hail had peppered down on the pretty red car. When she was standing on the top of it, she looked right at Bridget.

"Bridget, *honey*, you had better never show your face at Bless My Bloomers ever again."

"Get off that car. You've already done thousands of dollars worth of damage. Sam is going to sue the hell out of you for this," Lenny shouted.

Sam, a robust man with a rim of gray hair, a belly that hung out over his belt, and five-thousand-dollar eel cowboy boots, rushed out into the showroom. "My God, Carlene, have you lost your mind?"

"She's gone crazy, Uncle Sam," Lenny said.

"You want to see freakin' crazy? I will show you crazy." She stepped down to the hood and did a stomp dance. By the time she finished, the showroom was full. She took a deep bow and hopped down from the hood. "When I'm done, you'll be damn lucky to have potatoes with your beans once a week, much less plan little weekend trips to honeymoon suites where you wallow around in a round bed with office girls rather than going to meetings. Dock his pay for the damage, Sam. You'd be wise to fire his ass, but since he's your nephew, that won't happen, will it?"

"Come on Carlene, it was just a fling. It only happened one time and I'll never do it again," Lenny whispered.

"Fling! Just a fling?" Bridget's voice was as loud as a fire siren. "You promised me that you were leaving her. You promised me an engagement ring with a two-carat diamond as soon as you left your fat wife. You promised me we would have our own apartment by the time the chili cook-off happens and I could be your cheerleader for the event and you'd hang our picture above all those trophies in your office."

"Well, he's not leaving his fat wife. I'm leaving his cheating ass and he's all yours. Better keep him on a short leash. He charming, but he's a two-timin' son of a bitch." Carlene's high heels sounded like fire crackers as she stormed out of the dealership.

She drove until she reached the outskirts of town, pulled over, and laid her head on the steering wheel. That lyin' cheating bag of shit didn't deserve her tears but they flowed down her cheeks anyway as she sat there with the engine running and the air conditioner turning her warm, salty tears as cold as her heart felt.

❦

Monday morning was Josie Vargas's favorite time of the week. She'd cooked all weekend, put up with whining grandkids and great-grandkids, sons in her living room arguing about football on the blaring television set, and

daughters-in-law sipping iced tea at her kitchen table
while they gossiped about people she didn't even know.
The most beautiful sight in the world was the taillights
as they all went home Sunday night after supper. Maybe
by Friday she'd be glad to see them again, but right then
she rolled her eyes toward the ceiling and gave thanks
that she'd only birthed two sons.

"Okay," she muttered at the ceiling. "They say they
are bringing the kids to see me so I don't get lonely
since Louis died. Me, I think they are coming home to
be waited on and to eat my cooking. Tell me I'm wrong.
No? You can't lie?"

She warmed two leftover waffles from the day
before in the microwave and drizzled a mixture of hot
butter and maple syrup over them. That and coffee
would keep her until she arrived at Bless My Bloomers
where she sewed fancy lingerie for all sizes of women.
Crazy women who wanted pearls and ribbons and
fancy crap all over their under-britches. Josie couldn't
imagine wearing the things that she made. Plain old
white cotton panties were good enough for her butt and
Louis had never complained one time when he took
them off.

He would turn over in his grave if he knew she'd
gone back to work. She'd retired at sixty-five and she
and Louis had twelve good years together before he
died. But she got lonely after he was gone, and when
Carlene came to ask her if she wanted a job at Bless My
Bloomers, she'd jumped at the chance.

She was ten minutes early and parked her twenty-
year-old car around back, leaving the curb space and
driveway for customers. She was a short woman with a

touch of gray in her hair and brown eyes set in a bed of wrinkles. She was eyeballing her eightieth birthday in another year and she loved those three girls she worked with as much as her own granddaughters. Before she got out of the car, she took out the little compact that Louis had given her for their first anniversary and reapplied her trademark bright-red lipstick.

No one else had arrived yet so she let herself in the back door with her key and headed straight to her little room. It had been the library when the house was a residence but nowadays it was her sewing room. The living room was the store. The parlor had been divided into four fitting rooms. The dining room was the stockroom and the walls were lined with basic bras, corsets, and panties in all sizes, shapes, and colors. There were three bedrooms upstairs, and sometimes the owners, Carlene, Alma Grace, and Patrice, kept extra stock up there if the dining room overflowed.

She'd been working on a fancy corset for a bride when she left Friday evening. She pulled up her rolling chair, picked up the pearls, and started sewing them one-by-one onto the lace panels between the boning. She'd always liked intricate work. Even as a child she was the one who loved embroidery and needlepoint.

"I don't remember Carlene ever being out sick before. I hope she ain't sick today. Alma Grace will have a prayin' fit if she has to fit all those choir women from her church without any help."

❧

Alma Grace stopped by her mama's house on the way to work every morning so they could have a mother/

daughter devotional. They read the daily pages from the
study Bible, said a prayer, and then had breakfast.

Few people in Cadillac even remembered the Fannin
sisters' real names. Sugar's birth certificate said Carolina
Sharmaine, but she'd always been called Sugar. The
same with Gigi; her real name was Virginia Carlene.
And Tansy had started out life the day she was born as
Georgia Anastasia. They'd each had a daughter within a
year of each other twenty-seven years before. Alma Grace
belonged to Sugar, Patrice to Tansy, and Carlene to Gigi.

"Are you planning a surprise for the Easter program
this year?" Her mother pushed a strand of ash-blond hair
back behind her delicate ears. Diamond studs glittered in
the morning sunlight. Both of her sisters told her that the
television show *Good Christian Bitches* had really been
modeled after Miz Sugar Magee. Those women damn
sure hadn't given up a bit of their bling or their style to
be religious and neither had Sugar or Alma Grace.

Alma Grace's curly blond hair, the color of fresh
straw, was held back that morning with a silver clasp.
Cute little cross earrings covered with sapphires matched
the necklace around her neck and her blue eyes.

"Now Mama, you know I never give away all my
secrets about the Easter program. That's why we have
such a crowd. Everyone knows it'll be spectacular and
even bigger than the year before. But I will tell you this
much. The teacher from the drama department at the
school is working on a gizmo to make me fly as I sing
the final song and there will be sparkles on my wings.
It's going to be breathtaking. They'll still be talking
about it at the chili cook-off. Maybe even at the festival
this fall."

Sugar's eyes misted. "It will be the best thing that's ever happened in our church, and when your sweet voice starts to sing the final song, it will be like the heavens open up and the angels are singing."

Alma Grace dropped a kiss on her mother's forehead. "Thank you, Mama. I've got to go to work."

Sugar sighed. "Lord, I wish you wouldn't have…"

Alma Grace laid a hand on her mother's arm. "I prayed about it, remember? And God told me it was just underwear. Carlene, Patrice, and I are making a good living at Bless My Bloomers. And just think of all the happy men in the world who are staying home with their wives because of our jobs."

Sugar nodded seriously. "That's the only thing that I take comfort in, darlin'. Now let us have a little prayer before you go. We'll pray the blood of Jesus will keep you pure as you work on all those hooker clothes."

"Mama!"

Sugar tilted her chin up. "Well, God didn't tell *me* that those things were fit for decent God-fearin' women so I intend to pray about it every day."

"I've got to go or I'll be late. Dinner at Miss Clawdy's at noon?" Alma Grace asked.

"Not today. Gigi and Tansy and I are going up to Sherman to look at a new car for Gigi. She's still driving one that's four years old. It's a disgrace, I tell you. She's got a son-in-law in the business and she drives a car that old. Why, honey, it's almost a sin. I guess I should be happy that she's driving a car instead of a truck, but honestly, four years old!"

"Well, y'all have a good time and bring the new car back by the shop for us to see. That Lenny is so good to his family. Maybe someday I'll find a husband like him. Carlene is one lucky woman."

Sugar waved from the front door. "Yes, she is."

Alma Grace parked the car beside Josie's and went in through the back door. "Hey, no coffee? Where's Carlene?" she yelled.

"Ain't here yet. Hope she ain't sick. Y'all have got all those church women coming for a fitting today."

Alma Grace rolled her eyes toward the ceiling. She'd forgotten about that appointment. Thank goodness, her mother was tied up with Aunt Gigi's new car business or she'd have had to cancel lunch with her. Sugar Fannin Magee pouted when she got all dolled up and didn't get to go out and it was not a pretty sight.

"Think I should call her?" Alma Grace asked.

"Hell, no! She'll call us if she's sick. Maybe she's finally pregnant and got the mornin' sickness."

"A baby." Alma Grace almost swooned.

"I didn't say that she was. I said that she might be, and if she is, she'll tell us when she damn well gets ready. Why don't you make coffee?"

"Because Carlene says that my coffee isn't fit to drink. I'll get the lights turned on and the doors opened. I'm sure she'll be along in a little while. Patrice is late all the time but I've never beat Carlene to work since we opened the shop last year."

⌦⌫

The alarm rattled around in Patrice's head like steel marbles banging against the edges of a tin soup can. She groaned and shoved a pillow over her eyes with one hand and used the other hand to slap the hell out of the clock, sending it scooting across the floor. That the plug came loose from the wall was the only thing that saved the damn clock from being stomped to death that morning.

Damn Monday mornings after a weekend of hell-raisin' sex and booze. Wine, beer, Jack Daniels and half a gallon of rocky road ice cream after the fight with her boyfriend did not make for a good start to a new week. Hangover, bloat, and tears were poor bed partners, especially on a Monday morning.

She kicked the covers off, took a warm shower, drank a cup of tomato juice laced with curry, ate half a can of chilled pineapple, and popped two aspirin. It was her special recipe to cure a hangover.

Her job at Bless My Bloomers was keeping books, inventory, and anything to do with a computer. Lord, she hated to face columns of numbers and deal with the wholesale sellers all morning with her head pounding like she was standing next to a jackhammer.

No one at the shop could help her, either. Alma Grace, bless her heart, could sell a blinged-out corset to a saint, but she could not add up a double column of figures even with a calculator. Carlene, God love her soul, could design something so sexy that the devil would hock his horns to buy it, but she was all thumbs when it came to keeping track of what went out and what came into the shop. If things got hectic in the sales room, Patrice could talk to customers, show them the merchandise, and even make a sale, but she didn't enjoy it.

The bathroom mirror brought about a loud groan. Her aqua-colored eyes looked like two piss holes in the snow and her platinum blond hair, straight from a bottle down at the Yellow Rose Beauty Shop, was only slightly better looking than a witch's stringy strands in a kid's movie. Hell, next week, she might cut it all off and wear it in a spike hairdo. It would damn sure be easier to fix than getting out the curling iron every damn morning.

"Grandma Fannin would have your hide if you did that," she whispered to her reflection.

When she'd done enough to cover up most of the hangover, she pulled a pair of skinny jeans from her closet, along with a tight-fitting shirt that hugged her double Ds and black, shiny, high-heeled shoes that she could kick off under her desk.

Evidently Lenny had brought Carlene to work that morning since her car wasn't parked out behind the shop. Patrice laid her head back against the headrest for a minute and shut her eyes against the blinding sun, vowing that she'd find her sunglasses before she stepped out into the sun again. She needed coffee, good black strong coffee, and lots of it. Thank goodness, Carlene always started a pot first thing in the morning.

Her head throbbed so bad, she'd almost be willing for Alma Grace to lay hands upon her and pray that God would heal her, but then she'd have to listen to her asking God to forgive her for drinking. She just needed something to relieve the headache. She hadn't killed her boyfriend so she didn't need forgiveness and even Jesus drank wine so Alma Grace could keep her preaching to herself.

"I'm never drinking again," she said as she made her way to the back door. But when she opened it, the aroma of fresh coffee did not greet her.

"Carlene?" Alma Grace yelled from the front of the house.

"It's Patrice, not Carlene. Where is our cousin? She's never late," Patrice said.

Josie poked her head out of the sewing room. "From the looks of your eyes, I'd say you have a supersized hangover."

Patrice held up a palm. "Guilty. Don't tell Alma Grace or she'll start praying."

"Come on in the kitchen. I'll fix you up," Josie said.

"I already did my magic."

"Did it work?" Josie pointed at the kitchen table.

Patrice shook her head and it hurt like hell.

"No." She sat down, put her head down on her arms, and poked her fingers in her ears when Josie started the blender.

"What is it?" she asked when Josie set a green drink that looked like ground-up bullfrogs in front of her.

"Don't ask and don't come up for air. Drink it all down without stopping," Josie said.

Patrice did and then slammed the glass on the table with enough force to rattle the salt shakers. "Holy damn shit! That's hotter than hell's blazes."

"Yep and it'll burn that hangover right out of you in five minutes. Now let's go to work. Carlene's not here. I hope she's not sick. Y'all have the church choir coming today for fittings."

"Dammit all to hell!" Patrice groaned. "I'm not in the mood for praisin' God and blessing souls or fitting bras to those holier-than-thou gossiping women."

"Me neither but they've got boobs that have to be roped down, so suck it up. Must have been a helluva weekend that you had." Josie smiled.

"I don't even want to talk about it until my head stops pounding. God, I hope Carlene isn't sick. I don't want to wait on customers today."

Alma Grace poked her head in the kitchen door. "I hope she's not sick, too, but it would be wonderful to have a baby in the family. My mama and your mama and Aunt Gigi are going to Lenny's this afternoon to look at a car. It'd be a shame if Carlene isn't here when they drive it by to show us."

❧

Carlene breezed in the back door of the shop with an armload of clothing, her head held high, her makeup repaired, and a vow that no one else would ever see her cry again. That damned Lenny Lovelle would never, ever know how much he'd broken her spirit and her heart with his cheating.

"I'd appreciate it if y'all would lend a hand and help me bring in all that stuff in my van before customers start coming into the shop."

Patrice peeked outside and frowned. "Good God, girl. You did more than clean out your closets while Lenny was gone this weekend. Did you buy out a store? Are we going into more than lingerie or what? And the look in your eyes is damn scary. What's going on? You look like you could commit homicide on a saint."

"I'm divorcing that two-timing sleazy sumbitch Lenny Joe Lovelle. I should never have married him in the first place. Aunt Tansy read my palm and told me that you can't change a skirt-chasin' bastard but would I listen? Hell, no! Now are y'all going to help or not? And if you start praying, Alma Grace, I'm going to slap the shit out of you," Carlene said. She sounded mean, but truth was she was just like those hollow chocolate Easter bunnies. If anyone pushed her, she'd crumble into a million pieces.

"Dear Lord," Alma Grace whispered.

Carlene shot her an evil look. "I forewarned you."

"I wasn't praying, although I should be. You want that unloaded up in one of the bedrooms or where? I can't believe you are talking about a divorce." She whispered the last word like it was something dirty.

"Just put everything on that old sofa up there in the first bedroom on the left. I'll decide which room I'm going to live in and hang them all up later."

"*Dios mío*, tell us what has happened," Josie said.

"Help me get the van unloaded first to give me some more time." Carlene pushed the screen door open and it slammed behind her as she led the way outside to the company van.

"Shit!" Patrice followed her.

"Fool must've gotten caught," Josie said.

"Until death parts us. I heard her say the words," Alma Grace whispered.

"Yeah, well, way I see it is that don't necessarily mean death of the body, girl," Josie said. "I'll be right here when y'all get that stuff all carried upstairs. I'm not making trips up and down those steps with these knees."

It took several trips up and down the stairs to get everything brought inside. When they'd finished, the bedroom looked like a tornado had struck a clothing store. The sofa was completely obliterated and Walmart bags bulging and overflowing with panties, bras, and nightgowns were lined up against the wall.

"Why in the hell didn't you pack in suitcases? I know you've got at least three sets," Patrice asked.

"I was so damn mad I didn't even think about suitcases. He promised her that he'd be living with her by the time the chili cook-off happens and that's only a few weeks from now. And that he'd hang their pictures above those damned trophies. He doesn't have a picture of me in his den, in his office at work, or even in his wallet." Her voice quivered but neither of her cousins heard it or Alma Grace would have started praying again and Patrice would have got out a sawed-off shotgun.

Alma Grace touched Carlene on the arm and said, "Okay, darlin', tell us what happened and we'll take it to the Lord in prayer."

"Coffee first and the Lord can't fix this so I'll be damned if I take it to Him. The person that I'm taking it to is Carson Culpepper and I hope that he's as good as everyone says he is when it comes to divorce court."

"Poor old Lenny." Patrice giggled then grabbed her aching head. Laughter and hangovers did not go together.

Carlene whipped around and glared at her. "He deserves it."

"Hell, yes, he deserves it and Carson will make him wish he'd never even looked cross-eyed at another woman. Who was it and how did you find out?" Patrice asked.

"Remember that cute little brunette who came in here and bought that red corset and matching bikinis? Bridget is her name and we laughed about her going to Vegas with her sugar daddy. Well, she works at the dealership and Lenny is the sugar daddy."

"Then go get him, darlin'. I'm right behind you. You want us to shoot his sorry ass? Ain't a one of us that can't handle a firearm, and we're strong enough to dig a six-foot hole," Patrice said.

"Now girls, there's two sides to every story." Alma Grace folded her hands in front of her, shut her eyes, and prayed. "Dear Lord, please help Carlene forgive and forget. Help Lenny to mend his ways *if* he has transgressed and help them to work this problem out because they have both made vows to you. Amen."

Carlene glared at her cousin. Not one time in the past hour had she thought Patrice and Alma Grace wouldn't both stand behind her in any decision she made. True, they were all different. Patrice with her wild ways and cussing. Alma Grace with her religion. Carlene with her business sense. But they were knitted together with blood that ran as deep as sisters. So why would Alma Grace want her to forgive a two-timin', cheatin' sumbitch like Lenny? She reached up and caught a tear as it escaped from the dam behind her eyelids.

"Why in the hell would you pray like that? You should be praying for God to strike him dead," Patrice said.

"There's two sides." Alma Grace squared her shoulders defensively.

"You got that right," Patrice said. "There's the truth and then there's the lyin', cheatin' bastard's story. Which family are you in anyway?"

"I'll put Carlene on the prayer list and we'll all pray that God will guide you to make the right decision and forgive poor old Lenny for being so weak," Alma Grace said. "Now let's go have some coffee."

"There is no coffee because Carlene is the only one

who knows how to make it, and if I was her, I'd poison yours," Patrice said.

Carlene was still amazed that Alma Grace hadn't supported her. Tears stung her eyes and her heart felt heavier than it had all morning. "Coffee might clear our heads," Carlene said as she started down the stairs.

They trooped into the big old kitchen: Carlene with curves that stretched a size sixteen; Alma Grace, the petite cousin; Patrice, the tallest one of the three at five feet eleven inches and slim as a runway model. Carlene put on a pot of coffee and then slumped in a chair. She started at the beginning. Surely when Alma Grace heard the whole story, she'd be more sympathetic.

"The sorry bastard. Let's poison him," Patrice said when she finished.

"You promised to love him through good times and bad. You need to give him a chance to make this all right," Alma Grace said.

Josie stood up from her chair, rounded the table, and hugged Carlene. "Honey, I'm not much younger than your Grandma Fannin would be and I got a feeling that she would tell you the same thing I'm about to tell you. Cut your losses right now and move on with your life. He's not worth it. Life's too short and hell ain't half full for you to put up with that kind of shit."

Alma Grace threw a hand over her eyes. "Dear God."

"You pray for me and I'll hurt you, girl. I swear I will," Carlene said.

"I wasn't praying. I promise that I wasn't. I just remembered that our mothers are going to Lenny's this morning to buy a new car," she said.

The sound that came out of Carlene's throat was

somewhere between a giggle and a sob. It quickly turned into nervous laughter, followed by a guffaw that echoed off the kitchen walls, and then tears flooded her cheeks again.

She could tell by the looks on her cousins' faces that they thought she was laughing until she cried.

Patrice threw a kitchen towel across the table toward Carlene. "Dab, don't wipe or you'll ruin your mascara. What do you bet that he runs the other way when the Fannin sisters come through the door? He won't remember that Aunt Gigi has been talking about a new car for weeks. Enough of this shit. We've got a business to run."

Carlene pushed the end of the towel up under her eye. "And I've got to call the furniture store and tell them to deliver a bedroom suite before dark or I'll be sleeping on the floor."

"You can stay with me," Alma Grace offered.

"Hell, no! I'm staying right here. All I have to do is walk down the stairs into the store every morning. It's a perfect setup until the divorce is settled. I hope he loses that damn chili cook-off trophy this year. It would serve him right after promising that bimbo that he would hang her picture above the trophies. I threw them across the room but they didn't break."

"You will make the coffee every morning, right?" Patrice asked.

Carlene shot a look across the table.

Patrice fended it off by putting both her palms up. "Don't be killin' me with your mean looks, woman. I didn't cheat on you and I'm supporting your decision to leave that scumbag. I can't believe he's so stupid he didn't even check his briefcase."

"I can't believe you are so stupid that you married him. Everyone knew he was a skirt chaser," Josie fussed.

"Well, I can't believe you aren't going to live up to the vows you said before all three of our mamas and God. And the fact that the trophies didn't break is a sign that your marriage isn't broken, just cracked, and that it can be mended," Alma Grace sniffed.

"I thought he meant it when he said his womanizing days were over, Josie. I hear the front door. Let's go to work," Carlene said, walking out of the kitchen.

"And he broke more vows than Carlene did, Alma Grace, so stop your sanctimonious shit. I hear the front door," Patrice said.

"It's going to be the ruin of us. The church didn't like it when I threw in with y'all to put in a lingerie shop but a divorced woman in the mix? I don't know what's going to happen to me," Alma Grace whispered.

"We've done got past the fifties, cousin. Divorce happens. Get over it and you better not ever let me hear you praying for that bastard again or I'll snatch you bald-headed," Patrice said.

Carlene returned with a white carryout box and opened it before she set it in the middle of the table. "That was Beulah from across the street. She ran over to Miss Clawdy's and brought us a dozen pecan tarts. Said that she'd heard the bad news and would be praying that me and Lenny could work things out. Don't you *even* roll your eyes at the ceiling Alma Grace! She said that she hoped that the tarts would help us get through the morning."

"Bad news travels fast," Josie said.

"Fat chance of working it out," Patrice said. "Lenny Joe has treated you horrible, Carlene. It's over."

Alma Grace reached for a tart. "You had these at your wedding. All arranged on a silver platter on the groom's table. You want one? Remember all the good times, Carlene. God wants you to forgive Lenny."

"I'd rather lick the white tops off of chicken shit." Carlene marched out of the room before she had another emotional outbreak just thinking about her wedding day.

The Blue-Ribbon Jalapeño Society Jubilee

by Carolyn Brown

~~~

Come early, eat until your buttons pop, and dance until you drop!

Miss Clawdy's Café has won the Jubilee blue ribbon every year since the dawn of time. This year, town matron Violet Prescott is going after that ribbon with an iron-clad determination only thinly disguised by her perfect coiffure and flawless manners, bless her heart.

It's time for café owners Cathy and Marty and their best friend Trixie to pull out their secret weapon. And this is where a lifetime of friendship, combined with just the right recipe at just the right time, might carry the day—or blow everything to smithereens.

Welcome to Cadillac, Texas, where the jalapeños are hot, the gossip is even hotter, and at the end of the day, it's the priceless friendships that are left standing...

~~~

"A high-spirited, romantic page turner."—*Kirkus*

"Brown keeps it lively with tart and raunchy dialogue and situations that will make you laugh out loud."—*Shelf Awareness*

For more Carolyn Brown, visit:

www.sourcebooks.com

About the Author

Carolyn Brown is a *New York Times* and *USA Today* bestselling author with more than sixty books published, and credits her eclectic family for her humor and writing ideas. Her books include the cowboy trilogy—*Lucky in Love*, *One Lucky Cowboy*, and *Getting Lucky*—the Honky Tonk series—*I Love This Bar*; *Hell, Yeah*; *Honky Tonk Christmas*; and *My Give a Damn's Busted*—and her bestselling Spikes & Spurs series—*Love Drunk Cowboy*, *Red's Hot Cowboy*, *Darn Good Cowboy Christmas*, *One Hot Cowboy Wedding*, *Mistletoe Cowboy*, *Just a Cowboy and His Baby*, and *Cowboy Seeks Bride*. Carolyn has launched into women's fiction as well with *The Blue-Ribbon Jalapeño Society Jubilee*. She was born in Texas but grew up in southern Oklahoma where she and her husband, Charles, a retired English teacher, make their home. They have three grown children and enough grandchildren to keep them young.

Praise for *Siege*

"I loved the heroes and heroines, I loved the emotional intensity, and I loved the way in which Frater uses allegory as—forgive the pun—biting social commentary. Anyone who calls themself a hard-core zombie-fiction fan who hasn't read the As the World Dies trilogy simply isn't a hard-core zombie-fiction fan. Bottom line: a must-read for anyone who enjoys zombie fiction and/or apocalyptic fiction."   —*Explorations*

"I found myself utterly amazed and thrilled while reading this . . . [and] going through so many emotions. Laughter, tears, joys, anger. When a book can evoke so many emotions, you know you are in for a hell of a ride. A very well-put-together blend of raw terror and relief to utter chaos . . . It is a real nail-biter. I loved the book in all of its beautiful intensity and raw emotion."

—*Livre De Amour*

"This book is E-P-I-C. I was filled with happiness, sorrow, and desperation while the survivors of the fort try to pull together a semblance of any sort of life after the end of the world. A highly emotional ride that I want to take over and over!"   —*The Bookish Brunette*

"I push these books on anyone who enjoys a good dramatic and horrific tale. The books are about zombies, but the essence of their very soul are the characters. I was completely smitten with this book. Frater excels at horrific storytelling. Isn't it about time you checked out this series, if you haven't already?"

—*Parajunkee*

"Intense is a complete understatement. Emotional doesn't begin to touch on how this book affected me. [Frater] does a great job at keeping the humor and touching moments in there, which make you smile even through the tears that will undoubtedly be streaming down your face! This is one of the most heart-pounding, tension-filled, emotional books I have ever read."

—*Book Loving Mom*